conflict of honors

sharon lee and steve miller

ACE BOOKS, NEW YORK

This is a work of fiction. Names, characters, places, and incidents either are the product of the author's imagination or are used fictitiously, and any resemblance to actual persons, living or dead, business establishments, events, or locales is entirely coincidental.

CONFLICT OF HONORS

An Ace Book / published by arrangement with
Meisha Merlin Publishing, Inc.

PRINTING HISTORY
DelRey mass-market edition / June 1988
In Meisha Merlin Publishing, Inc. hardcover and trade paperback editions of
Partners in Necessity / February 2000
Ace mass-market edition / August 2002

Visit our website at
www.penguinputnam.com
Check out the ACE Science Fiction & Fantasy newsletter!

ISBN: 0-441-00964-6

ACE®
Ace Books are published by The Berkley Publishing Group,
a division of Penguin Putnam Inc.,
375 Hudson Street, New York, New York 10014.
ACE and the "A" design
are trademarks belonging to Penguin Putnam Inc.

PRINTED IN THE UNITED STATES OF AMERICA

10 9 8 7 6 5 4 3 2 1

"LEE AND MILLER STRIKE
—Robin Wayne

Praise for

Conflict of Honors

and Sharon Lee and Steve Miller's
novels of the Liaden Universe . . .

"The plot threads are intricately interwoven. . . . The plotting is careful and well-balanced . . . the great excellence lies in the relationships."　　　　　　　　　　　　　　　—*Analog*

"I was mesmerized, awed, and totally entertained. Only rarely do I read a book that I literally can't put down, that draws me so deeply into the world created by the authors that I feel a part of it and don't want to let it go. It happened with *Local Custom*. I loved the action, the conflict of cultures, the characters, and the romance. But best of all, and what makes each story enduringly special to me, is the strong sense of honor that impels the actions of the main characters and is often the basis of the conflicts among them. The Liaden world is an admirable world." —Mary Balogh, author of *More Than A Mistress*

"One of the never-failing joys of *Local Custom* is the crisp language, the well-turned phrases, the very exciting action, not to mention the confrontation of two vastly different cultures."　　　　　　　—Anne McCaffrey, author of *Freedom's Ransom*

"Space opera isn't just ripsnortin' adventure, though Lee and Miller give us plenty of that. The thing about space opera is it's more than nifty science, the clash of customs, the evolution of ideas, interesting planets, cool tech, and new pioneers, it's also and above all about character . . . and one cares about the characters, about their further adventures, and their families' adventures, and even about the villains. The Liaden Universe stories are very good space opera."
　　　　　　　—Sherwood Smith, author of *Journey to Otherwhere*

continued . . .

Eight Chants past Midsong: twilight.

In the plaza around Maidenstairs a crowd began to gather: men and women in brightly colored work clothes; here and there the sapphire or silver flutter of Circle robes.

The last echo of Eighthchant faded from the blank walls of Circle House, and the crowd quieted expectantly.

In a thin pass-street halfway down the plaza, a slim figure stirred. She adjusted the cord of the bag over her shoulder, but her eyes were fixed on Maidenstairs, where two of the Inmost Circle stood.

The shorter of the two raised her arms, calling for silence. The crowd held its breath, while across the plaza a dust devil swirled to life. The watcher in the by-street shivered, hunching closer to the wall.

"We are gathered," cried the larger of the two upon the stairs, "to commend to the Mother the spirit of our sister, our daughter, our friend. For there is gone from us this day the one called Moonhawk." He raised his arms as the other lowered hers to intone the second part of the ritual.

"Do not grieve, for Moonhawk is gathered into the care of She who is Mother of us all, who will instruct and make her ready for her next stay among us. Rejoice, indeed, and be made glad by the fortune of our sister Moonhawk, called so soon to the Mother's side."

The crowd spoke a faint "Ollee," and the shorter Witch continued, her voice taking on the mesmerizing quality appropriate to the speaking of strong magic.

"Gone to the Mother, to learn and to grow, Moonhawk walks among us no more. For the span of a full lifetime shall she sit at the feet of the Mother, absorbing the glory, seen by us no more. In this Wheel-turn none shall see Moonhawk again. She is gone. So mote it be."

"So mote it be," echoed the larger speaker.

"So more it be," the crowd cried, full-voiced and on familiar ground.

The slim watcher said nothing at all, though she ducked a little farther back into the byway. The dust devil found her there and made momentary sport of her newly shorn hair before going in search of other amusements.

A tall woman at the edge of the crowd made a sharp movement, quickly arrested. The watcher leaned forward, lips shaping a word: *Mother.* She dropped back, the word unspoken.

It was useless. Moonhawk was dead, by order of she who was Moonhawk's mother during this turn of the Wheel. The funeral pyre of her possessions had been ignited at Midsong while the mother looked on with icy face and sand-dry eyes. The watcher had been there, too. She had cried—perhaps enough for the mother, as well. But there were no tears now.

In the bag over her shoulder were such belongings as she had been able to bring away from her cell in the Maidens' wing of Circle House. The clothes she wore were bought in a secondhand store near the river: a dark, soft shirt with too-long sleeves that chafed nipples unused to confinement; skintight leggings, also dark, except for the light patch at the right knee; and outworlder boots with worn heels. The earrings were her own, set in place years ago by old hands trembling with pride of her. The seven silver bracelets in the pack were not hers. In the shirt's sleeve pocket was a single coin: a Terran tenbit.

The two of the Inmost Circle left the stairs; the crowd fragmented and grew louder. The watcher quietly faded down the skinny by-street, trying to form some less desperate plan for the future.

Moonhawk is dead. So mote it be.

At the end of the by-street the watcher turned left, toward a distant reddish glow.

You might, she thought to herself diffidently, go to the Silent Sisters at Caleitha. They won't ask your name, or where you're from, or why you've come. You can stay with them, never speaking, never leaving the Sisterhouse, never touching another human being . . .

"I'd rather be dead!" she snapped at the night, at herself—and began to laugh.

The sound was horrible in her ears: jagged, unnatural. She knotted her fingers in the ridiculous mop of curls, yanking until tears came to replace the awful laughter. Then she continued on her way, the rosy glow ever brighter before her.

"**Liadens! Gods-benighted, smooth-faced lying** sons and daughters of *curs!*"

A crumpled wad of clothing was thrown toward the gape-mouthed duffel with more passion than accuracy. From her station by the cot, Priscilla fielded it and gently dropped it in the bag. This act failed to draw Shelly's usual comments about Priscilla's wasted speed and talent.

"Miserable, stinking half bit of a ship!" Shelly continued at the top of her range, which was considerable. "One shift on, one shift off; Terrans to the back, *please,* and mind your words when you're speaking to a Liaden! Fines for this, fines for that . . . no damn shore leave, no damn privacy, nothing to do but work your shift, sleep your shift, work your shift . . . *hell!*"

She shoved the last of her clothing ruthlessly into the duffel, slammed a box of booktapes on top, and sealed the carry-all with a violence that made Priscilla wince.

"First mate's a crook; second mate's a rounder . . . here!" She slapped a thick buff envelope into Priscilla's hand.

The younger woman blinked. "What's this?"

"Copy of my contract and the buy-out fee—in cantra, as specified. Think I'm gonna let either the first or the second get their paws on it? Cleaned me out good and proper, it has. But no savings and no job is better than one more port o' call on this tub, and that I'll swear to!" She paused and leaned toward the other woman, punctuating her points with stabs of a long forefinger. "You give that envelope to the Trader, girl-o, and let 'im know I'm gone. You got the sense I think you got, you'll hand in your own with it."

Priscilla shook her head. "I don't have the buy out, Shelly."

"But you'd go if you did, eh?" The big woman sighed. "Well, you're forewarned, at least. Can you last 'til the run's over, girl?"

"It's only another six months, Standard." She touched the other woman's arm. "I'll be fine."

"Hmmph." Shelly shouldered her bag and took the two strides necessary to get her from cot to door. In the hall, she turned again. "Take care of yourself, then, girl-o. Sorry we didn't meet in better times."

"Take care, Shelly," Priscilla responded. It seemed that she was hovering on the edge of something else, but the other woman had turned and was stomping off, shoulders rounded and head bent in mute protest of the short ceiling.

Priscilla turned in the opposite direction—toward the Trader's room—her own head slightly bent. She was not tall as Terrans went, and the ceiling was a good three inches above her curls; there just seemed something about *Daxflan* that demanded bowed heads.

Nonsense, she told herself firmly, rounding the corner by the shuttlebay.

But it wasn't nonsense. All that Shelly had said was true—and more. To be Terran was to be a second-class citizen on *Daxflan,* with quarters beyond the cargo holds and meals served half-cold in a cafeteria rigged out of what had once been a storage pod. The Trader didn't speak Terran at all, though the captain had a few words, and issued his orders in abrupt Trade unburdened with such niceties as "please" and "thank you."

Priscilla sighed. She had served with Liadens on other trade ships, though never on a Liaden ship. She wondered if conditions were the same on all of them. Her thoughts went back to Shelly, who had sworn she would never serve on another Liaden ship; though Shelly had done okay until the Healer had left two ports ago, to be replaced by a simple robotic medkit. That move had been called temporary. "More Liaden lies!" she had said. "They're liars. *All* liars!"

The first mate was a crook and the second a rounder—whatever, Priscilla amended, a rounder was. Liaden and Terran, respectively, and as alike as if the same mother had born them.

Perhaps, Priscilla thought, the Trader only hired a certain type of person to serve him. She wondered what that said about Priscilla Mendoza, so eager for a berth as cargo master that she had not stopped first to look about her. Yet she *had* been eager. In a mere ten years she had gone from Food Service Technician—which meant little more than scullery maid—to General Crew, and then into cargo handling. Among her goals was a pilot's certificate, though certainly there was no hope for furthering *that* aim while on *Daxflan*.

The Trader's room was locked; no voice bade her enter when she laid her hand against the plate. So, then. She shook her head as the 1100 bell rang. She would be short of sleep *this* shift.

The captain, she decided, would do just as well. She continued down the hall to the bridge, then paused, hearing voices to her right—a man's, raised in outrage; a woman's, soothing.

Priscilla turned her steps in that direction, Shelly's envelope heavy in her hand.

The door to the Liaden lounge was open. Heedless, Sav Rid Olanek flung the paper at his cousin, Captain Chelsa yo 'Vaade.

"Denied!" he cried, the High Tongue crackling with rage.

"They dare! When all my life I have left this finger free to bear only the ring of a Master of Trade!" He waved gem-laden fingers also at Chelsea, who blinked, automatically cataloging Line-gem, school-gems, Clan-gem among the glittering array of others less important to Sav Rid's melant'i.

"They say you might reapply, cousin," she offered hesitantly. "You need only wait a Standard."

"Bah!" Sav Rid cried, as she might have known he would. "Reapply? *That* for their reapplication!" He snatched the letter back and rent it twice before flinging the pieces away. "They think me unworthy? They shall be schooled. We shall show them, *Daxflan* and I, how it is a *true* master of the craft goes about his business!" He turned then, eyes catching on the shadow at the door.

"You, there!" he snapped in Trade, crossing the room in four short strides. "What is it, Mendoza?"

Priscilla bowed, offering the envelope. "I did not wish to disturb you, sir," she replied in Trade, "but Shelly van Whitkin bade me give you this."

"So." He tore the envelope open, glanced at the paper with no great interest, and fingered the coin idly before slipping it into his belt.

One cantra, Priscilla saw, her stomach sinking. A sum so far beyond her resources that it was absurd to consider following Shelly's example. She might, she supposed, jump ship, but the thought of the dishonor attached to such an action cramped her stomach further.

"You may go, Mendoza," the Trader told her, and she bowed again before turning away. As she stepped into the hallway, she heard him address another comment in High Liaden to Captain yo'Vaade, something about having made a cantra and lost a big mouth to feed.

Daxflan **was two days out of Alcyone, and dinner** looked terrible. Cargo Master Mendoza meekly accepted her tray and carried it into the crowded, steamy Terran mess hall. Peripheral vision showed Second Mate Dagmar Collier waving to her from a table near the door. Face averted, Priscilla moved to a newly vacated corner table. Self-preservation would not allow her to sit with her back to the noisy room, but the temptation was strong.

She frowned at the greasy soup and put her spoon down, then picked up the chipped plastic mug. Grinning, she sipped the tepid coffeetoot, recalling that Shelly had never sat down to a meal on *Daxflan* without indulging in a rant, the salient point of which was always the economic infeasibility of a tradeship serving 'toot instead of the real bean.

It had been Shelly's belief that serving 'toot to the Terrans was another deliberate snipe from the Trader. However, Priscilla had overheard Liaden crew members complaining that the beverage called tea aboard *Daxflan* had never seen Solcintra. Shelly had only a spacer's handful of Liaden, High or Low, and had just shaken her head at

Priscilla's theory that perhaps *none* of the crew was treated very well.

Resolutely, the cargo master put the 'toot from her and picked up her spoon. Horrible as it looked, the soup was dinner and she would get no better; the alternative was the sodden breadroll and the sticky lump of cheese she knew from experience to be inedible to the point of nausea. It would have to be the soup.

Taking a gelid spoonful, Priscilla found her mind turning, as it had these last two shifts, back to the containers they had taken on at Alcyone Prime. Sealed cargo. Nothing unusual in that; she had the manifests listing the items the sealed hold contained, their weights and distributions. All according to book. And yet there was something . . .

With a scrape and a *thump!* the second mate was with her. Priscilla jumped, splashing greasy soup on her sleeve. Clamping her teeth, she patiently daubed at the spot, avoiding Dagmar's eyes. The second grinned and leaned back in the chair, flinging her legs out before her.

"Scare you, Prissy?"

Priscilla's slim shoulders stiffened. Dagmar's grin widened.

"I was thinking." There was no emotion in the cargo master's soft, level voice.

"That's our Prissy," Dagmar said indulgently. "Always thinking." She leaned across the tiny table and touched the back of a slender hand, delighting in the slight withdrawal. "What about after dinner, though? What say I bring along something to keep you from thinking, and we have fun?"

"I'm sorry," Priscilla said, hoping she sounded like it, "but the distribution charts are behind. I'm going to have to spend some of this off-shift getting caught up."

Dagmar shook her head, secretly pleased at Prissy's seemingly endless supply of excuses. The game had run three months now. Dagmar considered the quarry worthy of an extended pursuit. It might be easier if the girl weren't so serious about her work—and so popular with the crew. The younger woman wasn't much on getting high or sleeping around. But Dagmar knew that Priscilla would have to relax and reveal a weak point one day—and when she finally did catch Prissy out, the spoils would be that much sweeter.

"That's all right," she said consolingly. "You work as hard as you want. Good to see that in a new hire. And at the end of the run—if you do *real* good—I'll give you a reward." She narrowed her eyes a bit, looking for signs of distress on the other woman's face. She detected none and played her ace.

"A reward," she repeated, and reached across the table to take one cool, slim hand in hers. "How 'bout . . . at the end of the run you and me go off—just us two—and have a Hundred Hours together? Huh? A hundred hours of loving and cuddling and fancy food and drink. Don't that sound nice?"

It did, Priscilla admitted to herself. Present company excluded.

She withdrew her hand carefully. "You're very generous," she murmured, "but I'm not—"

The second recaptured her hand. "Think it over. Got plenty of time." She squeezed the hand until she heard knuckles crack and then released it. "Nice, long fingers. You ought to wear rings." She smiled again, tipping her own hand so that light glittered sullenly across the dirty gems worn three deep on each fat finger. "I'll buy you a ring," she finished softly, "after our Hundred Hours."

Priscilla drew a deep breath, trying to drown a sudden, flaring urge to mayhem. She stood.

"Going so soon?"

The cargo master nodded. "Those calculations are going to take awhile." She fled the mess hall.

A *ring!* Holy Mother! Priscilla became aware that she was breathing hard, nearly running down the lowering corridor. She slowed, willed her hands to unclench at her side, and continued with outward serenity toward her quarters.

Inwardly she still raged. Day after day of the second's pursuit was bad enough, though at least *she* could be put off with excuses, but only this past shift had First Mate Pimm tel'Jadis come to her in the master's cubicle, and the less thought of *that* encounter the better.

Caught between the two of them, powerful as they were, with neither the Trader nor the captain willing to take the part of a Terran against a Liaden, or of one Terran against another . . . Priscilla slapped the palmplate and thumbed the light switch to HIGH before entering her tiny cabin.

The room was empty.

Of course, she jeered at herself, stepping in and locking the door. She leaned her head against the door frame and closed her eyes briefly. Stress, poor food, little sleep—she was getting nervous, fanciful. Surely the first mate would not secret himself in her cabin and wait to surprise her.

Not yet.

"Damn!" she said violently. She moved to the cramped 'fresher cubicle. Stripping off her clothes, she shoved them into the cleanbot and twisted the dial to SUPERCLEAN. More carefully, she removed the silver and opal drops from her ears and put them on the shelf under the short mirror. Then she dialed the unit temp to HOT, the intensity to NEEDLE, and stepped under the deluge.

Priscilla rubbed dry eyes and sat back, frowning at the screen. She was right. At first, she had mistrusted her equations and so rechecked everything a second time, and a third. There was no doubt. She wondered what she was going to do now. Contraband drugs were certainly nothing she wanted to be involved with—and as cargo master, she had signed for them!

Shaking her head, she leaned over the keyboard again.

First, she told herself, you're going to seal this data under the cargo master's "Confidential" code. Then you're going to take a cold needle shower and hope it'll make up for a sleepless night—you're on duty in an hour! She rose and stretched.

She would make no decisions until she had had at least a shift's sleep. It was important not to make a mistake.

"The following personnel," blared the speaker over the door, "will report to Shuttlebay Two at 20.00 hours: Second Mate Dagmar Collier, Pilot Bern dea'Maan, Cargo Master Priscilla Mendoza, Cargo-hand Tailly Zeld, Cargo-hand Nik Laz Galradin."

"What?" Priscilla demanded, spinning to stare at the

speaker. Bay 2 at 20.00 hours? That was less than ten minutes from now!

She spun back to the desk and cleared the screen, then spun again to rake her gaze around the closet-sized room, tallying her meager possessions. There was nothing she would need on Jankalim here. Smoothing her hands over her hair, she left the room.

It was only as she was striding toward Bay 2 that it occurred to her to wonder why she was needed at all. Jankalim was a drop-only, the sort of thing most commonly handled by the first or second and a couple of hands.

Maybe there had been a mistake? There had been no trip worldside listed on her schedule last shift, of that she was certain. Come to think of it, it was *silly* to send the cargo master on a trip like this one. Almost as silly as sending the Trader.

She rounded the corner into the bay corridor at a spanking pace and brought herself up sharply to avoid walking over the small man just ahead.

Trader Olanek turned his head and inclined it in unsmiling recognition. "Mendoza. Punctual, as always." The words were in Trade and heavily accented.

"Thank you, sir," she said, politely shortening her stride to match his. Somehow, she had never managed to inform the Trader that she had limited fluency in his language. She glanced at his profile and shrugged mentally. The Trader's temper was legend on *Daxflan,* but he seemed to be in as amiable a mood as she had ever seen him.

"Are *you* going worldside, sir?" she ventured respectfully.

"Of course I am going worldside, Mendoza. Why else should I be here?"

Priscilla ignored the irritation in his voice and plunged on. "Has there been a change in schedule, then? My last information was that Jankalim is only a drop point. If we're going to take cargo on—"

"I must therefore assume, Mendoza," the Trader cut in, clearly irritated, "that your information is not complete."

Priscilla bit her lip. It was folly to goad him further. She inclined her head and dropped back to allow him to precede her into the shuttle. Then, sighing, she slipped into the first unoccupied seat, eyelids dropping. Half an hour, ship to world. At least she would get a nap.

"Hi there, Prissy," an unwelcome voice said in her ear. "You're not asleep, are you?" A hand was placed high on her thigh.

Gritting her teeth, Priscilla opened her eyes and sat up straight.

Jankalim possessed one spaceport, situated on the easternmost tip of the southernmost continent, within a stone's throw of the planetary sea and the edge of the world's second city.

As spaceports went, this one was subaverage, Priscilla decided, watching Tailly and Nik Laz unload the few containers and pallets that represented their reason for stopping here at all. The spaceport boasted three hot-pads for in-system ships, four shuttle cradles, and a double-dozen steel warehouses. All the pads were empty, though there was a surprisingly well-kept shuttle in the end cradle.

She glanced at the corrugated metal building to her right. A lopsided sign proclaimed it to be the port master's office. Trader Olanek had disappeared within it immediately upon setdown, Dagmar trailing behind like a double-sized shadow.

As if summoned by the thought, the second appeared in the doorway, jerking her head as she crossed the yard. "Gimme a hand, willya, Prissy? Trader wants a couple boxes from that end house. Ought to be able to get 'em fine between us."

Raising her eyebrows, Priscilla looked back at burly Tailly and miniature Nik Laz, who were just setting the last pallet in place.

"Aah, give 'em a break, Prissy," Dagmar growled. "They worked plenty hard already."

Kindness was uncharacteristic of the second mate. Probably the woman wanted a little privacy to press her suit further. Trapped without a reasonable excuse, Priscilla nodded and fell into step beside her, keeping a cautious distance between them.

The lights came up as they entered the first warehouse. Dagmar turned confidently to the right; Priscilla, a few steps behind, let her lead the way. Several more turns led them to a musty-smelling hall, somewhat dimmer than the previous corridors, flanked with blank metal doors.

Priscilla wondered what the Trader could possibly want from a section of warehouse that was clearly abandoned, then she shrugged. She was cargo master. It was her job to stow what the Trader contracted for.

It just would have been nice, she stormed to herself, if the Trader had seen fit to inform his cargo master that he expected to take on goods at Jankalim.

Dagmar moved slowly down the hallway—counting doors, Priscilla thought—then stopped and slid a card into a doorslot.

The light in the frame lit, but nothing else happened. Dagmar grunted. "You're real good with computers. You try it."

The tone of voice made Priscilla uneasy. She took the card, inserted it, and was rewarded with both a light and a clicking noise from within.

Dagmar pushed at the door, then grunted again. "Damn thing's stuck. Come round here, Prissy—that's right. Now, I'm gonna pull back on the door an' get it started in the track. When it starts to slide, you get yourself between an' *push*, okay?"

"Okay."

Dagmar laid her hands against the door and exerted force. For a moment it looked as if the mechanism would resist. Then Priscilla saw a crack appear. She slipped her fingers into the slender opening as the crack began to widen, adding her own pressure to the enterprise. The gap widened farther. She slid her body into the opening and shoved.

As she pushed, there was a shadowy movement behind her, and she heard Dagmar say, "Can't be all that smart now, can ya, Prissy?" Then something clipped her behind the ear, and she crumpled sideways, tasting salt.

There was a window high in the sidewall, and that was good. The door was locked from the outside, and that was bad. Her head ached, and that, she decided, was worst of all. Neither the soreness of her face nor the pain in her shoulder came near it, though the throb of her ribs ran a close second.

Moving with extreme care, Priscilla went to the window and stood on tiptoe, craning. No way out there: the pane was solid blast-glass, and even had she the means to break it, the opening itself was too small even for her lanky frame.

Outside, the well-kept shuttle was still in its ratty cradle.

Daxflan's shuttle was gone.

Left me, she thought through the fog of dizziness and pain. And then, with a gasp that sent knifing fire down her side, the reality hit her. *Left me! Here,* with the door locked and no way out and *how* could they have left me? Surely the Trader would have missed me . . . or if not me—but how could they *not* have missed me! Tailly, Nik Laz, Bern . . . how could they have *left* . . .

She took a deep, deliberate breath, ignoring the pain.

"I will not," she informed the room austerely, "sanction hysterics."

Her voice came back to her from the empty walls, deep and oddly comforting. Priscilla closed her eyes and concentrated on breathing until the panic stilled.

I have to get out, she told herself, forming the thought carefully.

She surveyed her prison. Empty. Dustless. Dim. What light there was came from the window. She would have to do whatever she did before day failed.

Leaning against the wall, she went through her pockets: stylus, pad of paper, ID, strapping tape, comb, two Terran wholebits, magnetic ruler, penknife, calculator—nothing heavy enough to break a triple-thick window or strong enough to jimmy the door.

She took another look outside. The yard was as empty as the room she stood in. She settled her shoulders against the wall and considered her resources.

Stylus. Not too likely. It went back into her pocket. Likewise the paper; also comb, ID, and money.

Tape? She kept it out for the time being. Penknife? Why not? Ruler? No—Yes. Yes, wait a minute—magnets . . . lock . . . jimmy the *lock!*

She knelt at the door to get the cardslot at eye level, then peered cautiously within. It just might be possible . . .

Sitting back on her heels, she unrolled the ruler and tried unsuccessfully to pry the thin rectangular magnets off with her fingers. The penknife did the trick—fifteen minutes later she had four flat magnets, each with its own long tail of tape, lined up on the door next to the cardslot.

With the tip of the knife she inserted them, one at a time, thanking the Goddess that there were only four contacts within the mechanism and that no one had expected the place to be used as a jail.

The last magnet was affixed. She withdrew the knife, holding her breath . . . but nothing happened.

Wrong combination, she told herself, and patiently inserted the knife point again, reversing the polarity of the magnet on the extreme left.

She had worked through twelve combinations, and multi-colored spots were shimmering before her eyes, when there was a soft click. Hardly daring to breathe, she looked up.

The light over the door frame was lit.

She scrambled to her feet, folding the knife automatically and dropping it into her pocket. Leaning forward, she put her hands against the panel and prepared to push—but suddenly the door slid open.

Priscilla twisted, gasping, and regained her balance before the man on the other side extended a hand to grab her.

"Hold there, now." The grip on her arm changed. "Who by hell are *you?*"

"Priscilla Mendoza—cargo master on *Daxflan.*"

"That's so, is it?" He eyed her. "Bit beyond yer territory, would say?"

"Without a doubt." She gritted her teeth against the pain and fought to keep the edge out of her voice. "There's been a—misunderstanding. I'm sure Trader Olanek will vouch for me. He was with the port master . . ."

"That be so," the man agreed. "Then he an' his went off. Nothin' was said about a missin' mate. Happen you'll have a better tale for Master Farley." He stepped back, keeping a firm hold on her arm. "We'll be walking this way now."

Priscilla clamped her jaw and matched his stride firmly.

The glare of sunshine made her gasp with quadrupled pain. She was abruptly thankful for the man's bruising hold—without his support she would have fallen.

Sunlight gave way to shadow. Her captor paused and laid his hand against a plate, and a door slid open. Obedient to his tug, Priscilla stepped into an echoing cavern of a room. Four dark terminals sat at intervals on the empty counter; the ship-board suspended above displayed one row of tired amber letters, brilliant in the gloom: DUTIFUL PASSAGE SOL-CINTRA LIAD.

She stopped, staring at the board. A Liaden ship, surely, but . . . dear Goddess, they *had* gone! They had left orbit, left the sector, without her. She had been abandoned deliberately on this quarter-bit world!

"Come along, mistress, we've not got all the day." The man jerked hard on her arm, and Priscilla went with him, blankly.

She should be angry, she knew, but the various pains and shocks seemed to cancel emotion. Her overwhelming desire was for sleep—but no. There was the port master to see, and an explanation to be made. She would need money—a job. Two Terran wholebits was hardly a fortune, no matter how backward the world.

"In here, mistress." He gave another tug. Priscilla ground her teeth against a snapped retort and obeyed.

Port Master Farley was a plump man with a dejected yellow mustache and apologetic blue eyes. He blinked at Priscilla and turned toward her captor. "Well, now, Liam. What have you here?"

The man holding her renewed his grip and straightened, giving the impression of having brought his heels smartly together. "Computer reported some tamperin' with the lock on door triple-ay, corridor seven, house one—one o' the empty sections, Master Farley."

The port master nodded.

"Went to check things out—thinkin' it'll be a malfunction, you understand." He yanked Priscilla forward. "Found this one on the *inside*. Tells the tale o' bein' Priscilla Mendoza, cargo master on *Daxflan* as just left us."

The port master blinked again. "But what were you doing in the warehouse, lass? Especially along that way—it's been empty for years."

Priscilla took a deep breath. The pain in her side was less, she noted, down to a persistent dull ache.

"Trader Olanek and Second Mate Collier came into this building to speak with you, sir," she said. "I was outside, supervising the unloading. After a time, the second mate came out and asked me to go with her to the warehouse. She said the Trader wanted something out of one of the rooms. When we arrived, she put a card in the lock and asked me to help her push the door open, since it was stuck—"

"Like as not," Liam muttered. "Damn thing hasn't been opened this tenyear."

"And then," Priscilla concluded, "she hit me over the head and left me there. When I came to, I tried to gimmick the lock with a couple magnets off my ruler."

Master Farley was staring. "Hit you over the head and left you? And you her mate? Why would she do such a thing?"

"How do *I* know?" Priscilla snapped, then dredged up a painful smile. "Look, do you mind if I sit down? My head *does* hurt."

"Surely, surely." He looked a little flustered. "Liam . . ."

The warehouseman loosed her with reluctance and placed the chair close to the desk before taking up a position directly behind it. She sat carefully, hands curled around the plastic armrests.

"Thank you."

"You're welcome." Master Farley sighed, drummed his fingers on the rubbed steel top of his desk, screwed his eyes shut, and opened them again. "You'll be having some ID on you, of course."

She nodded, earning a flash of pain and a renewed flurry of dots. The hand that held her identification out trembled, she noted, and she was aware of a flicker of anger.

Master Farley took the packet and fed the cards one by one into the unit beside his desk. He studied the screen carefully, sighed, and turned back to her.

"Well, your papers are in order. Cargo master for *Daxflan,* out of Chonselta City, Liad—plain as rain." He shook his head. "I'll be right out with you, lass. I can't see the why of leaving you like this. A cargo master is an important part of a trade vessel. All this about being hit on the head and left—it don't add up. And I'll tell you what else: Trader Olanek was here, and we had a very pleasant chat. But I never saw this second mate you be speaking of. Nor I never saw you."

"You don't believe me, in fact."

He waved his hands soothingly. "Now, lass. Admit it don't seem so likely."

"I *do* admit it," Priscilla told him. "I don't know why it was done any more than you do. Perhaps the second felt she had a grudge—but nothing to warrant cracking my skull." Which means the Trader ordered it, she thought suddenly, crystally. Dagmar wouldn't have mugged her and left her—not without orders. It was more in her style to try rape, if she had thought Priscilla had insulted her. And if the Trader had ordered it, that meant . . .

Master Farley's chair creaked as he changed position. "Well, then, lass, I'm just bound to say that done's done. There doesn't seem to be any harm you've done—is that so, Liam?"

"Yessir," the warehouseman said regretfully. "Happens that's so."

The port master nodded. "Then the wisest thing to do is give you back your ID and send you on your way." He pushed her cards across the desk.

Priscilla stared at him. "Send me on my way," she repeated blankly. "I'm *stranded*. I don't have any money. I don't know anybody here." The Trader had ordered it. Which meant that her deduction was correct: *Daxflan* had been carrying illegal drugs in enormous quantity. Never mind how he had gotten at her data, locked under her personal code. He had found it, given her credit for being able to make the deduction—and acted to remove a known danger.

"Best you go to the embassy," Master Farley was saying with apologetic kindness. "Likely they'll send you home."

Home? "No," she said, suddenly breathless. "I want to go—I must get to Arsdred." That was *Daxflan*'s next port of call. And then? she asked herself, wondering at her own urgency. She shoved the question away for the present. She would take one thing at a time.

"Arsdred," she repeated firmly.

He looked doubtful. "Well, if you must, lass, you must.

But I'm not the one to know how you'll go about it. You said you'd no money . . ."

"The ship in orbit now—*Dutiful Passage?* Is she a trader?"

He nodded, blinking in confusion.

"Good." She took a deep breath and forced her aching head to work. "Master Farley, you owe me no favors, I know. But I want to apply for work on *Dutiful Passage*. Will you help me?"

"It's not me you need to speak to about that, lass. It'll be Mr. Saunderson, who's the agent." He puffed his chest out a little. "*Dutiful Passage* stops here every three years, regular."

A ship that listed Jankalim among its regular ports of call? And a Liaden ship, too. Priscilla paused, trying to picture conditions less appealing than *Daxflan*'s. Imagination failed her, and she smiled tightly at the port master.

"How do I get in touch with Mr. Saunderson?"

"His office is just in the city," Liam said from behind her. "Anyone can tell you the way."

"That's so," Master Farley agreed slowly. Then he squared his shoulders and stiffened his mustache. "You can use the comm to call him from here, if you like to."

Her smile was genuine this time, if no less painful. "Thank you so much."

"That's all right, lass. Pleased to be of help," he muttered, cheeks going pink. "Liam here will show you to the comm room." He made a show of turning back to the unit beside his desk, and Priscilla stood.

Liam looked as if he would have liked to grab her arm again, but satisfied himself with walking close behind her down the short hall to the communication room. He showed her the local screen and, after a moment's hesitation, punched up Mr. Saunderson's code. Priscilla smiled at him, and he flushed dull red.

Mr. Saunderson was old, his face a translucent network of wrinkles from which a pair of obsidian eyes glittered. He listened to her name and the statement that she had been employed until recently on *Daxflan* and heard her say that she was interested in employment on the orbiting ship.

"It is my understanding, Ms. Mendoza, that *Dutiful Passage* is fully staffed. However, if you would care to hold on for a few moments, I will ascertain whether this understanding is correct."

"Thank you, sir. I appreciate your trouble."

"Not at all. One moment, please." The elderly face was replaced with an image of an unlikely landscape, portrayed in various shades of tangerine and aqua. The picture had not been calculated to soothe raging headaches, and Priscilla closed her eyes against it.

"Ms. Mendoza?"

Priscilla snapped her eyes open, cheeks flaming.

Mr. Saunderson smiled at her. "The captain professes himself interested in an interview, Ms. Mendoza, and wonders if you would honor him by a visit." He cleared his throat with the utmost gentility. "He does indicate that *Dutiful Passage* employs a very able cargo master. He does not wish you to visit under a misapprehension, or if you cannot accept any position except that of cargo master."

Priscilla hesitated, wondering what positions the captain had in mind. But she was determined to get to Arsdred.

She looked at Mr. Saunderson, who was patiently waiting in the screen, and tried to visualize him whetting the captain's supposed appetite with a glowing description of her, bruised face and all. The vision brought forth a grin.

"You're very kind," she told the old gentleman carefully. "I am willing to accept any crewing work that might be available on *Dutiful Passage*. When and where may I visit the captain?"

"I shall send 'round Ms. Dyson, our pilot. Is twenty minutes convenient? Good. She will convey you to *Dutiful Passage*. I will inform Captain yos'Galan of your coming."

"You're very kind," she said again.

"Not at all." Mr. Saunderson smiled. "Good luck, Ms. Mendoza." He cut the connection.

Priscilla sighed and leaned back in her chair. She had twenty minutes until Pilot Dyson came to collect her. She looked at Liam. "Is there someplace where I can wash my face and hands?"

He snorted and jerked his head. "Down the hall, first door on the left. Nothin' fancy, it isn't."

"As long as it's functional." She levered herself up and went past him into the hall. He followed and leaned against the wall, arms crossed over his chest, watching as she opened the door and entered the 'fresher.

There was no shower, which was a shame. She had rather hoped for a hot deluge to ease some of the crankiness from her bruises. There was a sink, water, and soap. She would make do.

Automatically, she reached up to remove her earrings, then froze in disbelief when her fingers encountered only naked earlobes. Slowly, she went over to the tiny square of mirror on the far wall.

Reflected back at her was a creamy oval face surmounted by a tangled cloud of ebony curls, black eyes very wide under slim brows, and nostrils distended with anger. The fragile ridge of the right cheek was already purpling. There was a small hole in each perfect earlobe; the left one showed a thin line of blood, as if it was torn just a little.

How dare she? she thought furiously. My earrings, given to me on my Womanday, that were my grandmother's! How dare—Rage, sudden and shocking, drove out pain and fears. Priscilla was abruptly trembling, wishing fiercely to have Dagmar's neck between her hands.

Arsdred, she told herself, trying to still the fury. I'll have them both. Just let me get to Arsdred.

Slowly the rage became manageable; she enclosed it, as she had been taught, banked and ready for the proper moment.

Woodenly she went to the sink, turned on the cold water, bent, and began to splash her face.

"Asleep, Mendoza?" Dyson inquired from the pilot's chair.

Priscilla opened her eyes and sat up straighter. "Just resting."

"Okay by me. End of the line in about five minutes. Word is you'll be met and escorted to the captain's office. Got it?"

"Yes. Thank you."

Dyson snorted. "Don't thank me, Mendoza; I'm just passing on the facts." She thumbed the comm, reeled off her numbers, and grunted at the acknowledgment before turning her full attention to the board.

Orbit and velocity were matched with an offhanded exactitude that earned Priscilla's silent praise even as she regretted her own uncompleted certificate.

There came assorted mechanical clankings and ringings before a final authoritative *thump*. Dyson locked the board with a sweep of her hand. "Okay, Mendoza. Roll on out."

"Okay." She unstrapped and stood. "Thanks."

"What they pay me for, Mendoza. Beat it, all right?"

Priscilla grinned. "See you around."

She went out the hatch and through the door—then stopped, blinking.

Carpet was beneath her feet; she was struck by the vaulting, the well-lit spaciousness . . . She was in a state reception room.

The identification was hard to refute. To her left and some twelve feet downroom was a grouping of chairs and loungers—Terran- and Liaden-sized in equal proportion. Farther on, a podium was shoved against the wall, directly beneath the mural of an enormous tree in full, green leaf. Hovering behind and a little above, nearly dwarfed by the tree it guarded, was a winged dragon, bronze and fierce, emerald eyes looking directly at her. There were words in Liaden characters beneath the roots of the tree.

Priscilla sighed slightly, recalling little Fin Ton, who had taught her Liaden in an even exchange for games of *Go*. But his lessons had not extended to reading. Priscilla turned her head carefully to the right wall, which held what appeared to be a collage of photographs and drawings.

Obviously she was in the wrong place. She had better return to the docking pod and see if there was another door that led onto a more reasonable area—one containing her escort to the captain.

Half a second later she had abandoned that plan. Over the door by which she had entered, the atmosphere lamp glowed clear ruby, indicating vacuum in the pod beyond.

Priscilla turned. The door directly across from her, then? Or a ship's intercom? Surely, in a room as spacious as this one she could find an intercom.

That thought brought to mind all kinds of interesting questions about the room itself. Tradeships did not, in her experience, devote space to ballrooms or auditoriums. Three of *Daxflan*'s holds would have fit comfortably into this area.

Priscilla put speculation from her mind. First, she had to find an intercom.

The door across from her opened, and a rather breathless

small person erupted into the room. He skidded to a stop about two feet away and executed an awkward bow.

Not Liaden, she noted with relief. But—a child?

"Are you Ms. Mendoza?" he asked, then swept on without waiting for an answer. "Crelm! I'm *awful* sorry. I was supposed to be here when you came in. Cap'n's gonna *skin* me!"

She grinned at him. He was a stocky Terran boy of perhaps eleven Standards, dressed in plain slacks and shirt. There was a smear of grease on his right sleeve and another on his chin. An embroidered badge on his left shoulder bore the legend "Arbuthnot."

"I've only been here a minute," she told him. "Surely he won't skin you for that?"

The boy gave it consideration, tipping his head birdlike to one side. "Well, he still might. He *told* me to be here, didn't he? And it's rude, you gettin' off the shuttle and there being nobody to meet you." He sighed. "I really *am* sorry. I *meant* to be here."

"I accept your apology," Priscilla said formally. "Are you my escort to the captain, by any chance?"

"Oh, crelm," the boy said again, and laughed. "I'm making a rare mingle of it! An' he told me to make sure I welcomed you onboard, too!" He looked at her out of hopeful brown eyes. "Did I do that?"

"Admirably," she assured him, fighting down a rare spurt of her own laughter.

"Good," he said, relieved. He turned, waving at her to accompany him. "My name's Gordy Arbuthnot. I'm cabin boy."

"Pleased to meet you," Priscilla said gravely, trying not to stare around the wide, well-lit hallway. *This* was the ship that visited Jankalim every three years on a regular basis? The little she had seen so far would contain most of *Daxflan*. She opened her mouth to ask Gordy how many holds *Dutiful Passage* could carry, then thought better of it and asked another question instead. "What *was* that room back there? I thought I'd made a wrong turn getting off the shuttle."

"Reception room," he explained offhandedly. "For when

we have visitors. Most of us just use the cargo docks when we come back on-ship."

"But I'm a guest?" She frowned. "Do you get a *lot* of visitors?"

Gordy shrugged. "Cap'n has parties sometimes. And sometimes people take passage with us—'cause we go where the liners don't, or 'cause we go there faster."

"Oh."

They entered a lift, and her guide punched a quick series of buttons. Shortly the door opened to a narrower hall, wide enough for four Liadens to walk abreast, Priscilla estimated. She smelled cinnamon, resin, and leather; she took a deep breath and held it a moment before sighing.

Gordy grinned. "Best place in the whole ship for smells. That's Number Six Hold." He pointed. "There's Cap'n's office."

Priscilla caught her breath sharply and bit her lip against a flare of pain in her head.

There's nothing to worry about, she told herself firmly. The captain wants an interview. The worst that can happen is that he has no job to offer. Time enough, when that happens, to think of another way to Arsdred.

Gordy laid his hand against the palmplate in the captain's bright red door. There was a chime, followed by a subdued "Come."

The door slid open.

Priscilla crossed the threshold on the boy's heels, then stopped and frankly stared.

Once again she was overwhelmed by spaciousness. Shelf after shelf of booktapes, bound books, and musictapes lined one wall. On another hung a tapestry worked in dark crimson, dull gold, jade, and azure, a twining geometric design at once restful and surprising. Below that was a unit bar; to one side of it was another shelf of tapes interspersed with bric-a-brac. Straight ahead, in the center of the room, two chairs faced a wooden desk supporting a computer screen and two untidy piles of hard copy. To the left of the desk was a closed door bearing a diagonal red stripe. A deep, hedonistic chair was placed at an angle to the corner, several books and a sketch pad were piled helter-skelter on the carpet nearby, while more books littered the nearer low table. The second of the set supported a chessboard. Seated on the edge of the sofa and bent over the board was a white-haired man in a dark blue shirt.

The captain was *old*. Priscilla found it somewhat easier to breathe.

Gordy Arbuthnot stepped to the table and cleared his throat. "Cap'n?" he said in Terran. "Here's Ms. Mendoza, come to see you."

"So soon? Pilot Dyson has outdone herself." The man sighed and shook his head at the chessmen. "I don't think this stupid position *has* a solution."

He rose and came forward a few paces before inclining his head. "I'm Shan yos'Galan, Ms. Mendoza."

He was tall—a giant among Liadens. Silver eyes thickly fringed with black lashes looked directly into hers. Nor was he old—the frostcolored hair had misled her. His face was that of a man near her own age.

But, Goddess, *what* a face! Big-nosed, jut-cheeked, wide-mouthed, with a broad forehead, triangular chin, and thin white brows set at a slant over the large eyes. Anything farther from the usual delicacy of Liaden features would be hard to find this side of the Yxtrang.

Recovering herself with a start, Priscilla bowed stiffly in the Terran mode. "Captain yos'Galan," she said with precision, "I'm glad to see you."

"Well, you'll be among the first," he commented, and his accent was of Terra's educated class, not of Liad at all. "Though my family professes something of the sort. Of course, they've had time to get used to me. Gordy, Ms. Mendoza wants something to drink. Also, my glass is missing—and wherever it is, it's probably empty. What do I pay you for?"

The boy grinned and moved toward the bar. Pausing, he looked back at Priscilla. "The red wine's best," he said seriously, "but I think the white's probably pretty good. And there's brandy—I'm not sure about that . . ."

"What do you know about it at all?" the man demanded. "Nipping my spirits while I'm not watching, Gordy? And who said the red's best? Your own trained palate?"

"*You* drink the red, Cap'n."

"Unprincipled brat. You don't offer brandy to a person who's come for a job interview. Strive for some polish."

"Yessir," Gordy said, not noticeably abashed by this rebuke. "Ms. Mendoza? There's red wine, white, canary, green, blue—I mean, misravot—and tea and coffee . . ."

Another alarming bubble of laughter was rising. Hysteria, thought Priscilla, and suppressed it firmly.

"White wine, please," she told the boy, and he nodded, turning to the bar.

"Come sit down," the captain invited, waving a big brown hand toward the chairs and the desk. Light glittered off the stone in his single ring—the large carved amethyst of a Master Trader.

Obediently, she followed him to the desk and sank gratefully into one of the chairs. Master Trader? This ugly, too-tall Liaden was a Master Trader? And captain, too? With an absent smile Priscilla took her drink from the cabin boy.

On *Daxflan,* Sav Rid Olanek—a mere Trader—and Captain yo'Vaade split administration of ship and crew between them. That had been the one thing about *Daxflan* that had followed the routine she knew from other ships. Captain was a full-time job, after all; Trader, somewhat more than that. Yet here was a man supposedly doing *both.* And more. There were perhaps a double-dexon—twice a dozen dozen—of Master Traders in all the galaxy.

"Gordy." His clear, rather beautiful voice held a mild note of exasperation. Priscilla brought her attention back to the present.

"Cap'n?" The boy froze in the act of handing the man his glass.

Shan yos'Galan sighed and laid a blunt forefinger on the grease-smeared sleeve. Gordy flushed and bit his lip.

"There's a matching one on your chin. Are we out of water? Or soap? Is there some atavistic or religious significance attached to going about with grease on your face? Maybe you put it there purposefully, after long thought, feeling that a little facial decoration would call Ms. Mendoza's attention to you more favorably? You hoped she would be so overcome by the artistry of the smear that she would fail to chide you for being late to meet her?"

"How did—" Gordy interrupted himself and raised his eyes to the man's face. "I'm not Liaden, Cap'n."

"I have independently noted the fact. No doubt you feel it has some bearing on the matter at hand." He took his glass and leaned back in the chair.

"Yessir."

"I'm intrigued. An explanation, please?"

"Yessir." Gordy took a breath and squared his round shoulders. "Liadens consider the face the—the *seat of character.* Because of that, Liadens don't use cosmetics on their faces, like Terrans might, to—to dress up or to make themselves more attractive." He paused. The captain raised his glass and waved at him to continue.

Gordy nodded. "Also, the face has an—*erotic*—significance to Liadens. There are certain social situations where it's okay to touch between Liadens where Terran code of behavior would forbid. But only extreme intimates—like family members—touch hand to face or face to face." He took another breath. "So it follows that Liadens would be *particularly* careful about keeping their faces clean. Terrans, whose cultures don't include a strong facial taboo, are less strict."

There was a small pause while Shan yos'Galan raised the glass to his lips. " 'Taboo' is rather strong," he commented. "I think perhaps 'tradition' does nicely. Liadens love tradition, while you're dealing in generalizations, Gordy." He raised his glass again, and this time, Priscilla saw, he drank.

"As far as it goes, your grasp of the information seems

sound," he continued thoughtfully. "However, I'm not sure your inferences are correct. That tends to happen when you extrapolate from general, rather than specific. In any case, I have found—again, through independent observation, not to say experience—that it *feels nicer* to be clean than it feels to be dirty. Also, I have found that I prefer looking at clean faces as opposed to dirty faces. This is, I believe, a personal preference. I may be wrong. Since I am captain of this ship, though, I think I have the rank to indulge in a few harmless eccentricities. So, for the fourth time: Gordon, I would very much prefer that you endeavor to keep your person as smear-free as possible." He raised the glass again. "The next time, I'll have to dock you. What do you think might be a reasonable sum?"

The boy looked down. He rubbed at his soiled sleeve, then looked up. "Tenbit?"

"Fair enough." The captain grinned. "I detect the makings of a gambler in you. Or a Trader. We'll want lunch in half an hour or so."

Gordy blinked. "Lunch?"

"Yes, *lunch*. Did I use the wrong word? Cheese, fruit, rolls—that sort of thing. Speak to BillyJo; I repose all faith in her ability to resolve the matter for you. Now jet."

"Yessir." And he was gone, the door sighing shut behind him.

Shan yos'Galan shook his head. "It's my fate to raise small boys." He lifted his glass. "Are you ready to be interviewed, Ms. Mendoza? Or have you changed your mind?"

Priscilla sipped her wine, then met his gaze straightly. "I'm ready to be interviewed, Captain."

"Brave heart." He extended a long arm and flipped two switches set along the desk top. "Your name, please, and planet of origin."

"My name is Priscilla Delacroix y Mendoza. I was born on Sintia. I am a Terran citizen."

"Do you honor the Goddess, then?" His face was sharp with interest. "Hold to her teaching exclusively?"

"I did," she said carefully. "After all, She's part of every-

day life . . . But I've been on trading ships since I was sixteen.
And the Goddess isn't as powerful in the galaxy as She is on
Sintia."

"Since you were sixteen," he repeated, abandoning the
Goddess abruptly. "What do you know?"

She raised her brows. "I know how to cook for a crew of
twenty, how to wash up for a crew of thirty-three, how to decode messages, how to code messages. I can drive a jitney,
calculate weight distributions, figure loading capacities.
Whenever possible, I've pursued pilot training. My marks-
manship rating is ninety percent accuracy at two hundred
paces with a standard pellet gun. I speak Trade, Terran, Cren-
ish, and Sintian. I understand Liaden better than I speak it. If
I have to, I can shoot astrogation."

He nodded. "Your last position?"

"Cargo master on *Daxflan,* out of Chonselta City."

"And you held that post how long?"

"Four months," she said with determined serenity. "I
signed on at Tulon."

"Did you?" He raised his glass to his lips. "And what
brings you to apply for work on the *Passage?*"

"I don't have any choice."

The slanted brows pulled together. "Has Mr. Saunderson
still got that impressment operation going? I did ask him to
stop, Ms. Mendoza, I give you my word."

For the third time in an hour Priscilla felt laughter rising.
She drowned it in a swallow of wine. "I'm sorry—that was
rude. What I meant to say was that I've been—dismissed—
from my post on *Daxflan.* Yours is the only ship in at
Jankalim now, so I'm applying here."

"I see." He sipped wine. "Your dismissal sounds abrupt."

"Extremely."

He nodded again, shifted in his chair, and rested his arms
on the desk top. "Ms. Mendoza, I have a copy of your record
here . . ." He spun the computer screen around.

Priscilla frowned, her eyes traveling automatically down

the lines of information. *Ladybird . . . As You Like It . . . Tyrunner . . . Selda . . . Dante . . . Daxflan.*

"Motherless, lying, spawn of a—" She gasped, and the rest was lost as the enormity of the thing hit her. *Ruin . . .* She met Shan yos'Galan's eyes. "It's a lie."

"Do you want to say so officially?" He spun the screen back. "It looks pretty bad, doesn't it? 'Suspected larceny. Jumped ship, Jankalim, Standard 1385.' " He leaned back in the chair and sipped wine, his eyes on her face. "*I* don't know of any reputable captain who would take on a person with a record containing that entry—even granting the overall excellence of the rest. What happened to your earrings?"

"The second mate hit me over the head," she said tonelessly, trying to conquer the shock. "They were gone when I came to."

"Odd sort of thing for a second mate to do," he commented. "But maybe there were extenuating circumstances. You disliked each other?"

"*I* disliked *her*. She liked me all too well." He was toying with her, drawing out the talking when there was no use in talking anymore. Priscilla tightened her grip on the wineglass, fighting to keep her face calm. On his ship, in his power . . . and who would miss a suspected thief who had jumped her last ship? Who would believe a suspected thief if she chose to tell outrageous lies about a Master Trader? He must have called up her record while speaking with Mr. Saunderson and seen that damning entry.

The man across from her shifted sharply. "And yet," he persisted, demanding her attention, "liking you so well, she hits you over the head and steals your earrings." He drank. "Forgive me, Ms. Mendoza, but *that* sounds even odder."

"The Trader ordered it," Priscilla said, clinging to serenity as if it were her last hope of salvation. Let him hear, Goddess, she begged silently. Let him believe the truth.

"Ah, dear Sav Rid." The expression on his face was one of mild puzzlement. "He will have his little joke, you know, Ms. Mendoza. But surely there were other avenues open to him, had he conceived a desire for your earrings. Why order the second mate to hit you over the head for them? Couldn't he merely have purchased them from you?" He snapped his fingers lightly. "He had offered a fair sum, and you refused to sell. Rendered desperate—"

"*Stop* it!" She snapped forward, eyes riveted on his. "Captain yos'Galan, please. It's imperative that I get to Arsdred. It's a large port—I'd hoped your ship would dock there. Any crewing duties you have—I'll work my passage to Arsdred as assistant mess cook, and you can lock me in a closet off-shift! You don't have to trust me—believe what you will. I *don't* think it's very funny to abandon someone and ruin their record, make it impossible to find—to find honorable work . . ." Her voice had developed a quaver. Horrified, she bit her lip and clenched her hands tightly to squeeze out the shaking. "I *must* get to Arsdred."

He broke her gaze and drank wine, then swirled the remainder in the glass. "Revenge," he told the glass softly, "is a highly appropriate desire. Among Liadens, revenge is something of an art form. There are strict rules. There are certain punishments which are not considered *proper* revenge." He glanced at her. "Death, for instance. At least, not directly from the hand of the vengeful party. Should the dishonor attending a balancing of accounts prove so vast that one has no other choice—" He shrugged. "Well." He set the glass aside and looked closely at her. "I will not have a murderer on this ship."

Priscilla stared at him. "But you *will* have a thief?"

"You said it was a lie. Or did I misunderstand? Perhaps something else was a lie?"

The shaking was worse, extending up her arms and down her legs. Did he believe her? Or the record? It was impossible to read the expression on his face.

"*Daxflan*'s record—that I was stealing and then jumped ship—*that's* the lie."

"Do you want to say so officially?" he asked again.

Priscilla shook her head. "I can't prove it—how can I?

'*Suspected* larceny'? His word against mine—and *he's* the Trader. 'Jumped ship'?" She produced a wan grin. "I'm not there now, am I? Though why anyone with three consecutive thoughts in her head would jump ship on a place like Jankalim, with twobits in her pocket . . ."

"And no earrings in her ears," he agreed. "But maybe you saw they were on to you and were frightened. Jankalim might have been your last chance for free flight—leg irons are so cumbersome. There are excuses for a bit of poor planning . . ." He tipped his head. "But why *did* Sav Rid order the second mate to hit you over the head, Ms. Mendoza? At your direction, I dismiss avaricious thoughts regarding your earrings."

"I can't prove it," she said again. "I *think* they were running contraband."

"Do you? What a peculiar thing to think. You told Sav Rid, and he was—quite understandably—annoyed. Thus the second mate, the warehouse . . ."

"I'm not *that* stupid," Priscilla muttered, and wondered why he grinned. "There was sealed cargo," she continued. "I had the manifests—I knew what was *supposed* to be there. But—something seemed wrong. I didn't know exactly what. So I got the idea of checking the piloting equations, just to prove to myself that I was imagining things."

"And you found that to be the case?"

"I found the equations were so far off that the captain had to be a reckless fool. Or she had to know exactly what she was doing." She took a breath. "So I checked the densities of the cargo."

"Did you?" He leaned forward. "Now why—no, you've had some pilot training. And I'm interrupting. Forgive me, Ms. Mendoza—you checked the densities, matched them to the captain's equations, and?"

"The captain knew what she was doing. The densities didn't match the substances that were *supposed* to be in the cargo. *Daxflan* ships mostly pharmaceuticals. I started going through the list, checking the numbers . . ." She shook her head. "I *think* there's Bellaquesa onboard. It's listed as Aserzerine on the manifest. Everything's all wrong for Aserzerine, though. Bellaquesa matches—but so does sugar. But why would you call sugar Aserzerine? . . ."

She shrugged. "It all *looked* interesting—but I can't *prove* any of it. I never *saw* the stuff. And I'll lay my last bit the data's not locked under my personal file anymore."

He nodded and leaned back in the chair again, staring blankly at the ceiling. Priscilla finished her wine and carefully put the glass aside. Now what? she wondered. She forced herself to sit loosely in the chair, hands relaxed on her knees.

Abruptly, he spun to face her. "We leave Jankalim in fourteen hours," he said slowly. "Before the two of us can discuss specifics, there are several tests required. They are rather lengthy, and, unfortunately, my presence is demanded worldside this evening. If you feel able, you may take the tests directly after lunch. The ship will extend a cabin for you to guest in, and we can speak again at Seventh Hour. Agreed?"

"Agreed."

He nodded and seemed about to speak further when the door opened to admit a clean-faced Gordy behind a wheeled cart piled high with eatables.

"In the nick of time!" Shan yos'Galan cried, flipping off the toggles. "*Now* you offer brandy, Gordy . . ."

Former Cargo Master Priscilla Mendoza leaned back in her chair, sipping at a mug of *real* coffee, the remains of an extremely edible meal on the table before her.

The tests had been lengthy—and rather odd. Among the standardized examinations had been random lists of words to define; questions regarding her personal tastes in books, music, sports, and art; and surveys soliciting her opinion on a surprising range of topics.

Priscilla sighed and sipped her coffee appreciatively. She was tired, her thoughts moving in hazy slow motion. Soon it would be time to look again at the map she had been given and puzzle out the route to her cabin. But having come to rest at last, with no immediate task before her, she was content to simply sit and sip, letting her eyes randomly scan the vast, nearly empty dining hall. She had gathered from the cook on duty that First Hour was not the usual time for people to be fed. He had laughed her apology aside and heaped a plate high, setting it on a tray with a steaming white mug.

"Start on that," he had told her, grinning broadly. "If you're still hungry when you're done, come on back and say so."

"Thank you," Priscilla said, blinking in confusion at the tray. It seemed to hold more food than she had seen at one time in months. The man laughed again and returned to his duties.

Her eyes were drooping closed. Odd, she thought drowsily, that I should feel so comfortable.

She sat up straight and drank the last of her coffee in a snap. After all, tomorrow's interview with the captain could end with her back on Jankalim, no better off—with the exception of a few good meals—than she had been this afternoon. So much depended on the tests, and on the captain. *Did* he believe her?

Why should he? she asked herself fiercely. She sighed and looked up.

A midsized Terran was standing across from her, coffee mug in hand, an expression of admiration on his round face.

Priscilla felt her stomach sink. Here we go again, she thought.

"Hi," the man said easily enough. "You must be the only person onboard who hasn't had a message to send this trip."

"That's because I'm not onboard," Priscilla told him, then grinned and shook her head. "No, *that* doesn't make sense. I mean that I'm only visiting . . ."

"Yeah?" he said interestedly, and extended a soft-palmed hand. "Rusty Morgenstern, radio tech. Pleased to meet you, Ms.—"

"Mendoza." She took the hand and shook lightly; she was agreeably surprised when he did not try to prolong the contact. "Priscilla Mendoza. Sir down?"

"Thanks." He slouched down and put his elbows on the table, fingers curled loosely about the mug. "Who're you visiting, if that's not too nosy? And how come they left you to eat by yourself?"

"I'm not explaining things too well. What I'm doing is applying for a job. I took some tests earlier, and I'm to see the captain at Seventh Hour to find out how I did." She sighed.

"The whole thing seems pointless, though. Mr. Saunderson—the agent on Jankalim—said the ship's fully staffed."

"Well, that's true." He paused to swallow coffee. "What's your line?"

"I was cargo master on my last ship."

Rusty shook his head. "Got a hell of a cargo master—old Ken Rik. Forty years older'n Satan and twice as slippery. Don't play cards with him." He drank more coffee. "But that doesn't mean much. If the cap'n figures you'll work out, there's bound to be something for you to do."

Priscilla blinked at him. "I'm sorry?"

"Well, it's like—" He pointed a finger at her. "Cabin boy. You met Gordy?"

She grinned. "He met me when I came on."

"Nice kid. Point is, we've had a couple different cabin boys. One was backup astrogator. 'Nother spent more time helping Ken Rik figure distributions than she did fetchin' wine. Last guy—seemed like all he did was play chess with the cap'n. Gordy—he's teaching the cap'n—aah, what is it? Restructured Gaelic? Some damn thing—old Terran dialect. Happens to be the everyday parley where Gordy's from."

"The captain's learning Old Terran from Gordy Arbuthnot?" Priscilla picked up her cup and frowned into it. "Why?"

Rusty shrugged. "Cap'n likes to talk."

"I noticed. But—Old Terran? And an obscure dialect, at that?"

"Better ask him—I don't know. But to get back—if the tests check out okay, you're in. And you'll work." He grinned. "*Every*body works."

"But it seems that cabin boy is filled," Priscilla pointed out.

"Cap'n'll think of something," Rusty said with decision. "More coffee?"

She smiled. "Thanks."

"No problem. How you like it? Black? Back in a sec."

He was back almost immediately, handing her a mug; he remained standing, eyeing her consideringly. Priscilla took a gingerly sip and hoped he wasn't about to say anything unfortunate.

"If you got a minute," he began as she clamped her jaw, "let's go 'round to the lounge. There's a screen there. We can call up the spec freight and you can give me lots of ideas for making money. Ought to be interesting, since you've been a cargo master and all."

Priscilla let out her breath and stood with a smile. "Okay."

"Right this way."

Matching his stride, Priscilla asked, "What's the spec freight?"

"Speculation," Rusty explained, and grinned at her blank look. "See, every crew member who wants to pledges a certain percentage each trip for speculation. Wood, say—that's what I'm interested in. Or perfume—that's pretty chancy, but Lina seems to do okay with it. Musical instruments—I don't know. Little while back we had some Grestwellin caviar—one of Gordy's finds. Sold out next port we put in." He shook his head. "That kid's gonna be one hell of a Trader. Knows what's gonna be hot next port, even if we don't know where next port *is*—here we are."

The door slid open at their approach, and Priscilla followed him over the threshold into comfortable dimness and subdued chatter. There was a card game going on in a bright corner—Rusty waved in that direction and got two or three absent responses—and a few other people were scattered about, some in conversational clusters, some alone, with books or handwork.

"There's Lina," Rusty said, and made a detour toward a single chair where a brown-haired Liaden woman was reading a bound book.

She glanced up and smiled. "Rah Stee. They let you from your cage so soon?"

"It's later than you think," he told her, waving Priscilla forward. "This is Priscilla Mendoza. She's a guest onboard this shift. Got an interview with the cap'n next. Priscilla, this is Lina Faaldom, chief librarian."

Honey-colored eyes considered her gravely. Prompted by an impulse she could not name, Priscilla did what she had never done to Sav Rid Olanek or any of the *Daxflan*'s crew—she performed the bow between equals, exactly as Fin Ton had shown her. "I am happy to meet you, Lina Faaldom," she said, with a careful ear to her accent.

The woman clapped her hands. "She speaks Liaden! See, now, Rah Stee, are you not ashamed?" She stood and returned the bow gracefully. "No happier than I am to meet you, Priscilla Mendoza." She straightened and added in Terran, "Perhaps you will prevail upon this lazy Rah Stee to learn, as well."

"Nag," Rusty said without heat. "I was going to call up the spec for Priscilla. Want to kibitz?"

"I do not know. What is it—kibitz?"

"It means to look over our shoulders," Priscilla explained. "Rusty wants me to give him ideas to make money."

"Money, money. Already Rah Stee has more money than he can gamble away. Why does he need more? But yes, I would like to kibitz. Thank you."

The screen was in the corner opposite the card game. Rusty waved his hand at the lightplate and entered his code. Lina perched on the arm of his chair, and Priscilla sat on the hassock to the left, legs curled under her.

"Here we are. Contents. Hold Six: twenty kilos mahogany; ten kilos yellow pine; fifty-eight gallons Endless Lust perfume—*Endless Lust*?" Rusty turned a pained face to the woman beside him.

"It is the *smell*," Lina told him with dignity, "not the name."

"You're the expert. Four hundred bushels raw cotton; and thirty-two dozen bottles Essence of Themngo." He shook his head. "That kid better be right this time . . . What do you think, Priscilla?"

"Impressive," she said sincerely. "You seem to have chosen well—mostly luxury items. I'm not an expert on woods, though. Thirty kilos sounds like either too much or too little."

"It is the artists," Lina explained. "Everywhere we go, there are the artists, always looking for something new. Rah Stee starts with the wood . . . oh, *long ago*, when the captain's father was captain. Now, we have orders. The wood becomes a—a usual thing. We are expected."

Priscilla nodded, struck by another thought. "You've got an entire hold tied up in the crew's speculative cargo? What about capacity fees?"

"Cap'n pledges that. On condition the ship gets her share first out of any profit. The ship shares any loss, too—it's a fair deal."

"More than fair." She sipped her cooling coffee. "Your captain sounds unusual."

"He is a good captain," Lina said.

"And the *Passage* is a profitable ship," Rusty added, turning back to the screen. "Most of the wood'll go at Arsdred— the Artisan's Guild put in a big order. We might pick up a few odds and ends there—not too likely, though, since almost everybody running this sector stops there. Number Six'll be empty for a while." He glanced at Priscilla. "Can't make money that way."

"But you just said the wood's an ordered item," she pointed out. "You've got a profit, right?"

"Yeah, I guess." He brightened. "Tell you what—let's try and get our shore leaves matched for Arsdred. Then we can go scouting together. Who knows? Something might turn for the spec. Or even for the ship."

Priscilla stared at him. "I might not be onboard at Arsdred, remember?" She drank the rest of her coffee and shook her head. "Do you *all* look for the ship, too? What's the Master Trader do?"

Lina laughed.

"He trades," Rusty said, his round face serious. "*We* don't trade. But anybody might see something. Cap'n's only one person—he could miss a deal just 'cause he can't be in three places at once. So as many of the crew as can go worldside. If you see something, you hotfoot to the nearest comm and call the cap'n or Kayzin Ne'Zame—first mate. If it turns out to be a go, there's a finder's fee." He blinked at her. "What's wrong?"

"Nothing. I—the last ship I was on didn't—encourage— the crew to go worldside. And the Trader did all the trading."

"Sounds like a stupid arrangement to me," the man said flatly.

"It does not make good sense," Lina agreed slowly. "The ship is everyone's venture. We all take a share of the profit. It is only sensible to work hard for a *big* profit." She looked carefully at Priscilla. "Perhaps you were not on such a good ship before."

"Perhaps I wasn't," Priscilla said dryly, and lifted a hand to cover a sudden yawn. "I'm sorry. It's been a long day. Better be finding my room . . ." She uncoiled her legs and stood.

With a nod, Rusty signed off and moved out of the alcove. One of the card players looked up and waved him over. "In a sec," he called, and turned back. "Priscilla, I bet you threebits you'll be on the *Passage* at Arsdred."

"I don't have threebits to bet," she said ruefully. "But I hope you're right. It was good to meet you."

"See you later," he responded, and drifted off toward the game.

"You should excuse Rah Stee," Lina said, waving a hand at his retreating back. "You know where your room is from here?"

"I have a map," Priscilla began, fishing in her pocket.

The smaller woman laughed. "The map is good, but it will take you by all the main halls. I know the short ways. If it does not offend, I can show you. It is time I went to sleep as well."

"I don't want to put you to any trouble . . ."

"It is no trouble," Lina assured her. "Only let me get my book."

They turned left from the door of the lounge rather than right, as the map directed, and pursued several short zigzagging corridors before regaining the main hall. They followed this past several closed doors, one marked GYM and another POOL, before turning into a slimmer, dimmer way.

Lina left her with a smile and a slight bow at the third door on the right. "Sleep well, Priscilla Mendoza. I will look for you tomorrow."

"Sleep you well also, Lina Faaldom," Priscilla answered softly in Liaden. "Thank you for your care."

The room was a blur to her overtired mind. She located the cleanbot and pushed her clothes into the slot, hoping that the black smear on one yellow cuff would come out in the cycle.

There was a clock on the shelf over the bed; she keyed in a request for Sixth Hour and curled into the luxuriously soft cushions with a sigh as she belatedly waved a hand at the lightplate.

She was asleep before the room was dark.

"Priscilla Mendoza?"

She started, almost spilling what was left of her coffee, and blinked at the small person who had appeared suddenly before her. The woman was a Liaden of middle years, with golden skin showing deep lines about eyes and mouth, and yellow hair going gray.

Priscilla smiled. "I am sorry. I was daydreaming. How may I serve you?"

The handsome face did not relax its austere lines. "The captain's compliments, Ms. Mendoza. He requests that you come to him, if you have broken your fast." She hesitated before inclining her head ever so slightly. "I am Kayzin Ne'Zame." The first mate.

Priscilla smiled again, despite the stiffness of her face, and pushed back her chair. "I've just finished this minute. I'll go to the captain as soon as I've cleaned up my tray." She was fairly confident of the route, having studied her map throughout breakfast.

"I shall escort you," Kayzin Ne'Zame said uncompromisingly.

Fear returned. Priscilla would be sent from the ship—or she would be required to remain—it was impossible to know which was the worse possibility. Breakfast was a handful of cold rock in her stomach; she abruptly remembered the woman she had met last night and wished they had had a chance to speak further.

Priscilla laid her tray gently on the conveyor belt and turned back to the first mate. "Thank you, Kayzin Ne'Zame. I am ready now."

The captain was behind the desk, fingers busy on the keypad. A glass of wine sat to hand, and the previous day's stacks of paper had given birth to two others like themselves.

"Captain," the first mate said formally. "Here is Priscilla Mendoza, come to speak with you."

He glanced up absently. "Ms. Mendoza. Good morning. I'll be with you in just a moment. Kayzin, old friend, will you come to me in an hour?"

"Certainly, Captain." She executed a disapproving bow, but he had already returned his attention to the screen, and Priscilla did not think he saw. Frowning, the mate turned on her heel; the automatic door did its best to bang shut behind her.

Priscilla stood, fighting cold nausea. Biting her lip, she studied the man behind the desk, combating fear with observation.

It was a puzzle, she decided. He was so tall, his skin warm brown rather than golden. Like all Liaden men she had seen, his face was as fine-grained as a child's, without a hint of beard. The white hair and brows made a vivid contrast; the lean cheeks and mobile mouth were not displeasing.

Really, she thought, if you don't expect him to look Liaden, he's not ugly at all.

Certainly he was not an ill-made person. Beneath the wide-sleeved shirt his shoulders were level and broad, his back straight without being rigid. The big hands moved with graceful economy on the keypad, and Priscilla did not think they would be babysoft like Rusty Morgenstern's.

Abruptly he nodded, leaned back, and extended a long arm for his glass. The slanting brows pulled sharply together as he looked up. "Does Sav Rid have delusions of grandeur? Sit, sit. Have you eaten? Will you drink? Did you sleep well?"

Priscilla considered him. "I don't know. Thank you. Yes. No. Very. Did *you*?"

"Not too badly," he said, raising his glass. "Though Mr. Saunderson's idea of a party *is* a bit risque. We played charades. And sang rounds. The youngest Ms. Saunderson attempted to elicit my promise to wed her when she comes of age." He shook his head. "Alas, it seems clear she is more enamored of adventuring about the galaxy than she is of my elegant person, so there's a brilliant match gone begging. I have your test scores. Are you interested in discussing them now?"

Priscilla made an effort to settle her stomach firmly in place. "Yes, sir."

He ran his fingers in a quick series over the keys. "Physics, math, astrogation—yes, yes, yes. Colors red, colors blue, taste in books—yes?" He glanced up. "Prebatout. You recall the question? 'How many toes should a prebatout have?' And here is Priscilla Mendoza saying, 'As many as it feels comfortable with.' I've only known one other person to answer that particular question that way."

"Have you?" Priscilla asked, hands ice cold. "Was she a suspected thief, too?"

"Thief? No, a scout. Though, come to think of it, the two trades might have some similarities. I've never considered it in that light. I'll ask, the next time I see him . . ." He returned to the screen, humming to himself.

Priscilla curled her fingers carefully around the armrests, refusing to rise to the bait—if it was bait—of his last comment. Let *him* talk, since he seemed to like it so much.

He moved his shoulders, gave the keypad a final tap, and leaned back. "You don't have a pilot's license? That won't do, will it? Let me see . . . forty-eight crew members, counting the captain—eight of them pilots. Too few by far. You'll have to study, Ms. Mendoza. I insist on it. Every ninth shift you'll be on the bridge for lessons."

"Wait a minute." She took a breath. "You're signing me on? As a pilot?"

"As a pilot?" he repeated blandly. "No, how could I do that? You're not a pilot, are you, Ms. Mendoza? That's why you'll need to take lessons. Certification's no problem. I'm rated master, all conditions—is something wrong?"

"Forgive me," she said carefully. "I thought you were captain. And Master Trader, of course. You're a pilot, too?"

"A little of this, a little of that. The *Passage* is a family enterprise, after all. Owned and operated by Clan Korval. And piloting runs in the blood, so to speak. I got my first class when I was sixteen Standards—been ratable for a few years before that, of course. Did my first solo on this ship when I was fourteen—but rules are rules, and they clearly state that no one may be certified until sixteen Standards. But I was saying—what *was* I saying? Oh, yes. Since I'm a master pilot, there won't be any delay once you earn your certification. Are you *certain* you haven't got a license, Ms. Mendoza? Third class, perhaps?"

"I'm certain, Captain." Things were moving too fast; the torrent of words was threatening to unmoor her fragile hold on serenity. "Just what will my position be?"

"Hmm? Oh—pet librarian."

"*Pet* librarian?"

"We have a very nice pet library," he told her gravely. "Now, details. We're nearly half done with the route. I can offer you flat rate from Jankalim to Solcintra—approximately a tenth-cantra upon docking. You'd be eligible for the low-man share of any bonus the ship might earn from this point on—finder's fees and special awards are the same for everyone, based on profit of found cargo and merit, as judged by the majority of the crew." He raised his glass. "Questions?"

She had a myriad of them, but only one was forthcoming.

"Why," she demanded irritably, "do you keep waving that glass around if you never drink from it?"

He grinned. "But I *do* drink from it. Sometimes. More questions?"

She sighed. "How much will the ship charge for pilot training?"

"If you fail to report for training every ninth shift, the captain will dock you twentybits. Three unexcused or unexplained absences will be grounds for immediate termination of your contract. Understand, please, Ms. Mendoza, that pilot training is an essential part of your duties while you are a member of this crew. I will not allow abandonment of that duty—the penalties are quite in earnest." He paused, his light eyes gauging her face. "You *do* understand?"

"Yes, Captain." She bit her lip. "It's that I've been charged for training on every other ship I served on—and pursued it during my free time. *Daxflan* denied me permission to continue training while I shipped on her."

"Sav Rid, Sav Rid." He shook his head. "However, this is not *Daxflan*, and her rules do not apply here. Now. Your supervisor—no. The ship will extend you credit for a Standard week's worth of clothing, to be reckoned against your share at the end of the route. Please draw what you need from general stores. Your supervisor will be Lina Faaldom, who is chief librarian."

"I met her last night—"

"Yes? She will introduce you to the residents of the pet library and acquaint you with your duties there. I don't believe the work to be arduous, so you'll be expected to take on other duties as necessary. Janice Weatherbee will be your piloting instructor. If she is called elsewhere upon occasion, I will take her place. I believe that's everything. Are the terms agreeable to you?"

"Since I was almost certain I'd be back on Jankalim this morning, yes, Captain, the terms are agreeable to me." She paused, studying his face. Sometime during the interview the fear had dissipated, leaving her limp and slowly warming. "Do you *really* need a pet librarian?"

"Well, we didn't have one," he said, spinning the screen toward her. "So I guess we do. Palmprint here, please."

Shan yos'Galan was tipped back in his chair, arms folded behind his head, eyes apparently resting on the crystalline mobile hanging in the far corner of the ceiling. The expression on his face was one of dreamy stupidity. He did not glance around at the hissing of the door; he did not even seem aware that he was no longer alone in the room.

Kayzin Ne'Zame knew better than to be deceived by appearances. She sat in the seat that Priscilla Mendoza had recently vacated, her spine two inches from the chair back, and frowned at his profile.

"You've signed her on?" she demanded in the High Tongue, each syllable icy with disapproval.

"I did say that it was my intention to sign her on," the man reminded the mobile gently and in Terran. He spun the chair lazily around, unfolded his arms, and sat up. "What is it, Kayzin?"

"She is too beautiful." The Terran words were no less cold.

"But that's not her fault, is it? People can't choose their faces, can they? If they can, I want to know why I wasn't told about it."

The older woman regarded him with something perilously close to amusement. "I am, in fact, to pity her."

"What harm can it do?"

"What harm! You ask it? Or is it the game again? Do not trouble yourself, I beg you . . ." She paused, visibly taking herself in hand. "And what harm is it—to the ship, to the crew, to your Clan, and to Shan yos'Galan—should Sav Rid Olanek prove clever as well as dishonorable? What harm, should this so-pitiful, so-beautiful woman prove to be a tool in his hands—a blade at your throat? What harm—"

"Kayzin . . ." The big hands made a soothing motion; concern for her showed in his face.

She slumped back in her chair. "Shan, it is my last trip. I prefer it to be an uneventful one."

"There's no reason for it to be otherwise, old friend. Why should Sav Rid want to plant a—what? spy? *assassin?*—on the *Passage*? He's had his coup—and a very fine laugh. There's no reason for him to go to such trouble. No reason to think of the affair at all, except to chuckle and extend the story in port taverns as proof of Shan yos'Galan's rabid foolishness." He grinned wryly. "And he's not too far off the mark, is he?"

She gestured, speechless.

"You worry too much, Kayzin—and without cause. Circumstance, synchronicity—I don't believe Sav Rid would *wish* Priscilla Mendoza here, assuming he wished her any place at all, except, perhaps, dead. I think it more likely that he acted twice as opportunity dictated. It's interesting—but not impossible—that the victims of both actions should come together."

"It is also not impossible that Olanek has grown wary—or even that he has grown greedy. What a coup for him, should he bring Korval entire to its knees . . ."

Shan's brows pulled together. "Do you really think he could? Not that he doesn't have the potential for being that greedy—or that reckless. Kayzin, the *Passage* proceeds as ever. For our years together and the time you spent raising me, I will attempt to keep the rest of the route as uneventful as possible. In the meantime, please try to be kind to Priscilla Mendoza." He picked up his glass and drank slowly. "And wouldn't you say it was better, Kayzin, to keep the knife—if there is a knife, of course—in our view rather than have it poised at our back?"

She smiled. "You will reward him properly?"

"Steps are being taken to bring accounts into balance," he promised, and finished his wine.

Glass in hand, Shan yos'Galan rounded the corner into the leisure section. Ahead was a slender figure, gay in raspberry tunic and celadon sash. He stretched his long legs and caught her by the intersection to the athletic hall.

"Well met, Lina."

She looked up, her smile radiant. "Shan. I'm glad to see you."

"And I'm glad to see you. As always. You're looking exceptionally lovely. Off to a party? Will you bring me with you? I promise not to brag of my exalted position. How do you find your assistant?"

She laughed. "But it is exactly of Priscilla that I wished to speak! Have you truly a moment? I know how busy it is to be captain. I hardly see you . . ."

"Languishing?" He raised his glass, his light eyes mocking. "By all means speak to me of Priscilla. Do the residents approve? Is she impossible for you? Shall I send her to Ken Rik?"

"Oh, no, not to Ken Rik. The small ones are each delighted—Master Frodo to the point of purrs. You knew he would be." She stopped, frowning up into his face. "Shan? What is wrong with her—do you know? There is joy—one can feel it—but she denies . . . suppresses . . . I like her very well. Don't you?"

"It would be enough to lower anyone's feelings, wouldn't it, to be hit over the head and deserted with no money, a ruined record, and no friends?"

"It is more than that," Lina insisted. "She wants Healing."

"Does she?" He sipped. "Is she impossible for you?"

"Not at all. Though perhaps *you* . . ."

"Me?" He laughed. "I'm not a Healer, Lina; I'm the captain."

"Bah!" She banished this quibble with a tiny contemptuous hand. "As if you haven't the skill and the training!" She tipped her head, considering information of which the expression on his face was only a small portion. "Shan?"

A lifted shoulder denied her. He frowned slightly. "What—perfume—are you wearing, Lina?"

"The one we bought—Endless Lust." She chuckled. "Rah Stee objects to the name."

"As well he might." He moved back a step or two. "Very potent, isn't it? I don't recall that you reported aphrodisiac qualities."

"It has none!" She grinned. "Are you certain it is the perfume?"

"Forgive me," he murmured. "I have admired you forever, Lina, but amorous thoughts were far from me this evening. If it *isn't* an aphrodisiac, it's the next best thing. Did anybody explain how it works?"

"It is the smell . . ." She sighed sharply, asked permission with a flicker of her hands, and slid into the Low Tongue, on the mode spoken between friends. "It is an enhancer of one's own odor. Thus, if you are attracted primarily, you will be more so when the perfume is used. Harmless, old friend, I assure you."

"I," the captain said in Terran, "am not convinced. There

are laws on certain worlds about perfumes and substances that—what *is* the official phrasing?—'take away volition and make pliable the will'? Something more or less pompous." He took a drink and drifted away yet another step. "Do me the favor of submitting what is left of your vial to Chemistry, Lina. I would so hate to break the law."

"It is harmless." She frowned. "It does *not* take away volition—no more than a Healer might, encouraging one to embrace joy . . ."

Shan grinned. "I believe you may be splitting hairs. *Are* you going to a party? I would like to accompany you—purely scientific, you understand. It might be very interesting to observe the effect of this perfume of yours on a roomful of unsuspecting persons."

"I," Lina said dampingly, "am going to watch a Ping-Pong match between Priscilla and Rah Stee. You may come, if you like. Though if you persist in backing away from me in that insulting manner . . ."

He laughed and offered an arm. "I have myself in hand now. Let us by all means inflict ourselves upon the Ping-Pong match."

Rusty was sweating and puffing with exertion, the expression on his round face one of harried doggedness.

In contrast, Priscilla was coolly serene, parrying his shots with absent smoothness, barely regarding the ball at all. Yet time after time she fractured his frenzied guard and piled up the points in her favor.

"Twenty-one," he said, his voice cracking slightly. "I don't believe it."

"No, Rah Stee, it *is* twenty-one for Priscilla," Lina said helpfully. "I counted also."

"That's what I don't believe." Rusty leaned heavily on the table, directing a sodden head shake at his opponent. "You're blowing me away! I don't get it. Half the time I don't even see the ball coming."

"That's because you have the reactions of a dead cow," Shan explained, not to be outdone in helpfulness.

The other man turned to glare at him. "Thanks a lot."

"Always of service . . ."

"Maybe," Priscilla offered, cutting off a scorching reply, "it's because you look for the ball. I almost never do that."

"Then how do you know where it *is?*" He ran a sleeve across his forehead and sighed hugely. "Dammit, 'Cilla, I'm good at Ping-Ping. Been playing for years!"

"But not against pilots," the captain said, sipping wine.

"What's that got to do with it?"

"A great deal, don't you think, Rusty? Your reaction time's slow; you move in a series of jerks rather than a smooth flow; you fail to apprehend where an object *will be.*" He raised his glass. "Don't feel too bad, my friend. We all have our niche to fill. After all, I could hardly fill your place in the tower, or operate the—"

"Like hell you can't," the other muttered, spinning his paddle clumsily on the table.

"I beg your pardon, Rusty?"

"Never mind." He turned suddenly and flipped the paddle to Shan, who caught it left-handed, lazily. "*You* play her."

The captain blinked. "Why?"

"You're a pilot. She's a pilot. Maybe I'll pick up some pointers." Grinning, Rusty retired from the field and flung himself into a sideline seat. "Besides, I need a break. You don't want me to keel over dead from exertion, do you?"

"Now, that would be a tragedy. So young, so handsome, so wealthy—he had all to live for . . . Ms. Mendoza? Are you interested in a game? Observe that you have the advantage of youth over dissipated old age."

Priscilla swallowed a laugh. Lina frowned.

"Certainly, Captain. I'll be happy to play with you. Will you offer me a handicap?"

"You should offer one to me," he said, setting his glass aside and wandering toward the table. "Remember that I'm frail, please, and easily bruised. You'll serve?"

She nodded, and the ball was even then skimming smoothly over the net . . . to be returned with casual force, heading toward the edge of the table, barely brushing; it was caught as it struck and sent backspinning over the net, to be returned again, barely inside her play zone, then flipped by a cunning paddle edge back into his court.

"Twenty-seven, twenty-five," Priscilla said nearly forty minutes later. She actually grinned at the man opposite. "Good game, Captain."

"Fighting for every point," he agreed, laying his paddle down and moving in the direction of his wine. "Notice, please, Rusty, that I barely won. *Have* you picked up any pointers?"

"Huh? I'm gonna retire to a home for the physically degenerate." The radio tech shook his head. "You're so fast! If I hadn't heard it hit, I'd've thought you were runnin' a scam: pretending to have a game with an invisible ball."

Priscilla drifted over to Lina's chair and sat carefully on an upholstered arm. The Liaden woman smiled up at her. "You played very well, my friend."

Friend. The word was unexceptional from Lina, yet Priscilla never heard it without a small thrill of warmth. She smiled gently. "Thank you." She moved her shoulders in response to a slight twinge. "No excuse for not sleeping tonight."

Lina shifted. "You have not been sleeping? On our ship?"

Priscilla allowed herself the luxury of another grin. "I sleep better on this ship than—than I sometimes do." She moved her shoulders again, half a shrug. "It's nothing. I get by."

"In two days we are at Scandalous," the smaller woman offered, apropos of nothing. "A drop only. Then, in three days more, we are at Arsdred. Do you like us, now that you have been here a whole week?"

"Has it been a week?" The question woke echoes of Shan

yos'Galan's voice in her mind's ear, and she smiled again, almost lazily. "I like you very much. Everyone's been kind . . ." Except Kayzin Ne'Zame, of course. What ailed the woman? She glanced down and saw Lina's small golden hand resting on the chair arm at her knee. It looked strong and capable and curiously pleasing. With hardly a thought except that it would be comforting to do so, Priscilla laid her own hand over it—and flicked her eyes, startled, to the other woman's face.

Lina smiled at her.

Priscilla sighed; the sound seemed to come from very far away. Friend, she thought, and her fingers tightened around Lina's. She received warm pressure in return and smiled for the fourth time in five minutes. From across the room she heard the soothing murmur of voices: Rusty and the captain, speaking between themselves. She shook her head. "I must be more tired than I thought . . ."

"Yes? Would you like to go to bed? I will walk with you, if you like."

Priscilla looked into the face of her friend. Goddess, it would be hard to tell Lina good-bye . . . "I'd like you to come with me," she said softly. "That would be good."

"I think so, too," Lina said, and stood, keeping their hands linked.

Across the room, Rusty suddenly sighed. "Here I thought she liked me," he complained, "and then she goes off with Lina!"

Shan glanced around absently. "I'm afraid you were outgunned. Lina was wearing that new perfume of hers."

"Was she?" He looked up, all interest. "Damn. That stuff's gonna make us *rich*."

They reached Priscilla's quarters and entered together when the door slid away. Just inside, Lina stopped and smiled up at her tall companion a little quizzically. Cautiously, she touched the bruise on the pale cheek. "I am sorry that they hurt you, my friend."

"It wasn't so bad. . . ." Priscilla murmured, gazing down into her face. Slowly, with a sense of inevitable tenderness, she bent and kissed Lina on the mouth.

Master Frodo the norbear burbled happily and ran to the port opening as fast as his bowed legs would carry him. His three companions came more slowly from their cozy-places and followed, Tiny uttering a small, dignified *bwrrr* of welcome.

Priscilla carefully measured out three portions and placed each in its appointed place. Tiny, Delm Briat, and Lady Selph fell to with a will, while Master Frodo stood by, fairly quivering with anticipation. As the last measure was placed, he extended a small clawed hand and snagged a fold of sleeve.

"Did you think I'd forgotten you?" Priscilla asked as he clambered into her hand. Master Frodo rubbed his head against her fingers.

Smiling, Priscilla brought him to her shoulder. He rolled off and sat up on hind legs, one hand clutching the curls over her ear while with the other he solemnly accepted pieces of corn and stuffed them into his cheek pouches.

"It's the tower for me today," Priscilla confided as Master

Frodo broke his fast. "I'm to report to Tonee sig'Ella by Twelfth Hour."

Her companion vouchsafed no direct reply, though he let her know by the quality of his eating that Tonee sig'Ella was not a bad sort, received everywhere by norbears of consequence.

Since Priscilla was able to verify by the sign-out that Tonee was no infrequent visitor to the norbears' hearth, this information was not startling. She thanked Master Frodo for his recommendation, however, and scratched him lightly between the ears before replacing him in the tank.

He settled to the sandy soil with a little sigh and twisted his head sideways, peering upward, one paw raised in supplication.

Priscilla grinned again. "No more for you," she said sternly, rubbing his belly with a gentle finger. "You're getting positively fat."

Master Frodo let it be known that among norbears a certain portliness of figure was considered attractive. Priscilla might, of course, think what she would. He did not like to mention it, but *she* could use a little extra corn to advantage.

Caught in the imagined dialogue, she shook her head. "I've always been scrawny," she said, closing the hatch and sealing it.

She shook her head again. Talking to yourself like a Seer. If anybody catches you, they'll have you down in sick bay before Master Frodo can give you a reference.

But the thought failed to alarm her. Lina had in fact caught her talking to Master Frodo a shift or two back. The Liaden woman's only response had been to tug on one rounded ear and warn Priscilla not to let the norbear charm her out of extra rations.

"He is a rogue, this one," Lina had explained, laughing at the creature's antics. "And you must not be taken in. He will exploit you shamelessly."

Priscilla left the pet library by way of the side door, which gave onto the library proper. Lina was at the desk, frowning

at her screen, but she glanced up with a smile. Still unused to
such warm and easy friendship, Priscilla caught her breath.
"Everyone's taken care of," she said, striving for serenity.
"I'm going up to the tower now."

"So? Call me to Tonee's attention. We have not met often
this trip." She touched the back of a slim pale hand. "Shall we
share prime meal, my friend?"

"Yes." She drew breath against the pounding of her heart.

Lina smiled. "I will see you at prime, then. Be you well,
Priscilla."

"Be you well, Lina."

The tower was opposite the library and up six levels, a dome
in the ship's center section exactly balancing the dome of the
main bridge, six levels below. Priscilla entered a lift and
punched her route, then leaned back into a corner.

Pet librarian. So far, she had spent only one shift performing the duties attached to that post. Her assignment was on her
cabin-screen when she awoke, always allowing her ample
time to see to the needs of the creatures she cared for. And
then she was sent elsewhere: to the maintenance bay to help
lanky Seth with an overhaul, to the kitchen to assist garrulous
BillyJo, to the holds to pore over distribution charts with
sharp-tongued old Ken Rik. And, of course, to the inner
bridge for piloting lessons with Janice Weatherbee, second
mate and first class pilot.

Only a week, and I must have worked everywhere but the
pet library, Priscilla thought. But she found she did not mind
the variety of work. Rather, it seemed to ease her in some
unidentified way, even as the mix of personalities exhilarated
her.

People. One might find friends here. She had found at least
one friend already. And since she had had no friends at all,
that was a treasure past any attempt at counting.

The lift stopped, and the door slid away to reveal a bright
yellow hallway. Priscilla walked to the end of it, feet sound-

less on the resilient floor, laid her hand upon the door, and entered.

Instruments were flickering; one console was clamoring for attention, while a screen set in the far wall flashed orange numbers: seven in series; pause; repeat.

No human occupant was apparent.

"Hello?"

"Hahlo! Yes! A moment!" There was a harried scrabbling from behind the center console. Priscilla started in that direction and almost bumped into the person coming the other way.

"You are Priscilla Mendoza, yes?"

"I'm Priscilla Mendoza," she agreed, bowing the bow between equals. "You are Tonee sig'Ella?"

"Who else? No, we have not met—you must not regard . . ." An abbreviated version of the courtesy was returned. She had a moment to wonder if Fin Ton would have approved before her hand was caught in a surprisingly strong grip and she was pulled toward the console.

"You are a decoder, yes? You have operated the bouncecomm and know the symbols? There is a difficulty with the in-ship, and I must have time, but the messages—you perceive? Do you but decode what arrives, encode what must be sent—I will have my time; we will not fall behind. All will be well!" the little tech finished triumphantly, pulling out the console chair.

Priscilla sat and flicked a glance at screens, transmitters, receivers. The equipment was standard; there should be no problem.

"How are we getting the messages to the proper people onboard?" she asked. "If the in-ship's out—"

"I have spoken with the captain," the other interrupted, rubbing wire-thin hands together. "The cabin boy will be dispatched to the tower and will carry messages as they are ready. It should not be long. You are familiar? You will contrive?"

"I will contrive." Priscilla made the assurance as solemn as she could, despite the rising wave of laughter. She swallowed firmly. "Lina Faaldom asked to be remembered to you. She says you haven't seen each other often this trip."

"Lina!" The gamin face lit, eyes sparkling. "I will call on her—say, to beg her forgiveness!" A quick laugh was accompanied by the lightest of touches of her shoulder. Then she was alone. On the other side of the tower, Tonee was removing the cover of the noisy console.

Priscilla shook her head and turned to the task at hand.

Gordy had just left with his third handful of messages. Priscilla heard the sound of the door cycling without assigning it importance, most of her attention captured by an unusually knotty translation.

Could it really be "desires your most religious custom?" she wondered, fingers poised over the keys. The message was directed to Master Trader, *Dutiful Passage*. It would be best to take a little time to be sure.

"What," demanded a heavily accented voice, "are you doing here?"

Priscilla glanced up, stomach sinking. Kayzin Ne'Zame stood before the console, and it was apparent she was in no mood to be pleased.

"I was assigned here," she began.

"You are not cleared for this work!" the first mate snapped. "Who assigns you?"

"My screen lists my duties at the beginning of each shift," Priscilla explained, keeping her voice even. "This shift, I was assigned to Tonee sig'Ella at Twelfth Hour."

"Who is your supervisor?" Kayzin asked awfully.

"Lina Faaldom."

"Lina Faaldom. And it is your belief that a librarian has the authority necessary to assign you to the tower as a decoder of messages?" There was no mistaking the sarcasm.

"She has apparently," Priscilla snapped, "had the authority to send me to the maintenance bay, the cargo holds, the kitchen, and hydroponics. Why should I assume this shift's assignment was different from those?"

"Has she?" There was an odd expression on the first mate's face. She turned, scanning the towers, eyes lighting on the hunched figure at the far corner. "Radio Tech!"

Tonee turned and hurried forward with a sigh. "First Mate?"

"How came this woman to you?"

The radio tech blinked. "Under orders, First Mate. She was expected. Twelfth Hour, so went the captain's word."

"The captain—"

"First Mate, she is required!" Tonee pleaded, as if suddenly perceiving where that line of questioning might lead. "She has been of utmost assistance. The in-ship is nearly repaired. Before we leave orbit, I promise it—but you must not take her now! The messages—surely you know the need!"

It was apparent from her expression that Kayzin *did* know the need. She looked from Tonee to Priscilla, rigid at the console, then inclined her head. "A question of clearance, Radio Tech. However, since you have the captain's word, there is no more to be said." With that, she turned on her heel and left the tower.

Priscilla and Tonee exchanged glances before the little tech flung both hands out in a gesture of wide amazement.

"You work well. When we leave orbit, the screens will be clear. The first mate . . ." There was a ripple of narrow shoulders. "Her temper is chancy, a little. Do not regard it."

With another delicate pat on the shoulder, Priscilla was left alone to conquer bewilderment and return to the matter at hand.

Priscilla whipped about—and froze. The alley be-hind her was full of men and women, hands ominously clenched, righteousness shining from each grim face. She fell back, forgetting the danger behind—

Until with a jerk the precious bag was torn from her grip and she was dealt such a blow between the shoulders that she fell to her knees in the alleyway.

She was up in a flash, facing Dagmar with fury. "That's mine! Give it back!"

"Yours?" the other woman sneered as Pimm tel'Jadis came laughing to her side. "That ain't the tale I heard, Prissy." She jerked open the bag and thrust her hand within, rummaging about. Then, uttering a crow of triumph, she raised high a fist in which were clutched the seven silver bangles of a Maiden-in-Circle.

The crowd shrieked.

The first rock caught Priscilla on the thigh as Dagmar brought a fist across her face.

The second rock slammed solidly into her right arm, breaking it with an audible crack.

The third took a rib, and she screamed, rolling into a ball on the filthy alley floor, trying to protect her head while the rocks struck with greater and greater force, and the crowd cried out her names: Liar! Coward! Unperson!

"Priscilla!"

She felt hands on her, and she struggled.

"Priscilla! No, denubia, you must not . . ." The voice was familiar, concerned.

"Lina?" She lay still, hardly daring to believe it.

"Of course, Lina. Who else?" The hands were soft on her face, her hair. "Open your eyes, denubia. Are you afraid to see me?"

"No, I . . ." She achieved it and beheld her friend's serious face. "I'm sorry, Lina."

"And I. Such *terror*, my friend. What was it?" The kind hands continued their caress; comfort like a healing warmth enclosed her. Priscilla sighed and shook her head.

"It was nothing. A bad dream."

"Yes?" Lina ran light fingers along Priscilla's jaw and down the slim throat, then laid her hand flat between rose-tipped breasts. "A very bad dream, I think. Your heart pounds."

"I dreamt—I dreamt I was being stoned." She shivered, drew a breath, and tried to recapture inner peace.

"Stoned?" Lina frowned. "I do not think—"

"It is the custom on my—on the world I'm from—to throw rocks at a criminal until she—until she dies."

"Qua'lechi!" The smaller woman sat up sharply and reached to trace the line of her friend's brow. "No wonder you were frightened." She tipped her head. "But this thing was not truly done to you?"

Priscilla managed a smile. "No, of course not." There, she had found the well-worn way to serenity and set her spirit feet upon it. "I'm not very brave," she told Lina softly.

As Priscilla's lashes drooped and her breathing evened, the Liaden woman frowned. Tentatively she unfurled a mental tendril, as one might with a fellow Healer, extended it along the least dangerous of the lines—and nearly cried out as Priscilla reached the place she had been seeking and firmly closed the door.

The library door slid open, and a tall, broad-shouldered person ambled to the center of the room and stood sipping from his glass, quietly regarding the figure hunched over the master terminal. It was perhaps five minutes before she sat back with a sharp sigh and spoke with the ease of long acquaintance. "Are there Healers among Terrans, old friend?"

He considered it, coming forward. "Not formally, I believe." He bent over her screen, frowning at the upside-down characters. "You want 'empath,' my precious. It's listed under 'paranormal.'"

"Paranormal!" Lina's head was up, eyes flashing.

"I didn't put it there," Shan pointed out mildly. "I only offer information. That's where it was when I searched it."

And, Lina realized, he would have done just such a search a few years ago. She smiled. "Forgive me. There was hard work done, if little accomplished. I am—edgy."

He bowed slightly. "I might offer aid."

"So you might." She smiled again and reached to touch his stark cheek. "I thank you, bed-friend and colleague. Grant me grace and offer another time."

"So I will." He drank wine. "Don't stay up all shift, please, Lina."

"Bah! And what of you! Or does the captain never sleep?" She chuckled, then sobered abruptly. "Kayzin was complaining to me that Priscilla is assigned where she has no right to be."

"I heard." Shan shook his head. "What did she want me to do? First she tells me this is her last trip and I must not ask her for decisions concerning future trips, then she takes me to *severe* task for daring to follow her instructions! I tell you, Lina, it's a hard life the captain lives!"

"Alas," she managed around a mouthful of laughter.

He grinned and raised his glass. "Search well, Master Librarian. Sleep well, too."

"Sleep well, Shan."

But he was already gone.

The *Dutiful Passage* broke orbit smoothly and proceeded down the carefully calculated normal space lane to the Jump point and passed without a quiver into hyperspace.

Priscilla ran through the last check, reaffirmed destination and time of arrival, locked the board, and leaned back, barely conquering her grin.

"Not too bad, Mendoza," Janice Weatherbee said from the copilot's seat. She glanced at the chronometer set in the board. "Quittin' time. See you 'round."

"Okay," Priscilla said absently, still watching the grayed screen. It was not the simulation screen this time—it was the prime piloting screen on the main bridge, and she had done it all. She, Priscilla Delacroix y Mendoza, had plotted the course, worked the equations, chosen the coords—done everything, out of her own knowledge and ability.

She closed her eyes against the screen, cherishing the solid wedge of belief in her own ability. For this little time, at least, it seemed not to matter that she was outcast and lawfully nameless, with no more right to call herself Mendoza than Rusty Morgenstern had.

"Sleeping, Ms. Mendoza? It's a very comfortable chair, I grant, but someone else might wish to use it."

She opened her eyes and grinned at the captain, who stood with one hip braced against the ledge and a glass of wine in his hand.

"Sorry, Captain. I was indulging in vulgar self-congratulation."

"Well, that's encouraging," he said, grinning back. "I was prepared to believe you had no faults at all. But now that you admit to gloating, I'm sure we'll get along very well together. Janice is a bit laconic, is she?"

"Maybe she's trying to make up for you," Priscilla suggested, then bit her lip in horror.

Shan yos'Galan laughed. "Could be. Could be. Someone should, I guess. Are you working a double shift? Even so, you're allowed an hour to eat—ship's policy. And there's really not much to do here now, is there?" He glanced vaguely at the gray screen. "Seems to be in hand. Why not take a shift or two for yourself?"

"Thank you, Captain," she said. "I will. Good shift."

"Good shift, Ms. Mendoza." He raised his glass to her.

She was to meet Lina and Rusty for prime at Seventeenth Hour. Priscilla turned left, away from the lift. There was time for a walk to stretch legs cramped by hours in the pilot's chair.

Hugging her recent accomplishment to herself, she wandered down a quarter mile of hallway, took a down-lift when the way deadended, and smiled at dour old Ken Rik when she stepped off one level below.

I feel good, she ventured, probing the thought as if it were a shattered bone. A mere quiver of pain answered, to be quickly blotted out by another warm thought.

I have a friend. The first real friend since her girlhood on Sintia. The friendship existed independently of the sudden physical relationship. She'd had bed-mates from time to random time, and it was very nice to be loved and petted and—made comfortable. And it was wholly delightful to be permitted to return that grace as best as she was able. But this was not the thing that was precious, that prompted her now to reexamine the plans she had laid out for herself.

Again she heard the sleepy voice of her friend: "Priscilla? Go back to sleep, denubia. All is well."

All is well. For the first time in many years she allowed herself to think that it could, in time, *be* well. If she remained a member of this ship, with its odd captain, and clumsy Rusty Morgenstern and Gordy and the old cargo master and Master Frodo and Lina—of course, Lina . . .

Perhaps, if she stayed there . . . if she put Sav Rid Olanek and Dagmar Collier out of mind and concentrated on a future full of friendship, where all might be well . . .

"What are you doing here?"

The sharp voice brought her up short. She blinked at the unfamiliar hallway to which her unheeded feet had brought her, then looked back at Kayzin Ne'Zame and inclined her head. "I'm very sorry. I was thinking and lost my way. Is it restricted? I'll go away."

"Will you?" The first mate was tight-lipped with anger. "You will just walk away, is it so? I *asked* what you are doing here. I expect an answer. Now."

"I am sorry, Kayzin Ne'Zame," she said carefully. "I gave you an answer: I was walking as I thought, and lost the way."

"And you so conveniently lost the way in such a manner that you come to the main computer bank. I will have truth from you, Priscilla Mendoza. Again—what do you here?"

"I don't think that's your business," Priscilla flared. "Since you won't believe the truth, why should I keep repeating it?"

"You!" If she had been angry before, the mate was livid now. "How much does he pay you?" she demanded, her accent thicker by the second.

The Terran looked at her in blank astonishment. "One-tenth cantra, when we reach Solcintra—"

"Have done!" There was a pause while Kayzin looked her up and down. The set lines of her face did not alter; she opened her mouth to speak further, then closed it, eyes going over Priscilla's shoulder.

"Go!" she snapped. "And mind you do not lose your way to this place again. Do you hear me?"

"I hear you, Kayzin Ne'Zame," Priscilla replied evenly. She inclined her head and turned away.

Shan yos'Galan was leaning against the wall, glass of wine held negligently in one hand, arms crossed over his chest.

Priscilla took a breath. "Good shift, Captain."

"Good shift, Ms. Mendoza," he said neutrally. She walked past him and down the intersecting hallway.

He turned to Kayzin. "Correct me if I'm wrong," he said softly. "The crew is allowed access to all portions of the ship?"

"Yes, Captain."

"Yes, Captain," he repeated, his eyes holding hers effortlessly. "Priscilla Mendoza is a member of the crew, Kayzin. I can't think how you came to forget it, but please strive to bear it in mind in the future. Also, it is just possible that you owe an apology."

She drew a deep, deep breath. "Say that you trust her!"

"I trust her," he said flatly, giving her the grace due an old friend.

"You are besotted!"

"Quite sober, I assure you," he said in icy Terran. Then he switched to the High Tongue, that of lord instructing oathsworn. "I act, having given consideration to laws of necessity."

Kayzin bowed low, pride of him glowing through her mortification. There were those who said that Er Thom yos'-Galan's lady had foisted a full-blooded Terran upon him as his eldest. If those could but see him, standing there, with the eyes spitting ice and the face just so! Who could behold him thus and say he was not Korval, blood and bone?

"Forgive me, Captain," she murmured. "It shall be as you have said."

"I am glad to hear it," he replied in Terran.

Arsdred Port roared. It pushed, yodeled, shoved, sang, shimmied, stripped gleaming naked, and swathed itself head to toe in bright colors and glittering gems. Much of the noise—and most of the color—was contributed by the people behind stalls, before storefronts, and beside carts piled high with Goddess knew what. These were Arsdredi, dark-skinned Terrans, doe-eyed, hook-nosed, and voluble. They wore layer upon layer of gauzy, brilliant cloth and hawked their wares, sweatless, in the glare of the midday suns.

Some of the clamor, to be sure, was generated by those for whom the wares were displayed. Thronging the narrow streets were members of half a dozen races: Terrans of all description; graceful Liadens, dark-lensed Peladins, hairless Trimuvat, silent Uhlvore. Priscilla started, catching a gigantic figure out of the corner of an eye, wondering if even the Yxtrang stopped here—but it was only a towering Aus, golden-haired and full-bearded, head bent as he addressed a booming remark to the tiny woman skipping at his side.

"Firegems, pretty lady? The finest here—for you—so pale

your skin, so black your hair! For *you*, beautiful lady, what else but azure? A mere twentybit—sacrificed on the altar of your beauty! Only try and see how it becomes you."

"Cloth, noble lady? Scarves? Crimson, gold, serpentine, xanthin, indigo! Wear them about your head, twist them around your waist—a fair price, noble."

"Porcelains, lady? Guidebooks . . . Ices . . . Incense . . . Gemstones . . ."

Peace.

Priscilla rounded a corner into a less traveled thorough-fare, breathing a sigh of relief. The roster had granted her leave this first day in port. Rusty and Lina had drawn time together on the third, a circumstance that brought a frown to the Liaden woman's face while Rusty shrugged. "Maybe next time."

Secretly, Priscilla was relieved. A leave-companion would have quickly discovered the state of her finances. She was pleased not to burden her friends with that particular information and perhaps be forced to endure kindhearted offers of a loan or, worse, an outright gift.

It was better this way, she thought, strolling along the hot little street. A day of rest before a trying tomorrow. For the roster's other news had been that she was to assist Cargo Master yo'Lanna with the worldside unloading next shift-worked.

She had come to the first cross street when a familiar voice intruded upon her.

"Hi, Ms. Mendoza! Is this your day, too? Want to partner?"

She turned, smiling down into Gordy Arbuthnot's round—and exquisitely clean—face. "I'm afraid I'd hold you down," she said carefully. Then she added more briskly, "You aren't here *by yourself,* are you, Gordy?"

He grimaced. "Well, sort of. Cap'n says he knows I got enough sense not to get in trouble, but that accidents happen an' my grandad'd break his nose for him if I came by one. So, we compromised." He tugged something off his belt and held it out for inspection: a portable comm.

"I've got the cap'n's direct beam-code. If I get in a

scrape—even a *little* one—I'm supposed to get on the beam
and *yell*." Gordy sighed, then looked up again, trying to put a
good face on it. "I guess that's not too bad, is it, Ms. Mendoza?"

"It sounds," Priscilla said truthfully, "very generous. And
reasonable. A great many people, you know, would think you
were only a little boy."

"Well, that's true," he agreed. "Even Ma said something
like that when Grandad told her he'd got everything fixed
with the cap'n, and she's usually—reasonable too. But Mor-
gan'd been talking her ears off about how Shan wasn't *really*
related to us—and Liaden, besides. I guess," Gordy concluded rather breathlessly, "that kind of thing'd be enough to
make *any*body unreasonable."

"It certainly sounds like it would be," she agreed with
amusement. "Is the captain related to you?"

Gordy nodded as he clipped the comm back to his belt.
"Shan's ma was Grandad's sister. So we're cousins—Shan
and Val Con and Nova and Anthora. Well, at least," he said
scrupulously, "not Val Con. He's a fosterling. But I call him
cousin, too. And he's *Shan's* cousin, so I guess we're related,
some way." He grinned at her. "Want to partner?" he asked
again.

Priscilla shook her head. "I think I'd rather just roam
around and get my thoughts in order, rest a little. I'm scheduled to help Ken Rik tomorrow."

Gordy laughed. "You better rest, then. Ken Rik's okay, but
he likes to make people squirm. Good at it, too. Tell you what:
I'm due at the shuttle Last Hour, shiptime. Let's go up together, okay, Ms. Mendoza?"

"Okay." She smiled at him. "You might as well call me
Priscilla. Everybody else does."

"Cap'n doesn't," Gordy pointed out, moving off. "I will,
though. See you later—Priscilla."

"See you later—Mr. Arbuthnot."

That drew another burst of laughter. Priscilla shook her

head, still smiling, and turned left down the cross street, away from the voice of the bazaar.

It was a little past Nineteenth Hour, shiptime. Priscilla, feeling very well in a lazy sort of way, had quit the municipal park some moments before and was sauntering down a thin avenue that curved in the general direction of the port.

Most of the shops along this way were closed, though she passed a brightly lit window displaying an extremely ornate chess set carved of red and white woods and set with faceted stones. She paused, considering the set and comparing it to the chessmen she had seen upon the captain's board. Those pieces had been carved of ebonwood and bonebar, but very plainly—a set for a person who played the game, not for a collector of the exotic.

She continued on her way. The next window, under a sign that read TEELA'S TREASURES, was crowded with an eye-dazzling collection of objects. A carved ivory fan lay next to a tawdry firegem tiara; a gold necklace with a greenish tinge lay as if flung across a bound book of possible worth and definite age; while a cut-plastic vase hobnobbed with an eggshell porcelain bowl down on its luck.

Fascinated, Priscilla bent closer to the window, trying to puzzle out more of its contents. A carved wooden box with a broken hinge; an antique pair of eyeglasses, untinted; a—her breath caught in her throat as she spied it, balanced precariously atop a stack of mismatched flowered saucers: a blown-crystal triglant, caught by the artist in a mood of pensiveness, wings half-furled, tail wrapped neatly around its front paws. A charming piece—and hers!

Hers. And of the few things she had been able to bring with her from Sintia, it had been the most treasured. *She* had commissioned the work, paid for it with the labor of her own hands.

She had built the velvet-lined box in which it had been lovingly displayed.

Perhaps the thief had thought the box worthless.

Priscilla stalked stiff-legged into the shop, twobits clenched in her fist. Fifteen minutes later, she came out, carefully tucking the paper-wrapped figurine in her pocket. Broke, she reminded herself, trying to call up fear.

But all she felt was warm contentment. She had the triglant. She had a berth on the *Passage*. She had a tenth-cantra waiting for her when they docked at Solcintra. It would suffice. She had a friend—perhaps even three. That was so much more than sufficient that she barely had room for the grief of leaving her other things in the hands of the proprietor of Teela's Treasures.

She took the first cross street, hurrying now toward the port. To her right, a shadow moved. She spun.

"Hello, Prissy," Dagmar said, grinning widely. She took two steps closer.

Goddess, aid me now . . . "Good-bye, Dagmar," she gritted through her teeth. She made to pass on.

The bigger woman blocked her way, grin widening. "Aw, now, honey, you ain't gonna let a little thing like a headache come between us, are you? I was just following orders, Prissy. And I sure am glad to see you again."

"I'm not glad to see you. Good-bye." She turned away.

Dagmar grabbed an arm and yanked Priscilla forward, while her other hand found a breast and squeezed.

Priscilla swung with all the force in her, slamming five knuckles backhanded across the other woman's leer as she twisted, just managing to get free.

Dagmar lunged, grabbing a handful of shirt. Priscilla continued her twist. The fabric tore, and Dagmar pitched backward, scrabbling for support.

It was time to run. Priscilla dived forward.

It was easy.

Dagmar was bigger—and no doubt stronger. Certainly she was more accustomed to this kind of business than was her prey.

But she was *slow*.

Priscilla had the measure of the game now. Moving with pilot swiftness, seeing with pilot eyes, she landed an astonishing number of blows, though the ones she received were telling.

She ducked back, slammed a ringing blow toward the ears that was only partially successful, and suffered a numbing crack to her right shoulder.

Several more passes and she saw how it might be ended— quickly and to her advantage. She began the spin to get into position—

The hum warned her, and she snapped backward, rolling heavily on her right side, wishing she had had the sense to run before.

Dagmar had pulled a vibroknife.

Gordy was late.

He streaked across the municipal park, causing consternation among the local duck-analogs, and careered into Parkton Way. He passed the window containing the chessmen without a glance, though he did slow as he came abreast Teela's Treasures, out of respect for the policeman half a block ahead.

A side street presented itself, wending portward. Gordy took it—and froze in disbelief.

Before him was Priscilla Mendoza, shirt torn nearly to the shoulder, bent forward like some two-legged, beautiful, and quite deadly predator, carefully circling a larger, broader woman, who circled in her turn.

The position of the two changed sufficiently for Gordy to see the rest: The larger woman held a knife.

Gulping, he turned and ran back the way he had come.

Priscilla considered the knife dispassionately. It could be done. She was fast. Dagmar was slow. Her objective was only to dispose of the blade—*she* was no knife fighter.

Priscilla moved.

Dagmar twisted—so slooow—and Priscilla's fingers swept through hers, dislodging the evil, humming thing and sending it spinning into the shadows. The larger woman finished her twist and slammed heavily into her opponent, trying to grab and hold two slender wrists in a big hand, hugging her tight, and Priscilla could not breathe . . .

"Here now, here now! That'll be enough of *that* kind of carrying on!" Strong hands grabbed and pulled—and breath returned.

Priscilla sagged backward, too grateful for the boon of air to resent the hand irons so competently slapped into place. Dagmar, she saw presently, was in worse shape. She had apparently taken a stunner charge and was retching against the wall, her face already beginning to purple.

The cop finished affixing irons and turned away—and his eyebrows went up with his stunner. "All right, my boy, fun's over. Give it to me, please."

Gordy blinked, reversed the vibroknife, and held it out. The cop took it gingerly, then jerked the comm from the boy's belt and clipped it to his own.

"That's mine!"

"Then you'll get it back after the trial. Hold out your hands."

"I won't wear irons." The round chin was rigid.

"Then you'll go unconscious, over my shoulder." The cop considered him. "Might drop you, though."

Gordy looked over the man's shoulder at Priscilla. She managed a ragged smile and a nod. He held out his hands.

The exhibits were on a table against the far left wall: a vibroknife, a portable comm, a pile of glittering shards that had once represented a triglant at rest.

The prisoners were to the right. The slender woman and the boy sat next to each other, as far away as possible from the bulky woman with the battered face. Sedatives had been administered to all, in keeping with the magistrate's order. Though there had been no renewal of hostilities, the arresting officer was keeping a sharp eye out. One never knew with outworlders.

Priscilla fought the tranquilizing haze, struggling for clear thought. They were waiting, the cop had said, for the arrival of a ranking officer from *Daxflan* and from *Dutiful Passage* so that the trial could commence.

Kayzin Ne'Zame, Priscilla thought laboriously. She dislikes me—here's a Goddess-sent opportunity for her to be rid of me altogether.

Lina. What would Lina think? Would Priscilla be allowed to speak with her, explain what had happened, before the *Passage* left orbit? She caught her breath, her mind suddenly clear of fog, aware of a nearly overmastering desire to fling herself down and sob.

Fool, she told herself harshly. You should have run.

There was a rustle of robes in the outer hallway, and Gordy shifted next to her. "Maybe that's the judge," he said drowsily, "I sure hope so. Crelm, Priscilla! Do you know how late we are? Shan's gonna *skin* me!"

Her reply was cut off by the arresting officer.

"All rise for Magistrate Kelbar!"

She stood; she started when Gordy slipped his hand into hers, and then squeezed his fingers.

"That's you, too!" the cop was telling Dagmar, who mumbled something and climbed to her feet.

Magistrate Kelbar swept into the room, an imposing figure in his sun-yellow robes of office. Out of stern brown eyes he considered the three of them before seating himself with a flourish upon his throne. He waved a hand in a languid gesture that the cop translated sharply.

"Prisoners sit!"

Dagmar grunted and slouched back onto her bench. Priscilla sat quietly, though Gordy heaved a sigh.

Let it be done quickly, Goddess, Priscilla prayed.

As if in answer to that thought, the door was opened from without, admitting a small, fair man.

Sav Rid Olanek had been called from a party, Priscilla thought: His shirt was shimmering rose silk; the pale trousers surely were velvet. Jewels glittered in his ears, on his hands, and from the buckle of his belt, and around his throat was a titanium collar worth double the pay she would never collect at Solcintra.

Recognizing a person of consequence, the magistrate snapped his fingers at the prisoners to rise and swept forward. "Good evening, gentle sir!" he said in affable Trade, extending a wide hand. "I am sorry to have had to summon you here. A small matter, I am sure, and easily settled, once your honored colleague arrives. I am Magistrate Kelbar."

He was accorded a flickering glance from bright blue eyes,

and the barest possible bow. "I am Sav Rid Olanek, Trader on *Daxflan*, out of Liad," he said coldly. "I am afraid you may be too optimistic, however." He pointed at Priscilla, who returned his gaze with determined serenity. "*That* person is a desperate criminal. She is without doubt a thief. What else she may be—"

"Good evening!" a voice called in cheerful Terran, preceding its owner into the room by a heartbeat. Sav Rid Olanek bit off the rest of his sentence, and Priscilla felt Gordy shift next to her.

It was not Kayzin Ne'Zame, after all.

He wore a shirt barely less bright than his hair, and soft black trousers. His belt buckle was merely silver, its design changing from a fanciful bird to an impossible flower as Priscilla watched. An amethyst drop exactly matching the color of the gem in his master's ring hung from his right ear.

He was the most welcome sight Priscilla had ever beheld. It'll be all right now, she told herself, and didn't even wonder why she thought so.

He smiled at the magistrate and bowed easily, then came forward with hand outstretched. "I'm Shan yos'Galan, sir. Am I very late? Forgive me, please. I was at Herr Sasoni's— but perhaps I should say no more. Except that I was on the verge of concluding a very—interesting—piece of business, so it was fortunate your message reached me when it did."

The magistrate actually laughed, taking the more slender hand in his. "But this is dreadful!" he cried. "Surely you were able to procure her key for later use? I should never forgive myself, sir—"

"No matter," the captain interrupted easily. "I'm sure we'll be able to clear this matter up in a moment or two, and I'll return—what *is* the matter, by the way, sir? I—" He turned his head, eyes alighting, apparently for the first time, on his glaring colleague.

"Good evening, Sav Rid," he said politely in the Liaden High Tongue.

"You!" the other snarled.

"Well, of course, me. I couldn't very well be anyone else, could I? Has this little inconvenience put you out of temper? I'm sure we'll be shut of it in a moment. The magistrate seems very amiable, don't you think? As I just said to him— but I've forgotten, you don't speak Terran, do you? A sad pity, since so many other people do, but no doubt you have your reasons."

"I do, and they are not yours to inquire into." Trader Olanek waved his hand in their direction, though his eyes did not leave the captain. "You might wish to turn your limited understanding to the matter at hand. It may be that you have undervalued the inconvenience."

"Yes?" The silver eyes swept the three of them vaguely. "Well, I must say, your crew member—I assume she is yours—looks as if she's taken rather a tumble. In her cups, perhaps. But you're too experienced a Trader to allow a little drunken sport among the crew to spoil your whole evening."

"Gentles?" Magistrate Kelbar said in firm Trade. "If we may get on with the hearing? I am certain we would all rather be elsewhere." He resumed his seat with another flourish and waved the prisoners forward. "Will you two gentlemen please identify these persons?"

Trader Olanek pointed. "That is Dagmar Collier, second mate on *Daxflan*." "And, as her superior officer, you are willing to speak for her?"

After a slight hesitation, the Trader said, "Yes."

"And the two remaining," the captain said cheerily, "are mine, sir. The young gentleman is Gordon Arbuthnot, cabin boy on the *Dutiful Passage* and my kinsman—"

"You mean to say you acknowledge that connection?" The Trader's High Liaden carried outrage. "It's full Terran! Have you no sense of the honor due your Clan?"

"Well, we're *half* Terran, after all," the captain said mildly. "You knew that, didn't you, when you propositioned my sister? And he's a good lad."

"You cannot be serious."

"He is under Korval's wing." The captain's inflection shifted subtly, his voice nearly cold. "Do not mistake me."

"Pah! Korval's wing unfurls too far for health. Does the same apply to the bitch beside him?"

She stiffened, outrage erupting—

"Priscilla!" the captain snapped, and she stilled, cheeks flaming.

"You keep it on a short leash," the Trader commented. "How much do you pay it? Or does it serve for the pleasure of looking at your beautiful face?"

The captain shook his head. "On Priscilla Mendoza's home world, Sav Rid, you would have just now uttered an insult demanding your death for balance. It's fortunate, isn't it, that her knowledge of our tongue is a scholar's? But I am forgetting my manners again! You are acquainted!" The light eyes were on her. "Have you no greeting for the honored Trader?"

She stared at him. Did he really expect her—And then she smiled, recalling another of Fin Ton's lessons. Loosing Gordy's hand, she bowed low.

"Forgive me the situation, Master Trader," she said in her careful High Liaden, "and believe me all joy to see you."

"What!" Sav Rid cried, visibly shaken. "How is it possible that—"

"Gentles," the magistrate said. "I must insist that we keep to the matter at hand."

"Of course, sir." The captain was contrite. "Do forgive us. My colleague is an avid student of lineage and sought enlightenment regarding Gordon's place in the family tree. To continue, indeed. The lady with the torn shirt is Priscilla Delacroix y Mendoza. She is under personal contract to the captain of the *Dutiful Passage*, serving as librarian, pilot, and apprentice second mate." He smiled. "I'm quite happy to speak for both of them."

What was this? Pilot? Second mate in training? Priscilla tried to recall the precise phrasing of her contract, but the magistrate's voice defeated the effort.

"As all three have someone in authority to speak for them,

the hearing now commences. What we know is this: Yonder knife is the property of Dagmar Collier. We have taken imprint readings and find it to be so. She does not deny it.

"It is important to note that two other sets of prints are found on the hilt, besides those of the arresting officer: those of Gordon Arbuthnot, and a faint, very blurred set which we believe to be those of Priscilla Mendoza." The magistrate paused to clear his throat importantly.

"We will hear from the arresting officer."

The cop's statement was brief and to the point. He had been hailed by Gordon Arbuthnot, who cried that there was a fight in Halvington Street. Arriving on the scene, he had found "those two persons there" in close embrace, the larger apparently engaged in squeezing the smaller breathless. The arresting officer was of the opinion that this project was near completion and so had administered a judicial stunner blast to the larger person, hand-ironed both combatants, and turned to find Gordon Arbuthnot with "that knife, there, sir," in his hand. So, in the interest of fair play, Gordy had been ironed as well, and all three brought in. The officer paused, scratched his head, and added that he had also taken from Gordon Arbuthnot a small rectangular object with a belt clip—very likely a portable comm and no harm to it. But at the time he had seen no reason to take unnecessary chances.

"Quite right," the captain said approvingly, and the cop grinned shyly.

The magistrate motioned him back. "We will now hear from Dagmar Collier."

Dagmar came forward slowly and darted a glance at Trader Olanek. He did not meet her eyes.

She made a woeful attempt to square her shoulders. Her voice when she spoke was hoarse, the words mushy. I hope I broke every tooth in her mouth, Priscilla thought.

"Prissy and me are old friends," Dagmar was telling the magistrate. "Used to serve on *Daxflan* together. It was just natural for me to go over and say 'hey' when I saw her walkin' down the street." She shrugged. "Must've been drunk, I guess, Your Honor, 'cause she just hauled off and hit me."

There was a short pause before the magistrate asked dryly, "Is that your statement of the affair?"

Dagmar blinked. "Yessir."

"I see. We are willing to hear you again, should something else occur to you after Priscilla Mendoza speaks."

Priscilla stood forward. "Ms. Collier and I were never friends," she began hotly. "She has stolen from me and sold my things to a—a *thrift shop* on Parkton—"

The magistrate raised his hand. "That is not the issue at trial here. Please limit your remarks to the incident in Halvington Street."

Priscilla bit her lip. "I saw Ms. Collier in Halvington Street," she began again, "as I was on my way back to the port. She spoke to me. I returned the greeting and tried to pass on. Ms. Collier blocked my way and grabbed me—I *believe* she intended rape, but that may be unjust. At the time it seemed exactly what she meant, and I—"she broke off, her eyes seeking the captain's. "I lost my temper," she said wryly. He nodded, and she turned back to the magistrate.

"I tried to defend myself against what I thought was an attack. Ms. Collier continued to block my way and at some point pulled a knife. I *did* disarm her, but she grabbed me. Which is how I came to be in the absurd situation from which the officer rescued me." She sighed. "That is my statement, sir."

"Very clear, Ms. Mendoza. Thank you."

"I would like to point out," Sav Rid Olanek said abruptly, "that the animosity between these two individuals seems of long standing—"

"Exactly," the captain interrupted. "in which case, Magistrate, I venture to say that each has had ample opportunity to vent her spleen. A fine, of course, is in order, for breaking the peace. But, since it is highly unlikely that they will meet again soon . . ."

Magistrate Kelbar beamed at him. "I am sure you can be

trusted to control the members of your crew during the rest of your time in port, sirs. My trust in your discretion prompts me not to demand that both individuals be rendered ship-bound for that period. They will, of course, be confined to the port proper. And, there *is* a fine." He coughed gently. "For engaging in fisticuffs in a public thoroughfare: one hundred bits each. Drawing a deadly weapon: two hundred fifty bits. Possession of said weapon without Arsdred certificate of permission: six hundred bits. Resisting arrest—" He looked up and smiled, first at Gordy, then at the captain. "I think we might dispense with that. Transport fee: fifty bits each.

"So then, owed from Dagmar Collier, through her superior, Sav Rid Olanek: one thousand bits. Owed from Priscilla Mendoza, through her superior, Shan yos'Galan: one hundred fifty bits. Owed from Gordon Arhuthnot from his superior, Shan yos'Galan: fifty bits. You may pay cash at the teller's cage as you leave, gentles." He arose and sailed from the room, the arresting officer in his wake.

Shan considered Olanek's set face. "One thousand bits," he murmured in sympathetic Trade. "Will it put you out of pocket, Sav Rid? I can extend a loan, if you like."

"Thank you, I think not!" the other snapped, jerking his head at his crew member.

Shan sighed. "So short-tempered, Sav Rid! Not sleeping well? I do hope you're not ill. At least we know you don't have a guilty conscience, don't we? By the way, Ms. Mendoza seems to have lost a very special pair of earrings. Do you know Calintak, on Medusa? Wonderful fellow, very good-tempered. And the things he can fit in just a *little* bit of space: built-in sensors, trackers—that sort of thing. If you're ever in the market for something, since you wear so *much* jewelry . . ."

Dagmar Collier was hovering close, eyes riveted. "Sensors?" she asked with a kind of fascinated dread. "How small a space?"

"Oh, are you interested? He's quite dear, you know—but hardly any space at all. An unexceptional earring, for instance, is all the room he needs to work in. An artist—" "Oh, have done!" Sav Rid snarled, turning on his heel. "Pay him no mind, he's a fool. Now, come!" He was gone, Dagmar following.

Shan shook his head and held out a hand to Gordy, who came and slid his own into it. "Well now, children—Ms. Mendoza?"

She was at the exhibit table, picking up the shards of crystal, one by careful one, and settling them in her palm.

"Crelm!" Gordy muttered, and went to her side. "Priscilla, what're you doing? It's busted."

She did not look away from her task. "It's all I own, anywhere, and I'm taking it with me." Her tone was perfectly flat, with an absence of emotion that raised the hairs on Shan's neck. He stepped forward quickly, pulled a square of silk from his sleeve, and dropped it in front of her.

"You'll cut yourself, Priscilla. Use this."

"Thank you." Her voice was still flat, though he fancied he detected a quiver of *something* . . .

Hand in hand, he and Gordy waited until she had finished and tied the silk into a knot. Gordy took her hand, and, so linked, they went out to pay the cashier.

"You will do me the favor, won't you, Gordy," the captain murmured, "of neglecting to inform your mother that you've been arrested?"

"Was I?" the boy asked hazily. "I mean, I wasn't *really*. They didn't do anything to me."

The man laughed. "Arrested, I assure you. The details may vary by world, but the larger outlines remain constant: irons, hearings, magistrates, fines—not at all the kind of thing mothers enjoy hearing of, even when it's carefully explained that you were completely without blame. Which reminds me—how did your imprints come to be on that thing?"

"Priscilla was losing," Gordy explained. "And the knife was just lying there. I was trying to figure out how it worked . . ."

"Yes? To what end, please?"

"Well, I thought if I cut Dagmar's arm, she'd let go."

"It's a theory," the captain admitted. "Report to Pallin Kornad after breakfast, please. I see it's time you learned how to protect yourself."

"Yes, Cap'n." He paused. "Shan?"

"Yes, acushla?"

"Is it—can I tell Grandad I was arrested? I didn't do anything *wrong* . . ." This last was spoken, it seemed to Priscilla, with considerable doubt.

A boot heel scraped on the pavement as the man went down on one knee, eyes level with Gordy's.

"You will *absolutely* tell your grandfather," he said firmly, his big hands on the boy's round shoulders. "He will be proud of you. You acted with forethought and with honor, coming to the aid of a shipmate and a friend." He cupped a soft cheek. "You did very well, Gordy. Thank you."

"Yes." Priscilla heard her own voice from far away. "Thank you, Gordy. You saved my life."

He blinked at her over his cousin's shoulder. "I *did?*" She nodded, not sure what her face was doing. "She really was winning. I couldn't breathe. You did exactly right."

She should, she thought vaguely, find something more to say, but it was unnecessary; doubt had vanished from the young face. He grinned. "I'm a hero."

"You're an impossible monkey." The captain stood and held out his hand. "And you're well behind your time to return to the ship. Come along."

They walked a little way in silence. The drug was gaining the upper hand again, and Priscilla stumbled; she caught herself and asked over Gordy's head, "What was that about your sister?"

"Sav Rid's little joke," the captain said easily. "It amused him to propose marriage to the eldest of my sisters." ·

"What!" Gordy was outraged. "That—person? To *Cousin Nova?*"

"Indeed, yes. Exactly Cousin Nova. Why? Do you think Anthora might suit him better? I admit it's a thought. He so fair and she so dark . . . But he was more enamored of fair with fair. You can't really blame him, Gordy; it's merely a matter of taste."

"What did you do?" Gordy demanded awfully, ignoring this flow of nonsense.

The man looked down at him. "What could I do? I was from home. Besides, Nova is well able to take care of herself. Simply told the fellow she'd rather mate with a Gehatian slimegrubber and sent him about his business." He sighed. "I'm afraid he didn't take it in very good part. Well, how was she to know he had a horror of the creatures? I'm sure she would have thought of something else just as revolting to compare him with, if she'd had the least idea. Very resourceful person, Cousin Nova. The more I think on it, the more certain I am that you're right, Gordy! Anthora would certainly suit him far better! A pity he didn't see it that way and allowed himself to be enraptured by a mere pretty face. Perhaps we should suggest—"

"Pretty!" the boy choked. "Cousin Nova's *beautiful!*"

"Well," the lady's brother conceded, "she is. But I wouldn't let it weigh too heavily with you. Gordy. Sort of thing that might happen to anyone. And she's really quite clever."

They came at length to the cradles and crossed to their shuttlepad in silence. A shadow loomed at the door, bringing two fingers up in a casual salute. "Evening, Cap'n."

"Good evening, Seth. Two passengers for you. Take good care of them, please; they both seem a bit yawnsome—is that a word?"

"Bound to be," the lanky pilot returned good-humoredly. "Not going up yourself?"

"Business, Seth. Duty calls."

"He has to get her key," Gordy said helpfully.

"Brat." His cousin sighed. "Don't forget Pallin next shift, Gordy." "No, Cap'n—at least, *yes*, Cap'n. I'll remember."

The captain laughed and began to move away, then checked himself and came back, fishing in his belt. "My terrible memory! I knew there was something else. Ms. Mendoza!"

She started. "Captain?"

He was holding out a flat rectangle, a card of some sort. She took it automatically.

"Do take care of it, Ms. Mendoza," he chided gently. "It's really not the sort of thing you want to leave lying around. Good evening." He was gone.

Priscilla frowned at the card, but the uncertain light or her sedative-fogged eyes defeated the attempt to identify it. She put it in her pocket with the knotted kerchief and followed Gordy into the shuttle.

Gordy was asleep when they docked. The snap of the board being locked jerked Priscilla out of her own doze, but even the most stringent effort she was able to make would not rouse her companion from his.

Sighing, she fumbled her webbing loose, then opened his. Her several attempts to pick him up should have roused one dead, she thought foggily, but Gordy only grumbled a few sleep syllables and tried to curl farther down into the chair. Priscilla rubbed her forehead with the back of a hand and tried to apply her mind to the problem.

"Out for the count," Seth commented from beside her. "I gotta get back down. Can you carry him, or should we call Vilt?"

Priscilla gave him what she hoped was a smile. "I can carry him. Getting him up is the problem."

"Naw. Not when somebody's that far out." He bent, grabbed an arm, heaved, turned, and offered Priscilla an armful of boy.

She took Gordy and allowed herself to be escorted to the door of the cargo dock. It slid open for her, and she stepped into the corridor, blinking a little in the directionless yellow light.

Before her she saw, with the vivid disconnection of a dream, a bronze-winged dragon hovering. No. It was a painting on the wall, a smaller reproduction of the design in the reception room. Under Korval's wing, Priscilla recalled. She shifted her burden and began the long walk to the crew's quarters.

She had made it, staggering only now and then, to the top of the corridor where Gordy had his room, when she heard quick steps behind her and an exclamation.

"Priscilla! Is that Gordon? What has—is all well, my friend?"

"Well?" She considered Lina muzzily. It took several seconds to formulate an appropriate response. "Gordy's all right. It's mostly that stupid stuff they injected us with at the police station. Makes you . . . makes you groggy. Half asleep, myself."

"Ah." The other woman fell in beside her. "The police station? Does the captain know?"

Priscilla nodded, then paused to regain her balance. "He came to bail us out—dear Goddess!" She stopped, arms closing convulsively around Gordy, who muttered. "Dear Goddess," she said again, though not, Lina thought, prayerfully. "One hundred fifty bits! Out of a tenth-cantra? And the clothes . . ." She took a hard breath and began to walk again. "Broke. No money at all."

Lina's worry increased, but she refrained from pursuing questions, merely remarking that they had reached Gordon's room and lifting his hand to lay it against the palmlock.

Priscilla laid him on the bed, pulled off his boots, straightened the blanket, and pulled it up. Lina stood by the door, watching and saying nothing.

The boy disposed comfortably, Priscilla glanced around the room, and nodded slightly, then bent and ruffled the silky hair.

"Ma?" Gordy inquired from the depths of sleep.

She started, then completed the caress. "It's only Priscilla, Gordy. Sleep well."

Lina followed her out, stretching her short legs to keep up with the pace her friend set, even half-drugged.

At the top of the hall Priscilla made to turn right. Lina caught her arm. "No, Priscilla. Your room is this way."

"Have to go to the library," she protested. "Now."

"Not now," Lina said with decision. "Now, you must rest. The library will be in place next shift."

Priscilla shook her head. "Have to see my contract."

"Your contract? Priscilla, it is—conselem—an absurdity! What good does your contract do when you must sleep? You are signed until Solcintra. You may look at your contract any time these next four months. Come to bed."

"He lied," Priscilla said flatly, a decidedly mulish look about her lovely mouth.

Lina sighed. "Who lied? And why must—The captain lied?" She stared up at her friend. "That is not much like him, denubia. Perhaps you misunderstood."

"I'm very tired," Priscilla said clearly, "of misunderstanding. I must see my contract."

"Of course you must," Lina agreed. "It would be very bad to have misunderstood the captain. Let us go to your room and access the file from there." She slipped her arm around the other's waist.

Priscilla stiffened and moved away—a very little. Lina's eyes widened, but she said nothing, only withdrew her arm. And waited.

"All right," Priscilla said presently, the mulish look much abated. "Let's do that. Thank you, Lina."

"I am happy to help," Lina said carefully as they turned left down the hall. "What happened, my friend?"

There was a long pause before the taller woman shook herself and answered, "I was attacked on the street. Gordy tried to help, and we all three got arrested. They called the captain out of a party to—to speak for us."

"Most proper," Lina said, and stopped, waiting for Priscilla to lay her palm against the lock.

It seemed for a moment that she did not recognize her own door. Then she shifted and placed her hand in the center; when the panel slid away, she entered, with Lina trailing after.

"Most proper," Priscilla repeated, standing in the middle of her cabin and staring around as if she had never seen the place before. She spun.

"It cost *one hundred fifty bits* to *speak* for me!" she cried with an unexpected but wholly gratifying flare of passion. "One hundred fifty! And I'll have earned a tenth-cantra by the time we reach Solcintra, and I already owe the ship for my clothes—and all my things—my things are gone . . ." Abruptly she sat on the bed, running violent fingers through the curly cloud of her hair.

Lina came forward, daring to lay her hand on a rigid shoulder. She frowned at the startled jerk. "I did not attack you on the street," she said severely.

Priscilla looked up, apology in her eyes. Lina smiled, lifting the tips of her fingers to a pale cheek.

"Of course I did not. I have been very well brought up." She tugged gently on an errant curl. "Of this other thing: The ship has a—*legal fund*. Since *you* were attacked, I think the fund will pay the expense of your bail. It is a thing you should speak of with the captain. Was he angry with you?"

Priscilla blinked. "I don't think so. Does he get angry?"

Lina laughed. "If he had been so, you would not be in doubt. So, then, I would not worry about my wages. It is very likely that they remain intact. Now, allow me to call your contract up." She went to the screen.

Behind her, Priscilla stood, moved unsteadily to the mirror shelf, and began to pull things from her pocket. The knotted silk she placed carefully to one side of the usual oddments. Patting her pocket to be sure it was empty, she felt a flat thickness—the card the captain had given her at the shuttlepad. She pulled it out and examined it, her breath catching.

"Lina!"

The Liaden woman was at her elbow instantly. "Yes?"

Priscilla held out the card in a hand that was not at all steady. "What is this, please?"

Lana subjected it to a brief, two-sided scrutiny and handed it back, smiling. "It is a provisional second class pilot's license in the name of Priscilla Delacroix y Mendoza. Ge'shada, my friend, you have done very well."

"I've done very well. Done well . . ." Priscilla stared and

suddenly threw back her head, uttering a sound so shattered that no one could have called it laughter. Then she bent double, torn with sobs.

Lina put her arms about her and probed with a Healer's sure instinct, evading weakened defenses and slashing at the protected reservoir of pain.

Priscilla cried out and went to her knees. Lina held her closer, withdrawing somewhat, content for the present to have the storm rage.

After a time, the sobbing eased and she coaxed her friend to the bed. When they were lying face to face, she probed again, projecting on all possible lines.

Priscilla stirred, sodden lashes lifting, then extended a tentative finger to trace the lines of her friend's face, exhausted wonderment on her own.

"I see you, sister," she murmured. Then her hand fell away, and she slept, bathed in warm affection and comfort.

"But why can't we sell the perfume here?" Rusty demanded, staring at Lina over a suspended forkful of ice-toast.

The Liaden woman sighed. "It is—bah! I have forgotten the word. It is to *force* one to love another, a . . ."

"Aphrodisiac," Priscilla supplied, looking up from her own breakfast. "Aphrodisiacs are illegal on some planets. I guess Arsdred's one of them."

Rusty scowled at his plate.

"Rah Stee, do not!" Lina was laughing. "You will spoil your food! It is not so bad. We will sell at another port." She shook a slender finger in mock severity. "You believe I have given us a loss! But I claim the dice for more than one throw. You will see, my friend: the perfume will sell—and at high profit!"

Rusty looked dubious, and Lina laughed again.

"Priscilla?" a breathless young voice asked at her elbow. She turned her head to discover the cabin boy, clutching a box.

"Good morning, Gordy," she said, offering him a storm-beaten smile. "I thought you were supposed to be learning self-defense first thing this shift."

"Crelm!" he said scornfully. "I did that an hour ago!" He held out the box, plainly expecting her to take it. She did, full of wonder.

"Cap'n's compliments," he said formally. "And his apologies for sending you planetside alone." Gordy tipped his head. "He said he was a fool, Priscilla, but he can't have meant me to tell you that, do you think?"

"Very likely not," she agreed. "So we'll pretend you didn't."

"Right. Gotta jet. Morning, Lina! Rusty!"

She sat holding the box in her lap until Rusty inquired, a little impatiently, if she wasn't going to open it.

"Yes, of course," she murmured, making no move to do so. Allowing me planetside alone? A test, Goddess? she wondered. To see if I would choose revenge, after all? It occurred to her to wonder if the captain's watch over her had been rather closer than she had supposed. She shook her head and reached for a blunt-edged jelly knife.

The sealing tape broke easily. She laid the knife aside and unfolded the flaps. The box contained several objects, each wrapped in bright gossamer paper.

Very slowly, she pulled out the first object. She unwrapped it as slowly, refusing to acknowledge what weight and shape told her until her eyes added irrefutable evidence.

The object was a rosewood comb, intricately carved with a pattern of stars and flowers, the tines satin-smooth from years of being pulled through a waist-length cascade and, more recently, a brief, unruly mop of hair.

Priscilla took a breath, laid the comb aside, and returned to the box. One by one she uncovered them: the brush and hand mirror that matched the comb, several fired-clay figurines, a thin folder of flatpix, a brass-bound kaleidoscope, four bound books, nine musictapes, and three thin silver bangles.

Priscilla held the bangles in her hand for a moment before laying them with the other things. Once, there had been

seven: the full complement of a Maiden-near-Wife. Four she
had sold at different times, as need had dictated. They would
have been worth far more as a set, sold to a collector of the
occult. She never let one go without a wrench that was almost
a physical illness.

She laid the bracelets carefully beside the other objects. In
the bottom of the box was one more item: a small red velvet
box. Frowning, she picked it up.

"What is all this?" Rusty demanded, breaking the silence
that had fallen on the three of them.

"My—things," Priscilla said hesitantly. "My personal
things that were left behind on *Daxflan*." She held out the red
box. "Except this. I don't know . . ." She lifted the lid.

Earrings.

Not *her* earrings, which had been ornate and old. These
were new, not at all ornate, just simple hoops; their plain design was deceptive, for the weight and sheen said platinum,
and the individual who had crafted them had signed each with
a proud flourish.

Priscilla looked at Lina. "They're not mine."

"Ah."

"Why?" Priscilla whispered.

Lina moved her shoulders. "He sent apologies. Perhaps he
felt you were owed. You should, perhaps, ask."

"Yes . . ." She closed the lid carefully and put the box with
the rest of the items.

Rusty picked up the kaleidoscope and peered through it.
"Nice," he murmured.

"Mother, look at the time!" Priscilla cried suddenly, pushing her chair back. "I'm as bad as Gordy! And Ken Rik *will*
skin me! Lina—"

"I will take care of them," her friend said, picking up the
mirror and beginning to rewrap it. She looked up with a fond
smile. "Go. Give Ken Rik a kiss for me."

"You do it, if you want him kissed," Priscilla retorted, and
was gone.

Rusty picked up a piece of tissue and clumsily crumpled it

around the kaleidoscope. "Funny sort of thing for the cap'n to do," he said thoughtfully.

Lina glanced up. "Do you think so?"

"Yah, I do." He looked at her closely before returning to the remains of his breakfast. "And don't try to bamboozle me into thinking you don't think so, either. We been on too many rounds together for that to pass."

"Well," Lina said conscientiously, "there are many reasons why he might do so."

Rusty grinned and drank the rest of his coffee. "Knew you were fuzzed," he said triumphantly, pushing back his chair. "You think of more than one, come on up to the tower and tell me what it is."

Ken Rik had done no more than glare at her rather breathless arrival. He slapped a clipboard in her hand and set her to supervising the emptying of Hold 4, adding a caustic rider to the effect that he hoped she knew enough to balance the load properly for the shuttle.

Priscilla rounded her eyes at him. "Thank you," she said in an awed whisper. "I would never have done it without a reminder. Lina said you were kind."

The old man looked at her suspiciously, saying he knew very well Lina had said no such thing. But Priscilla thought he sounded somewhat less cross.

Hold 4 contained the agricultural plants belmekit and trasveld, both stasis-held items; both on their way—so the clipboard informed her—to the warehouses of one Herr Polifant Sasoni, Offworld Bazaar, Arsdred. The last pallet came up on her board as "samples." She followed the jitney bearing it to the shuttlebay, her mind on breakfast.

Ken Rik took the clipboard, rechecked her figures, approved the weight distributions with a sniff, and waved her into the shuttle.

Automatically, Priscilla started for the copilot's place, to be sharply called to book by her companion.

"Are you a moonling?" he demanded, dropping into the co's chair himself. Priscilla stared at him until he snorted in exasperation and pointed at the board. "Come along, woman! Don't waste my time."

"You want *me* to take us down?"

"No, I want the shuttle to fly itself," Ken Rik snapped with relish. "I am told you are a pilot. You will, therefore, pilot." He folded his arms over chest and webbing, leaned back, and closed his eyes.

Priscilla webbed into the pilot's chair. Slowly at first, then with more assurance, she ran her fingers over the board, calling up rotations, distance, wind speeds, upper atmosphere. Then she chose her approach, cleared the site, and signaled ready.

They left the *Passage* in a neat tumble, skimming toward the planet in a matching arc, hit atmosphere a little later with the barest possible bump, and slid into the approach approved by Arsdred Port. The wind gave her a little trouble, but she managed to hold the craft steady, her teeth indenting her lower lip, her hand unfaltering over the board.

In a glass-smooth glide, they settled on the pad. Priscilla rechecked and locked the board, then flipped the toggles that unsealed the hatch and snapped her webbing loose.

Ken Rik was already standing. "Not too bad," he allowed grumpily, "for a first attempt."

Priscilla grinned. "Praise, indeed."

"Hmmph," Ken Rik said, and turned away.

"In addition," said the fat man in the electric purple overrobe, "we have fourteen dozens of the finest quality firegems in a multitude—a double rainbow!—of colors. It is certain that the honored Trader must feel impelled to acquire so worthy an item."

Shan took a careful puff on the hookah that his host had so graciously provided for him. The smoke was narcotic—mildly to the individual across from him, rather more than that to even a large Liaden well fortified with anti-intoxicants.

"Firegems," he said, blowing a thoughtful smoke ring. "But surely the honored merchant jests. Why should I wish to purchase firegems of any quality, when all the galaxy carries them? More profitable to ship ice. Or atmosphere."

The fat man smiled with unimpaired good humor. "I see the honored Trader is a man of discrimination, with an eye for the beautiful and the rare. Now, it happens that we also have in our warehouses Tusodian silks of the first looming, elbam liqueur, essence of joberkerney, praqilly furleng, tobacco such as we now enjoy . . ."

The honored trader yawned and blew another ring. "Herr Minata, do, please, forgive me! When Herr Sasoni spoke of

you—of your warehouses, the rarities—but I misunderstood!
My command of your language falls short. A thousand apologies for having wasted your time, sir! Believe me, your most
obedient . . ." He stood, bowed with more courtesy than abjectness, and turned to go.

"Master Trader!"

He turned back, concern apparent in his face. "Yes, Herr
Minata? How may I serve you?"

The fat man dropped his eyes and toyed with a fold of his
robe. "Perhaps we might speak again," he suggested delicately.

"That would be pleasant," Shan said with apparent delight.
"We will have our pavilion in Ochre Square within the port,
as always. Anyone will tell you the way. Please do come. I
will be most happy to see you there."

He bowed again and turned away. This time the merchant
let him go.

Outside, Shan took a deep breath of double-baked air and
allowed himself a moment of self-congratulation. *That* fish
was well netted and no mistake. Praqilly furleng—essence
that was mere perfume for some, and a religious necessity for
others—Tusodian silks   a vivid mind picture of Priscilla
Mendoza draped in diaphanous garnet silk presented itself for
his inspection.

That will do, he told himself sternly, banishing the picture
and merging with the flow of pedestrians heading toward the
Outworld Bazaar. The sample case would be down by now,
and Ken Rik would surely have something choice to say if his
captain were not present at the raising of the pavilion in Ochre
Square.

The shipment had been taken to Herr Sasoni's warehouse and
handed over to a capable-looking young man who inspected
the packing and gravely counted the crates before signing the
receipt and handing it back.

Returning to Ochre Square and Ken Rik, Priscilla maintained a sedate pace through the bustling pedestrian and jitney traffic, prolonging her first opportunity for quiet thought since the previous evening's encounter with Dagmar.

The second class provisional in her pocket had proved to be neither counterfeit nor imaginary. Sworn to by Master Pilot Shan yos'Galan, it had been issued and registered at the Arsdred branch of the Galactic Pilots Commission yesterday.

A pilot—even a provisional second class pilot—could always find work, she thought, steering her jitney carefully through a crowded corner. The red and yellow plastic card in her pocket represented a solid, respectable future; it represented a breathing space, if she required one when they hit Solcintra, before looking about for another berth.

She slowed as she reached another knot of traffic, then stopped as it became apparent that the driver of the jitney stuck sideways across the thoroughfare was going to be some time in righting his error. Sighing, she leaned back and ran her eyes absently along the crowded street.

What a difference from Jankalim! The air was filled with the whine of jitney motors and the deeper throbbing hum of the monotrains running on the maze of catwalks and rails that roofed the whole of the port. And, of course, voices: raised in conversation, song, argument.

Priscilla yawned and reached for the thread of her thoughts. She had not yet reviewed her contract. That was the first thing to be attended to, next off-shift. Then she would speak with the captain.

With her eyes on the bustling, bright crowds, it occurred to her that she had several things to speak with the captain about. That he should restore her belongings was a puzzle. Lina had said something about owing, but that made no sense. She was Terran; no Liaden could feel honor-bound to balance accounts with her. And if honor had not prompted him to return her things, what in Her name did a gift of earrings mean?

Priscilla sat up suddenly, eyes sharpening on the crowd, catching sight of a familiar bulky figure just turning the corner into Tourmaline Way.

Dagmar.

Her hands clenched the steering rod convulsively even as her breath hissed out between her teeth. Stop it! she ordered herself sharply. That one who has been in the service of the Goddess should feel hatred for a fellow being . . .

She swallowed hard and sent her thoughts back to the comfort of her friend—to meet with mockery even there. Done well, Lina?

"C'mon, honey—move that thing! Coast's clear!" Priscilla shook herself, automatically shifted into gear, and sent the jitney forward again, resolutely declining to think of anything at all.

"Took your time, did you?" Ken Rik asked, though not with the air of one who expected an answer. "Found the warehouseman amusing?"

"There was a jitney jammed across Coral Square," Priscilla said tonelessly, sliding out of the seat and offering him the clipboard.

He took the board and glanced at her sharply. Priscilla shrugged. Sharp glances, after all, were not unusual in the old cargo master.

"All right," he said after a moment. "Help me with the samples. When the captain arrives, the pavilion will be raised."

"And the captain *has* arrived, so work may proceed without interruption," concluded that gentleman, walking toward them with a grin. "Thank the gods. I was certain I was late and living in terror of a tongue-lashing, Master Ken Rik!"

"You're a bad boy, Captain," the old man said repressively.

"My expectations fulfilled! Thank you, old friend. Now—" He spun slowly on one heel, surveying the immediate neighborhood. "Wonderful, a temporary-permanent next door. We shall ignore it, secure in the knowledge of our superior taste. The southeast corner, I think, Ken Rik, and we'll have the nerligig for catching eyes. Herr Sasoni's order has been safely delivered?"

"Priscilla Mendoza has just returned from the warehouse. The trip down was unexceptional."

"Unexceptional?" Priscilla demanded. "You told me it wasn't too bad."

Ken Rik sniffed and burrowed into the depths of the sample crate.

"Carried away by exuberance," the captain explained. "It's the sort of thing that happens to Ken Rik rather often. My father had to speak to him frequently."

The subject of this palpable untruth turned his head to glare. "Are you going to help raise this pavilion or not?"

"Absolutely! Nothing could induce me to miss such an undertaking! I was only just now having the most delightful chat with Merchant Herr Minata. We could have gone on for hours, so at one did we find ourselves on all matters of importance. But no, I said to him, making my excuse, I *must* go and help raise the pavilion, for Master Ken Rik rules me with an iron hand."

A small sound escaped Priscilla, somewhere between a sneeze and a cough. The captain looked at her curiously.

"Are you well, Ms. Mendoza?"

"Perfectly, sir. Thank you." She took hold of the slippery pavilion cloth and kept her eyes lowered.

"Now," Ken Rik said, shoving a portion of fabric into the captain's hands, "we begin."

It took some time to arrange the corners to Ken Rik's satisfaction. Eventually it was accomplished; the valves were closed, and the pavilion began to inflate.

Priscilla, standing a little way back and watching the first wriggling upheaval, caught sight of a tip of bronze against the bright yellow fabric and inclined her head, as if welcoming a friend.

"Is Korval the dragon or the tree?" she wondered to no one in particular.

"Neither," the captain said. "Or both. The Tree is Jelaza

Kazone, originally the cipher for Clan Torvin—Line yos'Phelium. The Dragon is Megelaar, for Clan Alkia—Line yos'-Galan. Together they're Clan Korval."

She frowned a little. "Two Clans merged to make one?"

"Oh, well," he said, smiling, "they really didn't have a choice. Cantra yos'Phelium was the only member of her Clan on the colony ship—when it landed on Liad, you understand—except for her unborn child. Tor An yos'Galan was in the same fix. At least, he wasn't pregnant, so perhaps his fix was worse. She had been pilot; he'd been co. When they finally raised a world—landed the ship safely—she asked him to raise her heir, should something happen to her. He accepted it, poor child, ready to abandon Alkia to the void and become Clan Torvin. But Cantra seems to have been a fair-minded sort of person, among her other faults, so Torvin *and* Alkia ceased to be, and Clan Korval emerged." He moved his shoulders. "Family history. But you asked for it."

"Yes, I did. Your Clan was made when the ship landed on Liad?" Priscilla was still frowning; it seemed a very long time.

"A young House," he said cheerfully. "An upstart. There are some who trace their ancestry back to the Old World. Sav Rid's family, for instance—"

"Captain?" Ken Rik said from the seat of the jitney. "I'll go to Thessel's now and see if there's news. Unless you would rather go?"

"I," the captain said, "would rather get my hands dirty setting up the nerligig. By all means go to Thessel. And *do* say all those polite things she seems to find so necessary to her comfort."

Unexpectedly, Ken Rik grinned. The jitney slid easily into the flow of traffic, heading west.

The captain wandered over to the sample case, rummaged about for a few moments, and emerged with a toolbox in one hand and a dark nerligig in the other.

Dropping the toolbox, he sat on a crate before the slowly inflating pavilion and put the nerligig on his knees.

"Might as well put waiting to work," he murmured with the air of quoting someone. "Why don't you take a walk, Ms. Mendoza? There's nothing for you to do here right now."

Priscilla hesitated, nettled by this casual dismissal. But his head was bent over the mechanism, and he was to all appearances absorbed in making the necessary adjustments, so she eventually stalked away.

Ochre Square was a crowded, busy block under the shadow of the monotrain station. Over the buzz of the track, the jitney traffic kept up a perpetual whine. Priscilla considered the other Traders' displays and tents from a distance that said she was not a potential customer. Several things tempted her, and she regretted her lost money. Presumably Dagmar had kept the cash she had found in Priscilla's cabin.

Shan was still concentrating on his work when Priscilla came leisurely back toward the fully inflated pavilion with its striking dragon and tree design. It was comforting, she thought suddenly, to see him there, patiently working, the big, clever hands manipulating the tools with precision.

Frowning, she shook her head. There was no reason at all for her to be comforted by the captain's presence, yet twice now she had distinctly had that sensation. She was not altogether certain she approved of it. Irritably, she looked away.

The jitney was driverless. It was speeding, helped along by the double load gripped in its front claw. And it was on a collision course with the *Passage*'s tent.

Later, Priscilla was never sure if she had run or merely flung herself across the distance that separated them. She struck the captain with brutal force and knocked him rolling from the crate, rolling herself as he twisted away, hearing sounds of destruction from too near at hand until she caught up, gasping, against the wall of the temporary-permanent.

She came to her knees, horror-filled.

He lay a little distance from her, his back against the wall, his eyes closed. If he was breathing, he was going about it very quietly.

"Captain?" she whispered. She laid her hand along his cheek.

The slanted brows contracted, and the dark lashes snapped up. "Don't do that, Priscilla."

"All right." She dropped her hand and looked at him uncertainly. "Are you hurt?"

"No," he said shortly. "I'm not hurt." He sat up and looked past her, his silver eyes enormous. Priscilla turned.

The pavilion was gone, tangled crazily about something that surged and tottered and whined like a netted wilmaby. A crowd was beginning to gather.

"Your arm please, Priscilla," said the captain, eyes still on the wreckage.

She rose and offered a hand. He accepted the aid and linked his arm in hers, his hand curved lightly about her wrist.

"Captain?" she said softly, hating to say it but certain it should be said. "I saw Dagmar earlier, on Tourmaline Way . . .

"She has a right to be here, Priscilla; this is the port. Ah, a policeman. How nice." He started toward that official, and, arm-linked, she went with him.

Thankfully, the library was empty. Priscilla had no wish to speak to anyone at the moment, not even Lina. She located an isolated screen by the door to the pet library and sat down, fumbling with the keys.

The interview with the policeman at the port had been interesting. Disentangled, the jitney was identified by an emaciated gentleman in cherry and white robes as belonging to his employer, one Herr Reyes. He had noticed its absence approximately twenty minutes before and had reported the disappearance to the police before undertaking a rather lengthy walk back into the city. By coincidence he had been turning into Ochre Square as the Tree and Dragon suddenly shrieked, shuddered, and folded in on itself.

A quick examination by the policeman at the site showed that the steering rod bore no imprints at all.

At that point Priscilla had opened her mouth. The captain's fingers tightened briefly on her wrist. Priscilla closed her mouth.

This happened three more times during the course of the captain's conversation with the cop and once as he was speaking with a visibly shaken Ken Rik. He then gave Priscilla into the cargo master's care and instructed him to escort her to the shuttle.

"What!" she cried. "*Why?*"

The captain returned her stare calmly. "You've had a hard shift, Priscilla. Take the rest of it off and come to me at prime. Be back as soon as you can, Ken Rik. There's a bit of cleanup to do. I'll be speaking with Merchant Reyes's clerk." He had turned away.

The screen chimed, bringing her back to the present. She fed in her request, then waited a few anxious moments until the proper file was retrieved and displayed.

SERVICE RECORD. PRISCILLA DELACROIX Y MENDOZA.

She began to scroll through it impatiently. Suddenly she hit PAUSE and went back a screen.

STANDARD 1385, TULON. TEMPORARY BERTH *DAXFLAN*, CARGO MASTER TRANSSHIP JANKALIM AS AGREED *DUTIFUL PASSAGE*, PILOT (PROV SEC), LIBRARIAN. NOTATION: COMMAND POTENTIAL; SECOND MATE TRAINING INSTITUTED.

She read it twice, each time going back to the beginning and scanning every line to the end. There was no mention of thievery or of jumping ship. TRANSSHIPPED JANKALIM AS AGREED.

At the end of the file she paused again, staring at the certification from the registry office on VanDyk.

It was dated one Standard Week ago.

"Impossible," she told the screen.

The words persisted. She read them again and keyed in her next request.

CONTRACT SIGNED BETWEEN PRISCILLA DELACROIX Y MENDOZA, FIRST PARTY, AND SHAN YOS'GALAN AS CAPTAIN, *DUTIFUL PASSAGE*, SECOND PARTY. FIRST PARTY SHALL AGREE TO PERFORM DUTIES INHERENT IN THE POST OF PET LIBRARIAN AND ALSO TO UNDERTAKE PILOT TRAINING ONE SHIP WATCH OF EVERY NINE, WITHOUT FAIL, AND ALSO TO UNDERTAKE ANY ADDITIONAL TRAINING OR DUTY DEEMED REASONABLE AND JUST BY SECOND PARTY.

Priscilla leaned back. There it was. She briefly and belat-edly recalled advice given a much younger Priscilla: "I tell you what, youngster. Don't you ever sign a Liaden's contract. I don't care how careful you read it. If he won't sign yours, let the deal go. Safer that way."

Still, there was nothing wrong with undergoing second mate's training. She would have appreciated being told, but she was sure that he had meant it for the best.

It was not until she had cleared the screen and left the li-brary that it occurred to her to wonder why she *should* be sure of it.

Priscilla exited the lift and walked resolutely toward the captain's office. She was dressed in the yellow shirt and khaki trousers she had worn when she first walked down this hall. In her pocket was the provisional second class. The rest of her belongings were in the cabin that had been hers, the clothes neatly folded and stacked beside the scrounged plastic box. She must remember to tell the captain to offer the bracelets to a collector. The price they would bring as curios would go far toward paying her debt to the ship.

She rounded the corner by Hold 6 and nearly walked into Kayzin Ne'Zame.

The first mate recovered first and swept a surprising bow, as deep as one would accord the captain, augmented by an odd little flourish that mystified Priscilla entirely.

"We are well met, Priscilla Mendoza," she said in a light, quick voice much unlike her usual manner of speech. "I have been remiss in offering you an apology for my behavior several shifts gone by, when we spoke near the central computer." She took a breath and looked up. "Pray forgive it. I was discourteous and in error."

Priscilla blinked, collected herself immediately, and bowed in turn, though not as deeply, nor did she attempt to copy the flourish.

"Do me the honor of putting the incident from your mind, Kayzin Ne'Zame. I shall do the same."

The Liaden woman inclined her head. "You are kind. It shall be as you have said. I leave you now."

"Be well, Kayzin Ne'Zame," Priscilla murmured, laying her hand against the captain's door.

"Come!"

He was standing, hands hooked in his belt, his bright head bent over a chess problem. It was a new one, Priscilla saw, and she wondered if the other had had a solution, after all. He glanced up as the door closed and smiled. "Hello, Priscilla. Did you rest well this past shift?"

"I visited Master Frodo for a while," she said, hesitating between desk chairs and couch.

"A very restful companion. I've always found him so, at any rate. Ken Rik labels him terminally cute. But Ken Rik likes snakes. What may I give you to drink?"

"Nothing, thank you, Captain." She decided on one of the chairs before his desk, drifted over, and perched on the arm.

"Nothing?" The slanted brows drew together as he crossed the rug. "Are you angry, Priscilla? Or am *I* angry? If it's me, I assure you that I'm not. And if it's you—but surely you knew I had to send you away? It would have been unforgivable to keep you by, especially when I'd put you in so much danger already."

"You put me in danger?" She stared at him. "It's the other way around, Captain. *I* put *you* in danger. Which is why I would rather not accept a drink. I'm not stopping long." She forced herself to meet his eyes calmly. "I think it would be wisest for me to leave the *Passage* immediately."

"Do you?" He paused. "What a very odd notion of wisdom. If you were staying long enough to have a drink, Priscilla, what would you prefer? Purely hypothetical, of course." The light eyes were mocking her.

"Idle speculation, since I'm not staying that long," she said crisply "I came only to say that—"

"It would be wisest for you to leave the *Passage* immediately," the captain interrupted, holding up his hands placatingly. "You *did* say it. I heard you. Now, Priscilla, please pay attention—this is very important. You might at least have some consideration for my feelings in the matter. I'm thirsty, and you're telling nonsense stories, which you could as easily tell while having a glass of wine with me like a civilized person." He tipped his head. "*Do* strive for some courtesy, Priscilla."

She felt laughter rising and clamped down, with limited success. A small sound woefully reminiscent of a hiccup emerged. "Red, please," she said, glaring.

"Red," he repeated, moving toward the bar. "An excellent choice, as even Gordy will tell you. Though, of course, there's nothing wrong with the white or the jade or the *blue*." He was back and handing her a cut-crystal glass. Her fingers curved around the stem automatically. "And the red won't ruin your taste for prime—you will have time to dine with me, won't you, Priscilla? I agree that I should have first found if your schedule was clear, but it did seem rude to ask you to come to speak with me at dinnertime and then rob you of dinner."

She sipped her wine and tried again. "Captain, surely you must see that the longer I stay with you—with the *Passage*—the more danger you're in? If I'm gone, then you—"

"Priscilla, you have a woeful tendency toward single-mindedness," he interrupted, sitting on the edge of the desk and swinging a leg.

She clamped her jaw and stood. "Thank you for all you've done, Captain, but I really must be going."

"You can't do that, Priscilla; you have a contract. You're bound to this ship until Solcintra. That's four months, as the route runs. You don't have the buy-out fee, do you? I didn't think so." He raised his glass. "It looks like you're stuck, child. Might as well sit down and finish your wine."

"I'm not a child!"

"Well, I can't be expected to know that, can I, if you persist in acting like one? You really must try to curb these tastes for melodrama and resignation."

"Melodrama!" She glared at him, her fingers ominously tight about the glass. "At least I'm not high-handed and—"

"High-handed!"

"*High*-handed," she asserted with relish. "And dictatorial. And *obstinate*. As if you couldn't see why—"

"High-handed! Of all the—Priscilla, when we reach Solcintra, I engage to introduce you to my brother's Aunt Kareen. Call *me* high-handed! Before that, you'd best improve your grasp of the High Tongue—your accent's *execrable*. And another thing! How dare you profess yourself all joy to see me? Have you no sense of propriety? I hardly know you."

"Nor will you know me any better," she stated, suddenly calm. She set her glass on the edge of his desk. "Because I'm leaving. Contract or not. Sue me."

"I won't. But I will arrest you, if you force me to it." He was in front of her, his face quite serious. "Priscilla, have some sense. Don't you realize you saved my life this afternoon?"

She gaped, aware of a strong desire to take him by the shoulders and shake. "Do *you* realize it? You act like—Captain yos'Galan, if you know it, then *let me go!* Surely you see that the sooner I'm gone, the sooner you're safe! People will stop trying to kill you—"

"No, wait." A big, warm hand closed around one of hers. "Priscilla, please—a favor. Come sit down . . . here's your wine. Now, you please, tell me what happened at the port today."

She sat carefully, accepted her glass, and took a sip, steadying heart rate and breathing, embracing serenity. "You know what happened, Captain. You were there."

"I was there," he agreed, back at his station on the edge of the desk. "But I'm Liaden. You're Terran. From what you've said, it seems clear we think that two different things occurred." He leaned forward, eyes intent on her face. "Tell me, Priscilla. Please?"

She took another sip and looked at him straightly. "Today someone deliberately tried to kill you by aiming a jitney at you, jamming the rod, and jumping out. By the grace of the Goddess, I was close enough to knock you out of the way." She took a breath. "I believe—though I have no proof—that Dagmar Collier made the attempt. I also believe that it was ordered by Sav Rid Olanek, striking at you because you gave me sanctuary. So, if I leave the *Passage,* show myself to be a free agent, no more attempts should be made on your life."

"There it is," he said softly, brows pulled slightly together. "Why sacrifice yourself to keep me safe, Priscilla? Assuming all of what you say is accurate, of course."

"I brought danger to you," she said patiently. "It's only just that I take it away again. It's what is honorable."

"Is it?" He raised his glass, reconsidered, and lowered it. "Then I'm afraid we have a conflict of honors. The code I was raised to follow says that, having been so careless as to have necessitated your saving my life, I am very much in your debt. Setting aside the fact that allowing you to go would be murder, if my assessment of Ms. Collier's character is correct, I owe you the protection of this ship—of my resources, say rather. To send you away—unprotected and unprepared—to decoy danger from me is lunacy. And also highly dishonorable. It makes far more sense, is within the limits of honor— and duty!—to stay where it is relatively safe and work to balance what is owed them!" He did drink this time, slowly, then lowered his glass and shook his head.

"The fact is, Priscilla, you don't know the rules. I grant that the admission of Ms. Collier and yourself into the game alters things somewhat, but not enough to matter. Certainly the larger points remain constant. Am I being sinister enough, or should I wrap myself in a cloak and snigger?"

"Can you snigger?" she asked with interest.

"Probably not." He grinned. "But I'll do my best if it takes that to convince you to let me have my high-handed, dictatorial, and—what was the other one?"

"Obstinate," Priscilla supplied, though she had the grace to blush.

"A fairly accurate reading of my faults. Though you omitted inquisitive and meddling. Your suspicion of Sav Rid does him less than justice, by the way. I don't think he ordered me eliminated. It's my belief Ms. Collier was acting on her own initiative. Sav Rid has his limitations, even in stupidity. And it would be extremely stupid to murder me." He drank. "Besides, I don't think I scared him that much."

She blinked. "Were you trying to—oh, the earrings?"

"The earrings. But that seems only to have frightened Ms. Collier into an indiscretion. Lamentable. Sav Rid really ought to screen his people more carefully. I saw Ms. Collier's record—idle curiosity, you understand. She had been a marine. Dishonorable discharge. Personnel complications." He tipped his head. "I said that she used to be a marine, Priscilla; please pay attention. How close did you come to killing her?"

"I didn't—" The lie choked her, and she looked down, then looked back at him. "She's so *slow.* But I misjudged the knife, so she almost killed me, not the other way around."

"An error of inexperience, I believe. I doubt it would happen again. Forgive me, Priscilla, it had seemed a good idea."

This was more than usually convoluted. She put it away for later thought. "What are the rules, Captain?"

"The rules are—" He paused and looked at her consideringly. "Whose life did you save, Priscilla?"

"Shan yos'Galan's," she said, wondering.

"Did you? Good. It makes things somewhat simpler. Now, what—oh, the rules. Wouldn't you rather have the story first? I always need something to hang the rules on, don't you? My dreadful memory. But maybe yours is better."

"It's awful," she told him seriously. "I'd better have the story."

He grinned. "Not too bad. Priscilla. With a bit of practice you should be quite convincing. More wine? No? Oh, well."

He finished his glass and set it aside, lacing his fingers around a knee.

"For the sake of argument," he said pensively, "we'll say that the story begins with Clan Plemia, Sav Rid's family. A very old, most respected House. And also one that's fallen on hard times these last hundred Standards or so, which makes money . . . oh, not as plentiful as it once was. Fortunes rise, fortunes fall, and Plemia's case, while no doubt uncomfortable, isn't *dire*. There's every reason to expect that a bit of careful husbandry will bring them about. In time." He paused, then shrugged.

"Unfortunately, Sav Rid doesn't seem a patient man. He wishes to restore Plemia to its pinnacle *now.* I assume that he cudgeled his brain and finally hit upon the happy plan of taking a lifemate. He possesses lineage, address, a comely face, an elegant person—an extremely eligible individual in all ways. It need not be said that one of Plemia might look where he chose."

Priscilla smiled. "Which is how he happened to propose to your sister."

The captain grinned. "Well, it does make a certain amount of sense, you know. Nova's of age; she might choose whatever husband or lifemate suits her. She has lineage, address, a comely face, an elegant person—and is, incidentally, of course, quite wealthy. There was no reason why they shouldn't have been very happy with each other."

A sound escaped Priscilla, neither a hiccup nor a sneeze—a chuckle, low and obviously delighted. "But she sent him off with a flea in his ear."

"So she did. But she was sadly provoked, you know. The silly creature wouldn't take no for an answer—kept asking and asking. The final time, he paid a morning call for the sole purpose of pleading his case once more. He sighed. "We none of us have gentle tempers—very hotheaded family, the yos'-Galans; and the yos'Pheliums are worse. At any rate, the morning call was the nether end of too much, and she threw him out." He looked at her earnestly. "I wouldn't have you think less of her, Priscilla. She really did try very hard to be civil."

"I'm sure she did. It's irritating when people won't believe what you tell them." Her grin faded. "But if there's a—vendetta—it would be on Trader Olanek's side, wouldn't it, Captain? If he wanted to believe your sister had insulted him?"

"I should have warned you," the captain said, picking up his empty glass and sighing, "that it's a rather long story. Will you have some more wine? Thirsty work, talking."

"I'd have thought you'd be used to it."

"You wrong me, Priscilla; I'm often quiet. Reports are that I hardly ever talk in my sleep, for instance." He was at the bar. She turned in her chair, considering the fit of his shirt and the worked leather of his belt, the gentle bell of cloth from knee to instep. He always dressed with immaculate simplicity. She saw now that the fabrics were costly, the tailoring precise—not readymades from valet or general stores.

He turned around, brows twitching. "Yes?"

"You had said your Clan—Korval—is an upstart?" She stopped short of all she wished to ask, unsure of the polite way to do so.

He grinned and handed her a glass. "Oh, we're respected enough. After all, we trace our lines to Torvin and Alkia, and thence to the Old World. It is, of course, to be regretted that my father should have seen fit to allow Terran blood into the Clan, but there's nothing wrong with Terran blood that I know of. Does its job just as well as anyone else's blood. Purists may frown, but not many Clans can recite a lineage that doesn't include the odd Terran or two. My brother tells me that the Clutch-turtles simply call everyone 'The Clans of Men' and let it go at that. In a little while—according to *their* view of things—we'll all be one race. No Terrans. No Liadens. No half-breeds." He raised his glass. "Ready for Chapter Two?"

"Please."

"Again we start with Sav Rid, I think. Why not? He and

Chelsa yo'Vaade, both of Clan Plemia. Chelsa isn't too bad a
pilot but doesn't have any brains to speak of. She does what
Sav Rid tells her to do. A pity.

"Also important to this story is Shan yos'Galan, who is,
please remember, a fool." He paused, brows twitching. "You
said, Priscilla?"

"I wanted to know how a fool became Master Trader," she
repeated.

He grinned. "It's easier than you might think. And my father would settle for nothing less from me." His face became
more serious. "Several people hold the opinion that Shan
yos'Galan is a fool, Priscilla. There's a certain advantage to
that. Several other people believe that Shan vos'Galan is *not*
a fool, if it comforts you, but Sav Rid isn't one of them.

"To continue. In the course of his trading, Sav Rid took on
a quantity of mezzik-root—highly perishable, but also highly
profitable, if one happens to be going to Brinix. Sav Rid was,
hence the root. He, in fact, jumped out of Tulon System,
pegged for Brinix. And returned just an hour or so after the
Passage docked at Tulon Prime. I met Sav Rid at the trade bar
a little time after that and heard his tale. *Daxflan* was urgently
required elsewhere on business of Clan Plemia. The mezzik-
root would pass its time before he had any hope of delivery.
Would I be going near Brinix? Would I consider buying the
shipment at a flat figure, thus helping a fellow Liaden and en-
riching myself?"

He shrugged. "It was an opportunity, and I took it. It does
occur that one is suddenly called away on Clan business and
must dispose of cargo as it's possible. I knew nothing of the
honored Trader except that he had annoyed my sister—easy
enough to do. She's seldom completely in charity with *me,* for
instance. The price was paid, the load transferred. Other business completed, the *Passage* jumped out-system, pegged for
Brinix—which was found to be under medical quarantine and
expected to remain so for the next local year, far past the time
when the mezzik-root would have started to deteriorate." He
paused to drink.

"The tower manager was polite—and astonished. *Daxflan*, under Captain yo'Vaade, had been in orbit not many days since and had promised to deliver news of the quarantine to Tulon."

Priscilla took a breath. "How much did you lose?"

"Forty cantra. But I did enhance and improve my reputation as a most wonderful fool, which must be counted a gain." He shook his head.

"By the time we got back into Tulon, the story was all over the trade bar. The report had been delivered two minutes after the *Passage* jumped out. *Daxflan* was gone, having hired a new cargo master."

"All that for—balance—for being insulted by your sister?" Priscilla was frowning.

"Now there," the captain said, "I'm not at all certain. Nova is old enough to mind her own honor. If Sav Rid had a quarrel with her reading of his character, then his satisfaction lies with her. He might have assumed that I forbade the match, as Head of Line, you see. I didn't, and probably wouldn't have, if she'd set her heart on him. It never came to me at all; I learned everything after the fact, and in pieces—which, come to think of it, is the only way you learn anything from him— from Val Con, who was kind enough to show Sav Rid the door on the occasion of his morning call." The movement of his shoulders was not quite a shrug.

"For whatever reason, a debt is owed—has been owing. Sav Rid's belief that I am too foolish to be considered an able—" He stopped, brows contracting. "Here's a thing that doesn't happen often," he murmured. "Forgive me, Priscilla; my Terran seems to be lacking. Can it be *debt-partner?*" He sipped wine, considering the carpet with absent intensity.

"Say debt-partner," he decided after a moment. "It makes less nonsense than the other possibilities."

Priscilla shifted in her chair. "This happened at Tulon?"

He glanced up. "Yes. At the beginning of our run."

"And you still owe him for—dear Goddess—forty cantra?" The amount of the loss was staggering.

"Forty cantra's the least of it. I owe him a lesson to treat me with courtesy and respect, not to mention honesty." He sipped, eyes on her face. "These things take time and planning, Priscilla."

"So it was lucky that I came here asking for a job," she said, making the connections rapidly. "I could be a very useful weapon."

"Now, Priscilla, for Spacesake, don't get into hyper again!" He was in front of her, hands spread-fingered and soothing. "I'd have given you a job if Sav Rid were my best friend! Only a lunatic would turn down someone of your potential." He grinned at her. "Foolish, yes. Crazed, no. And it's not a question of giving. You're earning your pay."

"Am I?" she demanded, refusing to give in to her desire to be mollified. "And when will I start training as second mate?"

"You've started," he told her, lowering his hands slowly. "Ken Rik thinks very well of you. So does Tonee. And Lina. And Seth, Vilobar, Gordy, BillyJo, Vilt, Rusty, and Master Frodo. If you keep on at this rate, you'll have the expertise by Solcintra. You already have the ability. Are you angry, Priscilla? Don't you want to learn the job?"

"Of course I want to learn it," she said irritably. "I just would have appreciated being told instead of finding out by accident."

"High-handed," he said mournfully. "I'll try to curb it, but don't expect miracles. I've been this way a long time."

"You're not much older than I am," she told him severely. "How did you manage that trick with my record—dated last week! And no mention of theft or jumping ship."

"Oh." He drifted back to the desk, hoisted himself up, and recaptured his glass. "More high-handedness, I'm afraid, Priscilla. Please try to bear with me." He drank. "I contacted the captain of *Dante* for a more specific recommendation, took every word as truth, and pin-beamed your updated record to VanDyk with a notation that it superseded all previously dated information."

He grinned at her. "Sav Rid had ruined your record within

the sector; but he's tight-fisted, and the courier bounce to VanDyk will take months. Just imagine his unhappiness when he finds his report of your nefarious activities returned to him marked 'Superseded by Data Attached.' Do you think he'll file an official complaint? And risk a hearing into the specifics of your so-called crimes? Will he insist that his very negative report be inserted next to all those glowing ones?" He raised his glass in salute. "I think not."

"You pin-beamed . . . Captain, do you know how expensive pin-beaming is?"

"No. Tell me." The silver eyes were laughing at her.

She frowned, rediscovered her glass, and took a healthy swallow.

"Don't worry about it, Priscilla We've got a pin-beam on board—Rusty's favorite toy. One of the services the *Passage* offers the more backward of our ports is the use of the pin-beam. For a fee, of course. I'm well paid, by contemplating the expression on Sav Rid's face when he reads 'Data Attached'— Dinner at long last!" he interrupted himself as the door chimed.

Gordy grinned from behind the serving table. "I'm on time," he pointed out with considerable pride. He parked the table and came around to Priscilla. "Now you're a hero, too."

"No," she said with decision. "I'm *not* a hero, Gordy."

He tipped his head, clearly puzzled, and turned to the captain. "Shan? Isn't she?"

"She just said she wasn't, didn't she, Gordy? People have a right to define who they are, don't they? If Priscilla doesn't want to be a hero right now, she doesn't have to be. It's probable that she's hungry. Very difficult to be heroic when you're hungry."

The boy laughed and went to the table to begin unfolding leaves, and releasing odors. Priscilla suddenly realized that she was very hungry.

"Ken Rik said to tell you the nerligig works fine," he said over you his shoulder.

The captain stared at him. "It does? He tried it on all settings?"

Gordy nodded. "The case is pretty dented, he said, but since it's for attention getting, that doesn't matter." He paused to glance at his cousin. "He really did say that."

"Of course he did. Ken Rik doesn't believe in curbing his tongue for anyone. I'd be seriously concerned for his health if he started now. Besides, he met me when I was younger than you are, and twice as clumsy. No doubt that makes it occasionally hard to proffer the appropriate respect. What about the tent? Has he gotten a new sample case together? And he'll—no, never mind; I'll wander over and speak with him later. Is prime ready yet?"

"Whist, now, Johnny Galen," Gordy murmured in an exaggerated accent.

The captain laughed and drank wine. "Intolerable puppy. I bear that from your grandfather. But I'm bigger than you are. Please try to keep it in mind."

"Bully," Gordy said, settling plates amid an amazing amount of clatter.

"High-handed," the captain corrected, and grinned at Priscilla, who dropped her eyes.

Gordy stepped back. "Ready. Should I stay?"

The captain glanced at him in surprise. "Did I ask you to dinner, Gordon? Forgive me, the invitation slipped my mind. I seem to recall a report that you've fallen behind in your studies, a circumstance your grandfather, my uncle, would not forgive me. We're due for a review, aren't we? At breakfast."

Gordy swallowed visibly. "Yessir."

"That bad?" He raised his glass. "Well, better see what you can catch up on beforehand. And mind you're in bed at a reasonable hour. I won't need you anymore."

"Yessir," Gordy said again, looking so comically crestfallen that Priscilla had to forcefully swallow the rising laughter. "G'night, Cap'n. G'night, Priscilla."

"Good night, Gordy," she said, smiling at him warmly.

"Good night, Gordy." The captain reached over to the boy and ruffled his hair lightly. "*Do* sleep well."

The boy smiled up at him, made an awkward bow, and departed, the door hissing closed behind him.

"Now, then, Priscilla, if you'll pull up the chairs, I'll serve us. I hope you're as hungry as I am."

A little time later, the edge of hunger blunted, she leaned back and considered the top of his head and the thick, well-cut hair gleaming in the room's soft light.

"Johnny Galen?" she wondered.

He glanced up, smiling. "It's my Uncle Richard's fancy that Liadens are the 'little people' of Old Terra's legends. Thus, Arthur Galen, Johnny, Nora, and Annie Galen. And their foster brother, the king of Elfland."

"Oh, no!" A chuckle escaped, but she didn't notice.

"Oh, yes," he assured her. "Complete with 'my Liege' and 'your Highness.' Pretty comical, actually. My father finally did manage to put a stop to it, but I think he had to resort to threats."

"But he let himself be called Arthur, and you Johnny?"

"Well, no, not exactly," he said, reaching for his glass. "He didn't *answer* to 'Arthur,' you see, so if Uncle Dick really wanted to speak with him, he had to use 'Er Thom.' I don't mind 'Johnny'— my mother called me 'Shannie' more often than not—and Anthora was *always* 'Annie.' To the best of my knowledge, Nova never did answer to 'Nora.'" He sipped. "I hope Val Con doesn't feel he owes balance for the king routine. I rather doubt it. Whatever his faults, Uncle Richard is a master storyteller. And Val Con's addicted to stories."

Priscilla frowned down at the table, then glanced up. "Captain? What is a debt-partner?"

He set his glass aside and picked up his tongs, readdressing dinner. Priscilla hesitated, then returned to her own plate, wondering if she had offended.

"A debt-partner," the captain said slowly, "is one with whom you are engaged in a balancing of accounts." He glanced at her quickly from beneath his lashes. "There are, as

I mentioned before, many rules governing revenge—balance—and how it might be achieved. One of them is that balance is only owing *respected persons*. Animals, for instance, may not claim debt-right." He paused, watching her face carefully.

"It," Priscilla whispered, her spoon forgotten halfway to her mouth. "He called us 'it,' Gordy and me."

"So he did," the captain agreed carefully. "One of the least attractive things about the High Tongue is that it's so easy to deny worth." He looked at her closely. "*I* didn't call you 'it,' Priscilla. Of all the people in the galaxy, I'd be among the last to do so. But Sav Rid believes that people who aren't Liaden aren't—people." He raised his glass and took a sip. "What he had done to you on Jankalim, he would never have ordered done to another Liaden. Even one he considered a fool of the first order, completely careless of his personal honor, the honor of his Line, and of his ship." He grinned. "He thought he'd gotten away clean, Priscilla. Imagine his depression when I not only turn up to bail you out, after he thought you safely disposed of, but uttering threats about earrings, guilty consciences—little enough. But he knows he's gotten away with nothing. He may still doubt my ability to do it, but he knows I'll attempt balance."

She laid her spoon down carefully. "But an—animal—has no recourse."

He sipped, eyes on her. "But you're not an animal, are you, Priscilla? Aren't you a person? Isn't respect due you? You can be an animal, if you choose to say you are. Or you can show him quite clearly that you are a resourceful, intelligent *person,* worthy of the dignity accorded all persons." He set the glass down, his big mouth tight.

"He has stolen from you—possessions, money, personhood. And you speak of taking on the role of an animal, sacrificing your life for mine. Priscilla, don't you see that you are owed? How *dare* he order violence against your person? How *dare* he steal the money you earned, the things you own, your reputation? And by what right did he place your personal honor in jeopardy in the first place, hiring you as master over a cargo of contraband?" He held out a hand. "Wouldn't you rather stay, Priscilla? We'll bring him payment together."

With no hesitation at all, she slid her hand into his.

"Yes," she said clearly. "We'll do that."

Priscilla laid her hand against the door. It slid away to a soft "Enter" from within.

Smiling, Lina bounced up from her seat at the desk. "Priscilla! How are you, my friend?"

"Fine," Priscilla smiled back, sliding her hands into the small ones stretched out to her. "You're busy? I'm not on urgent business."

"No, come and talk with me! If I look at that terrible report another minute, I shall develop a *severe* headache." She laughed, tugging on Priscilla's hands. "Save me!"

They sat on the bed, Lina cross-legged in the center and Priscilla on the edge.

"So, now, what is this not-urgent business?"

"I'm afraid it isn't going to make any sense," Priscilla apologized, toying with the quilt. "At least, I can't think of a sensible way to ask it. Lina, isn't Shan yos'Galan the captain?"

The smaller woman blinked. "Of course he is. Are you having a joke, my friend?"

"I said it didn't make sense," Priscilla pointed out. "I just had dinner with the captain—" She stopped. Lina folded her hands together, waiting.

"I had dinner with the captain," Priscilla repeated slowly. "As I was leaving, I asked him about having returned my things. He said the ship bore the expense of buying them back, that I was to consider it my bonus for having been put in danger." She paused, frowning a little. "Then I asked about the earrings, because they *weren't* mine."

"And?" Lina prompted softly.

"He said the earrings were a gift from Shan yos'Galan, and the captain had nothing to do with it."

"He said so?" Lina moved her shoulders. "Then it is true."

Priscilla sighed. "Yes, I'm sure it is. But Lina, if Shan yos'-Galan is the captain . . ."

"Surely you know that the captain speaks—acts—for the ship," her friend said carefully. "Yes? So, Shan speaks for himself. It is—I do not know the Terran word. Shan yos'-Galan has many . . . roles! He is captain, Master Trader, pilot—three voices with which to speak on the *Passage*. On Liad he is also Lord yos'Galan. He only made certain that you understood which face he used—from which role he acted—when he gifted you."

Priscilla stared at her. "It makes a difference? But he's the same man, no matter what title he's using!"

"Of course he is. But the captain has specific duties, responsibilities, different duties than the Master Trader. A pilot has yet another set." Lina chewed her lip uncertainly. "It is only melant'i, Priscilla." She sighed at the blank look on her friend's face and tried once more. "It is true that Shan yos'Galan is the captain. But the captain is not Shan yos'-Galan."

"I'll work on it," Priscilla said, smiling apologetically. "There might not be a Terran word, Lina." She tipped her head. "Is my Liaden accent horrible?" "No. Who said it was? You are very careful and listen hard, but it is true you are just learning."

"The captain—at least I *think* it was the captain, but it

might have been Shan yos'Galan—told me my accent was execrable and that he was going to introduce me to his aunt—his brother's aunt."

"To Lady Kareen? Illanga kilachi—no. Priscilla, did he *promise* that he would do so?"

"He said he would *engage* to," she said, somewhat amused. "How awful can she be?"

"You cannot imagine. She is very proper—ah, he is bad! We will practice, the two of us, very hard. And tomorrow I will choose enhancement tapes. You can sleep-learn? Good. Also protocol lessons." She looked up at her friend, hands fluttering. "What made him say such a thing? To Lady Kareen—"

"I told him he was high-handed," Priscilla confessed.

"So he now wishes to show you what that is." Lina grinned. "You are well served, then. However did you come to say something so rude?"

"It slipped out right after he told me I had a tendency toward melodrama."

Lina laughed. "It sounds as if you had a fine dinner! Compliments all around."

"Protocol lessons are a necessity," Priscilla agreed, smiling. She sobered. "Lina? Why is it wrong for me to tell the captain—the Master Trader—that I am all joy to see him?"

Lina looked at her in horror. "You said that? To Shan? In public?"

"And in the High Tongue," her friend admitted sheepishly. "Am I beyond redemption?"

"No wonder he gives you earrings!" Lina cried, taking her hand. "Priscilla, you must never do so again! It is a phrase reserved for . . . a brother, perhaps, or an individual one has grown up with . . . a lifemate."

"Really? I'm glad I said it, then. It was exactly right."

"Priscilla," Lina pleaded. "It is most improper! You must not do so again."

"All right," she agreed sunnily. "I don't think I'll ever need to again." She laughed then, very softly, and Lina held her breath. "Poor Sav Rid!"

Lina found Shan in the gym. Just inside, she stopped to watch him swing the paddle, strike the ball, spin, connect, dive, connect—faster and even faster, the ball a white blur trapped between wall and paddle, the man moving with lithe intensity, never missing, never pausing.

After a moment, she walked forward, angling toward the wall, then heard the ball strike just beyond her shoulder.

"Lina! Are you courting suicide? You could have been hit!"

"No," she told him calmly, changing her course. "You are far too quick for that, my friend."

"Accidents happen." Shan walked to meet her, paddle in one hand, ball in the other. His hair stuck in wet points to his forehead, lending him a slightly satanic air; he was breathing hard, and the wine-colored shirt showed darker patches. Lina set aside a spurt of fond sympathy; she stopped at precisely the proper distance and looked sternly up at him.

"You are meddling!" She spoke in the High Tongue, as senior to junior.

"I always meddle," he returned in mild Terran. "You know that."

"You will cease to do so in this instance. Immediately." Her words were still in the High Tongue, commanding, as was proper.

"Dear me," Shan murmured, looking down with a fine show of bewildered stupidity. "Do you mind if we sit down?"

She laughed and turned with him toward the side benches. "You are impossible!" she told him in Terran. "You deserve to be scolded!"

"Often," he agreed cordially, flipping paddle and ball into the wall slot and dropping into the first chair he came to. He thrust his long legs out before him. "Scold me."

She frowned. He was in a chancy mood. She began tentatively. "Shan, it is serious. Please. You could do harm." She extended a mental tendril.

She was met with opposition, the familiar Healer's barrier. He rarely took such complete refuge; never in all their years of friendship had he done so with her. Not at the time his mother had died so tragically, nor when Er Thom yos'Galan had turned his face from kin and from duty to follow her.

Lina withdrew the tendril and considered him quietly. "It is a bad thing," she offered, "for Healers to argue over a proper approach. Most especially when Healing has begun."

"I agree," Shan said.

"That is good. Now, I will tell you that I am puzzled. We spoke, did we not? And it was agreed that I should proceed, though Priscilla was drawn as much to you as to me. You insisted, old friend, saying you were captain, not Healer."

"True. I do not act as Healer in the matter."

Lina stifled a sigh. This was Shan at his least tractable, showing the streak of stubborn reticence that characterized Korval at the fore. In a way it was a blessing—if she could not read him through the protective barrier, neither could he read her. The Wall, like so much of healing, was reciprocal.

She considered that last thought. One did tend to become entangled with those one Healed. Priscilla . . . He may have feared reciprocity, having felt the strength of her—even half-crazed with pain. And if he had been drawn enough to fear the Healing process . . .

"What is it that you want, old friend?" she asked.

He stirred. "I want to be her friend."

So. "And her lover!" She put a lash to that. If he did not yet know . . .

"I am not," Shan said carefully, "made of stone. You will have noticed this."

"Better you should have taken her to Heal yourself, then! The bond was there, from the beginning! Healing across sex is more rapid—you know that! Why—"

"And have her think herself hired to be the captain's slut? Thank you, no." There was Korval ice in that.

Lina blinked and gave a flickering thought to her own protections. "Why should she have thought so, old friend?"

Shan sighed. "She came to me—as captain—for protection. One Liaden had already robbed her of status as a person. It would not have seemed at all wonderful to her if another continued—" He shifted irritably. "Priscilla's Terran, Lina. She wasn't raised to melant'i. I *am* the captain to Priscilla. She believes it. It would have been nothing short of rape, a violation of trust so basic . . ." He took a breath and ran his fingers through his hair, standing it up in sticky spikes. "I was in error, old friend. I act as Healer in the matter, in that I refused to act as one."

"I am Liaden," Lina said softly. "I am her superior."

"You are also friends. And I believe that the amount of influence a senior librarian exercises over a junior is somewhat less than what a captain may exercise over a crew member."

There was a silence that grew lengthy. Then Shan leaned forward abruptly and took her hands between his.

"I want her to be well. Joyful and complete. That most. I want her friendship, but I don't—won't—force it. A pair of earrings? Call it restitution for another wrong done her by Trader Olanek, if you like, Lina. If it will make all easier—"

"You have already said they are your gift to her," she reminded him. "But I do not think harm was done." She smiled warmly. "It is a good thing to have friends."

"I think so, too." He leaned back. "I leave the Healing in your hands. My word on it."

"So, then," she said, satisfied. She brought a finger to the side of her head. "I had almost forgotten the other. She did not mean it, Shan, when she welcomed you in esteem. I have explained, and it will not happen again. You must not be angry with her."

"Angry with her?" He laughed. "I'm delighted with her! She would have done no better if I'd coached her beforehand. What a devastating setdown for poor Sav Rid! The look on his face! I could have kissed her."

"You must not encourage her to behave improperly," she

scolded him. "You talk of being her friend! It is important that she learn to behave with propriety. Especially if you will present her to Lady Kareen!"

"Yes, Lina," he said with wholly unconvincing meekness.

She shook her head. "No, *that* will not do. I know you. Priscilla and I will work on her accent, and she will use sleep tapes. Lady Kareen will find her above reproach."

"A matter of your own pride, in fact?"

She laughed and stood. "Completely impossible. Good night, old friend." She touched his cheek, very gently, noting that the Wall was yet in place. "Sleep well."

He did *not* sleep well. Nor did his interview with Gordy do anything to mend his badly frayed temper. He had begun by snarling at the boy, and his mood was not improved by the realization that he sounded rather like his father in that tone.

Irritably, he crossed to the bar and poured himself a glass of morning wine. There were a few things to attend to here before going worldside to begin a local week of trading. He dropped into his chair and spun the screen around.

Buzzzz!

Shan looked up, not quite placing the sound.

Buzzzz!

Brutally, he rearranged the mob of documents on top of the desk and eventually uncovered a shiny blue pad set with two unmarked keys. He depressed one at random. "Yes?"

Buzzzz!

Shan sighed and pushed the other key. "Yes?"

"Cap'n? Rusty here. Sorry to bother you."

"Rusty? Aren't you scheduled for world leave today? I

thought you'd be dancing in the streets with a lover on each arm."

"Well, I'd planned on it," Rusty said seriously. "But when we hit port, there were two—oh, individuals—waiting for us. They say nobody from the *Passage* is allowed on-world and that they're coming up." There was a tiny pause. "They say they've got a warrant, Cap'n."

"Do they? What are we to do with that very interesting piece of information, I wonder? And what does it have to do with the crew's leave? Do strive for clarity, Rusty—I'm afraid I'm a bit dense this morning."

"Well, they say they want to see you. I guess they'll explain it personally."

"Wonderful. What sort of . . . individuals, Rusty? Ambassadorial? Mere policepersons? Concerned citizens?"

"Ummm . . ." Rusty's voice drifted, then came back. "Didn't Cap'n Er Thom used to say that if your host wore a dagger, you should wear a dagger and a dirk?"

"It sounds very like him."

"By those rules, you ought to wear three daggers and a machete."

Shan grinned. "And these very formidable persons wish to call on me? How pleasant. Do me the favor, please, Rusty, of asking Seth to bring our visitors up as quickly as possible. Gordy will meet them and serve as escort. You needn't bear them company, if you'd rather not."

"Right you are. I'm not losing *my* breakfast. I'll catch a lift with Ken Rik, since they're evacuating him, too."

"Marvelous. Thank you for the call, Rusty. You always have such cheerful topics of discussion."

The other laughed and broke the connection.

Shan spun in his chair, hit the toggle that would summon Gordy, opened a drawer, and began to sweep papers into it.

The door opened to admit a subdued and rather pale cabin boy. "Yessir?"

Ruefully, Shan stretched out a hand. "Forgive me, acushla.

My dreadful temper. I swear I didn't mean it to sound half as fierce as it did."

Gordy actually produced a grin, albeit a faint one. "That's okay. I should've been workin' at it all along. Guess I deserved to get my head bit off."

"That for me!" his cousin cried, snapping his fingers with a grin. Sobering, he shook his head. "An emergency, Gordy. Run to Selna and get a piece of the sample wood—so." He squared it off in the air with big, capable hands. "On your way back, stop and ask Calypso for the loan of his antique. Jet!"

Gordy was gone.

In an amazingly short time he was back, armed with the required items, which he placed on the pristine desk.

"Good," Shan said, surveying things. "Another task. Shortly there will be two individuals in the reception hall. Please bring them here."

"Yessir," the boy said, moving toward the door.

"Oh, Gordy!"

"Yes, Cap'n?"

Shan grinned. "Take your time."

The visitors were not pleased. They followed Gordy with rustling aloofness, their sulfur-colored robes brushing the sidewalls, and kept their hands on the hilts of their swords. They came finally to the red door—after having traversed the length of the ship twice, had they but known it—and Gordy activated the annunciator.

"Come!" Shan's clear voice was followed by a peculiar heavy *thump* just as the door slid open.

Gordy stepped into the room. Shan was lounging back in the chair behind the desk, which was clear except for a block of oak with a wooden-handled hatchet buried in it. He raised his glass and lifted his brows.

Mindful of the proprieties, Gordy bowed. "Cap'n yos'-Galan, here are Budoc and Relgis come to speak with you."

"Good day; gentles. A pleasant one, isn't it? How might I serve you?"

Relgis, who was bald, stepped around Gordy and executed a grudging bow. "Good day, Captain," he replied in hoarse Terran. "We are officials of Arsdred Court. It is my duty to inform you that we carry papers denying your crew access to the planet surface for the amount of time required for the municipality of Arsdred to inspect and verify your cargo. Under this same order, you are banned from trade activities until such time as investigation retires charges brought against the *Dutiful Passage*, tradeship, and Shan yos'Galan, captain and Master Trader." He paused to glare sternly from beneath bushy eyebrows. Shan sipped wine.

"The charge," Relgis continued in a goaded voice, "is smuggling illicit pharmaceuticals and proscribed animals."

"The *Dutiful Passage* is accused of running contraband?" the captain inquired in the mildest possible tone. "May I know the name of the accuser?"

Relgis looked at him with suspicion, apparently formulating a reply. Into the silence stepped his partner, saying with ponderous affability that no such thing as *charges* had been leveled at ship or master.

"Relgis made a slip of the tongue, sir. The thing is, a complaint has been lodged with the court, citing *suspicion* of contraband. I'm sure you'll agree that this is a very serious thing."

"Oh, I do," Shan said, raising his glass, "Especially when suspicion names my ship."

Budoc had the grace to look discomfited. "Well, of course you're bound to feel that way," he allowed after exchanging a startled glance with his partner. "I'm sure it will be inconvenient for you to deny your crew leave and forfeit a few days' trading. But if you're innocent—as I'm certain you are—then there's no harm done, is there? You'll be allowed to go about your business, just as you normally would."

"The municipality," Relgis stated, revolted by this conciliating speech, "must be certain of either the truth or falsity of a suspicion of contraband. We cannot be too careful."

"I see. Any other suspicions, sir? Or is this the awful whole?" Once again Relgis found that tone of vacuous amiability disconcerting. Budoc took over, clearing his throat noisily.

"We also bear a warrant for the detention of one Priscilla Delacroix y Mendoza, of the crew of the *Dutiful Passage*. She is to be questioned under deep probe and held, pending arrival of further information."

"On what charge?" Shan queried gently, leaning forward and setting the glass aside.

"Suspected thievery." Relgis was back in the game.

"Really?" Shan looked at him with interest. "Now I have found her to be scrupulously—no, make that excessively—honest. Who accuses her?"

"Trader Sav Rid Olanek brought the matter to the attention of the court, sir. When the balance of his information arrives, determination shall be made as to whether the matter would be most properly handled by local or galactic authorities."

"And if she's innocent?" Shan asked, resting his chin on his left hand. His right lay next to the wooden block.

"If she's innocent," Budoc said magnanimously, "she will be released."

"Which will," Shan said dulcetly, "do her a great deal of good if the *Passage* has moved on in the meantime." He ran an absent finger down the hatchet haft. "What is she suspected of stealing from Trader Olanek? The clothes on her back? She had nothing else when she came to me."

The two officials exchanged glances. "No doubt that will be included in—"

"Trader Olanek's further information," Shan concluded. "Of course. May I see the papers you carry, sirs? I must say that I think it extremely unlikely that Ms. Mendoza is a thief. As to allowing her to be removed from this vessel and placed in a detention block for—how long before this information comes forth? Stupid of me, but I don't seem to recall . . ."

"We didn't say," Relgis said quellingly. "No longer than ten days, local."

"Captain," Budoc added, with a warning glance at his partner.

Relgis glowered, produced the papers from the depths of his robe, and handed them over with scant grace.

"Thank you," Shan said, receiving them in the spirit in which they were offered. He glanced at the hovering cabin boy. "Gordon, fetch Ms. Mendoza, if you please."

"Oh, no you don't!" Relgis snapped, leaping between Gordy and the door is a swirl of fabric. He fingered his sword hilt menacingly. "A very sly idea, Captain, but it won't work! Send the boy for her! Warn her, more likely! Next we'll be hearing from him that she's escaped!"

"Escaped?" Shan blinked at him, striving for his best look of foolish interest. "Now, where would she escape to, I wonder? I do seem to recall rather clearly a statement to the effect that none of my crew would be allowed worldside." He picked up his glass and took a thoughtful sip. "Of course, the *Passage* is a large ship," he conceded. "But not that large, do you think? I'm sure you could run her to ground if she took a notion to hide from you."

Perceiving a sheen of dew on Relgis's bald pate, he relented somewhat. "Go for Ms. Mendoza," he instructed Gordy gently. "Say that I wish to see her immediately. Please do not mention the presence of these two persons."

Gordy goggled at him, then recovered enough to bow and mutter "Yessir" before turning toward the door.

Speared by a glance from his partner, Relgis let him go.

Shan had another sip of wine and began a leisurely perusal of the court's documents.

In just under five minutes, the door chime sounded.

"Come!" Shan called, eyes still on the documents he had already committed to memory.

The two officials turned, hands on swords, ready to confront the desperate criminal herself as she stepped unescorted into the room.

Relgis preserved his countenance. Budoc visibly gaped.

Priscilla gave each a friendly, though curious, smile and stepped around them. "You wanted to see me, Captain?"

He glanced up, sternly subduing the pang he felt upon seeing her ears yet unadorned. "Good morning, Ms. Mendoza. I'm sorry to have to call you to me so abruptly. These gentlemen, however—" He nodded at Budoc and Relgis and paused, frowning. "My terrible manners! Ms. Mendoza, these are Relgis and Budoc, officials of Arsdred Court. They have come to deliver this paper to you." He held it out.

She took it, directing a sharp glance at his face before beginning to read. Her cheeks flushed, then went white. Shan overrode the impulse to hold out his hand to her; instead, he picked up his glass and brought before his inner eye a Wall.

"Will he never stop?" Priscilla cried, slapping the paper onto his desk. "He hounds me, names me criminal, leaves me for dead—and now has me arrested! Questioned under deep probe! What good can he think it will do him? Trader on a ship crewed by lechers and motherless fools!" She spun, approaching the two officials with a tigerish tread. Relgis gave ground by a step. Budoc licked his lips.

"Whose palm was greased?" she demanded awfully. "*Suspicion* of theft? Information *forthcoming?* And I'm to be detained and questioned, treated like a thief on the strength of information that will never arrive, and so I swear!" She straightened haughtily. "I'm not going anywhere with you."

"Well," Budoc said carefully, "you've got no choice, miss. We've got the warrant, and you've got to come. It's the Law."

Priscilla sniffed. "This is a Liaden ship. You have no authority here."

"*You're* Terran," Budoc pointed out with a fair semblance of rationality.

"I should perhaps explain," Shan broke in apologetically, "that Ms. Mendoza serves on this ship because of a personal contract between her and the Heir Apparent of Clan Korval."

There was a moment's silence. Then, in accents between dread and wonder, Budoc asked if that wasn't the Tree and Dragon Family, trade representative for Trellen's World?

"Exactly the Tree and Dragon." Shan beamed at him. "Precisely Trellen's World. The contract between us extends back nearly two hundred Standards. How clever of you!"

That information might have impressed his partner, but to Relgis it conveyed nothing more than a blatant attempt to thwart the law. He stiffened his resolve and advanced upon Priscilla's position by one step.

"Be that as it may," he said sternly, "the Law is still the Law. This woman's Terran, and she goes with us." He shifted his eyes to the man behind the desk and thrust out his chin. "She's not Liaden, even if this heir or whatever it is, is. We don't have a warrant for her contract—we've got a warrant for her!"

"Heir Apparent," Shan corrected gently. "Not, praise gods, the Heir. Ms. Mendoza is correct, you know. A personal contract of this kind assures her of the Heir Apparent's protection. Which amounts to the protection of Clan Korval. And Clan Korval is a legal Liaden entity." He finished his wine and set the glass aside. "An interesting point, isn't it? I'm sure the lawyers would be able to argue it for much more than ten local days, don't you?"

"Now, Captain," Budoc said nervously, "be reasonable. No one wants to get into that kind of protracted debate. Think of the expense! Better to just let her come along with us. Maybe the judge will allow her back right after the questioning—in light of her contract, you know!" He licked his lips again. "I'm sure we can work something out."

"Are you?" Shan asked. "Good. I think so, too." He picked up the disdained warrant and made a show of frowning perusal. "There doesn't seem to be anything here about bail," he murmured, feeling Priscilla's gaze bent on him in speculation. "An oversight on the part of the judge, no doubt. Who was— oh! Judge Zahre? What a delightful circumstance!" He smiled

with exquisite stupidity at the two officials and avoided
Priscilla's eye.

"We'll have everything settled soon!" he said gaily. "I'm
acquainted with Judge Zahre. What a fortunate circumstance!" He flipped a toggle on the panel by his desk.

"Tower," a crisp voice informed him.

"Good shift, tower. Are you busy? Would it be possible for
you to find Judge Abrahanthan Zahre of Port City, Arsdred,
for me? I'd like to speak to him."

"Right away. Captain. Route the call to the office screen?"

"That will be perfect, tower, thank you. Do hurry. We have
guests, and I seem to be wasting their time."

"Yes, sir." The connection was cut.

Shan nodded to himself and called the commlink from its
slot, then turned to the infoscreen and tapped in a quick series.
Out of the corner of his eye he saw Priscilla drift over and
perch on the arm of the nearer chair, dividing her attention between the two officials and her captain.

Budoc and Relgis exchanged glances and remained un-
comfortably silent. Relgis nurtured the hope that the judge
would drop one of his thundering lectures on the heads of
both captain and crew member.

The commlink buzzed gently.

Shan spun his chair, tapped the violet key set along the left
margin of the screen, and inclined his head to the austere individual in ruby-colored robes. The other man also wore a
ruby turban, held by a glittering nelaphan brooch. His eyes
were dark and deep-set, and the authority of his nose ex-
ceeded that of Shan's own.

"I am Judge Zahre," he said emotionlessly.

"Yes, sir," Shan agreed easily. "We are acquainted, though
I doubt you remember me. My father, Er Thom yos'Galan,
and I guested you aboard *Dutiful Passage* several Standards
ago, upon the occasion of your Honesty's succession to office."

The face in the screen thawed somewhat; the lips bent a trifle.

"Indeed, I do remember you, sir, and most kindly. How does your father do? It would honor me if you and he would dine at my residence, if the length of your stay permits it."

Shan took a breath, hardly aware that it was deeper than the one before it. After so many repetitions, the phrase had become merely rote, and the inward voice that had keened "My father is dead!" was now but a wordless flicker of pain.

"I regret to be the first to inform you," he said evenly, pulling the words verbatim from the High Tongue, "that my father's heart ceased its labor nearly three Standards gone by."

The lines about the judge's mouth grew deeper as he bowed his head. "It grieves me to hear it. I am richer for having had his acquaintance, though it was for so brief a time."

"I will tell my family you said so, sir. Thank you."

The older man nodded. "Now, tell me what I may do for Er Thom yos'Galan's son."

Shan smiled. "A misunderstanding has occurred. At least, I think it must be a misunderstanding." He held the warrant up so that the other could read it. "This was delivered by two officials of Arsdred Court—Budoc and Relgis. It's a warrant for the detention and questioning of one of my crew members, Priscilla Delacroix y Mendoza. Apparently Trader Sav Rid Olanek accuses her of theft."

Judge Zaire nodded. "I remember him. I admit I did not like to let him swear out such a thing and then immediately depart the sector, but he pleaded urgent business and paid penalty and swear-charge. All was according to Law, as he promised further information by bouncecomm, within ten local days. I performed my office, as set out in the Book."

"I am certain you did," Shan said soothingly. "However, there are several points of which you could not have been aware. One is that Trader Olanek has taken Ms. Mendoza in severe dislike. I am not certain of the cause. It is a fact, however, that far from her stealing from him, he has stolen from her. A member of his command has within the last local day sold personal articles belonging to Ms. Mendoza at a shop in

Parkton Way—Teela's Treasures. The proprietor is Frau Pometraf. She has a very good memory."

The judge inclined his head. "I am grateful. The information, of course, will be verified." He looked up, his deep eyes shrewd. "You have yet to say what I might do for you, Shan yos'Galan."

"A small thing, correction of an oversight." He rustled the paper. "There doesn't seem to be any mention of bail here, sir. Now, Ms. Mendoza is an important member of my crew. I can't spare her for ten days. Not for ten minutes! What shall I do?"

The older man's lips twitched, though he gravely agreed that it *did* seem to be an oversight. "You must understand that a warrant has been sworn to, sir. The Law must be served."

"Of course it must." Shan spun the infoscreen around. "I had nearly forgotten! This is Ms. Mendoza's record, sir. Now, I ask you: Is it likely that a person possessing such a record would sully her honor by stealing?"

After a longish pause, the judge said, "I believe bail of one cantra—cash, of course—is sufficient to this case. You will guarantee Ms. Mendoza's presence, should the matter in fact go to trail?"

"Korval guarantees," Shan said formally, and jerked his head at the gaped-mouth officials. "These two gentles may take the money with them? It will be secure?"

"Relgis and Budoc are completely trustworthy."

"I'm sure they are. No thought of their venality crossed my mind, sir, It's only—a cantra, you said? You're certain they won't want an armed guard to escort them?"

Relgis made an outraged noise; the man on the screen smiled.

"I believe that no guard will be necessary, sir. I appreciate your concern."

"One cannot be too careful," Shan said earnestly. "What with innocent persons being attacked by ruffians in the streets of the city." He sighed and spread his hands. "You've been very kind, sir. I find it necessary to impose upon you still further." He held the second document up.

The judge scanned it quickly and shook his head. "This matter is out of my jurisdiction. However, I am acquainted with Judge Bearmert, who is among those signed. Allow me to call him and ask if he will speak with you."

"You're very kind, sir," Shan said again. "Forgive me the trouble."

"There is no trouble. It is my duty to see that the Law is served, not that the innocent suffer." He bowed stiffly. "Be well, Shan yos'Galan. Will you come to dine tomorrow evening?"

"I would like nothing better, sir. But I believe that the ban on my crew visiting your pleasant world applies to me as well."

"Nonsense," the judge said crisply. "I will send my yacht for you, sir. You will be conveyed directly to my home. You will experience no difficulty."

Shan grinned. "In that case, of course. I'll be delighted."

"Good. Until then." The screen went dark.

Shan thumbed the yellow stud, and the screen slid back into the desk. Absently, he pulled open a small drawer on the right side and fished out a battered lacquer box.

"Cantra," he muttered, and dumped the box over.

Coins *tinged* and tumbled, rolled in tight circles, and sped away to catch against the block of wood supporting the hatchet: Terran bits of all denominations, Liaden coins, local money of half a dozen worlds, several rough-cut citrines, and a loop of pierced malachite.

"Cantra," Shan murmured again, conscious that Budoc was drawing closer. With clumsy care, he selected ten tenth-cantra from the jumble of money and beckoned the man still closer.

"One, two, three . . ." He counted all ten carefully into the sweaty palm and nodded. "Ten, are we agreed?"

"Yes, Captain," Budoc breathed.

"Good." He pointed at Relgis. "You, sir. A receipt, please."

Relgis glowered but did as he was bidden. Shan flipped a toggle by the desk. The door chimed instantly and slid away on his word to admit a grim-faced Gordy.

Shan smiled. "These gentles are leaving now, Gordon. Please conduct them to the reception hall and arrange for refreshment. Seth will conduct them worldside in good time." He turned his smile to the officials, striving for complete vacuity. "Thank you so much for your visit, sirs. I enjoyed it immensely. Good day."

"Good day, Captain," Budoc said, bowing low. Relgis sniffed and bowed, silently and slightly. Both turned and followed Gordy out.

The door closed, and Priscilla stood, holding out a hand. "May I refill your glass, Captain?"

He considered her warily. "Thank you, Priscilla. The red, please. And pour yourself something."

Priscilla stared a moment at the hatchet in the block of wood, then turned to busy herself at the bar.

"It's Pendragon," she announced suddenly.

Shan frowned at her beck. "Pendragon? Oh, the fellow with the table. One of Val Con's favorite stories, I recall. Named one of his infernal felines Merlin." His frown deepened. "It's only Uncle Richard's fancy, Priscilla. Coincidence. Dragon-analogs are fairly common around the galaxy, you know."

She nodded and handed him a glass before settling into the chair across.

"One hundred bits the night before last, a terrible scare yesterday, a cantra today. What am I to cost you tomorrow?" Her tone was mild, but her eyes were very bright.

Shan considered the Wall; he left it in place and raised his glass.

"I don't expect you'll cost me anything tomorrow, Priscilla. You didn't really cost me anything today. Sav Rid's thought was to cause me discomfort—so it seems I'm taken seriously! How gratifying." He sipped. "He has accused the

Passage of running contraband. That's creative of him, isn't it? We're to be investigated—by officials of Arsdred Court."

"Unless the friend of your friend brings his authority to bear," she said dryly.

"Well, I don't think he will, do you? It's worth a try, of course. No sense rousing Mr. dea'Gauss until we need him. My sister the First Speaker prefers our man of business to stay close to hand. His tact and finesse are a good balance for her temper, you see. By the way, you were magnificent."

"I thought that was it." She considered him for a moment out of half-angry black eyes, then shook her head and smiled a little. "*Are* you Heir Apparent to Korval?"

"Of course I am. It's not the sort of thing one lies about, after all. You could find yourself in a great deal of trouble if you did. Besides that, if you want truth, I'd rather not be Heir Apparent. Especially with Val Con adventuring around the universe, busy being a scout and making no push at all to place an heir of his body between myself and destiny." He sighed. "I'm afraid I wouldn't be a very good Delm."

There was a pause while Priscilla tasted the wine, her eyes on the hatchet. Shifting her gaze to his face, she asked, carefully, he thought, "Will you do me a favor?"

"I'll certainly *try*, Priscilla," he said with matching caution. "What is it?"

"I wonder if you wouldn't make me a list of all the people you are, so I know who to ask for."

He grinned. "I'm afraid it might get a bit lengthy. And a few are so close that only a Liaden would make a distinction." He set the glass aside and began to count on his fingers. "Head of Line yos'Galan. Heir Apparent to Korval. Guardian to the Heir Lineal—that's a joke. Brother to Val Con, Nova, Anthora. Cousin to Val Con. Guardian to Anthora. Father to Padi. Master pilot . . ."

He sighed. "This is too tedious, Priscilla. You could call me Shan if you get confused, and I'll sort it out for you."

"Why don't I just call you Captain?"

"I *knew* you were going to say that," he complained.

Surprisingly, she grinned and pointed at the hatchet. "What's the idea?"

"My father used to say—so I was informed earlier—that if your host wears a dagger, you should wear a dagger and a dirk. I think he might have meant it in some other context. but Rusty did me the favor of calling it to mind this morning when he told me of the presence of our visitors." He wrenched the hatchet free, sending two sundered chunks of wood skittering across the polished desk top.

"My brother, now, says there's nothing will give one pause like the sight of a naked blade." He extended it, and Priscilla leaned back in her chair. "He's right, I see. That's comforting. I thought I would give our visitors a visible reminder of might." He grinned. "Liaden tricks, Priscilla. Forgive me."

She shrugged. "It worked, didn't it? And *they* were using tricks, too. Blustering and acting as if all justice were on their side."

"High-handed, in fact."

"I'll never live it down." She sighed. "Will it help if I say I'm sorry?"

"*Are* you sorry? You might ask me to forgive it, if you think I'm offended. But Liadens don't in general say that they're sorry. It's an admission of guilt, you see. Asking forgiveness acknowledges the other person's right to feel slighted, hurt, or offended without endangering your right to act as you find necessary."

She blinked at him. "Which is why Kayzin Ne'Zame was so infuriated with me when we met at the main computer! I kept saying I was *sorry . . .* " She sipped, working on the concept in silence.

Shan toyed with the weapon, turning it this way and that, taking note of its balance and the feel of it in his palm. Laying it aside, he took up his glass again and sipped, allowing himself the luxury of watching her face.

As if she felt his eyes on her, she glanced up, a slight smile on her lips. "Is there anything else, Captain? I'm supposed to be having a piloting lesson."

"Teaching me how to run my ship?" He waved his glass toward the door. "Go back to work, then. And thank you for your assistance."

"You're welcome, Captain," she said serenely. "It was no trouble at all."

Mr. dea'Gauss leaned back in the seat and allowed himself a moment of self-congratulation. Progress thus far was satisfactory. Not, he reminded himself, that he was in any way reconciled to being shipped harum-scarum off Liad and flung out into the galaxy with barely an hour's notice. If his heir had not just recently entered into a contract marriage that tied her to the planet, Korval would have found itself represented by the younger, less-tried dea'Gauss: and so the elder had informed Korval's First Speaker.

Lady Nova had acknowledged that statement with a slight tip of the head and continued outlining his task in her calm, clear voice. Mr. dea'Gauss experienced a reminiscent glow of warmth in the region of his mid-chest. She was a great deal like her father, and competent beyond her years.

She'll do, Mr. dea'Gauss thought with satisfaction. They would *all* do eventually. It was simply a sad pity that so powerful a Clan as Korval should have been left untimely in the hands of persons too young for the duty. Even the eldest, Shan, now Thodelm yos'Galan, had not attained his full majority. And young Val Con, the Delm-to-be, was barely more than a halfling, no matter how gifted a scout he might be.

The old gentleman laid his head against the cushion. It was his duty to ensure that all continued as it should during this period of readjustment, just as Line dea'Gauss had kept Korval's business for generations—to mutual profit.

They were intelligent children, after all, he reminded himself with a shade of avuncular pride, and quick to learn. He and his would be unworthy indeed of the post they had held so long if Korval were to lose ground before Val Con placed the Clan Ring upon his finger.

The taxi glided to a stop. Mr. dea'Gauss opened his eyes and glanced out the window. Satisfied, he gathered up portfolio and travel desk, slipped the proper Terran coin into the meter's maw, and exited the cab as the door elevated. He blinked once at the din and the colors and the smells of the Offworld Bazaar, then turned his steps with calm dignity toward the shuttlecradles.

There was an armed guard before Cradle 712. Mr. dea'Gauss was untroubled; he had expected no less. What did puzzle him was the presence of two additional individuals engaged in vociferation with the guard.

"I don't care," the fat woman with the jeweled braids was saying loudly, "if you've got orders from the Four Thousand Heavenly Hosts! I am Ambassador Grittle of Skansion! You've seen my identification. You've verified my identification. I have urgent business onboard the *Dutiful Passage*—"

"Off limits," the guard interrupted laconically. "Judge Bearmert's orders."

The fat woman's face turned a curious purple color that contrasted not unpleasingly with the silver lines drawn around her eyes. The second individual addressed the guard.

"I am Chon Lyle, sector agent for Trellen's World. It is imperative that I be allowed onboard the *Dutiful Passage*. Clan Korval is the licensed representative of Trellen's World in matters of offworld trade. A charge of illicit dealing brought against its flagship must also be thought a charge brought against my world."

Mr. dea'Gauss's brow cleared. Unmistakable, here was the hand of Korval's First Speaker. He stepped forward, affording the guard a tip of the head, as was proper for a person of consequence addressing a mere hireling.

She surveyed him with boredom. "Don't tell me. You want to get up to the *Dutiful Passage*."

"Precisely," he said, undeceived by the apparent readiness of her understanding. He proffered a piece of orange parchment folded thrice. "I have here a manifest from Judge Bearmert allowing me that privilege, and also whomever I deem necessary to the commission of my duties." He moved a hand, encompassing ambassador and agent. "These persons are such. Pray verify the document. I am in haste."

The guard sighed, took the paper, and unfolded it with a flick of the wrist. Her eyes moved rapidly down the few lines, then returned to the top and moved downward more slowly. Eyes still on the page, she unhooked her belt-comm, thumbed it on, spoke into it briefly, then listened. She nodded.

"Okay, shorty," she said, handing the paper back to Mr. dea'Gauss, who folded it precisely and replaced it in his sleeve, "you're legit." She craned her head around the entranceway. "Hey, Seth! Customers!" Then she took up her official stance again, arms folded under her bosom, legs wide.

A tall, rat-faced Terran appeared at the edge of the ramp and glanced at the three before bowing to the elderly Liaden. "Yessir?"

He was awarded a slight smile and an actual, if shallow, bow. Korval employed persons of worth. It was as it should be.

"I am Mr. dea'Gauss, Korval's man of business. Lord yos'-Galan expects me." He indicated his companions. "These are Ambassador Grittle of Skansion and Agent Chon Lyle of Trellen's World. His Lordship will be most gratified to receive them."

Seth nodded and stepped aside. "Welcome aboard, sirs, ma'am. We'll be lifting as soon as the tower clears us."

"That cargo is sealed!"

The taller of the two inspectors turned and sighed down at the cargo master before repeating for the ninth time that their duty was to inspect and—

"Verify the holds, goods, equipment, and general cargo of the *Dutiful Passage*, out of Solcintra, Liad, under the captaincy of Shan yos'Galan, Master Trader," Ken Rik singsonged, and threw up his hands in exasperation. "I *know*. I also know that this cargo is sealed. Do you understand what sealed means?

"Sealed means—one, that this cargo was delivered by the agency that leased the hold, made secure to their satisfaction and sealed with their lock.

"Two. It means that, having sealed the cargo at their end, the agency expects—has paid for the certainty—that the hold will still be sealed when the cargo reaches its destination.

"Three. It means that, if you two—people—unseal that hold, the *Dutiful Passage* will lose a shipping fee of approximately fifteen cantra—that's five hundred twenty-five thousand bits to you!—and very likely ten times that amount in commissions she will not receive for shipment of sealed cargoes in the future."

The taller inspector sighed. "I am aware of the exchange rate, sir. I am also aware of my duty. Surely you understand that in cases of contraband, to rely upon the ship's own records is sheer folly."

Ken Rik gasped. "How *dare*—" The Terran words were insufficient, he realized suddenly. Setting his jaw, he marched forward, placed himself before the hold in question, crossed his arms, and rooted his boot heels to the floor. "This hold is sealed," he said with a calmness his captain would have instantly recognized as highly dangerous. "And it will remain sealed."

"Quite proper," a dry voice said from the left. "Unless, of course, one of these individuals is a certified representative of the company whose seal is upon the cargo."

"Mr. dea'Gauss!"

Korval's man of business bowed. "Mr. yo'Lanna. I am pleased to see you well."

"And I'm pleased to see *you*, sir," Ken Rik said, throwing a grin of pure malice over his shoulder at the inspectors. "How may I serve you, Mr. dea'Gauss?"

The other man considered. "I will need a place to work. I apprehend these persons are inspectors from, ah, *Arsdred Court?*"

"Indeed, we are," the taller one asserted, coming forward with hand held out. "I am Jenner Halothi; my associate is Krys William. It is our duty to—" He cast a wary eye in the cargo master's direction. "—search this vessel for contraband and illegal goods."

"But not, I think," Mr. dea'Gauss said, ignoring the hand, "the holds sealed by companies independent of Korval or the *Dutiful Passage* unless a representative of that company is present." He surveyed the inspectors with the air of one sizing up the opposition. "The purpose of this, of course, is twofold. The representative will be present to oversee the unsealing and search of the cargo and will be able to make testimony that it is, in truth, the proper cargo. Also, should the cargo prove to be—or to contain—illegal items, you, sirs, will have your culprit. Is there a representative of—" He glanced at the device on the hatch. "—Pinglit Manufacturing Company on board, Mr. yo'Lanna?"

"No, sir, there is not," the cargo master replied happily. "There is, however, Ambassador May of Winegeld, Pinglit's world of origin. Also Ambassadors Sharpe, Suganaki, and Gomez, from trade-linked planets."

"Excellent, excellent." The old gentleman's eyes were seen to glow with what Ken Rik knew to be the light of battle. "If these gentles will but follow—Mr. yo'Lanna, I regret. Is there a place I may work?"

"You may use my office, sir," Ken Rik offered with exquisite cordiality. "This way, please."

"With all due respect, Mr.—umm—dea'Gauss?—we have our duty."

"Of course you do," he agreed. "We each of us have our duties. At this present, however, yours must wait upon mine." He executed a stiff, barely civil bow. "Attend us, please, sirs."

Shan yos'Galan rounded the corner with lazy haste, a glass of wine in his right hand and a large green plant cradled in his left arm. Suddenly he stopped, plant fronds swaying over his head, and blinked with consummate stupidity.

"Have the inspectors gone, Ken Rik? Or is it time for your midshift tea? Please don't think I begrudge you anything, but—"

Ken Rik grinned at him. "Mr. dea'Gauss is here."

"Is he? How delightful for us. Has he been shown his room? Oh, are you going visiting? Silly of me—of course you are. Very proper, since the two of you are such fast friends. A game or two of counterchance, a few glasses of wine, a bit of gossip. But the *inspectors,* Ken Rik?"

"Mr. dea'Gauss is with the inspectors. He came directly to the holds, looking for your Lordship, and has taken matters into his hand. I am sent for a ship-to and a colorcomp, that he may do his work the better."

"You left the inspectors *alone* with Mr. dea'Gauss?" Shan grinned widely. "Poor inspectors. Should I succor them, do you think, Ken Rik? It wouldn't do if a charge of cruelty to those of limited understanding were lodged."

"Mr. dea'Gauss summoned four ambassadors pertinent to the present situation to my office, where he is instructing the inspectors. I think they'll be safe enough for this while." He sniffed. "Did you know that we've engaged the services of a local accounting firm to tally the losses to port and to ship while the *Passage* is off limits?"

Shan regarded him with awe. "Have we? That was clever of us, wasn't it? How did we do it?"

"We put an advertisement," the older man explained, a bit unsteadily, "in the port business publication."

Shan gave a shout of laughter, the plant shivering alarmingly in his arms. "Oh, dear. Oh, *no!* In the port business paper? Ken Rik, we have a blot upon our immortal souls: We've brought an expert to an amateur's game! Speaking of which, I believe I should be present, as referee. My Lordship wouldn't miss such a show for—never mind." He held the plant out. "Do me the favor of taking this along to Ambassador Kelmik's quarters. She tells me that she cannot feel comfortable without a bit of greenery about."

Ken Rik sighed. "How are matters in the pet library?"

"Lina and Priscilla seem to be holding their own. Really, we have a most remarkable crew. When I left, the inspectors were bloody, but game. Neither of the ladies had yet been touched."

"Nor will they be," the cargo master predicted with delight. "Please tell Mr. dea'Gauss that I have not forgotten him, and that he will have his equipment very soon."

"I will, indeed," Shan promised, moving off with his big, loose stride. Ken Rik grinned and proceeded toward the guesting hall, plant fronds bouncing over his head with each step.

• • •

"**Also,**" Mr. dea'Gauss was telling an attentive audience when Shan entered the cargo master's sanctum, "it must be taken into account that persons employed by Clan Korval receive wages that are between ten and fifteen percent higher than wages received by persons employed in similar positions on other vessels. This, of course, means greater in-port spending on the part of Korval's crews. I expect to have the precise extrapolations in—your Lordship." He rose immediately and bowed low.

Shan stilled a sigh and inclined his head. "Mr. dea'Gauss. I am happy to see you. Forgive that I was not on hand to greet you personally when you came aboard."

"Your Lordship is gracious. It is understood that there are many demands upon your attention. Mr. yo'Lanna has seen to my needs. I believe it is not overoptimistic to state that matters progress well and an end to this misunderstanding will be speedily attained."

"I am sure we all hope for that," his Lordship responded gravely. "Please continue. It's always an inspiration to watch you at your work."

Mr. dea'Gauss acknowledged this with a tip of the head and reseated himself. Shan drifted to the left, exchanged polite smiles with the four ambassadors, and took up a position where he could watch the faces of the inspectors and Mr. dea'Gauss's workscreen.

"We should shortly," Korval's man of business resumed, "have a response from Pinglit Manufacturing Company. If they agree to the proposal offered—that is, your Lordship, to allow the presence of these four persons, Ambassadors May, Sharpe, Gomez and Suganaki, to equal the presence of one of their agents—then we will proceed with the unsealing and inspection of Hold Forty-three. In the meantime, sirs . . ." He turned to the befuddled inspectors. "I shall require from you a list of areas inspected and a certification for each."

"Certification, sir?" queried the shorter one—Inspector William, Shan recalled—with trepidation. "What sort of certification?"

Mr. dea'Gauss regarded him from under drawn brows. "Why, certification that you found nothing illegal within the stated area, of course. I do not ask if that was indeed the case. It could not have been otherwise."

Inspector William exchanged a glance with his partner.

"Was it otherwise?" Mr. dea'Gauss demanded.

The shorter inspector swallowed. "No, sir, of course—that is to say, we found no illegal substances in the holds thus far inspected. However, sir, it is our instruction to search the vessel entire and issue certification at the end."

"Insufficient," Mr. dea'Gauss judged, turning back to the screen. "Also, I find it incredible that two teams of inspectors are assigned to this task. A vessel the size of the *Dutiful Passage*—it is laughable. And while you pursue your efforts, Korval loses on the order of—" He touched a key with the reverence another man night reserve for stroking the cheek of his beloved. "Seven cantra per trade-night. Arsdred Port loses four point eight cantra per trade-night. This does not include the loss to those merchants who have offered guaranteed delivery for the goods we carry, based on our reliability. We must have at least two more teams of inspectors."

"I," Ambassador Suganaki said quietly, "would consider it an honor to be allowed to supervise one of those teams. It is absurd that the crew bear all the burden when there are so many of my colleagues here, pledged to aid. I am sure the crew has its scheduled round of duties, which must go on, regardless."

Shan bowed. "I thank you, ma'am. That's exactly the sort of assistance we do require. If I'd had any indication that the *Passage* was to have been boarded in this way, I would have signed on extra crew at the beginning of the trip."

"It is, of course, an unlooked for and unprecedented event, Captain," Suganaki agreed gravely, though there was a twinkle in her eye. "Perhaps an announcement at the reception this evening will alert my colleagues to the need." She turned to Korval's man of business. "It is possible, I think, sir, that even *four* more teams may not be excessive. The *Dutiful Passage* is a large ship."

"A worthy suggestion, Ambassador. My thanks to you. I shall inquire of Judge Bearmert how best to obtain additional inspectors. Now—" The in-slip buzzed, and Mr. dea'Gauss tapped the speak key. "Yes?"

"Tower here, Mr. dea'Gauss," Rusty's voice said formally. "Pinglit Manufacturing Company agrees to your suggestion. Hard-copy verification arrives via courier ship soonest. If there is anything else they may do, they beg you not to hesitate."

"Excellent, tower. My thanks to you." He cut the connection and gazed around in satisfaction. "Let us repair to Hold Forty-three."

Much later, after the inspectors had departed for the night, Shan walked with Mr. dea'Gauss toward the guesting hall.

"I have a message from the First Speaker, your Lordship," the old gentleman murmured in the High Tongue. "She bade me inform you that the Clan bears all expense in this situation, since the blow seems aimed at Korval entire, not only at the *Passage*—or yourself."

Shan nodded absently. "The First Speaker, my sister, is generous."

His response was most proper. Mr. dea'Gauss cleared his throat as a prelude to speaking further. It was not often that one found his Lordship so biddable. He did not at the moment recall that every period of docility he had previously observed in Shan's career had been immediately followed by some mad start. "I have also a message from Lord yos'Phelium."

The big mouth curved in a smile. "Do you? And what has my brother to say?"

Korval's man of business paused. The message was an odd one—flippant to the point of outrage. However, it seemed certain that young Val Con had inherited his father's devious directness, and Mr. dea'Gauss believed the true message lay far within the one he was bidden to deliver. Carefully, striving for the original phrasing, he said, "He asked me to tell you that he believes a successful scout and a successful thief must share certain vital characteristics. He thanks you for the suggestion of an avocation and asks further what he may be honored to steal for you first."

Shan laughed. "Renegade. He should have been drowned at birth. How long does he stop at home?"

Mr. dea'Gauss allowed himself a sniff to indicate his disapproval of this manner of speaking of Korval's Heir and replied stiffly. "He had been on Liad a bare quarter relumma when he was suddenly recalled to his duties as scout. He left the planet, I believe, the very day I was called before the First Speaker. It was only by chance that I was privileged to see him for a moment and exchange greetings."

Shan considered him. "Suddenly recalled by the scouts, was he?"

"Yes, my lord, and a sad blow it was to Lady Nova. She had invited Lady Imelda to guest. I believe she looked for a contract marriage in that direction, so that his Lordship might fulfill his duty to the Clan."

"Is she feeling better now?" Shan asked solicitously.

Mr. dea'Gauss blinked. "I beg pardon, your Lordship? Is who feeling better?"

"My sister. Of all the ladies she might have tried to force down Val Con's throat!"

"Lady Imelda," the old gentleman said severely, "is from a good Clan. She is honorable and quite complaisant."

"*Quite* complaisant. And neither stupid enough nor brilliant enough to pull it off. Val Con would have been at the screaming point within a relumma." They paused by an indigo-colored door. "I will give you any odds you name, sir, that that sudden recall by the scouts came after a personal request to be recalled."

There were several answers to this, none of them proper. Mr. dea'Gauss maintained an icy silence. His Lordship grinned and bowed. "Your room, sir. I trust you will find everything exactly as you wish it. The ambassadorial reception will be at Twenty Hours. I hope to see you among the merrymakers."

There was nothing for Mr. dea'Gauss but to make his bow and enter his room.

Shan moved toward his own quarters, his long stride eating distance while he frowned in thought.

It was true that the lad must do his duty to the Clan. Everyone must provide the Clan with his or her personal heir. Even Shan, the reprobate, the cynic, had given Korval a daughter who would in time take his place at the head of Line yos'-Galan; at the head of the *Passage* . . . Damn them both for being such loggerheads! If only Nova would try to enlist Val Con to the task of discovering some suitable lady, all might yet come out right.

Shan sighed, stopped in the middle of his sleeping room, closed his eyes, and breathed deeply and evenly, as he had been taught so long ago by the Master Healers. Slowly, the worries—familial, professional, personal—stilled.

One thing at a time, he reminded himself with forceful calm.

An image of Priscilla as he had last seen her, the light of battle in her face as she confronted two harried inspectors, rose before his inner eye.

With a groan, he dropped onto the bed and closed his eyes.

You want too much, your Lordship, he told himself. Try to be worthy of her friendship. If you're very lucky, you'll manage it.

He rose from the bed and wandered toward the 'fresher, stripping off his clothes as he went. He stepped into the needle spray, resolutely turning his thoughts to the coming reception and what profit might be earned from it.

"You must have a dress!"

"Lina—"

"No!" the small woman cried, taking her friend's hand. "You attend the reception properly attired. I will hear no more!"

Priscilla stood her ground and bit her lip. "Lina, I'm sorry—*truly* sorry. But I don't have any money, my dear. None. And I'm already into my wages for the cost of the clothes I'm wearing now. A—party—dress . . ."

"Bah!" Lina flung up a tiny hand, then swung close, pressing lightly against the taller woman's side. "I shall provide the dress, and you shall wear it to please me, eh?" She smiled. "All is arranged!"

Priscilla smiled and shook her head. "I can't ask you to do that, Lina. Why should you—"

"Why should I not?" Lina interrupted. "We are sisters— you said it yourself! Should I allow my sister to go improperly clad? And far from asking, you make it astonishingly difficult to gift you!" She laughed and pulled on Priscilla's hand, urging her to the entrance of the general stores. "Come, denubia. You must learn to accept a gift with grace.

The Terran woman chuckled. "Another protocol lesson? Next you'll be telling me to wear the earrings the captain gave me!"

"And why should you not?" Lina demanded. "The design is pleasing; I think they will look very well on you. Shan is honorable—he does not gift and then cry 'owed!'" She looked up into her friend's face. "The earrings are *yours,* Priscilla. A gift, freely given. No hurt can come from wearing them." She pulled her companion through the first storeroom, past the working clothes and everyday boots, past even the festive tunics and softshoes, into the room beyond, where dream fabrics drew the eye from all directions and the air smelled of Festival-time.

"I don't think . . ." Priscilla began, staring about her like a thing half-wild.

"Bah!" Lina said again, allowing no time for refusals. "Why should you not have a dress that becomes you?" She came close once more and extended both a hand and a mental touch of comfort to still the beginning panic. "Priscilla, you are lovely. It is added joy that you are so. Why not pleasure yourself—and those who see you—by wearing beautiful clothes? The occasion demands it!"

But Priscilla was no longer listening. She bent and stroked Lina's hair lightly, then slid a hand beneath the small chin and tipped her face so the light fell on it. Lina met the sparkling black gaze calmly, all Roads open and clear, the Wall at her back.

"You are of the Circle," Priscilla murmured, perhaps to herself. "I can feel the warmth coming out of you, like a hearth fire, my friend. And before—the pain—then the healing . . ." The hand withdrew; Lina kept her face tipped fully up, eyes steady.

"Are you Wife, Lina? Or Witch?"

"I have been a wife—twice by contract, as is proper. And I am mother of two sons: Bey Lor and Zac. By trade I am librarian; by training I am Healer. I do not know what a Witch is, my friend."

"Healer?" Priscilla frowned. "A Healer is—Soul-weaver, we say, on Sintia. When someone is sick in spirit . . ."

"When one does not accept joy," Lina agreed. "Shan says the proper Terran word is 'empath.'" She hesitated. "I am not sure. It seemed from my readings—for a Healer may not aid everyone. There are those I cannot feel at all. And there is training to be undergone, protections to be learned, techniques to be mastered."

"Yes, of course." Priscilla was still frowning. "But I—"

"You," Lina interrupted, "were fighting joy, denying both laughter and the possibility of kindness. It could not continue so! I had the means to aid you. Why should I not?" She swayed close, regardless of other persons in the room, all Roads open yet. "Priscilla? Sisters. You said it. I do not deny it."

There was a flare of pain like thrown acid, followed by a surge of joy nearly as searing. Lina put her arms around her friend's waist and hugged her tight, feeling Priscilla's arms pull her tighter.

"Sister and friend . . ." After a final, nearly bone-crushing squeeze, Lina felt herself released and realized that the Roads bore the other woman's clear, singing happiness; she retained enough wit to shut herself away from the intoxication.

"Come," she said, smiling and taking Priscilla's hand. "Let us choose you a *magnificent* dress!"

Long after Lina left, Priscilla stood before the mirror, oscillating between terror and delight.

The dress *was* magnificent: black shimmersilk, shot with random silver bolts that glittered and danced as she moved. The fabric covered her from knee to neck, from shoulder to wrist, meticulously reproducing every line it adhered to. The slit on the right side made her accustomed stride possible while allowing a tantalizing glimpse of creamy thigh. Goddess knew how much it had cost. Lina had not answered when Priscilla had asked.

She frowned at her reflection. She wore her three remaining bracelets on her right wrist, and a blue enameled ring borrowed from Lina on her left hand. A silver ribbon wove like lightning through her storm-cloud curls. Yet there was something missing.

Slowly she went back to the wardrobe and rummaged within. The velvet of the box was warm in her hand. She worked the catch on her way back to the mirror, then carefully hung a hoop in each ear and stepped back to observe the effect.

In a moment she nodded, which set the hoops dancing; laying the box aside, she left the room.

Rusty frankly stared before coming forward and offering his arm. " 'Cilla, you're gorgeous. How 'bout a cohab contract?"

She grinned. "You've been in the tower too long, friend."

"Well, that's true," he said morosely. "Between the cap'n and Mr. dea'Gauss, I thought I'd never get off that damn beam! We've got the fourteen prime points covered, I swear."

"Sounds rough," she sympathized. "Try coming to the pet library and defending Master Frodo's right to live."

Rusty snorted. "Busybodies. Why don't they find something real to do? As if we'd ship contraband! Must've lost all their aces to try and pin that on the *Passage*."

Just then Lina approached, arm in arm with an elderly Liaden gentleman in formal dark tunic and strictly correct ash-colored trousers. "Priscilla, here is Mr. dea'Gauss, Clan Korval's man of business," she said with a stateliness made tolerable by her smile. Turning to the gentleman, she repeated the formula. "Mr. dea'Gauss, here is Priscilla Mendoza, my good friend."

Both pet librarian and man of business bowed.

Straightening, Mr. dea'Gauss was seen to smile. "Lady Mendoza, I am delighted to make your acquaintance. Lady Faaldom has spoken most warmly of you."

"I am happy to meet you, Mr. dea'Gauss," Priscilla said cordially; she added a diplomatic rider. "I am certain that Lina's friendship must be a bond between us."

"So I thought, as well," the old gentleman said, delighted to find her so well spoken. He inclined his head to her escort. "Mr. Morgenstern. How do you go on?"

"Pretty well, sir," Rusty returned as if he had not spent the greater part of his day executing the old man's instructions. "How are you?"

"I find myself in the best of good health, thank you, sir, in spite of the fact that I have recently been constrained to travel.

Ah, there is Ambassador Kung." He executed a nicely gauged bow between Priscilla and Lina. "I beg to be excused. Duty must ever come before pleasure."

"Pity Ambassador Kung," Rusty muttered as Mr. dea'-Gauss moved off after his quarry.

Lina laughed. "Ah, he is not so bad, the old gentleman. He sincerely tries to care for people. It is not his fault that he loves work more."

"If you say so," Rusty said doubtfully. "At least he's not as strung-up as Lady Whatsis—Kareen? You remember that run we had her and her son? I don't think Shan showed his nose in the halls the whole time she was here! Even Captain Er Thom looked nervous."

Lina smiled. "But it was only for a few weeks, after all. And the rest of the trip was very nice. Bah! Now *I* must ask to be excused! I did promise to speak with Mr. Lyle. And it is true that we should be pleasant, since we wish them to work for us." She executed the bow between equals and slanted a grin up at Priscilla. "Lady Mendoza. Mr. Morgenstern."

Rusty shook his head and sighed down at Priscilla. "Well, she's right. I'd better find that silly woman who was so excited about the pin-beam and show off my manners." He raised a hand, grinning ruefully. "See you later."

Priscilla looked about her. Mr. dea'Gauss was in earnest conversation with an emaciated and exceedingly tall Terran. Janice Weatherbee and Tonee had engaged the attention of three or four lesser officials; the conversation was liberally laced with laughter. Ken Rik listened politely to a fat woman with a painted face and a multitude of jewel-tipped braids, while Lina smiled winningly up at a clearly captivated gentleman who was, Priscilla supposed, Mr. Lyle. Rusty had disappeared into the crowded back of the room. And she did not see the other person she was looking for.

Irritably, she shrugged her shoulders and moved at random into the crowd. What difference did it make to her if Shan yos'Galan chose to absent himself from the reception?

"It would, of course, be unfortunate," Ambassador Gomez

was saying confidentially to an elder in the robes of an Ars-dredi, "should Clan Korval send word to its allies and trade-partners that it no longer stops here."

"Generations to recover," another person murmured as Priscilla eased by. "Economic tragedy . . . second-rate port . . ."

Was Clan Korval as powerful as that? she wondered, slipping by Janice and Tonee with a smile. Could they ruin a spaceport? Make thousands jobless? By refusing to stop? Merely by letting it be known that they would no longer stop there? It seemed incredible. And yet Shan yos'Galan had lost a middling fortune at the hands of Sàv Rid Olanek and claimed the money as the least part.

He's a truthful person, Priscilla thought. He'd have told me if the coin-loss was desperate.

Spying a lone ambassador, important in beribboned tunic and sash-belt, she smiled and bowed. "Good evening. I am Priscilla Mendoza, of the crew of the *Dutiful Passage*."

The ambassador, it turned out, had a thirst for knowledge. He wished to know everything concerning the *Passage*, her captain, Clan Korval, the pet library, and the crew. Priscilla obliged him, editing where it seemed appropriate, thankful for once that the possession of a comely face allowed her room to be just a trifle stupid. While she could not feel that her interpretation of the role was as inspired as Shan yos'Galan's, it was perfectly adequate for the audience.

The patterns of the party altered, partnering Priscilla's ambassador with one of his own. Liberated, she moved off. She saw Seth bent almost double, speaking into Tonee's ear; Rusty was near the bank of green plants with Kayzin Ne'Zame, his stance formal as he spoke to a half circle of listeners.

And leaning against the far wall, beneath the very wings of the dragon, closely attending a blond woman in ambassadorial dress, was Shan yos'Galan. He wore a blend of Liaden and Terran formality: ruffled white shirt, brocade jacket, dark, form-fitting trousers. The amethyst drop hung in his right ear.

Priscilla was aware of a feeling of relief and took an unconscious step in his direction,

He glanced up, his big mouth curved in a smile. Priscilla froze, feeling her face flush.

"Ms. Mendoza?" The voice at her elbow was unpleasantly shrill.

She turned and smiled at the fat woman of the many braids. "Yes? How may I serve you, ma'am?"

The woman smiled, creasing the intricate pattern of her facial decoration, and made a jerky forward motion, which Priscilla interpreted as a bow. "I am Ambassador Dia Grittle of Skansion. Cargo Master yo'Lanna tells me you are a native of Sintia."

Her smile felt stiff on her face, and she was certain that she had lost color. Fortunately, Ambassador Grittle did not appear to notice.

Priscilla cleared her throat. "Indeed I am, ma'am . . ." She let the sentence trail to a tiny note of inquiry.

The ambassador nodded sharply. "Thought as much when I saw you walk in. Got the look of your mother."

Priscilla took a breath, forcing air down her constricted throat. Not here, Goddess, she prayed. Not now.

"Lady Mendoza. Ambassador Grittle. Forgive the interruption. I have here one who is anxious to meet you, lady." The speaker was Mr. dea'Gauss. Priscilla felt her knees sag in relief. Silently she thanked the Goddess.

The smile she gave Korval's man of business was genuine. "Of course, sir." Ambassador Grittle muttered something inarticulate but no doubt proper. Mr. dea'Gauss bowed, indicating the gentleman at his side.

"Priscilla, Lady Mendoza, may I make you known to Judge Abrahanthan Zahre."

The gentleman stepped forward, his ruby-red robes rustling, and held out a smooth, thin hand. "I am pleased to meet you, Lady Mendoza. Especially as it affords me the opportunity to make my apologies in person."

"Apologies, sir?" Priscilla's forehead puckered, then

cleared. "The warrant!" she exclaimed, striving for a look of vacuous enlightenment. "I had forgotten, sir. Please do the same."

"You are kind." The judge bowed, smiling. "But I do wish you to know that it is not my practice to brand one a thief on such flimsy evidence as was presented to me by Trader Olanek. He was very persuasive, it is true. But I serve the Law, and I hold myself responsible. That warrant should never have been issued."

"Warrant!" Ambassador Grittle was staring at the judge in what seemed to be disbelief. "You issued a warrant! Did you take no time to *think,* sir? Did you take no time to consider with whom you dealt?" She took a deep breath, her voice rising ever more shrilly over the room at large. "To think that a *Mendoza of Sintia* might be a thief—it is an outrage, sir! We of Skansion are trade-partnered with Sintia. I am myself acquainted with the Mendoza family. It is an insult, sir! And one nearly past bearing! Of all—was there bail set?" she shot at the white-faced and rigid Priscilla.

"A cantra was set as bail," the judge murmured in a moment, "and has been paid by *Dutiful Passage.* Clan Korval guarantees Lady Mendoza's appearance, should the matter go to trial." He smiled faintly. "Which I am certain it will not."

"A Mendoza of Sintia needs no one to guarantee her word!" the ambassador snapped. She reached into the velvet pouch hung at her ample waist, produced a single dully shimmering coin, and slapped it in the judge's hand. "Skansion doubles the bond! Thus do we stand by our allies!"

Priscilla ran her tongue over dry lips, then opened her mouth to say—what?

Again Mr. dea'Gauss rescued her. He stepped forward and offered the ambassador his arm, smiling coolly. "Lady Mendoza is fortunate indeed that her home-world has so staunch a trade-partner. Allow me to procure a glass of wine for you, Ambassador."

Priscilla inclined her head to Judge Zahre, then raised her

eyes to find him smiling in real amusement. Her own lips bent in response. "Now I must beg *your* pardon!"

His smile widened into a grin. "Without cause, Lady Mendoza. *You* were not rude." He glanced over her shoulder. "I see that refreshments have arrived. Allow me to escort you."

"You're kind," she said breathlessly, "but I—I must see someone just now. Perhaps we'll talk again later."

The judge's face turned quizzical. "Yes, perhaps we will." Bowing formally, he left her.

Moving with pilot swiftness, pilot grace, she slipped through the press of people and into the corridor. She strode down the hall, turned a corner, and leaned against the wall, listening to the pounding of her heart.

That dreadful woman! Who had heard? The entire room, most likely. And she claimed acquaintance with Anmary Mendoza! Allmother, what shall I do?

"Good evening, Priscilla. Asleep? It's a terrible crush, isn't it? My Lordship isn't good for much of this kind of thing. I'm a sad trial to my sister—no manners, no address."

She opened her eyes, breath snagging. "Captain."

"Sometimes," he agreed, light eyes mocking. "Don't you like the party? Mr. dea'Gauss seems very impressed."

Her face relaxed a little, her mouth curving toward a smile. "I didn't have the nerve to tell him I'm not a lady," she confessed, striving for lightness. "I'm afraid it would embarrass him."

Shan laughed. "Mr. dea'Gauss never errs in these matters. I suggest you accommodate yourself to ladyhood." He tipped his head. "That won't be so hard, will it, Priscilla? After all, a Mendoza of Sintia—"

Her face went white, eyes widening, one hand moving up and out, warding him away. "No."

"Priscilla!" He snapped forward, hand outstretched. "Priscilla, it was a joke! I—I never wanted to distress you!" He took another step as he bit his lip. "I'm *sorry*, Priscilla."

Her hand wavered, fell, and closed about his. "It's all

right," she said unevenly. Her hand trembled in his as she took a ragged breath. "Please, you mustn't ask . . ."

"I don't ask. I have no right to ask, Priscilla. It was only a joke. You looked as if you needed to laugh so badly." He smiled ruefully. "My wretched tongue!"

Her mouth wobbled on the edge of a smile. "Ambassador Grittle . . ."

"Makes you stop and wonder, doesn't it? How could she have become an ambassador? Do you think she might have assassinated someone?"

"There's a chance, if she did." The smile was there, finally; nor did she take her hand from his. "Maybe someone will assassinate *her*."

Shan laughed. "We can hope." Then he sighed. "My Lordship is expected to return to the festivities. Will you come with me? Or are you retiring?"

She removed her hand, though the smile remained. "I'll stay here for a moment or two, I think. Then I'll go back."

"All right," he said, moving reluctantly away. At the corner he turned back. "Priscilla?"

"Yes, Captain?"

A shadow crossed his face but was gone before she could name it. He bowed slightly. "It was nothing. I'll see you later, Priscilla." She was alone.

Leaning against the wall, she closed her eyes and breathed in the way that was taught to every Initiate: breathe in serenity, breathe out confusion. Breathe in strength, breathe out weakness. Breathe in hope, breathe out despair.

In a little while she opened her eyes, stood away from the wall, and went back to the reception.

Shan groaned and rolled over. One long arm swung out, smacking the alarmplate unerringly. Obedient to this prompt, the cabin lights came up and music began to play. Loudly.

"Give me a break," he muttered, sitting up and running his fingers through his hair. The music abated somewhat, a boon to his pounding head. "Damn that stuff! Floats you on a cloud, then hits you over the head with a rock. Why would *any*body want to smoke it?"

The room offered no answer.

Well, it had been a profitable week of trading, with the Arsdredi seemingly bent on recouping every cantra of "loss" the port business paper had kept such careful track of. It was merely a sad pity that profit had not yet been known to cure a headache.

Shan groaned again, and the pounding intensified as memory returned. Mr. dea'Gauss wished to speak with his Lordship this morning on business concerning Clan Korval. Wonderful.

He placed his feet carefully and stood, grimacing. Perhaps

it's not too late to resign as a lordship? But there was no conviction in the thought. His brother and sisters needed him, so a lord Shan would be.

"A shower," he told himself firmly. "And breakfast. Coffee. Lovely, hot coffee."

Breakfast had been the right idea. Coffee had been inspired. Armed with a second steaming mugful, Shan moved back toward his office, nodding to and exchanging greetings with the crew members he encountered.

The good news, he reflected, laying his hand against the plate, was that his interview with Korval's man of business must of necessity be brief. The *Passage* had received permission to leave Arsdred orbit in one ship's hour.

The bad news was that Mr. dea'Gauss could pack more well-mannered moralizing into an hour than a Moreleki proselytizer. The phrase "business of Clan Korval" was especially ominous.

Unless he very much mistook the matter, Shan was in for a masterly rake-down.

It was odd, he thought, setting his cup on the desk and disposing himself comfortably in the captain's chair, how lordhood's vaunted powers and privileges did nothing at all to protect one from the righteous nagging of those who held one's best interests at heart.

The door chimed, and Shan sighed. He toyed briefly with the notion of remaining silent, then regretfully decided that it would not be seemly and picked up his mug. "Come."

Mr. dea'Gauss walked three steps into the room and bowed low, as agent to lord.

Shan inclined his head and took a sip of scalding coffee. "Mr. dea'Gauss. How delightful to see you looking so well! Adversity always did agree with you, sir. Please, sit down."

"Your Lordship will have his joke, I suppose," the older man said repressively. "The business I come on is quite serious, however. I am certain that your Lordship will give me the closest attention for the next several moments."

"Of course." Shan murmured politely.

Mr. dea'Gauss regarded Shan steadily, feet flat on the carpet, hands folded, spine stiff and inches from the back of the chair. "In the course of following the instructions laid upon me by Korval's First Speaker," he said crisply, "I found that which seems to indicate that you have undertaken debt-balance with Sav Rid Olanek of Clan Plemia. I ask if this is so."

Here it comes, Shan thought. He inclined his head slightly. "It is so."

Mr. dea'Gauss exhaled sharply. "It is perhaps unfortunate," he suggested, though Shan failed to observe any note of delicacy in his tone, "that your Lordship took it upon himself to enter into such an enterprise without first consulting those of us who are more knowledgeable in affairs of this nature. If I had been apprised of the situation at its first occurrence, balance might have been quickly and, I will say, cleanly achieved. As it stands—"

"As it stands," Shan interrupted, allowing an edge of irritation to be heard, "I am captain of this vessel. As captain, it is my duty to guard her honor, the honor of the crew, and my own honor *as* captain."

"Very true," Mr. dea'Gauss agreed. "However, the situation is not so clear. It is not your responsibility as captain to plunge ship and crew into debt-balance without making the First Speaker aware. It is the First Speaker's duty, after all, to protect the honor of the Clan. And I believe this to be a strike at Korval entire." He paused, rubbing his hands together dryly. "You are aware, I think, that Sav Rid Olanek had previously given your sister, the First Speaker, cause to feel that she was owed?"

Shan drank coffee and shrugged. "I think the case is that my sister, the First Speaker, gave Sav Rid Olanek cause to feel that *he* was owed. But, yes, I was aware. It did not appear to alter things significantly."

"Wherein," the old gentleman said with asperity, "lies the meat of my comments. I have grown old minding Korval's interests. It is vainglory for one as young and as inexperienced as yourself to think he might take up so weighty a matter, unaided by older, wiser counsel." He paused. It occurred to him that perhaps this was not the best tone to take with Shan, who was well known for his unpredictability.

"It is true," he continued in a more conciliating mode, "that your Lordship is yet young. Experience comes with age, with observing the actions of one's elders and studying their thoughts. It is my dearest wish to aid you, your Line, your Clan. I have done so my life long. If I speak too freely, it is from the knowledge that youth errs most greatly when it strives to do what is most proper."

There was a pause long enough to inspire Mr. dea'Gauss with the fear that he had indeed badly overstepped himself. It was within Shan's power—and certainly within the scope of his character—to refuse the aid offered and send his man of business straightaway back to Liad. In such a case, Mr. dea'-Gauss's interview with the First Speaker could only be painful. Nova yos'Galan had a clear sense of her duty as First Speaker in Trust. She would not brook failure.

"So, then," Shan said conversationally. "What do you want from me, sir? Shall I give the captaincy of the *Passage* over to your capable self? Or call a halt to the balancing with what has already been done and hope that it suffices?"

Shan's unpredictability, Mr. dea'Gauss reminded himself carefully, could run both ways. "I hear from all only that you are a most excellent captain," he answered quietly. "A Trader of the first rank. For this present . . . If your Lordship would apprise me of what steps have been taken?"

"Pin-beams have been sent to four hundred twenty-eight worlds, issuing social and civil warning and citing *Daxflan*'s unfortunate link with port violence. To date, three hundred have responded positively, via pin-beam and bouncecomm. The Trade Commission has likewise been notified and responds with thanks and a promise to investigate." He paused. "I trust you find these efforts not completely ineffective."

Mr. dea'Gauss drew a careful breath. "I will, of course, desire to study your Lordship's records, for my own edification." He considered a moment before venturing further. "Lady Mendoza is partnered in this enterprise?"

"Lady Mendoza," Shan said, his mouth suddenly tight and grim, "has had her person abused and her honor jeopardized—by order and by direct action of Sav Rid Olanek. You may find the details in her file." He leaned forward, tapped a one-fingered sequence into the keypad, and rose to his towering height. "If you will sit at the desk, sir, you will see what efforts have been made thus far. I hope you won't find them entirely without merit." He bowed slightly. "I'm sure you'll forgive me, sir. Duty calls me to the bridge. The *Passage* leaves orbit shortly."

"Certainly, your Lordship," Mr. dea'Gauss said, coming to his feet. He bowed as Shan swept out of the room and then moved behind the desk, pulling a notecorder from his sleeve.

"Leaving Arsdred orbit," Rusty said pensively.
"'Bout time. I tell you, 'Cilla, I don't think I've ever been so
sick of a port before. Lost money hand over fist—well, not
the *ship*. Kayzin was saying at breakfast that the port-profit
appeared to be adequate." He grinned. "That means 'the cap'n
made a killing.' "

Priscilla gave one of her nearly noiseless laughs. "But
that's good news, isn't it? Your share will be more at Solcintra. And you didn't lose money on the spec cargo, did you? I
thought the wood was preordered."

"Yeah, that's all okay. Point is, we had to pay a stiff fine
to—umm, convince the inspectors that Lina's damn perfume
wasn't illegal in *some* places, even if it is on Arsdred, and that
we never had any intention of trading it on Arsdred." He
stopped, a riveted expression on his round face. "You know
what, though? We'd been going to try and trade some here,
except the cap'n nixed it. Whew! Close one! I tell you what,
'Cilla: Shan's damn good."

"Well," Priscilla said as the door to the bridge slid aside to
admit them, "he *is* a Master Trader."

"Sure is. What're you doing after shift? Want to pick up Lina and have a picnic in the garden? My treat."

"That sounds good. But Lina might have other plans."

Rusty set his coffee cup on the comm island. "I'll check before we get started. See you later, Pilot."

"Carry on, Radio Tech." She continued across the bridge, past Navigation and around Meteorology to Piloting. Smiling, she slid into the chair and inclined her head to Third Mate Gil Don Balatrin. He returned an absent half bow.

"Early, aren't you, Mendoza?" Janice Weatherbee asked; she, too, was early. "Might as well start calculating." She leaned back in her chair and folded her arms over her chest elaborately, her eyes ostensibly on the blank screen over the co-pilot's board.

Priscilla nodded, slid her card into the slot, logged on and began to run the figures, building an image on her screen. She checked it frowningly, made several adjustments, checked again, and nodded. A slim finger touched the send key and the image coalesced on the coscreen. Priscilla leaned back and deliberately closed her eyes.

"Looks okay to me, Mendoza. Feed it and look it."

She nodded, stifling a sigh as her fingers flew across the board. "Looks okay to me" was an accolade when Janice said it. It's childish, Priscilla thought, but it would be nice to hear that I'd done this or that *well*.

A chime sounded, and the minor hum of voices faded, to be replaced by one voice, clear and soul-warming "Good morning, all. Station reports, please. I assume everyone's ready to leave?"

The screen was a uniform gray except for the red digits in the bottom right-hand corner, busy counting the "real time" they spent in hyperspace.

Priscilla shifted in the pilot's chair, conscious of a glow in the vicinity of her stomach. From orbit-break to Jump-entry, the piloting had been hers. Janice had sat, watchful, throughout the shift but had given neither instruction nor assistance.

Janice stood and stretched. "Okay, Mendoza. I'm gonna run down and snag a cup of coffee. Should be back before Jump-end. If not, you go ahead. This place is a real backwater. Nothing tough. You want anything?"

"No, thanks."

The second mate nodded. "Okay. Back in a couple minutes."

"**Your** Lordship? May I speak with you a moment?"

Shan sighed and stopped, waiting for Mr. dea'Gauss to come alongside. "Good afternoon, sir," he said politely. "How may I assist you?"

"A few words on the matter lying between Korval and Sav Rid Olanek, your Lordship. I have taken the liberty of ordering credit checks on *Daxflan* at all ports in this sector. This is in the nature of a supportive effort to your Lordship's own tactic."

Shan raised a hand. "Mr. dea'Gauss, I regret. We are due to break into normal space in less than five minutes. Duty calls me again to the bridge."

"Of course," the old gentleman murmured. "May I walk with your Lordship?"

There was no escape. Shan inclined his head. "Certainly, sir." He began to move, sternly suppressing a desire to continue at his usual long stride.

"I am certain," Mr. dea'Gauss said, "that your Lordship will inform Lady Mendoza of the action I have taken. Also, it is necessary to ascertain whether she has notified her House of the fact that it is partnered with Korval in a venture of honor. I retain the impression that upon Sintia, Mendoza is a House of power, enclosing a varied melant'i. It would be wise to establish amicable relations." He paused, and Shan nodded absently. Matching the old gentleman's pace had kept him from reaching the bridge before Jump; the Jump alert sounded peacefully.

They rounded a corner, entering the long hallway that led to the bridge. Mr. dea'Gauss cleared his throat as the tingle of pretransition raced though the ship.

"Your Lordship has done quite well in the initial moves. The warnings will cost Trader Olanek much in time, in flexibility, in money. Of course, in this, as in chess, which I believe your Lordship studies, it is important for us to cast our minds ahead, considering the possible countermove open to our opponent."

The Jump-quiver came. From nowhere, from everywhere—the shriek of a siren. Above Shan's head, a lightplate snapped from yellow to red—and Shan himself was suddenly gone, running flat out toward the bridge.

The digits in the corner of the screen told their final tally and faded as the break-Jump chime rang across the bridge. Priscilla extended a hand toward the board.

COLLISION COURSE the red letters screamed. Abruptly her hands were flashing over the keys, calling up defense screens, demanding data as her eyes scanned the instruments, assessing what it was, how big, how fast and—

HOSTILE ACTION

Second screens up, Jump alert, coords locked back in, coils—Hurry up, coils! She saw it now, the screen providing maximum amplification: a tiny ship, bristling guns, in position for a second run-by. Coils . . . coils—up!

Her hand was at the Jump control, eyes on the distance dial. There was enough room—just. Now . . .

"Well done, Priscilla." A big hand closed around her wrist, pulling her away from the switch even as he slammed into the copilot's chair and rammed his card into the slot. "Series A29, shunt 42—second screens up? Of course . . ."

Priscilla's fingers flew in obedience, assigning control to

him; she heard him snap an order to Rusty for a visual and another to someone unknown, regarding Turret 7.

"Hurry up, please, Rusty."

"Got 'em, Cap'n—your screen."

The image filled both their screens: the bridge of the other vessel, smaller than the *Passage* by several magnitudes. A man was at the board. From off-screen, a woman's voice, initially inaudible, was becoming rapidly clear: ". . . tell Jury to start her run?"

"You will observe," the captain said from Priscilla's side, "the position of the gun turret on our off side."

The pilot of the other ship looked up in shock, made lightning adjustments to his unseen board, and swore. "Tell Jury to hang where she is!" he snapped over his shoulder.

"A wise choice," the captain said gently. "I hate to belabor the point, but I believe we now have five turrets trained on your vessel. Do correct me if I'm wrong."

The man took a deep breath. "You're right." He glanced behind him as another man came into the screen, a man older than the pilot, hard-faced and calm.

"What goes, Klaus?"

Wordlessly, the pilot pointed at something out of the range of the watchers on the *Passage*. The boss considered for a moment before turning back to the screen and inclining his head.

"Nothing personal, Captain. A contract."

"A contract," Shan repeated. "With whom?"

The boss grinned and shook his head "Confidential. But I'll tell you this: he wanted you out of the race real bad."

"Did he? I hope you got your money in cash and up front, sir. No?" He shook his head at the look of sudden dismay on the mercenary captain's face. "That was careless of you. I suppose you're sure that you have the right ship?"

"He gave me your break-in pattern, a time frame for arrival, approximate mass—real approximate."

"But he gave you no name? And you didn't ask—no, why should you? This is the *Dutiful Passage*, sir. Clan Korval.

Tree and Dragon Family. Stop me when you hear something familiar."

"*I Dare.*" The voice of the unseen woman was breathless with awe.

"A student of heraldry? Exactly. 'I Dare.'"

The other captain seemed uncomfortable. His eyes strayed from the screen back to the pilot's unseen instruments, then came back to the screen again. "All right, Captain, what's the deal? You've got weaponry and the mass to back it. You gonna use it?"

"That depends on you, doesn't it? I suppose you wouldn't be betraying a confidence if I asked if the name of the man you dealt with was Olanek or the ship *Daxflan*? You needn't say yes, only no."

There was silence.

Shan shook his head. "I hope you got at least half of your money in advance, sir. No? Forty percent? Thirty? *Twenty-five?*" He laughed suddenly at the acute distress on the other man's face. "I'm ashamed of you sir! Didn't your mother tell you never to sign a Liaden's contract? Twenty-five percent down on a job that would mark you all for the rest of your lives? Ask your crew member there if she believes a family with 'I Dare' for a motto would let you rest if you'd completed your mission successfully."

The mercenary captain shrugged. "There wasn't a contract," he said sheepishly. "It was a gentleman's agreement. But I know where to find him."

"No doubt you do," Shan said cordially "I should perhaps mention that *Daxflan* is also capably armed. And the captain is counted a very fair shot."

The boss bowed his head. "What's the price?"

"Get out of here," the captain snapped, his voice suddenly hard-edged and cold. "We have your ships recorded and filed. The information is being pin-beamed this moment to the Federated Trade Commission. I advise you to take up a different line of work."

The boss glanced over his shoulder. "Tell Jury and Sal to scram. We'll do the same, if the captain'll deflect his guns."

The last ship reached its Jump point and blinked out of existence. Priscilla's instruments showed empty space around the *Dutiful Passage* for several light-minutes in all directions. In the chair beside her, Shan yos'Galan took a deep breath and spoke, voice glacial. "Second Mate."

There was a slight hesitation before Janice answered from directly behind them.

"Captain?"

"You will report to the captain's office immediately before prime. You will bring hard copy of your contract. Dismissed to quarters."

Priscilla caught her breath at the other woman's shock; she thought for a heartbeat that one of them would cry in protest.

The second mate cleared her throat. "Yes, Captain." And Priscilla heard her go.

Relief flooded through her, shocking in its intensity, mixed with outrage, pain, and near-manic glee. She gripped the arms of the chair, seeking serenity, buffeted by emotion. Adrenaline high, she told herself, keeping to the search for the path.

"Ms. Mendoza."

She took a breath and found her voice. "Yes, Captain?"

"On behalf of this ship and of Clan Korval, Ms. Mendoza, all thanks. I could have done no better in your place, given the resources at your command. I only hope I would have done as well." He pulled his card from the slot and tucked it absently into his belt. "There will be a meeting of the crew immediately after prime. I would like to see you in my office following it, please."

"Of course, Captain." The inner chaos was subsiding somewhat. Daring to turn her head, Priscilla met a pair of quizzical pale eyes even as the feeling hit her again—differently, though as intense—an overwhelming impulse to fling back her head and laugh, to embrace the man beside her . . .

Just as she knew she must be lost, she found the pathway. She flew down the inner way, found the door, and slammed it hard behind her.

Beside her, Shan sighed sharply and snapped to his feet, spinning to face the incoming relief pilots. "Your boards," he said curtly.

Vilobar bowed. "The shift changes, Pilots." Priscilla pushed herself out of the chair, still giddy from too much emotion experienced too quickly. But she found her path blocked by the captain, who was glaring down at Mr. dea'-Gauss.

"Well, sir?" Shan demanded.

The old gentleman inclined his head. "Shall I draft a message to the First Speaker, your Lordship?"

"I believe," Shan said icily, "that is the captain's duty. I thank you for your concern."

Mr. dea'Gauss bowed low. "Forgive my presumption, your Lordship. It is, of course, exactly as you say."

"I'm pleased to hear it," the captain snapped, and swept by, heading for Communications.

Priscilla watched him leave; realizing that she was watching, she moved her eyes, cheeks flaming, but found her instinctive step away hindered.

Mr. dea'Gauss bowed to her, not as deeply as for the captain but with a hand flourish indicating profound respect. Priscilla forced herself to be still, to form the proper Liaden phrase.

"Mr. dea'Gauss. How may I serve you?"

"It is I who wish to serve your Ladyship. Will you accept my aid in contacting your family? They should, perhaps, be apprised of what transpires." He looked at her closely. "I ask indulgence, my lady, if the offer offends."

Priscilla stared at him blankly, then recovered herself and inclined her head. "You are all kindness, sir. I thank you for thought and offer, but no. There is no need to trouble House Mendoza with my affairs."

Mr. dea'Gauss hesitated fractionally. Then, recent contact with Lord yos'Galan having rendered him wary, he bowed again with no less respect. "As you will, my lady," he murmured. He stepped aside to let her pass.

"No," Gordy answered Lina, "I don't." He took an appallingly large swallow of milk. "I guess I'm just dumb, or way too weak. No matter how hard I try, I just *can't* hold on. Every day I go to the exercise room, grab on to the bar, and Pallin tries to pry me loose." He sighed. "Does it every time. And he keeps saying I've got to think about my strength being a river, all running down my arm and pooling in the hand that's hanging on, but you know what? That don't—doesn't—make any sense at all! Rivers don't hang on."

"Indeed they do not," Lina agreed seriously. "But perhaps Pallin only wishes you to understand that strength is a fluid thing. A—a variable."

Gordy stared at her blankly. "That doesn't make sense either," he decided. "You're either strong or you're not. I'm pretty fast, but Pallin says I've got to learn to hold on before I learn how to hit back or run."

"Ah," Lina murmured, momentarily stumped. She picked up her teacup and glanced at the third member of the dinner party.

Priscilla sat with her hands curved around a cup of coffee,

her eyes plumbing the dark depths. She had put her dinner aside untasted and had appeared lost in her own thoughts. But now she looked up, giving the boy frowning attention. "I know something that might help," she said softly. "It might sound silly to you, but it works."

"I'll try *any*thing," Gordy said, thumping his glass on the table for emphasis. "Nothing can be sillier than trying to think about a river making you strong."

Priscilla smiled faintly and sipped coffee. "To do this," she said slowly, "you should close your eyes and sit up straight, but not stiffly, and take two deep breaths."

He followed her instructions, shifting to set both feet on the floor and squaring his round shoulders.

Lina froze, regarding both with Healer's senses. Gordy radiated trust and boy-love, untainted by alarm. And Priscilla . . .

Gone were the grays and browns of unjoy, the coldness of unbelonging. Priscilla was a flame—a torch—of assurance, compassion. It was as if a door hidden within a dark and joyless cellar had been flung open to the full glory of a sun. Lina watched as Priscilla extended herself and surrounded the child's love and trust, saw her pluck one well-anchored thread of confidence from the glittering array of Gordy's emotions and expertly begin the weaving.

"Now," she said, and it seemed to Lina that her voice had also taken on depth; a vibrancy that had not been there a heartbeat before. "You're going to become a tree, Gordy. First think of a tree—a strong, vigorous tree at the height of its growth. A tree no wind will bend, no snow will break."

The boy's brows pulled together. "Like Korval's Tree."

"Yes," Priscilla agreed, still in that supremely assured voice, "exactly like Korval's Tree. Think of it alive, with its roots sunk deep into the soil, pulling strength from the ground, rain from the sky. Think hard upon this prince of trees. Walk close to it in your thoughts. Lay your hand upon its trunk. Smell the greenness, the strength of it." She paused, watching Gordy's face closely.

Lina carefully set her cup aside, watching the weaving with amazement, A Master of the Hall of Healers would do exactly what Priscilla was . . .

The boy's face went from concentration to pleasure. "It's my *friend*."

"Your friend," Priscilla reiterated. "Your second self. Walk closer. Lean your back against the trunk. Feel how strong your friend is. Lean closer; let the Tree take you, make you one with it. Feel how strong you are—you and your friend. Your back like a trunk, the strength running in you drawn up from the deep—clean, green, absolutely certain strength. You're so strong . . ."

There was a small silence as Gordy sat, face joyful, wrapped in love, taking the image into himself. Lina heard the image strike home then, with a chime so pure that outer ears could not have heard it, and felt it click into place in the next instant. Priscilla withdrew slowly; Lina could see nothing in the fabric of the boy's pattern to indicate the new weaving.

Beside her, Priscilla extended a hand to sketch a sign in the air before the boy's face.

"It's time to say good-bye to your friend now, Gordy. Take another shared breath . . . take a step . . . another . . . you may come to visit as often as you like. Your friend will always welcome you."

She picked up her coffee cup and took a sip. "Don't you want dessert, Gordy?" she asked, and her voice was entirely normal.

The boy's lashes lifted. He grinned. "Pretty good," he said, still grinning. "Do it for me again tomorrow?"

She lifted her brows. "Me? I didn't do anything, Gordy. You did it. All you have to do is close your eyes and think about your Tree whenever you need to renew your strength." She smiled. "Try it on Pallin tomorrow."

"Crelm! Won't he be surprised when he *can't* yank me loose?" Gordy laughed, then glanced at the clock. "Guess I won't have dessert, though. Got to get to the meeting room and make sure everything's okay before the crew gets there. See you later, Lina! Thanks, Priscilla!" He was gone.

"Will it work?" Lina asked carefully.

Priscilla smiled. "It usually does. A small spell, but very useful. It's one of the first things an Initiate's taught when she's brought to the Circle for training."

"Spell?" She was unsure of the word. Inwardly, Priscilla had shielded the flame, not hidden it. Lina wondered if her friend yet understood.

"That's what it's called at—on Sintia," Priscilla was saying apologetically. "A spell. Other people would call it hypnotism, maybe, or voice tricks and psychology. Whatever the right name is, it *does* work. The image is so easy and so strong." She smiled again.

"Is it so important for an—Initiate?—to be strong?" Lina wondered, feeling her way, taking care to keep all incoming paths open in case the other should reach out, Healer to Healer.

Priscilla sipped coffee and nodded. "Learning to make decisions, learning to use your voice, the power symbols . . . and later, the larger magics that might require the woven concentration of ten or twelve of the Circle. It's very important to be strong."

Lina tipped her head, groping for the best phrasing. The chime announcing the end of the prime sliced across her thoughts.

Priscilla stood and held out a slim hand. "Come to the meeting with me, friend?"

Lina smiled and slid her hand into her friend's larger one. The inner roads were empty. Priscilla would not approach her that way. "Of course," she murmured, standing. "We should also save a seat for poor Rah Stee. He is always late."

Janice had been stoic.

Yes, she understood the reason for her dismissal. Negligence of duty was a serious matter. No, she did not think she would accept a position as shuttle pilot on one of Korval's lesser ships, though she appreciated the captain's offer. She had friends on Angelus, fourth planet in the system they had just entered; she thought she would pay them a visit before looking for another job. After a small silence, she offered the opinion that Mendoza was a damn good pilot—ripe for first class.

Shan nodded, counting out the coins that bought back her contract. Janice informed him that she was packed and could leave the *Passage* immediately. She had no good-byes to say.

Again Shan nodded as he flipped a toggle and spoke quietly to Seth in the shuttlebay. Janice's departure was scheduled for Fourteenth Hour. They would be within shuttle distance of Angelus then.

The door chimed, and he whirled about, snapping to his feet. "Come!"

Kayzin Ne'Zame entered the room, checked, and bowed profoundly. "Captain."

"If you've come to remind me that I'm to attend the crew meeting, Kayzin, you'd no need. My memory is quite sharp, though I daresay it will begin to deteriorate very soon."

Covering her shock, her face neutral, she bowed again.

Shan sighed sharply and strode past her to the bar. Glancing over his shoulder as he poured a cup of misravot, he strove for a happier tone. "Kayzin? Will you drink?"

"Thank you," she said formally, "but no." She waited until he turned his face to her fully before continuing. "If it does not offend, Captain, I ask to walk with you. There is a thing to be discussed. A matter of reassignment of duty, to accommodate the lack of a second mate."

"Very well." He moved to the door and bowed her through before him. That was highly improper: rank earned *him* that privilege. But what could she do when he waved at her so imperiously?

"The case is," Kayzin pursued through her prickling hurt, "that the third mate does not wish promotion to second. He feels he lacks the proper qualifications, that his reaction time is insufficient to demands such as those present upon the bridge this shift just passed." She paused. Shan said nothing.

"I agree with his assessment of his strengths—and his weaknesses. He is willing to extend his hand to those duties of administration for which the second mate is responsible." She looked up at him gravely. "It is the first mate's recommendation to the captain that this be done. For a short time. And conditionally."

"The captain hears," Shan said unencouragingly. "The conditions?"

Another nuance had developed in the symphony of emotion that was Kayzin. A chilly fogging . . . embarrassment, Shan identified, and was amazed.

"In view of the first mate's imminent retirement," she said levelly, "and the lack of a second mate, coupled with the third mate's inability to step into that position, it is in the best in-

terest of the ship that another be trained in the line of command as soon as may be. I request that the captain assign
Priscilla Mendoza to the first mate, that she may be strenu-
ously schooled in the duties of the second."

"Reasoning, please."

"She has the ability. You yourself placed her in a training
position. I admit that track is not as rigorous as this proposed
will be. However, it has been my observation that Priscilla
Mendoza possesses a strong character, quick understanding,
and sure judgment. I believe she may do well for the ship,
were she but offered the means. And if she does not," Kayzin
shrugged, "the ship is no worse off than it is at this present."

"There is a phenomenon which Terrans call 'personality
conflict.' The captain has seen indications of this phenomenon between the first mate and Priscilla Mendoza."

"The first mate has mastered herself."

Shan nodded. "Your recommendations have merit. They
will be put into effect tomorrow First Hour, assuming Ms.
Mendoza's acquiescence. The captain will require from the
first mate a daily report of training and progress—or lack."
He paused at the door of the meeting room and bowed. "Forgive my hapless tongue, old friend. I regret having caused you
pain."

Her relief was like a puff of Arsdredi smoke. She smiled
and returned his bow. "It is forgotten."

"By both," he answered properly, and preceded her into the
room.

Shan leaned back in his chair and sipped. The room was full.
Those of the crew whose duties prevented their physical presence watched by monitor from their stations. The general
hubbub indicated good spirits and confidence.

He considered his inner Wall, then carefully allowed the
merest slit to part its impenetrable fabric.

Hot, scintillating, brilliant iciness assaulted him. He took a
breath, narrowed the slit, and began a Sort of the larger

threads, flickering among webs of burning color, neither apart from nor completely of them.

Satisfied, he closed the slit, took some wine, and held it for a moment in a mouth dry with effort. The crew was outraged, of course, by the attack. But there was no trace of panic, of terror.

They were certain of their ship—of their captain.

He wished he shared their certainty.

He moved a hand, and the room's lights dimmed as the central screen glowed to life. The crew's chatter died.

"You are all aware," Shan began conversationally, "of the day's *second* Jump alarm. I'd like you to watch a tape of what led up to the pilot's activation of the alarm." From the corner of his eye he saw Priscilla start. Lina reached out, and the taller woman settled back, her expression wary.

"We're at minus twenty seconds of the final transition from the scheduled Jump. Pilot Mendoza is at the board. Now—normal space."

COLLISION COURSE the screen shouted as Priscilla's hands flickered, hitting the screens up. "First defense barriers active." HOSTILE ACTION "Second screens up, coords fed, alarm on. We're waiting for the coils to come back up. Coils up and we're ready to go." On the screen his own hand stopped completion of the exercise. The action froze and faded as the room lights came on.

"Reaction time." Shan said for the benefit of the pilots watching. "From time of first warning to full defense: one and one-half seconds. From full defense to Jump-ready, two seconds. We were ready to depart twenty-four seconds after the initial alarm. Most of that time was spent waiting for the coils to renew themselves."

The silence in the meeting room was broken by the soft flutter of pilot hands over imaginary boards as pilot brains counted seconds.

Over to the right, Seth stood. Shan nodded to him.

"Yes?"

"I move that Priscilla Mendoza be given an up-share

bonus. She got us out of a tough one. That bomb was right on the drive sections. Would've done real damage if it'd hit."

Rusty was on his feet before Seth was off his. "Second."

"Third," Ken Rik said. "And a call for ship-points, Captain. The debt lies there."

Gil Don Balatrin seconded that diffidently.

Shan nodded. "Any comments? Disapprovals? Discussions? No? Show of hands, in favor?

"First Mate?"

"Unanimous, Captain."

"So I counted, also. Thank you." He initialed a paper on his pad. "Recorded and done." He smiled slightly over the room. "Also recorded and done—two points hazard pay for all crew, payable at Solcintra. More business?"

There was none.

"Thank you. Dismissed."

There was tension in the air, prickling the short hairs on her arm. She focused her attention on the tapestry over the bar.

"Brandy, Priscilla?"

She started, then managed a smile. "Thank you."

"You're welcome." He handed her the glass and went by, heading for the desk.

She followed and settled into the right-hand chair, with the tension still singing around her.

The captain took a sip of his drink. "Gordy tells me you've taught him to be a tree," he commented. "I don't say it's a *bad* idea, Priscilla. I only wonder how his mother will react if I deliver him into her arms all green and leafy."

Laughter escaped her, softly. "No, an inner tree. Pallin keeps telling Gordy to think of his strength as a river. But Gordy believes that strong is strong, without variation."

"I see." The light eyes were speculative. He inclined his head. "It was kind of you, Priscilla. Thank you for your care of my kinsman."

She moved a hand in a gesture learned from the tapes Lina

had provided. "It's not a *kindness*. I like him. He reminds me of Brand—my younger brother—the last time I saw him."

"My sympathy to you. But perhaps you'll find he's grown into a young gentleman when you go home next. I remember when that particular metamorphosis overtook Val Con." He laughed, and the tension shimmered. "*Truly* terrifying."

She laughed also, softly and unconvincingly. Sipping, she noticed an undercurrent of warm admiration such as she had not felt since her days as a Sister at Temple.

"The reason I asked you to come to me," the captain was saying, "is to discuss the new administrative structure of the ship."

She waited.

He sighed. "Janice Weatherbee has left us, leaving the post of second mate vacant. A problem, you will admit. The third mate has been approached and has graciously—one might say with comic haste—declined the promotion. The first mate has thus applied to the captain for another trainee." He leveled a blunt forefinger. "You."

"Me?" She stared at him. "I'm not qualified to be second mate."

"Did I say you were? I do beg your pardon, Priscilla. What I meant to say was that Kayzin had asked me to assign you to her so she could teach you to be second mate. What *is* the phrase? My dreadful, dreadful memory—aha!" He snapped his fingers. "On-the-job training."

To tension and admiration was added confusion. Priscilla drank. "I don't—why me?"

"Why not you? You were in the track already, after all. I do admit that the training Kayzin proposes will be more demanding, but it's the same training. Merely a difference in intensity." He stopped. "Kayzin is a very good teacher, Priscilla. She's been on the *Passage* for over fifty years, first mate for thirty. And she handled much of my own training, thankless task that it was."

Priscilla took a breath. "She dislikes me."

"No. She distrusted you, I believe. But I also believe that

it's passed. Even if it hasn't, Kayzin is not one to let mere personal prejudice stand in the way of doing the best she can for the ship." He sipped, eyes quizzical. "Well, Priscilla? Do you want the job?"

Want the job? Like she wanted breath. Shocked, she looked within and found the same surety that had allowed Gordy to find the Tree. "Yes," she said.

"Good. Now, then, there are a few things to be explained." He paused, then nodded. "First, it is imperative that you acquire your first class license. You will come to the bridge every day immediately following your duty shift. I'll teach you. There's no reason why you shouldn't be a first class pilot by the time we reach Solcintra."

She considered it. "Shan?"

The tension altered in some indefinable way, though the warmth was constant. "Yes, Priscilla?"

"Won't it work out . . ." She sighed and began again. "The captain."

"What of the captain, my friend?"

"If I'm to report for piloting lessons on my first off-shift, won't the captain be pulling a triple shift?"

"Occasionally." He grinned. "The captain's made of stern stuff. When I was learning the ship, I often ran double shifts, between tutoring from Kayzin and tutoring from my father—and then stayed up half the sleep shift studying for the next day." He tipped his head. "Do you object to the captain's instruction, Priscilla?"

"No, of course not . . ." She felt an echo of tension and an echo of warmth. The echo would overwhelm her if she did not take care.

"Fine, then that's settled. Other points: Second mate signs a standard ship contract. That means you'll no longer be under my protection, but under the protection of the *Dutiful Passage* . . ."

Not under his protection? Panic added a sheen of ice to the echoes. No longer to be under Korval's wing, where there was comfort and friendship and aid? To be cast out? To be—

"Priscilla." His voice was a flame of common sense, licking at the ice. "The *Passage* is owned and operated by Clan Korval. A ship's contract guarantees you assistance that a personal contract with Shan yos'Galan cannot. You will, of course, read it before you sign it."

"Yes, of course . . ." Feeling foolish, she drank.

"You'll want to know the rate of pay." He tapped on the keypad as he turned the screen to face her. "Second mate draws three cantra flat for the short run, plus one-half ship-share. Bonuses and increments—not applicable at present. You will, of course, be starting at the low end. We've got four months to go, so that's prorated . . . plus the amount owed under previous contract . . . crew's hazard pay . . . ship's points, can't forget them . . . oh, and the upshare . . . subtract ship-debt. Well, some of this can't be finalized until we hit Liad, but I think that's everything, Priscilla: the minimum. Is the sum agreeable to you?"

It was staggering. The glowing amber letters named more money than she had ever seen at once. Enough to repurchase her bartered bracelets three times over. She could buy a hundred hours for Lina and herself, and still there would be money for clothing, for books, for tapes, for lodging, for food. It might be more money than she had made in her life . . . for one trip!

"That can't—*can't*—be right."

"Can't it?" Shan frowned and turned the screen around. "Well, then, let's do it again. Base pay for second, prorated . . ."

She felt wave after wave of emotion: admiration, nervousness, exhilaration, exhaustion. Priscilla felt herself expanding under the assault, taking it in, sending it out, over and over. The exhilaration built, as it had not built since she and Moonhawk . . .

Moonhawk was dead.

And the echoes came faster, where there should never have been sound. Where there could be no motion. Dear Goddess . . . she pictured the Tree. She took a breath, hearing

Shan's voice as he muttered the figures over and leaned into the familiarity—the comfort—of it. The Tree had worked. The Gyre might work, as well.

She began the opening sequence and felt the image click into place and take on its own momentum. Thank you, Goddess. She would need to be in her quarters within the hour. Sleep was the room beyond Serenity: the end of the Gyre's dance.

"No, Priscilla, I'm afraid the figure is correct. You do have to realize that this is the short run, and that we're less than four months out of Solcintra. If you renew your contract at the end of the trip, you'll net more. Simple matter of mathematics. You'll be on from beginning to end, and the next trip's the long one. Takes a year to finish the circuit. Priscilla?"

She had passed through the First and Second Doors. The next was the Door to Serenity, where she would abide awhile before she came to Sleep.

"The sum is more than adequate, Captain," she murmured. "I was surprised because it seemed like such a lot of money."

"Oh, well, the *Passage* is the flagship of Korval's fleet, after all. You wouldn't want us to pay on the same scale as an ore shuttle, would you?"

"No, Captain." Serenity was in sight . . . then achieved. Priscilla took a relaxed breath and a drink.

Across from her, the captain stiffened: he shook his head sharply and stood. "I think those are the important points, Priscilla. You'll begin your training with Kayzin at First Hour. I will see you on the bridge for pilot training at Sixth. There will be a copy of the second mate's contract on your screen when you wake. Good night."

Such abruptness was hardly like him. But he must be tired, too, she thought, and offered him a smile as she bowed.

"Good night, Captain." The door closed behind her, and Shan's knees gave way. He hit the chair with a gasp and hid his face in his hands.

He mastered himself with an effort, levered out of the

chair, and turned toward the red-striped door to his personal quarters. Then he stopped.

Turning away, he crossed the room and went down the hall.

The crew hall was quiet and dimly lit: a blessing to his pounding head. He found the door by instinct and laid his hand against the plate.

For a moment he despaired. She was not there . . . The door slid aside. Honey-brown eyes blinked up at him. "Shan?" Then she slid her arm about his waist and drew him within. "My poor friend! What has happened? Ahh, denubia . . ."

Allowing himself to be seated on the bed, he pushed his face into the warm hollow between her shoulder and neck and he felt the Healing begin.

"She shut me out, Lina. Twice, she shut me *out*."

The contract was extremely clear; attached was an addendum providing the amount the second mate was due at Solcintra and the formula by which it had been figured. The addendum stated that the sum was not fixed and would be refigured upon final docking using the same formula and taking into account any additional bonuses, finder's fees, shippoints, or debts.

Priscilla placed her hand against the screen and felt the slight electric prickle against her palm as the machine recorded the print. *Beep!* Contract sealed.

Her hand curled into a loose fist as she took it away from the screen; she stared at it. Then, grinning, she turned to put on her shirt.

Lina's door was opening as Priscilla rounded the corner; she lengthened her stride.

"Good morning."

"Priscilla! Well met, my friend. I thought myself exiled to eating this meal alone, so slugabed have I been!"

It had done her good, Priscilla thought. Lina was glowing; eyes sparkling, mouth softly curving, she radiated satisfied pleasure. "You're beautiful," she said suddenly, reaching out to take a small golden hand.

Lina laughed. "As much as it naturally must grieve me to differ with a friend, I feel it necessary to inform you that among the Clans one is judged to be but moderately attractive."

"Blind people," Priscilla muttered, and Lina laughed again.

"But I have heard you are to begin as second mate in only an hour!" she said gaily. "Ge'shada, denubia. Kayzin is very careful, but she is not a warm person. It is her way. Do not regard it."

"No, I won't," Priscilla agreed, looking at her friend in awe.

"It is a shame that you will not have time to come regularly to the pet library now," Lina was rattling on. "You have done so much good there. I never thought to see the younger sylfok tamed at all. Others have remarked the difference there as well. Why, Shan said only this morning—"

Priscilla gasped against the flare of pain, and flung away from jealousy toward serenity— To find her way barred and a small hand tight around her wrist as Lina cried out, "Do not!"

She froze, within and without. "All right."

"Good." Lina smiled. "Shan and I are old friends, Priscilla. Who else might he come to, when he was injured and in need? And you—denubia, you must not shield yourself so abruptly, without the courtesy of a warning! It *hurts*. Surely you know . . . surely your instructors never taught you to treat a fellow Healer so?"

"Fellow—" She struggled with it and surrendered to the first absurdity. "Do you mean you're open *all the time?*"

Lina blinked. "Should I huddle behind the Wall forever, afraid to use what is mine? Do you deliberately choose blindness, rather than use your eyes? I am a Healer! How else should I be but open?"

Priscilla was bombarded with puzzlement-affection-exasperation-lingering pleasure. She fought for footing against the onslaught and heard her friend sigh.

"There is no need to befuddle yourself. Can you close partially? It is not this moment necessary for you to scan every nuance."

She found the technique and fumbled it into place like a novice. The pounding broadcast faded into the background. She took a breath, her mind already busy with the second absurdity. "Shan is a . . . Healer? A *man?*"

Lina's mouth curved in a creampot smile. "It is very true that Shan is a man," she murmured, while Priscilla felt the green knife twist in her again. "It is also true that he is a trained and skilled Healer. Do I love you less, denubia, because I also love others?"

"No . . ." She took another breath, pursuing the absurdity. "It—on Sintia. men, even those initiated to the Circle, are not Soulweavers. It's taught that they don't have the ability."

"Perhaps on Sintia they do not," Lina commented dryly. "Shan is Liaden, after all, and Sintia's teaching has not yet reached us. Those of us who may bear it are taught to pay attention, to use the information provided by each of our senses. Shan is not one of those who may do nothing but learn to erect the Wall and keep their sanity by never looking beyond; nor am I. And it hurts, denubia, to be in rapport with someone, only to be—without cause and without warning—shut out. You must not do so again. An emergency is another matter: you act to save yourself. Should you find that you must shield yourself from another Healer, it is proper to say, 'Forgive me, I require privacy,' before going behind the Wall."

Priscilla hung her head. "I didn't mean to hurt him. I meant to *shield* him. I thought I was generating a—false echo, because I was tired."

Reassurance, warmth, and affection flowed in. Priscilla

felt her chest muscles loosen and looked up to find Lina smiling.

"He knows that the hurt was not deliberate. The best balance is simply not to do it again." She held out a hand. "Come, we will have to gulp our food!"

Taam Olanek took another appreciative sip of ex-cellent brandy. Nova yos'Galan had been called from the party some minutes ago. "Business," she had murmured to El-dema Glodae, with whom she had been speaking. Olanek al-lowed himself the indulgence of wondering what sort of business might keep the First Speaker of Liad's first Clan—why, after all, dress the thing up in party clothes?—so long from the entertainment of which she was host.

True, there was Lady Anthora, barely out of university and comporting herself with the ease of one ten years her senior. She was at present listening with pretty gravity to Lady yo'Hatha. He toyed with the idea of rescuing the child from the old woman's clutches, but even as he did, Anthora man-aged the thing with a grace that filled him with admiration. Not the beauty her sister was—too full of breast and hip for the general taste—but no lack of brains or flair.

No lack of that sort in any of them, Olanek admitted to himself. Even the gargoyle eldest had wit sharp enough to cut.

Their fault—collectively and individually—lay in their youth. Gods willing, they would outgrow, or outmaneuver, that particular failing without mishap, and Korval would continue bright and unwavering upon its pinnacle.

While Plemia continued its slow descent into oblivion.

Olanek sipped irritably. It seemed somehow unjust.

"Eldema Olanek?" a soft, seductive voice said at his elbow. He turned and made his bow, no deeper than was strictly necessary, but without resentment. That she should address him as First Speaker rather than Lord Olanek or Delm Plemia was worthy of note.

He smiled. "Eldema yos'Galan. How may I serve you?"

"By your patience, sir," Nova murmured, pale lips curving in what passed for her smile. "I deeply regret the need. Is it possible that you might allow a moment of business to intrude upon your pleasure?"

Odder and odder. He inclined his head. "I am entirely at your disposal." Clearly Nova wished to treat with him as a colleague. Now, why should Korval wish to discuss business with Plemia when they moved in such different spheres? And why at such a time, in the midst of this vast and enjoyable entertainment? Why not a call to his office tomorrow morning? Surely the matter was not so urgent as that?

Still, he walked with her from the room, declining to have his glass refreshed. They went side by side and silent down the wide hallway to another, where the woman turned right.

This portion of the house was older, Olanek saw. Its doors were of wood, with large, ornate knobs set into their centers. Nova yos'Galan stopped at the second, turned the knob, and stepped aside, bowing him in before her.

The gesture was graceful—one could not accuse Korval of flattery. What could they possibly gain? Olanek inclined his head and passed through.

He stopped just inside to consider the room. It was a study or office, warm with wood and patterned crimson carpeting. Korval's device, the venerable Tree and Dragon, hung above the flickering hearth. He took a step toward the fire, heard a rustle, and turned instead to face his host.

She gestured an apology—a flicker of slender hands—and moved to the desk. Olanek followed.

"If you would have the kindness to read this message. I should say that it has been pin-beamed and arrived only recently."

GREETINGS FROM CAPTAIN SHAN YOS'GALAN TO ELDEMA NOVA YOS'GALAN, the bright amber letters read. It was a formal beginning for a message from brother to sister, surely—but this was business. Olanek sipped his remaining brandy and read further.

Finished, he stood silently. When he did speak, it was in icy outrage and in the highest possible dialect. "Plemia is not diverted by the jest, Eldema. We demand—"

"No," she interrupted composedly, "you do not. It is conceivable that my brother could frame and execute such a jest. It is not conceivable that he would bring formal charge in this manner, as captain of the *Dutiful Passage*, begging guidance from his First Speaker." She drew breath, and the sapphire rope glittered about her throat. "My brother is not a fool, Eldema. He understands actions and the consequences of actions. As was shown, I think, when he was himself First Speaker.

"You should know that Mr. dea'Gauss was on the bridge of the *Passage* at the time of the attack. I leave it to you to judge whether he, at least, would be party to such a thing, were not every reported particular correct."

"I would speak with Mr. dea'Gauss."

"Of course," she replied calmly. "I have sent word, recalling him for that purpose."

"It might be wise for you to recall your brother's ship as well," he suggested ominously.

She raised her brows. "I see no cause. The route is nearly done. Captain yos'Galan has received the tuition of his First Speaker, as requested. For this present, of course." She looked at him out of meaningful violet eyes. "It does not need to be said that Plemia will act with honor and good judgment, listening with all ears, seeing with all eyes. Korval depends upon it."

To be thus schooled by a mere child, when he had been First Speaker—aye, and Delm!—longer than she had had breath! He gained control of himself, essayed a small sip of his dwindling refreshment, then inclined his head.

"Plemia wishes only to make judgment for itself, as is proper, before negotiating further with Korval." He paused. "I would ask, if Korval's First Speaker has not yet in her wisdom done this thing, that Captain yos'Galan be . . . entreated . . . to stay his hand until the precise circumstances have been made clear to all concerned."

Nova yos'Galan inclined her fair head. "Such was the essence of the First Speaker's instruction to Captain yos'-Galan. I am certain that Plemia will instruct Captain yo'Vaade in like manner."

"Of course," he said through gritted teeth.

The woman bowed and smiled. "Business is then completed, Eldema. My thanks for the gift of your patience. Do enjoy the rest of the party."

Somehow, Olanek doubted he would.

Kayzın Ne'Zame was a thorough teacher—and a determined one. Priscilla's head felt crammed to the splitting point already. And there was so much more to learn!

She was in a hurry, lest she be late for her piloting lesson with the captain.

The captain! She dodged into the lift and punched the direction for the core and inner bridge. Rattled for the last six hours by a storm of information, she had nearly forgotten about the captain.

He was a Healer—a Soulweaver—though no man she had ever heard of was master of that skill. He was constantly open, always reading, aware . . .

Aware of her emotions. From the very beginning, he had scanned her and touched her feelings—and knew her as intimately as a . . . Sister-in-Power.

No! It was not done. It was improper, blasphemous! The power to read souls came from the Goddess, through Her chosen agents. Moonhawk, who was dead, had been such an agent, and Priscilla Mendoza her willing vessel. To use the power consciously, without divine direction . . .

The door slid open, and Priscilla escaped into the corridor; she dived into the first service hall she saw and froze, heart pounding.

Mother, help me, she cried silently. Help me . . . I'm lost . . .

The Tree, the Gyre, the Room Serenity, the Place of Watching—each had she used within the past day. She, who was nothing and no one, save that once a saint had lived within her.

Heedless of time, she closed her eyes and quested in the Inner Places, where the Old One's soul had sung in time gone past.

Moonhawk?

Silence surrounded the echo of the thought. There was no one there but Priscilla.

Priscilla knew no magic.

Magic had worked. She held to that thought and opened her eyes. Three times—four!—magic had worked. And the promise she had given Lina had held no taint of unsurety. She would not close the captain out. She would hold the Hood ready to muffle any strong outburst and spare him as much pain as she could.

The hour bell sounded, and she gasped.

Tarlin Skepelter, on her way to Service Hall 28 to replace a faulty sensor, was treated to the interesting sight of the new second mate running at top speed away from her, toward the inner bridge.

"No! Completely useless!"

She knew it before he said so and barely caught the blaze of self-fury in time to muffle it. Beside her, the captain snapped forward and swept his big hand across the board. He was out of his chair in a blur and towering over her.

"Are you *angry,* Priscilla?"

She winced at the volume and kept a firm hold on the Hood. "Yes."

"Then be angry! You're a better pilot than that! *Gordy's*

better than that! Of all the inexcusable, sloppy, *ground~ grubber* piloting I have ever seen—"

"And I suppose you could do better—keeping the board in half your mind and watching for echoes, too!"

"Did I tell you to watch for echoes? I told you to mind that board, Pilot! If you can't keep your whole mind right there and nowhere else, we'll suspend all lessons, now! I'll not have this ship endangered because the pilot at the board was thinking about some thing besides the business at hand!" He was a glittering buzz of anger. Priscilla fielded it unconsciously, even as the hold on her own rage slipped.

"I didn't ask to be on the board with a full-open empath! What am I supposed to do? Forget about the spill? What about—"

"Yes! That's precisely what you're supposed to do! Damn it—" He slammed into the copilot's chair and flung his hands out. "Priscilla, am I made of glass? Will I break, do you think, at the touch of a little well-earned self-rage?"

She was silent, seething without attempting to contain it.

The captain sighed, his pattern now containing less anger than frustration overlaying interest-admiration-warmth-friendship. "I'm not wide open, Priscilla. I don't need to be. You're coming through quite clearly without it. Also, I am not a cretin. I can adjust the level of reception, if things are so intense I find my mind wandering. Further, I am a pilot! I've worked with *dozens* of people since I began training. One of the finest pilots I ever knew was terrified every moment of duty. Another I worked with fairly often was as nearly asleep as she could be, no matter what the emergency—and her reactions were perfect. Ask her why she had done a certain thing, though, and she'd panic . . ." He shifted, offering a smile. "I'm not fragile, friend. My word on it."

It was a temptation to extend herself, to grasp his warmth and cuddle it about her. She shook her head. "I—Lina said that—Healers are open, except for emergency. On—I was taught to remain closed unless Soul-weaving was required, and to return to Serenity once the duty was done."

His response was outraged puzzlement. "Then how do you make love?"

"It's not for that!"

The captain moved his shoulders. "Forgive me, Priscilla. It seems our training has been very different. For *this* training, however, please be assured that I can take care of myself—except against slamming doors! You are here for lessons in piloting. The next time we meet, I expect your mind to be only on piloting! If you choose to remain outside of Serenity, then don't try to damp every little twitch of irritation or jubilation. If you wish to be closed, then please make sure you are behind your Wall before you arrive."

He stood. "Today's lesson is done. I'll see you tomorrow, Priscilla."

Taam Olanek was finding the way to truth uneasy. Even the testimony of so irreproachable a witness as Mr. dea'Gauss was insufficient to rescue him from his quandary.

In charity, Nova sat silent, though they had covered the salient points again and again. She found patience for the task by recalling the countless times Shan had befuddled her. When the charm of these palled, she could begin to list the occasions on which he had sent their father into fury with his ways.

All the world knew of the unpredictability of Thodelm yos'Galan. Recrimination was useless, of course. To remind Shan of his position as Head of Line yos'Galan was to invite a blizzard of outrageous behavior, all calculated, one would swear, to bring her to the blush.

But it never had been said that Thodelm yos'Galan was less than honorable.

Still, she thought, how much easier, in Taam Olanek's place, might it be to suppose that Shan had crossed finally into dishonor than to believe that Plemia had fired upon Korval?

"This person Mendoza," Olanek said to Mr. dea'Gauss now. "I do not properly understand, I think. Who is she, sir? What is her claim in the matter?"

So, they were at last beyond Shan and into deeper questions. Matters were progressing, she assured herself. Well and good.

Mr. dea'Gauss cleared his throat. "Lady Mendoza is of a high House on the world of Sintia, in the Thardom Sector. Ship's records indicate that she has been offered reasoned harm by Clan Plemia, in the person of Sav Rid Olanek. Or by those to whom he stands as lord. Verification is being sought. I am certain, however, that we will find the records from the *Dutiful Passage* accurate." He paused.

Delm Plemia inclined his head with Nova's silent approval. A lesser person would have murmured "Of course" to Mr. dea'Gauss in such a face. Plemia merely awaited further explanation.

It came. "There appear to be considerations of melant'i involved. Lady Mendoza is of Terran extraction; thus, it may be some while before matters become sensible. Word has been sent to House Mendoza, informing them of the situation as it was before my return to Llad. A response has not yet reached me. In the interim, Lady Mendoza is content to walk Korval's path, so I speak for her, as well."

"Her position?" Olanek pursued. "Some melant'i must be obvious, sir. For an instance: here it is said that she serves under personal contract. Do I learn from this that Captain yos'Galan extends the protection of Korval entire to a pleasure-love?"

A reasonable question, Nova admitted, from one unfamiliar with Shan's habit of rescuing every lame puppy and kitten in the galaxy. Certainly nothing so untoward that Mr. dea'-Gauss should stiffen and draw sharp breath.

"At the time of my departure," he informed Plemia in accents of ice, "Lady Mendoza served the *Dutiful Passage* in the capacities of apprentice d second mate and second class pilot. It was she who was the pilot of duty when the attack came against the *Passage*, and she who prevented damage and life-loss. That she honors Captain yos'Galan with her friendship is clear. Lady Faaldom enjoys like regard. The person we speak of could bestow no honorless esteem."

Great gods, what a paean! Nova very nearly stared at Korval's man of business.

Taam Olanek gestured peace, light sliding off the bright enamel work of his Clan ring. "I meant no disrespect to the lady or to the captain, sir. In the service of clarity, the question demanded asking. You yourself mentioned complications of melant'i."

Mr. dea'Gauss inclined his head. "Melant'i enters in another guise, sir. Information from House Mendoza will no doubt make matters more obvious. Are there other questions that demand the asking? Is there a way in which I might serve you further?"

Olanek wiped his screen with a sharp wrist twist and sighed. "I believe the questions remaining are those best asked of my kin. Eldema, I will go to *Daxflan* and ascertain what has, and what has not, been done. I ask, in the interest of both Korval and Plemia, that Mr. dea'Gauss be allowed to accompany me."

"I am," the old gentleman murmured, as one giving just warning, "Korval's eyes and ears."

"For that reason do I crave your company. sir. You are known as a person of long sight and careful counsel. In such a tangle as this, it is wisdom to see that Plemia will require both."

"Korval," Nova said calmly, "has no objection."

Mr. dea'Gauss caught her eye for a brief moment; almost it seemed that he smiled. He inclined his head to Olanek, gesturing his willingness to serve. "I am ready to travel at Plemia's word."

Priscilla came to him with pilot grace, one slim hand extended, a smile of dawning delight upon her face. Scarcely breathing, he waited, dizzy and joy-filled. She had erected no Wall, shut no door—and this her choice, freely made! He turned his face into the caress, eyelashes kissing her palm even as he moved outside his own defenses.

There was an intake of breath, expelled on soft laughter.

"Shan . . ." Her hand slid along the other cheek, cupping his face for enrapt inspection. The feeling sang between them, soaring unbearably. He felt his heart pounding and knew that hers kept pace.

She kissed him.

For a frenzied heartbeat he simply stood there, prisoned in reflected rapture, then he felt her question and turned his mouth more sharply; he stroking her body closer to his as their shared songs twisted each about the other, creating one.

An alarm began to scream.

She started—and was gone, even as he tried to hold her. "Priscilla!"

His own cry woke him, though the alarm's din was louder.

Snapping around in the tumbled bed, he slammed a violent palm against the shutoff and collapsed, eyes screwed tight against the rising lights. "Damn, damn, damn, *damn!*"

The music came up: Artelma's "Festival Delights," rendered with passion on the omnichora, by his brother Val Con.

"Damn," Shan said once more, and headed for the 'fresher.

Some time later he passed through the dining hall on his way back from the cargo master's office. Ken Rik had been a bit less testy this morning. Perhaps he was getting over his pet at Mr. dea'Gauss's abrupt summons back to Liad.

Priscilla and Rusty were sitting with their heads together at a corner table. Belly tight with jealousy, he helped himself to a cup of coffee and a ripe strafle melon.

Healer! he jeered at himself. You can't even control your own emotions. And what does she project that you dare be jealous? Friendship? Those small bursts of appreciation, of comfort perceived, of desire . . . He drew a hard breath and bit into the fruit with a snap. Those are the sorts of things one might feel about anyone. Do strive for some conduct, Shan.

"How do, Cap'n!" BillyJo greeted him from the door of the galley. "You'll be havin' a real breakfast, won't you? Can't live 'til luncheon on an apple."

He grinned at her, talked a few moments about kitchen operations, accepted the sweet roll she pressed upon him, and refilled his cup. He left the dining hall by the side door, resolutely keeping his eyes away from the private corner.

The message-waiting light was blinking on the captain's screen. He put the sweet roll on the edge of the bar and hit GO as he slid into the chair.

No more pin-beams from his sister, he noted. That was one fear laid to rest. He sipped coffee and scanned the directly. Nothing urgent. Well, tag the letter from Dortha Cayle. Maybe this time they had a deal. What was this?

A pin-beam from Sintia, directed to Mr. dea'Gauss?

He queried the item, frowning, found it was in reply to a

message sent, and called it up, his memory stirring. Priscilla was from a powerful family, wasn't that it? Mr. dea'Gauss had wished to apprise them of circumstances.

TO DEA'GAUSS CARE OF TRADE VESSEL *DUTIFUL PASSAGE*. FROM HOUSE MENDOZA CIRCLE RIVER SINTIA. RE QUERY PRISCILLA DELACROIX Y MENDOZA. DAUGHTER OF HOUSE BEARING THAT NAME BORN (LOCAL) YEAR 986, COMMENDED TO GODDESS (LOCAL) YEAR 1002. MESSAGE ENDS.

He stared at the screen. "Commended to the Goddess"? *Dead?* His heart stuttered as he thought of Priscilla dead, then he shook his head sharply.

"Don't be stupid, Shan."

He cleared the screen and demanded Priscilla's filed identifications as well as those requested from Terran census as a matter of mindless form.

The figures appeared side by side on the screen: retinal pattern, fingerprints, blood type, gene map.

The woman who called herself Priscilla Delacroix y Mendoza *was* Priscilla Delacroix y Mendoza, to a factor of .999.

A Mendoza of Sintia . . . He remembered the clammy wave of desperation, Priscilla's colorless face, her hand, warding him away: "You mustn't ask . . ."

But Mr. dea'Gauss had asked, damn him, and the answer returned was worse than none at all.

He had an impulse to destroy the message. But he knew that was childish—and useless. If a reply did not arrive within a reasonable time, Mr. dea'Gauss would merely query again.

Well, she was rather active for a corpse. He sipped coffee, staring at nothing in particular. Save the captain. Save the ship . . .

"What in space can she have done?"

He sighed and finished his coffee.

The easiest—simplest—explanation was that she had run away. It was not hard to see how Priscilla might have become disillusioned in a rigid societal structure, with all power belonging to the priestesshood.

So, then. The young Priscilla departs; her family declares

her dead, for honor's sake. What choice, after all, would they have? The local records reflect the "fact."

But Terran census, above mere local politics, still carries one Priscilla Delacroix y Mendoza alive, alive-oh.

Simple. Comforting. Even logical. Except something was missing.

"She could be a criminal," he told the room loudly. "I don't believe it. Lina wouldn't believe it. Mr. dea'Gauss, with no hint of empathy about him, wouldn't believe it. Ah, *hell* . . ."

Local crimes were varied and interesting, as any space traveler could attest. A felony on one planet was conduct that on the next would not cause even the mildest of middle-class grandmothers to blanch.

Ostracism. A crime earning that punishment would have to be extreme.

From world to world there was some variation in the most heinous crimes. Not much.

Kin slaying. Rape. Child stealing. Murder. Mind tampering. Enslavement. Blasphemy.

Murder? She had certainly been ready to wreak mayhem upon Sav Rid Olanek. He retained a vivid memory of that initial interview with its racket of fury, terror, and exhaustion. Murder was possible.

Kin slaying?

Child stealing?

Mind tampering? Enslavement? She was an empath—and a powerful one. Those crimes, too, were possible.

Blasphemy?

He sighed. Wonderful word, blasphemy. It might mean anything.

An exact definition of her crimes was required—for the ship, and for the Clan. Korval owed her much. It was vital that the person to whom the Clan was in debt be known—in fullness. Priscilla Mendoza had demonstrated aboard the *Dutiful Passage* a melant'i both graceful and strong. She had not, however, come into existence two months ago, much as he might wish it. The captain of the *Passage* could order the necessary actions, or Mr. dea'Gauss could order them, for the good of Korval. In either case, Shan yos'Galan's wishes and desires meant nothing. Necessity existed.

Hating necessity, he tapped in a new sequence and turned to issue instructions to the tower.

"**Priscilla?**" **Gordy interrupted apologetically.** "Morning, Rusty. Priscilla, I was thinking. Could you teach me to be a dragon?"

Rusty glowered; she caught the flicker of his irritation and let it pass.

"Dragons are possible," she admitted, considering the radiance of the boy's anticipation, "but very difficult. Some people work for years and never achieve the Dragon. It requires study and discipline." And the soul of a saint? Lina had been at pains these last busy weeks to demonstrate how empaths conducted themselves in the wide universe. Melant'i figured prominently in these lessons. Souls did not.

At her elbow, Gordy sighed. "But *you* know how, don't you?"

Did she? The Dragon was a spell of the Inmost Circle—but Moonhawk's soul was an old one. She had known the way . . .

Before her mind's eye the pattern rolled forth; the Inner

Ear caught the first rasp of leather wings against the air. She took a breath and reversed the pattern.

"Yes," she said, around her own wonder, "I know how. If you truly want to learn, I can begin to teach you. But there's a lot of study between the Tree and the Dragon, Gordy, and no guarantee that you'll be able to master it."

"Could Rusty be a dragon?" Gordy asked, trying perhaps to establish a range.

"I don't *want* to be a dragon," that person announced with spirit. "I like being a radio tech just fine. Don't you have someplace you need to be, kid?"

"Not right now. I've gotta help Ken Rik in twenty minutes. Priscilla, how come not everybody can learn this dragon thing? The Tree's easy."

"So it is." The Tree, the Room Serenity—anyone might learn these. The larger magics? Lina claimed no soul but her own. "The Tree is a very simple spell, Gordy. Only a good thing. The Dragon is both—a weapon and a shield. It's not to be used lightly. You could live a whole life without knowing need great enough to call the Dragon."

He frowned. "You mean the dragon is a good thing *and* a bad thing? That's as goofy as Pallin's river."

"Paradox is powerful magic. The River of Strength is a basic paradox. The Dragon is immensely complex, Gordy. You must learn to balance the good against the evil, the strength that preserves against the fire that consumes. You must be careful that the fire does not consume your will, or sheer strength override your . . . heart. You must not—soar—too close to the sun."

Rusty's uneasiness pierced the wordnet. She pushed away from the table and smiled at them both. "Or be late for your piloting lesson with the captain. Talk with me more later, Gordy. If you're still interested. Rusty, thank you, my friend. I won't see you at prime, I'm afraid. My schedule's blocked out for the next two shifts."

He whistled. "That's some piloting lesson."

"No time with Kayzin Ne'Zame today." She grinned. "A vacation."

Rusty's laughter escorted her to the door.

She reached the shuttlebay before him. Just.

"Good morning, Priscilla! On time, as usual."

"Good morning, Captain."

He stopped in his tracks, swept a bow that the carryall slung over his shoulder should have made impossible. "Second Mate. Good things find you this day. I perceive that I am in disgrace."

"As if it would matter to you if you were!" she retorted, receiving the first rays of his pattern with something akin to thirst. Two weeks ago she would have wondered at such temerity. It was incredible how quickly she had come to depend on a sense that could not be hers.

"It would matter a great deal," he said, waving her into the bay before him. "Nice day for a shuttle trip, don't you think?"

It was at least reasonable. The *Passage* was currently in normal space, ponderously approaching Dayan in the Irrobi System.

"If, in the judgment of the master pilot, one requires more board-time in shuttle," she said.

"High in the boughs today, aren't you? Practice makes perfect, as Uncle Dick is wont to say. Roll in, Priscilla. Won't do to be late."

He dropped the carryall by the copilot's chair and slid in, his eyes on the board as he adjusted the webbing. Priscilla strapped herself into the pilot's seat, feeling his excitement as if it were her own: sheer schoolboy glee at finagling a day without tutors or overseers, the thrill of some further anticipation riding above his usual pervasive delight. And a glimmer of something else, which she had first taken for his well-leashed nervous energy but now perceived as an edge, almost like worry.

"Board to me, please," he murmured, hands busy over the keys.

Obedient, she shunted control of the ship to the copilot's board and leaned back, watching.

Lights glowed and darkened; chimes, beeps, and buzzes sounded as he ran the checks with a rapidity that would have dizzied any but another pilot. Air was evacuated from the bay; the hatch in the *Passage*'s outer hull slid down, and they were tumbling away. Shan laughed softly, executed a swift series of maneuvers, cleared screens and instruments with the same flourish, and reassigned the board to her.

"Screen, please."

She provided it, wary now that it was too late.

The *Dutiful Passage* was ridiculously far away, big as a moon in the bottom left grid. Irrobi's four little worlds hung placidly beneath her.

Shan pointed at the second planet. "I want to be there, please. In—" He paused for a swift silver glance at the board-clock. "—eight hours, I wish to be docking at Swunaket Port. See to it." He spun the chair, snapped the webbing back, and reached for the carryall. At his touch it became a portable screen and desk. Radiating unconcern, he began to work.

Priscilla clamped her jaw on a caustic remark and began the dreary task of determining where exactly they were in relation to where the captain wished them to be.

"**Swunaket Port, Captain. The pilot regrets that** we have landed five Standard Minutes beforetime."

He looked up, blinking absently. Since his pattern for the past two hours had been the steady buzz of concentration—as perhaps when one played chess—this ploy failed to deceive her.

"Still steamed, Priscilla?" The absent look faded into a grin.

She willed her lips into a straight line. "It was a *rotten* trick."

"I remember thinking so when my father pulled it on me," he said sympathetically. "Other things, too. Most of them sadly unfilial. You did quite well, by the way, especially when we hit that bit of turbulence—all the lovely hailstones! Really, the local weather has cooperated beautifully!"

The laughter caught her unaware, filling her belly and chest, heart and head, and, finally, the cabin. "You are a dreadful person!"

Shan sighed and began to reassemble the portable desk. "My brother's aunt, my eldest sister—now you. I bow to accumulated wisdom, Priscilla."

"I should think so!" The webbing snapped back into its roller as she stood. "The pilot awaits the captain's further orders."

He set the box aside and stood, stretching with evident enjoyment. "The captain does not require the pilot's services at present, thank you. He does, however, desire the second mate to accompany him to a certain place in the town where business is to be conducted."

She regarded him suspiciously. "What sort of business?"

"Come, come, Priscilla, I'm a Trader. I have to trade *some*-time, don't I? To preserve the illusion, if nothing else."

He bowed slightly, ironically. "And I have need of your—countenance—here. I will be walking a proper distance behind you. The address we go to is in Tralutha Siamn. The name of the firm is Fasholt and Daughters." He waved a big hand, ring glinting. "Lead on!"

She stopped in the shadow of the gate, Shan close behind her, and stared into the street.

Bathed in the butter-yellow light of the smaller sun, women hurried or strolled, singly or in pairs. Behind each, at a respectful three-pace distance, came a man or boy, sometimes two. One elderly woman strolled by on the arm of a younger one, both expensively jeweled and dressed, followed by a train of six boys, each heartbreakingly lovely in sober tunic and slacks.

Priscilla frowned after them. The boys radiated a uniform contentment. Playthings, she thought. Well cared for—perhaps even beloved—pets.

"Well, Priscilla?" His voice was very quiet, with mischief and something more sober spilling from him.

She turned her head to glare. "Am I suppose to *own* you?" He nodded. "But don't repine." He felt the fabric of his wide sleeve between two judgmental fingers, tapped the master's ring and the intricate silver belt buckle, and stroked light fingers down a soft-clad thigh. "You obviously pamper me."

She flushed. "I can't think why."

"Unkind, Priscilla. I'm counted not unskilled. Also, I'm a pilot, a mechanic, a good judge of wines, fabrics, spices—"

"And an incurable gabster!" she finished with half-amused vehemence. "If you were mine, I'd have you beaten!"

The slanted brows lifted. "Violence? You might damage the goods, exalted lady. Best to attempt to barter for one less noisy if this one's voice displeases you."

"Don't," she begged him, "tempt me." Back stiff, she turned and marched off.

Head down to hide his grin, Shan followed.

Lomar Fasholt was round-faced and rumpled; her tunic was a particularly pleasing shade of pink. She smiled widely and dismissed her daughter with a nod as Priscilla entered her office.

"A good day to you, Sister Mendoza," Lomar said heartily, coming around the gleaming thurlwood desk and extending a fragrant hand. Priscilla took it and grinned with relief.

"A good day to you, also, sister."

Lomar laughed gently, her eyes going over Priscilla's shoulder. "Shannie! What a sight for old eyes you are! Have you decided to marry me, after all? Your room stands ready."

He laughed and came forward to bow: the bow of honored esteem, Priscilla saw. "It's good to see you, Lomar," he said gently. "How many husbands do you have now?"

"Eight—can you believe it? But it's no use, Shannie, I can't *not* make money! And the more I make, the more husbands they insist I take." She shook her head. "The newest is only a cub, the same age as my youngest daughter! What do they—" Her hands fluttered. "Oh, well, I've set him to be schooled, poor lamb. Though it's hard to find tutors who don't feel it below their dignity to teach a boy. But here I'm rambling on, and you both standing! Come, sit down."

"I don't think I'd do well, do you," Shan pursued, "as the ninth? There are certain freedoms I'm accustomed to." He grinned and slouched into a chair, legs thrust out before him. "Besides, I have a minor skill at making money, too. How many husbands can you support?"

"Oh, a few more, certainly. Though not as many as they'll insist upon. If I were twenty years younger, I'd leave this silly planet and set up somewhere else. I don't know why my daughters stay—true speech!" She sat, embracing them with her smile. "Well, I thought you'd say no, my dear, but one can hope. You'd certainly keep me laughing. Why are you here, Shannie?"

Priscilla caught the flicker of his puzzlement before he replied.

"I'm here because I have items to trade. Korval has traded with Fasholt these last two generations."

"And will do so no more. I'd hoped my message was clear." The round face turned sad. "It's true, isn't it, Shannie, that your family—your Clan—is headed by a man?"

He frowned and straightened a little in the chair. "Val Con is Heir Lineal, surely—Delm-to-be. But the yos'Pheliums aren't traders, Lamar; the yos'Galans are. Two different lines."

She considered that for a moment, then: "Who is the mother of your—Line—then, Shannie? No, that's wrong, isn't it? I don't know the right word."

"Thodelm," he supplied, his puzzlement increasing. "I am, Lamar, what is this? Have we slighted you in some way? Have you complaint of our policy, our price? Surely it can be mended. We've dealt together so long."

"Do you think I don't know it? Long, mutually profitable, and always such pleasant visits! Your father, always willing to sit, take a glass or two, and tell me about goings-on in the wide galaxy. You the same as he . . ." She smiled wistfully. "Things would have been better, Shannie, if you had been a girl."

Shan was sitting very tall, intent on the woman's face. "Lomar, I'm at a loss. I've been male all my life, and my father before me! The trade has always gone well."

"Didn't I say so?" She sighed, radiating grief and affection. "It's a new law, Shannie. From the temple. The thrice-blessed have instructed us to have no trade with any families but those who are properly headed by a female. To trade with no ship, except when captain and Trader are women." She fidgeted with an oddment of stone on her desk, then looked up sharply. "It's *Law,* Shannie."

"Lomar." Shan was speaking very carefully. "The contract between Clan Korval and the Fasholt family dates back to our grandmothers. It reads—if memory will serve me today— yes: 'Between Petrella yos'Galan, or assignees, and Tuleth Fasholt, or assignees.'" He moved his shoulders—not quite a shrug—and smiled. "Assignees, both."

"I know," she said, shaking her head. "It seems to hold some hope, doesn't it? I put the case forth, adding that it is the custom among outworlders to consider women and men equal." She grimaced. "The thrice-blessed were quite clear: trade is permitted only with those families or ships which are now headed by women. Because outworlders follow unnatural custom is no reason for us to do the same."

"After all," Shan said softly, "the Goddess made us all in Her image."

"Don't blaspheme, Shannie."

Priscilla stirred. "That is what we are taught—on Sintia."

The older woman smiled sadly. "This is not Sintia, sister. Here we follow the temple's instructions. Or find ourselves broken into bits and scattered, mother from daughter, and sister from sister, across the world."

Priscilla raised her hand and traced the Sign to Forefend in the air between them. Lomar nodded.

"So, I hope, as well. But it seems that my wishes are not to be fulfilled in this lifetime. Perhaps the next turn of the Wheel will find me in a happier time."

"So might it be," Priscilla murmured and Lomar bowed her head.

Shan cleared his throat. "Is it permitted by the—thrice-blessed?—that I speak to you of an item which belongs to a member of my crew? Lady Faaldom, who is Head of her Line—and female! Priscilla will attest my word. Or shall we go away?"

She considered him. "Is this item truly the possession of Lady Faaldom, Shannie? Why didn't she come to me herself?"

He looked, Priscilla thought, a little hurt. "Of course it's Lina's cargo. I said so, didn't I? As to why she didn't come herself, why should she? I'm Master Trader, she's librarian. It's reasonable that I speak for her in the matter."

Lomar shook her head. "If she's sworn to you, Head of her Family or not—I'm sorry, Shannie. The Law is the Law. I don't dare."

With a flash of vivid concern, Shan leaned forward abruptly, extending a hand across the desk. "Lomar, come away!"

She reached out and patted his hand. "There, now, dear . . . What a good boy you are, Shannie! But it will be all right."

"It will not be all right!" he snapped. "You know and I know that it will become less and less right. Cut off trade with half the galaxy? It's insanity—worse! Suicidal. You'll starve. If the luck rides your shoulder. If not—a society that enslaves half its population? Lomar, what happens when the slaves see the masters are weak?"

"Revolution," Priscilla said in a low voice, feeling prophecy stir within her. "War. Hatred. Death."

"I have read history, sister." Lomar sighed and stroked Shan's hand again. "Should I go without a bit to buy a guidebook, Shannie? My assets must be liquidated. That takes time, careful planning. And my daughters. It's not possible. Not now." She sat back. Priscilla thought she looked older all at once.

Shan sat poised, tension singing through him. Then he, too, sat back, sighing. "Of course. You'll do as you think wise. Do you have my pin-beam code, Lomar?"

She laughed a little. "Your personal code and the code for the *Dutiful Passage*. Why?"

"A favor, for the friendship we hold each other. When you're ready, call me. Transport will he provided. Also, I'll engage to be second partner in any business you care to establish."

She laughed. "Absurd creature! Why, again?"

Shan did not even smile. "Your credit is here. To set up elsewhere, you'll need local credit. With me as your second partner, there will be no problem." He did smile then, tiredly. "You do make money, Lomar. I know it. Why shouldn't I lend you aid in return for a profit I don't have to work for?"

She shook her head. "But you're local on Liad, Shannie. I don't—"

"Korval's credit," he interrupted gently, "is local everywhere. Except, perhaps, here."

There was a brief pause before she spread her hands. "A silent partner, then. For; say, five years? Ten, it had better be. Then I'll buy you out."

He nodded. "Easily arranged. But a mere business matter. The important thing is that you move you and yours as soon as may be—forgive my presumption, old friend. Line yos'-Galan will be happy—joyful—to guest you for a time, so you may look about and make informed decisions."

"You're a good boy, Shannie," she said again. "I'll remember. Now, my dear, I'm afraid I'm going to have to bid you both good-bye."

"Have we endangered you, sister?" Priscilla asked as they moved toward the door.

Lomar smiled and patted her hand, too. "Bless you, child, things aren't that bad yet. But it's best not to push what Shannie calls 'the luck.' Walk in Her smile, now, both of you."

•   •   •

Priscilla set a rapid pace through the morning streets, with Shan's uneasiness feeding her own. She felt the chill of worry at her back, eclipsing his warmth.

Mother, grant us safety, she prayed.

The port gate loomed, and she increased her stride, breathing a sigh of relief as she crossed into the outworlder's preserve. At her back, Shan's worry diminished somewhat.

Thank you, Goddess, she breathed silently. Then she sensed startlement—and outrage like a zag of lightning.

She spun in time to see the white-robed woman shake Shan sharply.

"Creature! How dare you pass by without obeisance?" Her staff snapped toward his head, calculated to cow, not to strike. Shan's fury flared, and the woman shook him again. "What are you called, soulless?"

"Frost, exalted lady." The quiet voice was in sharp contrast to the din of his rage.

"Frost, is it? Exalted lady, is it? Have you no manners, creature, or are you too stupid to know one of the temple when you see her?"

Priscilla felt a surge of bruising power. Aspect! She extended herself, deflected the other woman's intention, and felt her own expansion . . .

"Enough!" she snapped.

Both spun, staring.

"Frost," she snapped. "An apology to the thrice-blessed. And then behind me!"

For a heartbeat she thought he would not play along. Then, stiffly, he bent, forehead brushing knees.

"Forgive this one, thrice-blessed. No insult was intended your holy self."

It was scarcely the most abject of abasements, with the highborn fury crackling from him like electricity. Nor was the thrice-blessed appeased. Her staff whipped out, slashing the air between him and escape.

"Forgiven, indeed. After punishments, as it is written. A public scourging—"

"I had said enough!" Priscilla cried, projecting stern authority, soul-strength, and awe. "Would you mete violence to this person, with the Mother's own mark upon him?" She extended a hand and traced the sign, glowing, before Shan's face for the other to read.

"This man is more than you can know. He has power, as a temple-sister might have it! Depth of learning, skill of use— a mystery. And more!"

The priestess was fairly caught—the wordnet enveloped her, glittering. Priscilla pulled strongly on awe, mystery, belief, and began to weave—then became aware of something else: a single, sustained note, building passion and power, swelling, scintillating, magnificent—a lance of greatness overwhelming in its majesty.

It was Shan, projecting on all levels.

Within the wordnet. the thrice-blessed gasped; she raised a hand to shield her eyes from his radiance.

The note built further as Priscilla made adjustments. He must be caught, held in the echo of the thrice-born's trap . . .

The note paused, then glissaded, power fading with each downward thrum until the last hung, vibrating rainbows . . . and was gone.

The thrice-blessed hung in her net of glamour, reverberating mystery. The man was merely a man, radiating nothing.

"So have you seen," Priscilla intoned, loosing the net carefully. "So have you heard. So shall it be. We live in blessed times, young sister, when mysteries and miracles abound. Look closely at all you see and trust that the Goddess holds each of us protected." "Ollee," the priestess murmured. "I am blessed beyond counting, having beheld this wonder. Elder sister, I ask pardon. And your blessing."

Priscilla's hand rose and traced the proper signs at eyes, ears, and heart. "In Her name, forgiveness, as She forgives each of Her children. Walk in Her grace. Live well. Serve long."

The other effaced herself, and Priscilla turned, motioning to Shan. Unhurriedly, and without looking behind, they walked away.

Shan collapsed into the copilot's chair, his head thumping into the headrest. He opened one silver eye. "I would appreciate warning, please, Priscilla, the next time you feel the need of such support." His voice held a thread of amusement, another of exhaustion. His pattern . . . his pattern—was gone.

No! She sat, graceless, and reached along the inner ways, seeking his warmth as a blind person would seek the sun's touch upon her face. The questing encountered smoothness, cool and slippery, like a mirror, denying without repelling. And he must be beyond it . . .

"Priscilla?"

She brought her attention to the outer ways, striving for calm. "I didn't think to ask. I thought—I was afraid you'd been caught in the echo."

He snorted. "I haven't been caught in an echo since I was twelve years old, Priscilla. Give me credit for some ability."

"Yes, of course . . ." But this was a nightmare, with him before her and she unable to hear, unable to *know* . . . "Shan—"

He leaned forward and extended a hand, the master's ring flashing its facets. "I'm here, my friend."

There was concern in his voice and on his face, while within there was only the horrible, unyielding coolness. She gripped his fingers, feeling that warmth. It was not enough. "Shan . . ."

"I'm tired, Priscilla," he said gently. "It's been a long time since I've needed to travel outward along all roads. Grant me rest." He considered her face, squeezed her hand. "I'm in your debt again."

"Please," she began, and drew a breath. She found a phrase in High Liaden. "Pray do not regard it."

He sat back, his fingers slipping out of hers. "Kayzin is a

thorough teacher, I see." A quick glance at the board took in the white proximity light. "The *Passage* is in orbit. Wonderful. Let's go home."

Home. Even with him locked behind his private mirror she felt a sense of relief, and heard the sound of need.

"Yes, Shan," she said, and then, in urgent correction, "Yes, Captain."

Ken Rik stared in disbelief, "Prepare Hold Thirty-two to receive cargo?" he asked finally.

Shan raised his eyebrows and looked down his nose for good measure. "You're up to the task, aren't you, Ken Rik? Or is Hold Thirty-two already full?"

"No, it's not full," the old man snapped. "As you well know. You're not taking on that—ah, damn this language!—that lanza pel'shek! *His* cargo!"

"I'm not? Well, I'm pleased to know that, Master Ken Rik, thank you. But, do you know, I had the impression that I *was* going to take it." He paused, then delivered the punch line gently. "I had the further impression that the cargo master takes orders from the captain."

Ken Rik had tears in his eyes. "Shan—he tried to kill the *Passage*." He spoke in the High Tongue now: elder to youngling of a different Clan. "Now you take up his cargo, guarantee delivery! Your father—"

"Would have done exactly the same!" Shan finished in ice-coated Terran. "This is outside of balance. The goods are needed—required—on Theopholis. The port master appealed to us because of need. We guarantee delivery—because of need. We're going to Theopholis, aren't we, Ken Rik? Have some sense, for pity's sake! A pretty set of sharks we'd look when it came known that the *Passage* was petitioned at Raggtown and refused to take the load."

"Yes, of course." The words were nearly whispered, but they were in Terran. He bowed the bow of one instructed to instructor. "Forgive—"

"Oh, bother, you annoying old man! You've been ripping up at me for years! Don't, I beg you, begin to act properly now!"

Ken Rik laughed. "It would be something of a strain, I admit." He made a second bow, as subordinate to superior. "With the captain's permission, I will now go to prepare Hold Thirty-two for cargo."

"Thank you, Ken Rik," Shan said gently. "I'd appreciate it."

Port Master Rominkoff eyed the elderly gentle-men. That they stood there at all spoke of resourcefulness as well as resources. The amount of cumshaw required to pass two persons up the ladder of subordinates and into her presence was no doubt large. She made a mental note to find out the current rate. One liked to know the value of one's services.

The younger of her two visitors bowed, not deeply. "I," he said in careful Trade, "am Taam Olanek, Delm Plemia. My Clan possesses a tradeship, called *Daxflan*, which was to have been in port at this present. I find it has not arrived."

The port master sat up. Perhaps the old gentlemen had not paid so much, after all. "I am in agreement with you, sir," she said urbanely. "*Daxflan* has not arrived."

"I had hoped," Taam Olanek, Delm Plemia, pursued, "that you might teach me what you know of circumstances. I have learned from other persons here that berthing space was reserved—that it was not canceled. That there are goods awaiting?"

"And goods awaited," she finished, shedding a little of her urbanity. "Just so. You seem to know all I can teach you of the situation, sir. *Daxflan* is late by some four local days. Reassure yourselves that nothing ill has overcome it, however. I have had reports of her within the sector, doing business at certain—ahh, *free-duty* ports. It appears previous commitments have not been recalled." She steepled her fingers in front of her. "This is unfortunate. It is, of course, unfortunate for you, but it is even more so for Theopholis. Among the things *Daxflan* was to deliver are two shipments from Raggtown, consisting of medical supplies imperative to the conclusion of our vaccination program, and the jewelry the regent will wear at his coronation next week. Our last information from Raggtown is that those shipments are still in the warehouses, awaiting pickup."

There was a moment's silence, during which the port master wondered if her explanation had been too rapid for the old gentleman to follow.

He bowed. "The situation is very serious. Plemia has guaranteed delivery. There will be delivery. If you would allow me use of your facilities, I will make arrangements to employ a subcontractor for the delivery of the goods from Raggtown."

Well, now. *Here* was something. The port master inclined her head. "I will have you escorted to the beam room, sir. One moment." Her hand approached the keypad, but hesitated as the door to her right clicked open, admitting a breathless adjunct.

"Port Master," he began. The belated sight of the two gentlemen gave him abrupt pause.

Master Rominkoff raised her brows. "Continue."

"Yes, Port Master. We have had a pin-beam from the tradeship *Dutiful Passage*. It tells us they carry the shipments from Raggtown." The adjunct took a deep breath and finished his message. "Anticipated docking time is within the next local day."

"So, then." She smiled at her visitors. "It seems the problem is solved for us, sirs."

But Taam Olanek did not seem appreciative of his good fortune. He rounded on the adjunct, his face set in anger. "How does *Dutiful Passage* carry *Daxflan*'s cargo?"

The boy blinked and looked for guidance. She nodded.

"The port—the port at Raggtown, gentle," he stammered. "*Dutiful Passage* was asked to transmit the goods that were urgent, that were perishable. There was room, and the—the captain did the kindness . . ."

"Quite proper," the second gentleman murmured surprisingly, and the first spun to stare at him. "I suggest that we await the morrow. Captain yos'Galan will certainly be happy to lay every detail before you."

There was a moment of singing tension before the first gentleman bowed to the second. "Even so" he said softly. He turned back to the port master and bowed more deeply this time. "I thank you for your kindness and ask forgiveness on behalf of my Clan. Contracts must, of course, be honored. I pledge that they will be so, in the future."

The port master thought without sympathy of *Daxflan*'s Trader. The wrath in the old gentleman's eyes was well earned.

"I am glad that the present crisis has been resolved in so timely a manner, of course. It will not be forgotten that your first thought was of that, sir, and of the solution." She stood and bowed to both. "It has been a pleasure speaking with you. May we meet again."

"May we meet again," the second gentleman echoed, performing his bow with precision. He offered an arm to his companion and guided him gently to the door.

The port master nodded at her adjunct. "Inform me when *Dutiful Passage* takes orbit. I think I should greet Captain yos'Galan— personally."

The sum was enormous. Standing at the Trader's shoulder, Captain yo'Vaade was hard put to maintain her countenance. The trade at Drethilit had not earned them half so much, besides having gone to the port master to pay for the unused berthing. And the goods were gone as well, so there would be that loss, and another bill was awaiting them at Theopholis.

"What do you mean," Sav Rid demanded, his voice beginning to rise in that way she dreaded, "that my cargo is not here? You give me a spurious invoice and in the same breath say that the goods are not in your warehouse? Where are they?"

The warehouseman shrugged his wide Terran shoulders. "You didn't show, the client got worried, asked somebody else to take the stuff along. Shipped out yesterday."

"By what right—*who?* What ship took my cargo? Because I say it is nothing less than theft!"

Again the man shrugged. "That's between you and your client, Mac. Tree and Dragon took the stuff. Now, about the—"

"Tree and Dragon," Sav Rid repeated blankly. Then he shouted, the Trade words nearly unintelligible. "yos'Galan! Thieves, whores, and idiots! My cargo! Mine! And you release it to yos'Galan? Fool!" He shredded the bill, flung the pieces into the man's startled face, and stormed away, looking neither to the right nor to the left. Chelsa yo'Vaade hesitated, tempted—strongly tempted—to let him go. Then she spun back to the warehouseman, tugging the nireline ring from her finger and stripping the heavy chased bracelet from her arm. "They are old," she said quickly, pressing them into his hands. "It will be enough, if you sell to a collector of antiquities." She left him then, running.

Sav Rid was striding across the shuttle field, Second Mate Collier hulking at his shoulder. He had not been unguarded, then. Chelsa was aware of a certain relief as she laid a hand on his sleeve. "Sav Rid? Cousin, I beg you—let it go. It is— you have let it prey upon your mind. End now. Cry balance."

"Balance?" He shook her off, lips tight, eyes glittering. "*Balance?* In favor of that frog-faced, half-Terran lackwit? yos'Galan is the reason we lose in every endeavor we undertake! yos'Galan steals our cargo, slurs our name, hounds us from port to port—there can be no balance!" He held out his hand, fingers clenched tight. "I will crush them—both of them! The idiot and his whore sister!" He paused. "And the Terran bitch who puts her cheek to his!"

Chelsa's stomach clenched with fear—of him? for him?— as she cupped his shaking fist in her hands. "Sav Rid, it is *Korval!* Let be. Let it all be," she pleaded suddenly, her eyes tear-filled. "Let us go home, cousin."

"Bah!" He jerked away, his rings tearing her palms. "Korval! A pack of half-grown brats, born to wealth and ease—no more! But you are like the rest—say *Korval,* and they tremble lest they offend." He spat into the dust and marched off, the second mate keeping pace. "Coward!"

The tears spilled over. She struggled for a moment, then achieved control and started slowly after him.

Dagmar fingered the knife and gave her quarry a
little lead time—but not too much. She had almost lost them,
right at the beginning, when she had still figured that there
was some kind of sense to their explorations, before she had
understood that they were simply following the boy's whim.

She eased out of the doorway and sauntered after them,
picking up speed as they turned a corner. The boy was tugging
on the woman's hand—they were heading toward the port.
Slowly, doubling back on their own tracks now and then, they
were completing a rough circle. Dagmar lengthened her
stride.

Soon. Soon Prissy would pay for setting the white-haired
half-breed on *Daxflan*, eating their profits—eating *Dagmar's*
profit. Dagmar's share. Yes, her share. Without her, the Trader
would not have thought of shipping the stuff. She had been
the one who had showed him how profitable it would be
for the ship, and for his precious Clan. She had been the one
with the contacts at first, the one who had shown him how to
play the game. So she got a piece of the action. A sweetheart
bargain. What a Liaden would call balance.

They had stopped again. Dagmar slid into an alley mouth,
then edged out to watch. Prissy was laughing and pointing to

something in the window of a shop six doors distant. The boy had his nose pressed against the glass.

It would be the boy. She had decided that. Satisfying as it would be to hurt Prissy, to purple that white skin, to snap fragile bones . . . Dagmar wiped wet palms down the sides of her trousers, savoring the thrust of desire that the image imparted. Maybe . . .

No. She would take the boy. That would cause the deepest hurt—both to Prissy and to her half-breed lover.

They were moving again. Dagmar fingered the knife and let them get a little ahead.

Dillibee's DIGITAL DELIGHTS, the sign read. Gordy checked and drifted closer to the glassed-in display, joy flowing out of him in a purr so strong that it was a marvel the outer ears did not hear it as well. Priscilla smiled and rested her hands lightly on his shoulders. He wriggled comfortably, his attention on the gaudy goings-on beyond the glass.

Five minutes went by without a sign that his rapture would soon pass off. Priscilla squeezed his shoulders. "Let's go, Gordy."

"Um."

She laughed softly and ruffled his hair. "Um, yourself. The shuttle leaves in exactly one ship's hour. Your credit with the captain may be up to missing it, but mine isn't. Let's go."

"Okay," he said, still gazing at the display.

Priscilla sighed and walked away by a step or two. "Gordy?"

"Yeah, okay."

Shaking her head, she went farther down the block, adjusting her awareness so that the matrix of his emotions remained clear.

A bolt of terror impaled her as his voice wrenched her about.

"Priscilla!"

Pilot-fast, she was moving back toward the woman and the

struggling child. A scant two steps away, the woman twisted, her shoulder against a garland-pole, the boy held across her thigh with one hand as the other snaked to the front over his shoulder and held something that gleamed beneath the up-tilted chin.

"Freeze, Prissy."

The gleam was a vibroknife, not yet live.

Priscilla froze.

"Good. That's real good, Prissy. You stay right there." Dagmar grinned. "Where's the white-haired boyfriend? Not gonna bail you out today?"

Fury and terror poured from Gordy. Priscilla shut him out. She opened a thin hallway: her heart to Dagmar's. Then she heard, tasted, and saw kill-lust, fear, rage, and desire, a frag-mented cacophony that held no pattern but shifted, froze, and broke apart again and again.

Dementia.

Gordy twitched in Dagmar's grip, then gasped as it tight-ened brutally.

"You be a good boy," she snarled, "and I'll let you live." She made a sound like a laugh. "Yeah, I'll let you live—a minute. Maybe two."

Seeking a tool, Priscilla groped within and found a rhythm; she picked it up even as she felt another stirring and saw a flicker of light and darkness, outlining the Dragon's broad head. The vast wings unfurled as she passed the spell-rhythm to her body; she swayed to the right, not quite a step.

"Stay there! You want this kid to have as many seconds as are coming to him, Prissy, you freeze and stay froze!" Dag-mar grinned and moved the knife but did not thumb it on. "An' don't you look away, honey. I want you to tell the boyfriend exactly what it looked like."

"All right," Priscilla agreed, her voice pitched for magic, the words like strands of sticky silk. "I'll watch. Dagmar. Of course I will. But should I tell him everything? That might not be wise. If I tell everything, then they'll have you, Dagmar. They'll know who you are. They'll know where to find you."

The faraway wings filled, then hesitated. She dared another half step, her eyes watching Dagmar's eyes as her heart watched Dagmar's heart.

"Best to let him go. Let him go, and they'll let you go. Let him go and be free. Let him go and rest. Rest and be peaceful. Free and at peace. Let him go. Walk away. No hunters. No hunted. Let him go . . ."

Dagmar's pattern was smoothing, coming together into something reminiscent of sanity. Far off, the Dragon hesitated, wings poised for flight.

A heavy-hauler slammed by in the street beyond, shattering the circle she had woven. The knife straightened in Dagmar's hand.

"Freeze!" she hissed.

Priscilla stood calm, her eyes on her enemy, not allowing her to look away. "Dagmar," she began again, taking up the thread of the weaving.

"Boyfriend buy your stuff back, Prissy?" Dagmar across her words. "He did, didn't he? Except not earrings. Not the earrings. Nobody'll see them again. Bugged, were they? Not now. Took a hammer, pounded 'em to dust. Spaced the dust." She gave a jagged bark of laughter. "Let him try and trace that! Tryin' to follow where we're goin'. Tryin' to catch us sellin' the stuff—but he didn't! Not so smart, after all, is he?"

"It was a trick," Priscilla murmured against the sudden whirlwind of a Dragon in flight. She was cold. She was hot. She resisted, trusting yet to the power of voice and words: "Only a trick, Dagmar. He wanted to scare you, that's all. Like you've scared me. I'll tell him how it was. I'll tell him you mean business. That you wanted balance. That you have balance. The score's settled now, Dagmar. You can let the boy go. Let him go, Dagmar. A little boy. Only a boy. He can't hurt you. Let him go and walk free."

Footsteps in the street beyond cut the fragile strand. Dagmar shifted her grip on her hostage. "Little public here. Move it, boy. Nice and slow. Prissy, you stay put 'til I tell you to move."

"No!" Gordy twisted, and one hand shot out to grip the garland-pole. In her mind's eye, Priscilla clearly saw a Tree, green and vital, roots sunk through paving stone, soil and magma, to the very soul of the world . . .

Dagmar swore and yanked at Gordy, her already mad pattern splintering into a thing hopeless of order. She yanked again, then gave it up—and thumbed the knife to life.

Priscilla heard it hum, low and evil.

And within, the sound of wings was like thunder as a hurtling body blocked out heart and sight and sense and soul, screaming like a lifetime's accumulated fury—Dragon's fire!

It will be interesting to see how she contrives to send Mr. dea'Gauss away without me, Shan thought, sipping wine. The port master's desire washed him with warmth, and he curled into it shamelessly. Mutual pleasure was intended, neither hinged upon old friendship nor waiting on richer desires—the very thing he needed.

Healer, he instructed himself wryly, heal yourself.

The wine was excellent.

"Confess then, Captain," the port master drawled lazily. "You're intrigued by the proposition."

That was a masterly move. They had been discussing a possible investment of her own, the talk shared evenly between himself and Mr. dea'Gauss. Shan smiled, slanting his eyes toward her face in a sweep of black lashes.

"I am always intrigued," he answered audaciously, "by a lady's proposition."

She laughed, well pleased with him. "Perhaps you and I might meet to discuss the matter more fully." She inclined her head, including the old gentleman in her smile. "Mr. dea'-Gauss must accompany you, of course. I'm sure we will both require his counsel."

He raised his glass. "The trading will keep me—tomorrow,

the next day. You understand, ma'am, that there are persons I must see, in the normal course of business."

"Of course," she said appreciatively. "Perhaps I should stop by your booth in the Grand Square in a day or so. By then you may know your commitments more fully."

"Why, that would be lovely!" he exclaimed, smiling widely. "I'd be delighted to see you there, ma'am." And so he would, though he would be more delighted to see her this night—as she yet intended.

"Then naturally I will come." She began to add something more, then checked herself as the door to her right opened, no doubt admitting the third course.

But the individual who stepped into the room bore no tray, pushed no cart, and looked not a little worried.

The port master frowned. "Yes?"

"1 beg your pardon, madam," her aide said formally. "Precinct Officer Velnik calls on your private line. He assures me the matter is one of urgency."

After a moment's frowning hesitation, a hand flick directed the aide toward the wallscreen. She turned back to the table. "Do excuse the interruption, sirs. This post has many privileges. Privacy is not one of them. It will be but a moment. Please do not regard it."

"That's quite all right," Shan assured her, smiling sympathetically. Mr. dea'Gauss inclined his head.

The precinct officer looked nervous. As well he might, Shan thought. The port master's displeasure was plain on her face.

"Well?"

The officer swallowed. "I'm sorry to disturb you, Thra Rominkoff," he said breathlessly. "It seems routine on the surface. But the boy insisted we call. Says he's the ward of a— Captain yos'Galan?"

Shan stiffened, all attention on the screen.

The port master nodded sharply. "He is here. Is the boy injured?"

Relief flooded Velnik's face. "No, Thra Rominkoff, he's just fine. But we've got a dead Terran female—"

No! And then he was expanding in all directions, an explosion of seek-strands, streaking past the port master's pattern, and Mr. dea'Gauss, and the liveried servant here, and those in the kitchen beyond, stretching, stretching as no Healer could, trying to read the city beyond the walls, searching for one signature, one life—*Priscilla!*

In his far-off body something snapped, followed by pain and more pain as the search slammed hard against its limits, rebounded . . .

He dropped the shattered stem next to the sharded crystal bowl in its puddle of bright wine and blood, and wrapped a napkin around his hand as the port master spun back to the screen, snapping her fingers.

"Quickly! Who has died?"

"Dagmar Collier, Port Master." The man was stumbling over his own words, his eyes flicking from Shan to the woman and back. "Native of Troit. Second Mate on *Daxflan*, out of Chonselta."

Which should not be here! Shan swallowed his curse and saw the thought reflected in the port master's face.

"Bring the boy here," she instructed the precinct officer.

He shook his head. "We have the woman who killed Collier, Thra Rominkoff. She confesses. But murder requires a formal trial, since rehabilitation is the fee—"

"No!" That was out before he could stop it.

The port master slanted a quick glance at Shan's face and returned her attention to the screen. "The woman who confesses is a friend of the boy's? He refuses to come away without her?"

"Yes, Thra Rominkoff."

"Port Master." Somehow he had control of his voice against the tearing pains in hand and head and the terror in his heart. "The person in question is a member of my crew. Am I not allowed to speak for her?" Rehabilitation. Gods, rehabilitation *here*. "It is possible that she does not understand. She is not native here. And perhaps not all of the—circumstances—have been made clear to the precinct officer."

She nodded. "It is, of course, your right to speak for your crew member, Captain." Her eyes were back on the officer. "We shall arrive within the hour. So inform the captain's ward. And arrange for the guard to pass us without delay."

"Port Master." He gave a formal salute, and the screen went dark. The port master rose.

"A medkit," she snapped at the frozen aide. The woman scurried off, returning in a bare moment. Mr. dea'Gauss took it from her and himself applied the lotion, sealed the sharp edge of the cut, and wrapped it in soft cloth, radiating concern.

The old gentleman's pattern set Shan's teeth on edge with anguish: the complex spill of rage, puzzlement, and—admiration?—from the port master nearly had him in tears. Painfully, he began the sequence to seal himself away, to leach the worst of the pain from the rebound shock so that he might unseal himself in an hour, perhaps even to some purpose.

"My car awaits, sirs," the port master said, concern her face.

"You are all kindness, ma'am." He managed the formula, stood, and made his bow.

"Nonsense!" she snapped. "It is my duty to monitor what goes on in this port, Captain. That includes seeing justice done." She indicated the patient aide. "Melecca will see you to the car. I will join you very shortly. There is an urgent matter I must attend to." She was gone in a swirl of bright fabric.

"*Daxflan*'s in port," Shan murmured to Mr. dea'Gauss as they followed Melecca to the car. "That's interesting, isn't it?"

"Very," the old gentleman agreed. He sighed.

There were far too many people in the room. Port Master Rominkoff paused to sort out the crowd. The young captain never broke his stride.

"Shan!"

The boy was smallish and pudgy, running pell-mell toward them. The young captain went down on one knee, caught the child as he skidded to a halt, and returned a hug just this side of savage.

"Gordy." He set the boy back, ran his hands rapidly over the plump frame, and touched a smooth cheek. "You're all right, acushla?"

"Crelm!" the boy snorted. "*I'm* okay." The round face clouded. "Shan—they wouldn't listen! I told them—I did! They wouldn't fix her arm and—"

"Hush." He stroked the boy's cheek again, then laid a gentle finger over his lips. "Gordy. Just relax for a moment, okay?" The small body lost some of its tension, as if those words were all it took. "Good. Where's Priscilla now?"

Tears filled the brown eyes. "I tried to make them not—" He took a ragged breath. "They put her in a cage."

"Here now, young man!" the precinct officer said, approaching warily, his eyes flicking from the port master's face to the man and boy, then back to her face. "Not a *cage!* Just a holding cell, I promise!"

The captain rose smoothly and inclined his head. "A holding cell," he repeated softly. The precinct officer ran his tongue over his lips. The port master forbade herself the smile.

"I am captain of the *Dutiful Passage*," Shan continued clearly. "Ms. Mendoza is a member of my crew. I am here to speak on her behalf, as set in the trade compacts. You will liberate her from the—holding cell—and guide her here so that all may be done . . . lawfully."

The port master denied the smile more sternly. Really, the young captain pleased her more and more.

The precinct officer was shaking his head. "I'm afraid I can't do that, Captain. She's a confessed murderer. We asked her twice, according to law. She understood the questions and answered them. Twice. She talked crazy about other stuff, but not about that. The law says in those circumstances, we hold the prisoner for a next-day trial. It's most likely the judge will rule rehabilitation in light of the confession, and lacking witnesses—"

"What do you mean, lacking witnesses?" the captain demanded. "The child says he told you what happened—and that you refused to listen!"

Officer Velnik held up a hand. "Not admissible, Captain. He's underage."

"On his home-world," came a dry voice from the port master's side, "Master Arbuthnot is of an age where his testimony is considered admissible."

"I'm sure it is, Mr.—ah?"

"dea'Gauss," the old man supplied, going forward. "I am the man of business for Clan Korval, of which Captain yos'-Galan and, by wardship, Master Arbuthnot are members. Pray elucidate the reason for your refusal to admit testimony from a witness of sound mind and honorable character. You have yourself cast doubt by stating that Lady Mendoza spoke irrationally of subjects other than the specific mischance. It behooves you to place before a judge all interpretations of the event that are available. Justice could hardly be served in any other way."

"See here—"

It was time for the port master to take a hand. "Mr. dea'-Gauss raises a valid point and asks a pertinent question," she drawled from the doorway. "Why is the boy forbidden to testify, Velnik? I have monitored trials where children much younger than he appears to be have spoken and been heard."

"Thra Rominkoff, it is law that all witnesses in cases of violent crime must testify under the same drug administered to the accused. Persons under majority—nineteen Standard Years—may not be compelled to submit to the drug."

"What drug?" the young captain asked very quietly.

"Pimmadrene," she replied. "It's been used for many years. The ego is temporarily dissolved, which nets quite truthful answers." She considered the precinct officer. "And yet it does still seem to me that I have seen very young children testify. The law speaks of 'impel.' What if free choice is offered?"

He moved his shoulders. "The parents gave permission for the drug in the cases you mention, Thra Rominkoff."

"Or guardian of record?"

He bowed.

"But it is dangerous?" the captain asked quietly.

"Dangerous? No. The doctor adjusts the dose to body weight and stays by to monitor. But it's unpleasant. Not the sort of thing to force on a person who can't—a child. The side effects are dizziness, stomach cramps, fever, disorientation. Some people go blind for a few days, but that's not common. Doc over there could tell you specifically."

"I'll do it," the boy said suddenly, and tugged on the captain's sleeve. "Shan? Tell them I'll do it. I'm your ward. Grandpa told me!"

"Acushla, think carefully. The side effects sound very bad.

And the intended effect isn't good, either. I'll do what you tell me to do. It's your decision. But be sure, Gordy."

"Shan, it's *Priscilla*." He grabbed on to a big hand, looking up worriedly. "They said—do you know what they're going to do to her, if the judge says she's got to be—to be rehabilitated?"

"I know, Gordy. Hush."

But Gordy would not be hushed. He hung on to the captain's hand and looked at Mr. dea'Gauss, making the explanation to him in a voice that washed against every wall in the room.

"They said—since she's a *murderer*—she'll go to the organ bank. They'll float her in a tank and feed her through tubes and stuff until somebody maybe needs an eye. Then they'll take one of Priscilla's eyes. And she'll float some more 'til somebody needs another eye, or a kidney, or a lung, or a leg, and they'll cut her up, piece by piece . . ."

"Gordy!" The captain was on his knees, pulling the boy tight against his shoulder and rubbing his face in the sandy hair. "Stop it, Gordy. Please."

There was silence.

The boy pulled back, lifted a tentative hand to the man's stark cheek, and snuffled. "Shan, you better tell them I'll be a witness. They can't—Priscilla's *good*."

"Yes," the captain murmured, coming slowly to his feet. "I know that, too."

He bowed to the precinct officer very slightly. "It has been determined that my ward will testify at Ms. Mendoza's trial. Please tell us its time and location, as well as the proper manner in which to present ourselves."

"There is no reason," the port master cut in, "why the trial should not be held at once. I am empowered to act as judge in affairs of the port—as soon as my robes arrive and a room is made available." She glanced at the desk officer, who hurriedly placed a call.

• • • •

The robes were heavy on her shoulders. Perhaps it was their unaccustomed weight: she rarely took part in such affairs, usually letting things run the legal course in their own time. Perhaps it was the boy's involvement, or the young captain's. They sat together by special permission, the giant, white-haired Liaden austere, and the boy with his empty, drug-toned eyes.

She sighed heavily, rang the bell to order, and read the preliminaries without expression. Having established the identities of those present, she glanced at the monitor; she nodded satisfaction and looked back at the boy. His face was slightly damp, eyes wide open, pupils dilated black with a thin ring of brown iris.

"What is your name, boy?"

"Gordy." His voice was blurry, like a sleep-talker's.

The port master consulted the card and frowned. She addressed the boy again. "All right, Gordy. What is your full, *legal* name?"

"Gordon Richard Arbuthnot."

She nodded. "What is your planet of origin?"

"New Dublin."

"In Standard Years, what is your age?"

"Eleven."

"What is your father's name?"

Silence.

She frowned. "Gordy, what is your father's name?"

"His father," Mr. dea'Gauss whispered in her ear, "is dead." "I see." Damn this drug! It was clumsy—misleading. "Gordy, what *was* your father's name?"

"Finn Gordon Arbuthnot."

That was another match. "What is your mother's name?"

"Katy-Rose Davis."

And another. She turned her head. "Doctor, have we established that the drug is in force?"

"Yes, Thra Rominkoff."

"Excellent. We shall proceed with the testimony."

She paused to order her thoughts, mindful of the drug's

limitation. "Gordy, when did you and Priscilla Mendoza arrive on-world?"

"First shuttle."

First shuttle? What sort of time was that? "Approximately Regent's Hour," the young captain said softly, and she nodded her thanks. "Why were you with Priscilla Mendoza, Gordy?"

"We were leave-partners."

"You were assigned to each other?"

"No."

She sighed. "How did you become leave-partners?"

"I asked Priscilla if she'd be partners, and she said okay."

"Who chose where you went in town?"

"I did."

"You chose to be in Nietzsche Street?"

"Yes."

"Why?"

"It looked interesting."

"Did Priscilla Mendoza ask you to go down Nietzsche Street?"

"No."

"Did Dagmar Collier ask you to go down Nietzsche Street?"

"No."

"Did Priscilla Mendoza kill Dagmar Collier, Gordy?"

"Yes."

She swallowed a curse at that simple damnation; she heard Velnik shift beside her, and saw the young captain's lips shape one word. She gave it voice.

"*Why* did Priscilla kill Dagmar, Gordy?"

"To save me."

On the other side, Mr. dea'Gauss leaned forward infinitesimally, his attention centered on the blurry young face.

"Were you in danger, Gordy?"

"Yes."

"How did you come to be in danger?"

"I didn't come when Priscilla said to."

The port master made a mental note to explore drugs other than Pimmadrene for use in interrogation.

"Gordy, I want you to tell me exactly what happened from the time you didn't go with Priscilla in Nietzsche Street to the time the arresting officer came."

"Priscilla said the shuttle was leaving in a ship's hour and if my credit with the captain was up to being late, hers wasn't and we had to leave. She went two steps away and said 'Gordy?' I said 'yeah,' and she went further away and I was getting ready to go with her when I got grabbed and it was Dagmar and she yanked and held on when I tried to run and held us against a pole and held me over her knee and Priscilla was running toward us and Dagmar had a knife and she said 'Freeze, Prissy.' And Priscilla stopped." There was a tiny pause as the boy licked his lips.

"Where did Dagmar hold the knife, Gordy?"

"Across my throat. Under my chin."

"All right, Gordy. Priscilla stopped. Then what?"

"Dagmar said Priscilla had to stay there. She asked where Shan was. I tried to get away again, and she—she hurt me. She said if I was good she'd let me live for a minute or two." There was another small pause. The port master snapped her fingers, never taking her eyes from that damp face.

"She said Priscilla had to watch. To tell Shan what it looked like." An aide arrived with a glass of water. The port master waved her to the boy.

"Rest a minute, Gordy, and drink."

He did, draining the glass thirstily.

"All right, Gordy. Dagmar said Priscilla had to watch, so she could tell Shan what it looked like. Then?"

"Priscilla started to talk. I don't remember what she said, but it made my head feel funny. She talked and walked forward a little bit and Dagmar's arm got loose and I thought about running away but then there was a noise in the next street and Dagmar's arm got tight again and she made Priscilla stop. Priscilla tried to talk some more, but Dagmar asked if Shan had bought Priscilla's things. She said she broke

Priscilla's earrings into dust and then spaced the dust. She said Shan wasn't smart and that he wouldn't catch them selling the stuff.

"Priscilla started to talk again and my head felt funny again and then there were footsteps and Dagmar tried to make me go with her 'cause it was too public, she said. But I was scared and I didn't want to go with her and I grabbed on to the pole and held on and thought about the Tree like Priscilla'd taught me and Dagmar turned on the knife. I heard it hum and I was scared and I hung on and thought about the Tree and I heard a—roar. Like a big animal. And Priscilla was running fast— faster than Shan runs and Dagmar let me go and Priscilla—it was so *fast!* She grabbed Dagmar and twisted and did something with her hands. I heard a snap, like a stick breaking. Dagmar fell down. Priscilla stood for a minute and then she fell down, too." He swallowed.

"I went and kicked the knife away from Dagmar and then I tried to make Priscilla get up. It was hard and I thought she was—I thought she was dead. But she woke up and called me 'Brand' and her voice was all funny, like it hurt her to talk. Then she stood up and told me to go back to the *Passage.* I told her Shan wouldn't like it if I left her alone when she was in a scrape and she hugged me and threw a stone into the window of Marcel's Tailoring Emporium. Then she said she'd killed Dagmar and the cops would come in a minute and arrest her for murder. She told me to leave again, but I wouldn't. Then the cop came."

The port master leaned back in her chair and counted to twenty-five, eyes closed. She opened her eyes.

"Precinct Officer Velnik," she said very carefully. "I will now see the recording of Priscilla Mendoza's . . . confession."

The woman was slim, middling tall by Terran standards, doubly dwarfed by Velnik and the arresting officer. Her hair was short and black and curly, her face dirt-smeared; her eyes were enormous, ebon—and exhausted. "Priscilla Delacroix y Mendoza," she answered the precinct officer. Her voice was a ragged whisper.

"Planet of origin?"

"Sintia."

"Are you employed on a trading vessel?"

"Yes."

"State the name of the vessel, its home port, your rank."

"*Dutiful Passage.* Solcintra, Liad. Pilot, first class pending. Second mate."

"Did you kill the woman Dagmar Collier?"

"Yes."

"Did you deliberately murder the woman Dagmar Collier?"

"Yes."

"Where did you kill Dagmar Collier?"

"In front of Dillibee's Digital Delights in Nietzsche Street in Crown City on Theopholis."

"When did you kill Dagmar Collier?"

"One hour ago."

"Did you attempt escape after you killed Dagmar Collier?"

"No."

"Why?"

"There was no place to go."

From the young captain came a wordless protest. As if cued by that slight sound, Precinct Officer Velnik asked Priscilla Mendoza, "Why didn't you return to the *Dutiful Passage*?"

"No murderers are allowed on the *Passage*." The captain drew a sharp breath. "Your name," the precinct officer pursued, "is Priscilla Delacroix y Mendoza?"

"Yes."

"Did you intentionally kill the woman Dagmar Collier?"

"Yes."

"Describe your actions that brought the death of Dagmar Collier."

"I called the Dragon. When it was with me, we roared and threw a fireball to distract Dagmar's attention from Gordy. Then I broke her neck."

There was a slight pause while precinct officer and cop exchanged glances.

"You, Priscilla Delacroix y Mendoza," the precinct officer said carefully, "broke the neck of Dagmar Collier, fully intending to bring about her death?"

"Yes."

"Are you a native of Troit?"

"No."

"What is your legal name?"

"Priscilla Delacroix y Mendoza."

"What is your planet of origin?"

"Sintia."

"Did you kill Dagmar Collier?"

"Yes."

There was a small pause. "Where is the Dragon now?"

"Above the Tree."

"How much is two plus two?"

"Four."

"Have you said any lies since you were brought here by the arresting officer?"

"No."

"Did the dragon kill Dagmar Collier?"

"No."

"Who killed Dagmar Collier?"

"I did."

"**You** see," Velnik said to the room in general as the lights came up.

"Dragons, trees . . ."

"The Tree and Dragon," Mr. dea'Gauss cut him off, "is the shield of Clan Korval. It depicts a dragon, guarding a full-leafed tree. The motto is 'I Dare.' Lady Mendoza is quite familiar with the shield. It is displayed prominently on the *Dutiful Passage.*"

"So they had meaning for her; she was self-aware."

"Yes," the port master snapped, coming to her feet. Velnik

retreated a step. "She knew what she was doing. The boy is alive. The person he names his potential assassin is dead. Priscilla Mendoza was not asked why she willfully and intentionally killed Dagmar Collier, Precinct Officer. Your interview was less than thorough."

Velnik licked his lips and came to rigid attention.

"Doctor, is the serum you gave Mendoza still in force?"

He shook his head. "It runs through the system pretty fast. She'll be on the downside by now." He glanced at the bench. "Can't give her another shot for two days. That's a medical fact. She mightn't recover."

She nodded. "It won't be required, thank you. My ruling in this case is that Priscilla Delacroix y Mendoza is found not guilty of murder. Defense of a child is not a crime here! Arresting Officer, bring Priscilla Mendoza here, so that she may be released into the care of her captain."

Mr. dea'Gauss caught the young captain's eye. "*Daxflan*—"

"My office is currently dealing with that difficulty, sirs," she said, turning back. "Granting even unheard of levels of inefficiency, it should at this moment be sealed in close orbit. And there, I think, we may all let it wait until the morrow."

The old gentleman bowed. "It is as you have said, madam. I should mention that the feud between Lady Mendoza and Dagmar Coller is one of long standing. Dagmar Coller threatened her ladyship and Master Arbuthnot with violence once before to my certain knowledge. On Arsdred."

"I would appreciate receiving the particulars of that event, sir. Also—Captain. I am deeply ashamed that my inefficiency has caused this circumstance. Dagmar Collier should never have been in this port. I am responsible, and I am grieved. Please consider me at your disposal in the resolution of the matter."

"You're very kind, ma'am," he replied, smiling wearily.

"Port Master," the arresting officer said, arriving alone and looking very nervous. "Port Master, she—won't move. I open the door and call, but she just sits, Port Master."

"I'll come." The young captain slid away from the boy, beckoning to the old gentleman. "By your kindness, sir."

"Certainly." Mr. dea'Gauss sat carefully and slid an unaccustomed arm about young shoulders, enduring the head resting upon his chest.

"Let's go," the captain snapped at the cop as he strode by. She had to run three steps to catch up.

The room was mercilessly bright—shadowless. In the center of the cot huddled a ragamuffin creature, legs crossed, arms hugging her waist, head leaning against left knee. She was trembling minutely and constantly.

"Let's go, Mendoza!" the cop called briskly, unlocking the cell port.

The bundle of misery did not stir.

The cop licked her lips and tried again. "Come on, Mendoza! Your boss is here!" Nothing.

Shan laid his hand on the cop's arm. "Leave us. I'll bring her."

She began to shake her head, lips parting to prate some senseless law.

"Go!" He augmented the command with a lash of fury. The cop jumped—and fled.

The anger was blue-hot in him—Korval rage. With an effort he contained it, banked it, and shut it away until it might be used. Calmed, he went to the edge of the cot. "Priscilla."

She flinched, and he caught his breath; he calmed himself again and hunkered down before her, his hands resting on the edge of the mattress. "Priscilla, it's Shan." "Shan." There was anguish like a knife in the ragged whisper. "Shan, there wasn't enough time to be sure!"

Her agony caught him by the throat, even shielded as he was. The next moment he had cast protection aside, spinning a line of comfort, of love . . .

He was met by terror-desire-longing-grief-shame-love—a whipping windstorm of emotion, punishing in its intensity. He gasped, fingers clawing into the mattress as he scrambled for the line he had spun for her—he gripped it, following it back into himself by painful jerks, and finally called up the Wall.

It slammed into place with a force that drew a soft moan from Priscilla, though she did not lift her head.

"My dear friend . . ." Slowly he unclenched his hands. "Priscilla, please look at me."

She was silent, motionless but for the constant shivering.

"Priscilla?"

"I'd rather—talk—to you. Please, Shan . . . They're going to—to kill me. I—can you stay with me? Please . . . Until they come . . ." She drew a shuddering breath. "You keep—going away . . ."

He forced his brain to work, to consider that last. "Have I been here before, Priscilla?"

"I think—yes. I was talking to you—trying to tell you . . . I tried to—to reach athetilu, but you were closed and I tried to—to hold you and you went away and I thought I'd made you angry . . ." She moved a fraction, tightening her arms about her waist. "Cama se mathra te ezo mi . . ."

Sintian. He was losing her, crippled as he was, not daring to step beyond the Wall. Shaking, he extended a hand and stroked the bedraggled curls.

"Priscilla, *please* look at me. I grant I'm hardly a feast for the eyes, but it would spare my feelings."

She gave no sign that she had heard him. Then, slowly, almost clumsily, she unbent and sat straight, her right arm cradled in her left, her eyes bottomless ebony pits in a filthy, exhausted face.

He smiled and dropped his hand from her hair to her knee.

"Thank you. Now, since I seem prone to this fading in and out—your hand, please, Priscilla."

It took a moment for her to manage the movement, but she held a quavering left hand out to him.

"Good." He tugged the master's ring from his finger and slid it onto her thumb, where it perched precariously. "If you find I've gone away again, notice that you have my ring. I'll come back for that, at least, won't I?"

She considered it. "Yes."

He sighed, holding her hand lightly. "What a brute I am! It's a wonder I'm allowed your friendship at all, Priscilla; I marvel at you. What's wrong with your arm?"

"I burned it."

"Throwing fireballs?"

She jerked. His fingers tightened on hers, and she relaxed, licking her lips. "Yes. I'm not—accustomed—to throwing fireballs."

"I'd think not. Are you well enough to walk?"

"Yes."

"Good." He stood. "Let's go."

She stared up at him, her hand moving in his. "Go where?"

"To the *Passage*. You're hurt and sick and tired, and I'm tired and Mr. dea'Gauss is tired and even Gordy's tired." He grinned. "The port master's tired, too, but she doesn't come with us."

She tried to pull her hand away. He did not allow it.

"I can't."

He frowned. "Can't?"

"Shan . . ." Tears welled out of her eyes and spilled over, making streaks down her face. "Shan, I killed Dagmar."

"Yes, I know." Bending to take her other hand, he found her face close, so that he might lay his cheek against her—*Priscilla, I love you* . . . He fought the emotion and found the control to address her gently. "I'm sorry, Priscilla. It should never have come to that. You should never have had the need. Forgive me, I've taken poor care of you."

"You said—"

"I said 'no murderers,' may my tongue be damned! But self-defense isn't murder—nor is protecting the life of a friend." He took a breath, cooling the sharpest of the pain. "Please, Priscilla— for the friendship we have between us— allow me to take you to the *Passage*. You need care, healing—a sheltered place to sleep. When you are able, I will personally escort you anywhere you choose to go. Let me aid you."

There was confusion in her face and in her eyes. She was silent.

He raised a hand to touch the platinum hoop in her right ear and stroke the curls above it. "Please, Priscilla."

"The trial . . ."

"Has been performed. Gordy testified. The port master sat as judge. You are acquitted of murder. No one is going to come and take you away to die. Only Shan is come, to take you home."

"Home." Her hands clutched his, then relaxed. She looked into his face, her expression unreadable through the grime. "Please, Shan, take me home."

"Yes, Priscilla."

She staggered when she stood, clutching his arm for support. "Are you well enough to walk, my friend? Or shall I ask the port master to provide a chair?"

"No." She straightened, face set.

"Very well." He slid his arm around her waist, turning her toward the door. "Mr. dea'Gauss," he predicted with a merriness he did not feel, "will be appalled."

If Mr. dea'Gauss was appalled, he hid it well. The bow he performed was profound. "Lady Mendoza."

She inclined her head, which was all that dizziness and Shan's arm about her waist allowed. "Mr. dea'Gauss. I'm pleased to see you."

"You are kind." He glanced at Shan. "The physician has given Master Arbuthnot a drug he feels may counteract the worst of the side effects, or at very least allow him to sleep through them. He has also provided a printout of the structure of both drugs."

"Well enough," Shan said calmly, as if it were no surprise that Gordy should be lying so white and quiet upon the bench.

"I don't—" She shifted, half intending to go to the boy. The arm tightened about her fractionally, and she turned to look into silver eyes. "He was all right! They were going to send him to the *Passage*."

"But he would not go without you," a new voice explained. "Afterward it became necessary that he be given the drug, that his testimony might be heard."

Priscilla blinked, clearing her vision. The tall, handsome woman in glittering evening dress smiled formally and bowed. "Ms.—Lady—Mendoza. I am Elyana Rominkoff, port master in the regent's service. Allow me to present my apologies: this should not have befallen you in the city under my care. When you are rested—at your convenience!—please contact me, that we may sit together and discuss fair recompense."

"Yes, of course," Priscilla mumbled, unable properly to attend to what the woman said to her. She was sinking into an indigo blur where the only realities were Shan's arm about her and the warm strength of his body steadying hers. Abruptly she pushed at the creeping indigo and reached out, tapping that near source of energy.

Strength flowed unstintingly from him to her, clear and bracing. She straightened as the room came back into focus and inclined her head to the woman before her. "Port Master, forgive me. I am—unwell—at the moment. I will call you, and we will talk."

"That is well, then." The woman shifted her gaze beyond Priscilla, smiling with warmth rather than mere formality. "Captain yos'Galan, remember what I have said. I am entirely at your disposal in this matter. My eyes and ears are yours to command at any hour." She bowed then and moved back, cutting off his reply with a wave of her hand. "At this hour, you have folk to care for. My car awaits you. If you allow, the precinct officer will carry the boy. Lady Mendoza, Mr. dea'-Gauss holds your license and your papers."

"Thank you," Shan said gently. "You're all kindness, ma'am."

The walk to the car was blessedly short. Priscilla settled into the seat, Shan's arm still about her waist, his strength buoying her. She curled her fingers around her thumb, gripping his ring tightly. Then she reached within and turned off the tap.

The last thing she remembered was resting her head upon his shoulder.

He poured unsteadily, brandy splashing the bar top and, incidentally, the cup. Gritting his teeth, he managed to fill the thing halfway and set the decanter decently back into the rack.

Priscilla was in sick bay, under Lina's capable eye, and Gordy was there too. Both were asleep and abed—which was where he should be, working through the exercise that would grant his pounding head relief and rest. Brandy was not the best cure for an empath in his condition.

He sipped, frowning in momentary puzzlement at the stain on his cuff. Blood.

Yes, of course. Must remember to send the port master a set of crystal. Stupid Shan. Doesn't know his own strength.

Sav Rid Olanek. Gods, to have his hands about Sav Rid Olanek's slim throat . . .

And then? He jeered at himself, drinking again. The flaming ice of Korval rage stirred behind the barriers he had built about it. And then he would pay balance with his life! Shall he threaten lady, fosterson, ship?

Priscilla. That punishing outage of self-hate, terror, and

confusion. A trace effect of the drug? Or something more permanent? Lina would know.

He stopped himself on the way to the comm. Lina would know, sooner or later. And when she knew, so would Shan yos'Galan.

He would do nothing now but distract her from an essential task.

"Go to bed. Shan," he told himself.

But he tarried, sipping his drink, staring sightlessly at the tapestry above the bar.

When the annunciator chimed, he jumped.

"Come!" he called.

Mr. dea'Gauss entered, papers rustling in hand, face full of import. It was indicative of his weariness or the value of his news that he broke at once into speech, neglecting even his bow.

"Your Lordship, I have received the report of Ms. Veltrad, whom you sent to Sintia on the matter of Lady Mendoza. It is—"

"No!"

Mr. dea'Gauss blinked. "I beg your Lordship's pardon?"

"I said," Shan explained, voice thin with strain, "no. No, I do not wish to hear Ximena's report. No, I do not wish to hear the name of the crime Priscilla is supposed to have committed. No, I do not wish to find the report on my screen next on-shift. No, I do not want Ximena to call or visit so that she may tell me in her own voice what she has reported. No."

Mr. dea'Gauss took stock. Shan stood near the center of the room, holding a quarter-full glass in his bandaged hand, the bloodstained ruff falling gracefully about taut knuckles. The stark brown face might have been hewn from strellwood, and there was a slightly mad look around the silver eyes.

"The report from Sintia," he began again, "indicates that—"

"No!" Shan was across the room in a blur, was towering over Mr. dea'Gauss, his face set in cold fury, the syllables of the High Tongue crackling. "I do not hear you! Go."

Mr. dea'Gauss gave no ground. He had seen this before—

from Er Thorn yos'Galan. The proper answer had never included giving ground.

He drew himself up and took a firmer grip on his papers. "Will you hear it from me? Or from your First Speaker? It is a matter of ship's debt. The captain's attention is required."

For perhaps a heartbeat Shan was utterly still. He turned, went to his desk and sat, placing the glass precisely aside.

"yos'Galan hears," he said in the High Tongue, Thodelm to hireling.

Mr. dea'Gauss walked forward. He was not waved carelessly to a chair. Shan's face was expressionless, waiting. Mr. dea'Gauss bowed.

"Thodelm, it becomes my knowledge through the words of Ximena Veltrad, who was offered coin in return for verified truth, that Priscilla Delacroix y Mendoza was ostracized from her world for the crime called 'blasphemy' ten Standard Years gone by. The details of this crime are covered most fully by Ms. Veltrad's report. I wished only to assure you at this present that Sintia's melant'i suffers greatly by the reported incident. Lady Mendoza's actions were, as always, above reproach."

"And yet someone reproached her. Strongly." The High Tongue exuded no warmth. "You will explain this paradox."

"Yes, Thodelm. I am not conversant with the depth of the situation reported by Ms. Veltrad. My understanding is that Lady Mendoza, as an apprentice in Circle House—what is called there a 'Maiden' or novice priestess—called recriminations upon herself for an act of heroism. I confess that I do not understand why the saving of three lives should have caused these recriminations. Ms. Veltrad's report indicates doctrinal, rather than rational, causes. In any wise, Lady Mendoza was called before the masters of the craft and offered a chance to disown her act and be properly chastised. Lady Mendoza refused to recant. She was then stripped of her goods and her title, and banned from the craft. In order to keep face, her House cast her forth as well." Mr. dea'Gauss paused, considering the icy eyes. "Politics, Thodelm. Not balance."

"So." Shan drank the rest of the brandy slowly, then replaced the glass. "yos'Galan has heard. You will leave the report with me. Have you anything else that I must hear at this present?"

"No, Thodelm."

"Good. You are dismissed."

Korval's man of business bowed, then turned away.

"Mr. dea'Gauss."

He turned back. "Thodelm?"

Shan smiled wearily, his bandaged hand resting on Ximena's report. "Sleep well, sir. And thank you."

Mr. dea'Gauss felt absurd relief as his lips bent in reply. "Sleep well, your Lordship. You are quite welcome."

Shan lifted his head, groping after the sound. Surely . . . Ah. The door chime.

"Come."

The door parted, and she entered, slight and small, her face Liaden gold. "Old friend."

"Lina." Memory returned with a force that shuddered pain through his misused head, and he was half out of the chair. "Priscilla—"

"Resting. And well." Her small hands flickered, soothing. He sank back as she came around the desk. "More—she is herself. We spoke. She is rational; she knows what has transpired; she knows that necessity existed and that she acted as best she might." Lina sighed. "Much of the confusion you reported must be counted an effect of the drug—and of despair. Life has taught her to expect neither rescue from trouble nor surcease from pain. Healing had gone far, but that lesson is not easy to unlearn."

Shan had closed his eyes. Now he opened them, and Lina felt shock at the depth of weariness there. "She'll be all right," he murmured, his beautiful voice blurred and uneven. "Thank you, Lina, for coming to tell me. This is your rest shift, isn't it?"

"And yours, as well," she said briskly. "Priscilla sent me to make sure you slept. You were angry, she said, and hurt."

He rubbed his forehead absently. "Stupid. Trying to scan the whole planet . . ." He tapped a sheaf of papers. "Had to read Ximena's report. Mr. dea'Gauss . . . An act of heroism. She'll have to stop that, Lina. Get herself hurt. Saves three lives, using some sort of thing she wasn't taught yet. But she said the old soul—give 'em old souls, the Initiates, with the old names attached. Priscilla's soul was named Moonhawk. Very powerful lady. Much respected. Said the old soul had done it, for the glory of the Goddess and—and . . . who knows? Long and short, she gets thrown out. All very well and good to have a tame dramliza on your hands, but when she starts demanding her due, that's dangerous."

Lina frowned, noting the empty glass by his hand. "Is Priscilla a wizard, Shan?"

"Very good chance. Should see her—no, I hope you don't see her. Does things above and beyond us mere Healers. Got a definite flair . . ." He rubbed at his face again. "Gods, gods, she's *strong*."

She leaned forward and stroked the warm, thick hair. "Shan. Come to bed."

He blinked at her. "Bed?"

"You are tired. You must rest, let yourself heal. How much brandy have you had?" "Half a beakful," he muttered, and then grinned. "But it's quite a beak, eh?"

She laughed, between frustration and relief. "Come to bed, denubia." She grabbed the unbandaged hand and tugged. "Shan, have pity! I have promised my cha'leket to see you resting. Would you have me turn my face from her need?"

"Cha'leket?"

"Priscilla herself named me sister. I find my heart agrees. *Will* you come to bed?"

"Since you ask so nicely. Not likely to do you much good though, my precious." He wobbled to his feet but would not lean his weight upon her. Unsteadily, he laid his hand against the inner door.

She coaxed him to lie flat, unsealed the tight dress shirt, then sat stroking his hair and murmuring, weaving a net of warm comfort and loading it with the desire to sleep deeply and long.

After a time his eyes closed, his breathing lengthened.

Lina continued her weaving and stroking until she sensed that he had reached the first depths, where prime healing begins. She slid from the bed and spread the coverlet gently over him, dimmed the lights, and disarmed the alarm. Kayzin had agreed that the captain's rest should not be interrupted untimely.

Affairs ordered to her satisfaction, Lina bent and stroked his cheek. "Sleep well, old friend." And then she was gone.

he cab pulled to the edge of the pedstrip and
topped. The driver looked over his shoulder and said some-
hing in a barbaric garble. Sav Rid stared at him coldly.

"The vehicle can go no farther," the driver announced in
abrupt Trade. "Pedestrian traffic only inside the port. The
'are's fivebit."

Sav Rid extended the proper coin silently and exited the
cab. Behind him the driver spat between his teeth and mut-
ered, "Louse!" But the action was beneath Sav Rid's notice,
he single word in Terran.

He walked cautiously through the crowded port, intensely
aware of his lack of guard. Dagmar Collier had not been at the
rendezvous point this morning. He wondered what might
have happened to the creature, then put the thought away with
an impatient shrug. Who, after all, really cared? If Dagmar
Collier chose to jump ship before the run was through, that
was certainly its own affair. *Daxflan* would make good use of
he unclaimed wages.

A man was coming purposefully toward him down the
pedstrip: older with more gray than black in his thinning hair.
Sav Rid froze.

His Delm continued briskly forward, then stopped at the

proper distance and inclined his head. "Kinsman. I give you good day."

He managed a bow. "As I give you good day, kinsman and Delm. It surprises me to find you here, so far from home and House."

"No more," the elder said dryly, "than it surprises me to find you here, when the port master reports *Daxflan* absent."

"We hold orbit about the fourth planet out, my Delm. It has been found more—convenient—to use another vessel to bring goods from *Daxflan* to prime orbit."

"Indeed." Taam Olanek extended an arm, smiling coolly. "Walk with me, I beg you. I am curious about this so convenient method. Have you subcontracted your cargoes to others, Sav Rid?"

They walked a few paces in silence.

"It became necessary," Sav Rid murmured, "for *Daxflan* to purchase a subsidiary vessel to act as shuttle from *Daxflan* to berth. The method is quite simple, sir, and serves us well."

"Am I to understand," Plemia demanded, "that you have made *Daxflan,* in essence, a *warehouse?*"

"Exactly so," Sav Rid said, pleased.

His Delm drew breath. "I see. Forgive my question, kinsman, but such a purchase as a trading vessel . . . It seems that I surely would have noted the passage of a so large a voucher across my desk. Yet I recall nothing."

Sav Rid smiled, triumphantly oblivious to the worry in the other's face. "It was a small matter, sir; there was no need to resort to credit vouchers. We paid cash."

"Cash," Plemia repeated tonelessly. He was silent a moment or two as they walked. Then he straightened abruptly, renewing his grip on Sav Rid's arm. "It only now returns to me, kinsman—the matter of which I wished to speak. I have heard from the port master that a member of your crew—one Dagmar Collier—has been found dead in the city outside the port."

"So, that is what became of it," Sav Rid said calmly. "I had wondered. Well, it always had a quarrelsome nature."

"Had she?" Taam asked softly around the sudden ice in his throat. "And how long had Dagmar Collier served you, kinsman?"

Sav Rid moved his shoulders. "Two or three trips, I believe."

"Ah." Taam stopped, whirling on the other. "Sav Rid, a woman who has been in your service these four years has died! Do you not at least go to the precinct house and claim the body, that it might be sent properly to her kin?"

There was honest puzzlement in the young face. "No, why should I? I doubt it had kin. It was Terran, you see," he explained more fully in the face of his Delm's further silence.

"Terrans are not all kinless folk, Sav Rid," Taam murmured, his eyes filling as pity unexpectedly overtook dread. "They are people, even as we are." Still there was only puzzled confusion in the eyes watching his. He touched the smooth cheek gently. "And if they were not, my child, *we* are people. It is our burden and our pride to behave with honor, always."

"Yes, surely. But a Terran, sir . . ."

"Never mind, child. It will be attended to." He took Sav Rid's arm again and resumed the walk. "I hear from Korval that you and young Shan attempt to balance some puppy accounts. Are you not too old for such mischief, Sav Rid?"

The arm in his had stiffened, as had the young face. "It is not mischief, sir; it is earnest. I will have yos'Galan on its knees—hideous brother and first sister! Aye, and young Val Con, as well! How dare he treat a guest so? It was sheer insult, sir! They gave no consideration to that due one of Plemia! They will learn—and not soon forget! 'Korval,' Chelsa bleats, with fear in her face! A rabble of ill-raised brats! There is balance owing, sir, and it will be obtained. That I promise!"

"I see," Taam said again sadly. He took a breath. "Then you will not be adverse, I think, to this other news I bring. Korval demands a meeting, in sight of port master and witnesses, to establish balance and put paid to all accounts. The time is set for this local evening, if you find yourself able to attend."

"Korval demands a meeting!" Sav Rid laughed. "But they must, after all! How could they allow the idiot eldest to ruin himself?" He disengaged and bowed gravely. "I will accompany you with the greatest pleasure, sir."

Sleep receded, and she opened her eyes. The room had an uncertain familiarity—not her own quarters, nor yet the prison cell . . . *Sick bay,* memory provided. Lina had sent her into sleep, riding the wave of one resounding note, to wake when the healing reverberation was at last still.

How many hours? she wondered without urgency. She stretched, catlike, where she lay, noticing the cramp in her right hand, her thumb tucked tightly into her fingers.

Slowly, she eased the tension, the great amethyst of the master's ring sparkling in the room's dim light. Priscilla smiled. Goddess bless you, my dear, for bringing me home.

She stretched again, relishing the sensation, then sat up, pushing the thin cover away. Time to be about, whatever time it was. And she was *starving*.

The door to her left opened with a soft sigh. "Morning, gorgeous!" She started, then grinned at the gangling medic. 'Vilt. Do you always terrify your patients when they wake up?"

"Makes sense," he pointed out, taking her arm and beginning to unwrap the gauzy dressing. "If they're gonna have a

heart attack, might as well have it here, where there's some
body to take care of 'em."

"Who?" she wondered, and he laughed, laying the dressing
aside.

"Go ahead, do your worst. Just remember who runs the in-
oculation program around here. Arm looks great. Damnedes
burn I've ever seen, though: inside, between wrist and
elbow." He shook his head. "How'd you do it?"

She looked him in the eye. "Throwing a fireball."

"That a fact? Lucky you didn't lose some fingers. Better
use a glove next time."

"Goddess willing, there won't be a next time."

"If you say so. How's the throat?"

"Okay."

Vilt shook his head in mock severity. "Think I'm taking
your word for it? Open up, gorgeous—and don't even think
about biting."

She submitted resentfully. Vilt made a thorough and, she
suspected, leisurely exam, then grunted and stepped back.

"Looks good. Be careful of the voice for a couple days
just in case."

"Let the captain do the talking," she suggested.

He laughed again. "He will, anyway. I've known Shan
since I was apprentice medic on this ship and he wasn't any
older than Gordy. Been talking nonstop all that time. Likely
born talking. His mother was a linguist, which probably accounts for it. Genes, you know," he explained sagely as
Priscilla chuckled. He stepped back, abruptly sober. "All
right, gorgeous, pay attention. Sometime between leave-time
yesterday and arrival time, you lost one-tenth of your mass.
The kitchen has been provided with special menus, just for
you. You will eat everything on your tray until you've regained that weight. And just to keep you honest, you'll weigh
in before you begin each duty-shift." He glanced at his watch.
"A tasty, high-caloric breakfast will be here in three minutes.
After you've eaten everything on the tray, you can use the

fresher across the hall. Lina put fresh clothes in there for you. Any questions?"

"No."

"Great." He slapped her shoulder lightly and grinned. "See ya later."

"Vilt!"

"Yah?"

"Is Gordy okay?"

He snorted. "That kid? Been up for hours. Demanded to see you. Lina took him off to help in the pet library. Said you'd call him there when you woke up."

"I'll do that, then."

"You'll eat that breakfast before you do anything. Aha!" He stepped triumphantly to one side, allowing the orderly to push the meal cart up to the bed. "Enjoy!"

Priscilla stepped out of the dry cycle, running her fingers through unruly curls and frowning at her reflection. Her teachers had ever been anxious about her slenderness, saying that her body—Moonhawk's vessel—was not robust enough to endure the working of larger magics.

True enough, by the mirror's testimony. Fourteen pounds lost meant countable ribs and jutting hipbones, the knobs at wrist and collar painfully apparent. She cupped a breast, sighing. She looked like a disaster victim. She turned sharply away to rummage in the closet.

The fresh clothes were unexpectedly fine. Priscilla wondered where Lina had gotten them, for they had the air of things handmade to personal specification rather than bought from general stores. Wonderingly, she unfolded the silky shirt, noting the flaring collar and the wide, pleated sleeves gathered tightly into ruffled cuffs. Its color was a pure and shimmering rose. The trousers were river-blue and soft. Velvet? she wondered, running light fingers down the nap. They belled slightly at the knee and fell precisely to the instep of the new black boots. She ran the tooled leather belt around her waist, fastened the rosy agate buckle, and turned again to her reflection.

"Thodelm," she breathed, touching the collar that framed her face and lent blush to her cheeks. Lina had provided clothing that the Head of a Liaden Line might wear when about the business of the Line.

Hesitantly she approached the mirror, and put out a finger to trace the features of her own face: the slender brows, the straight nose and startling cheekbones, the stubborn chin, the full mouth, and all around them the tumbling mass of midnight curls, relieved at each ear by the pure curve of a platinum hoop.

"Priscilla Mendoza," she said aloud.

On her hand the borrowed amethyst glittered—and that was wrong. She was not Master Trader.

Nor was she outcast.

She stared into the purple depths, considering that thought. "Moonhawk is returned to the Mother."

Truth.

And what did that truth mean, after ten years, a double-dozen worlds—a death? What did it mean here, in the place her heart called home, surrounded by friends, buoyed by a power she thought had fled?

Lady Mendoza, the old gentleman invariably addressed her with profound respect. Lina had not found it unusual that her friend possessed power, only that she had not been taught courtesy in its use. Shan . . .

But it was not possible to think clearly of Shan. Certainly he regarded her abilities, like his own, as natural and acceptable. "How do you make love?" she recalled him asking, and she put a hand to a cheek suddenly flaming. Don't do that Priscilla . . .

Last night . . . How much had been drug-dream, how much true actions? He had come—she wore the proof on her hand even now! He had brought her home. What else besides these was fact?

Disturbed, she turned slowly and left the 'fresher.

In the hall she hesitated. It was time she reported for duty.
Yet Vilt had not released her, and the finery she wore was not
meant to withstand a second mate's rounds.

"Hello, Priscilla. Can you spare me a few moments?"
Shan's voice interrupted her thoughts.

"All the moments you like," she told him gladly even as
he groped for his pattern.

It was subdued, though she caught an indefinable jolt of
something as he paused and looked at her closely.

"Are you well, Priscilla? Tell me the truth, please—no
heroics."

"Well," she caught doubt and drifted an unconscious step
forward, smiling reassuringly. "I lost some weight—strong
magics have that effect. Vilt has me eating the most incredible amount of food! But I am well. In fact, I was getting ready
to sign out of here and go back on duty."

"Duty? Priscilla . . ." He paused, glancing about. "Is that
the room you were in? Do you mind if we speak there? I . . ."

Something was wrong. She expanded her scope, trying to
read it from his pattern, but received only a discord of pain,
bitterness, anger, despair—a medley so unlike Shan that she
would hardly have known him had her outer eyes been closed.

"Of course."

He stood aside to let her enter first, then closed the door
behind them and dropped into the single chair. Uncertainly,
she sat on the bed.

The silence was uneasy; scanning was worse than useless.
She pulled the Master Trader's ring from her thumb and held
it out.

He stared, despair increasing: taking the ring, he sat holding it between thumb and forefinger, toying with the lights
among its facets.

"Have you decided." he asked, looking at the ring, his
voice husky, "where it is I shall take you?"

She stared at him, ice blossoming in chest and belly.

"Why," she managed, "should you take me anywhere?"

"I gave my word," he told the amethyst. "You only said you would stay until you were—*well*, Priscilla."

Through the isolated, tangled scenes of the night before she recalled it and licked her lips. "You said you—had come to take me home."

"Did I?" Still he did not meet her eyes, but stared at the ring in his hand. "I will then, Priscilla. But you must tell me where that is. Home."

"Shan!" Anguish knifed through her; she made no attempt to damp it, and felt his answering surge of concern as he at last raised his face.

"You don't want me to go!" she cried, knowing it was truth. "Why—"

"It doesn't matter what I want, Priscilla! What matters is what you want! If there is a place that is home to you, where you know, if you are in need, that there is someone—anyone!—who will aid you, I'll take you there. See you safe settled . . ." His voice cracked on the unaccustomed harshness. Instantly the black lashes flicked down, shielding him.

He took a breath, then another, his emotions an unreadable riot. "That a member of this ship's complement should feel there was no place to go when she was in direst need . . . I am ashamed, Priscilla. I've failed you as a captain . . . and as a friend."

"I want to stay." Her words came as barely a breath of sound. She gripped the mattress and tried again. "Captain, please. You never failed me. I failed, by not learning soon enough . . . by not understanding what it means to be a crew member." Tears ran her cheeks, unheeded. "Shan, by the Mother! The *Passage* is my home. Don't—don't make me leave!" She drew a shuddering breath and loosed the mattress to wipe her face with shaking fingertips.

"Really, Priscilla, you might tell me in advance if I'm expected to provide handkerchiefs for us both."

She gave a startled gasp, groping perhaps toward a laugh, and took the proffered cloth. "Thank you."

"Don't give it a thought. I have dozens. I just don't happen to have them all with me at the moment." He leaned back, his face less bleak, his pattern showing a glimmer of what might be hope.

"The ship would miss the services of the second mate," he said carefully. "The captain's information is that the second mate progresses excellently in her training, taking over more responsibilities each shift. The first mate is pleased. The captain is also pleased."

Melant'i. She drew a deliberately even breath, relaxing tight chest muscles as she recalled sleep-lessons and Lina's tutoring. "The second mate wishes with all her heart to continue serving the ship and the captain."

Relief like a draught of ice-cold water cascaded from him to her. "Good. You will take your duties up again in four shifts." He raised a hand to still her protest. "There is a meeting at local midnight in the port master's office, Priscilla. Since you are intimately involved, it's best that you be there. Also present will be Delm Plemia, Sav Rid Olanek, Port Master Rominkoff, Shan yos'Galan, Gordon Arbuthnot, Mr. dea-Gauss, and Lina Faaldom, as observer."

"Balance?"

"Balance, indeed. Which reminds me. Thodelm. Mr. dea'-Gauss wishes to meet with you in a very few moments now to ascertain the extent of debt owed you by Plemia and Korval—"

"Korval owes me nothing!" she cried. "If anything. I owe Korval for giving me a job, for—"

"Priscilla, do be reasonable. If you hadn't been on this ship, there quite possibly wouldn't be a ship right now, whether or not there was a captain. Ship's debt exists. As well as a personal debt."

"No," she said stubbornly. "I won't take payment from you. There's no debt now, if there ever was one." She leaned forward, extending a tentative hand. "Shan? You gave me—a life. I gave you a life. Balance."

He hesitated, then put his hand into hers. "Balance, then,

Priscilla." He smiled. "You drive a hard bargain. Mr. dea'-Gauss awaits us. May I escort your Ladyship to the meeting?"

"No," she said, gripping his hand and drinking in his lightening pattern with giddy joy. "But you may escort your friend."

Shan grinned and stood. "Much better, I agree." He flourished the bow between equals. "After you, Priscilla."

Ten minutes before the hour.

Taam Olanek sternly forbade himself the luxury of fidgeting with the papers before him. It was not expected that a Delm betray uneasiness. At his right hand, Sav Rid sat silent. He still did not grasp it, Taam knew, pity warring with anger. He wondered briefly what had caused the younger man's madness, and set wonder aside. It hardly mattered.

Across the room, Mr. dea'Gauss was in quiet conversation with Port Master Rominkoff. The balance of the group had yet to arrive.

The door buzzed and was opened by the guard stationed there.

Taam Olanek felt his breath snag.

A plain-faced Liaden woman in the costume of Thodelm entered, a tow-headed Terran child at her side. Taam Olanek's breathing eased. Of course Korval would arrive last. It was proper.

"I'm not sitting at the same table with him!"

The child had stopped, eyes fixed on—*Me?* Taam thought. No. On Sav Rid.

The woman had her hand on the boy's arm and was speaking in gentle Terran. "Gordon? We are here to settle past difference. You know this. To do so we must sit and speak together."

"I'm not," Gordon said through clenched teeth, "sitting at a table with him. He called me 'it,' and he said Priscilla was a thief."

With a feeling of infinite sadness, Taam Olanek rose and went across the room. A child, Sav Rid? he thought.

He and Mr. dea'Gauss reached the spot at the same moment. Asking permission with a flicker of fingers, Taam bowed to the child: elder to young person of rank. The boy eyed him narrowly but returned the bow properly, then straightened and stood waiting.

"I am," Taam said, speaking the unaccustomed tongue with great care, "Taam Olanek. The person you object to is one who will obey my word. Will it satisfy you, young sir, if I pledge that my kinsman Sav Rid will behave with fitting courtesy during the time we meet together?"

The brown eyes looked into his: a weighing glance. Taam returned it calmly. The boy looked to Mr. dea'Gauss.

"Is that true?" There was no insult in the tone; he was merely requesting information. Taam Olanek found himself amused.

Mr. dea'Gauss inclined his head. "The word of Delm Plemia is above reproach, Master Arbuthnot. What he has said will be."

"Okay." The boy inclined his head. "Thank you, Delm Plemia."

Taam bowed graciously. "Thank *you*, Master Arbuthnot."

Mr. dea'Gauss indicated the patient woman. "Plemia, here is Thodelm Faaldom, Clan Deshnol."

He inclined his head. "Thodelm, I am pleased to meet you."

She bowed, as Head of Line to Delm of another Clan. "I am pleased to meet you, Plemia." Neither voice nor face betrayed her thoughts. Her behavior was most proper.

As observer, Thodelm Faaldom sat at the bottom left of the table. The boy sat to her right, near Mr. dea'Gauss. Sav

Rid eyed both coldly; he made neither overture nor introduction.

The hour struck on the clock above the door, nearly covering the sound of the door buzzer.

The woman was tall, though not much taller than Shan yos'Galan, who walked just behind her right shoulder, and black-haired and slender. But for its paleness, her face might have been Liaden. She wore calm authority like a silken cloak over the clothing of Thodelm.

Gliding, she crossed to the port master and bowed as between equals.

Pilot, Taam Olanek thought, seeing the woman's grace mirrored in her white-haired escort. He understood now Mr. dea'Gauss's moment of outrage. Pleasure-love she might be, but this regal lady was no one's plaything.

"Port Master," she was saying, her voice soft and deeper than one expected, "I'm happy to see you again. Please accept my gratitude now for your kindness to myself and my friend."

The port master smiled in momentary pleasure, then waved a dismissing hand. "You owe me no gratitude, Lady Mendoza. My duty was clear. I believe there are still amends to be made; we must meet again before you leave."

The black-haired woman murmured assent and stepped aside.

Shan yos'Galan made his bow to the port master. "I'm pleased to see you again, ma'am. Please accept my gratitude as well, to be flung aside with Lady Mendoza's."

She laughed. "A lesson in manners, Captain? Very well, I accept the gratitude of all—including the boy's, though he hasn't offered it. Perhaps he's a realist." She indicated the rest of the table. "We are all gathered now. Mr. dea'Gauss?"

Korval's man of business rose to his spare height and bowed profoundly to the two just arrived.

"Thodelm yos'Galan. Thodelm Mendoza. Here are Elyana Rominkoff, port master; Taam Olanek, Delm Plemia; Lina

Faaldom, Thodelm and observer; Gordon Arbuthnot, fosterson and witness; Sav Rid Olanek, Trader."

Plemia inclined his head. Beside him, Sav Rid shifted and
snapped, "*Lady* Mendoza!"

The woman's face remained coolly serene; she might not
have heard. Certainly yos'Galan had heard; the light eyes glittered steel.

Plemia turned his face. Deliberately, using the Command
mode of the High Tongue, he instructed for the ears of all,
"You will exercise fitting courtesy here!"

Impossibly, Sav Rid looked hurt. "Certainly, sir."

Taam sighed to himself and saw a flicker of a reaction
cross Lady Faaldom's face. At the top of the table, Lady Mendoza sat, Lord yos'Galan at her right. Plemia very nearly
sighed aloud. Korval thus demonstrated its support of Thodelm Mendoza's demands and subordination of its claims to
hers.

"It must be known," Mr. dea'Gauss announced, "that a
pin-beam has been received from Eldema yos'Galan. It reads
thus—" He plucked a sheet of hard copy from the pile before
him. "'In the present affair between Plemia and Korval, it
shall be that Thodelm yos'Galan speaks with the very voice
of Korval. I, Nova yos'Galan, First Speaker in Trust, Clan
Korval.'"

yos'Galan inclined his white head, his ugly face austere.
"It shall be done as the First Speaker instructs."

Mr. dea'Gauss laid the sheet aside. "For the purpose of balance, it shall be considered that Priscilla Delacroix y Mendoza is indeed Thodelm. Since she has chosen to disassociate
herself from House Mendoza, Sintia, she must also be considered Delm Mendoza Offworld—"

"Offworld?" Sav Rid cried, cutting the old gentleman off.
"Outlaw, more like!"

"Sav Rid!" Plemia allowed irritation to be heard. "I remind
you again that I will have courtesy from you, for every person
here."

"What difference," the younger man demanded, eyes glittering fever-bright, "if the bitch chooses to style itself Thodelm? Our business is with Korval, which has the ill judgment to allow the fool to speak for it—":

"You are silent!"

A wave of heat washed past Taam's cheek, gone even as he understood the words to be in the High Tongue—ultimate authority to rankless person—and recognized the voice to belong to Thodelm Mendoza.

Beside him, Sav Rid opened his mouth, throat working. No sound emerged.

"Your Delm," the woman continued in faultless Liaden, "will speak for you. When your words are required, you will be permitted speech."

"Most proper," Mr. dea'Gauss murmured.

Taam looked quickly around the table. Shan yos'Galan was expressionless; the port master was puzzled but unshaken. Gordon Arbuthnot's brown eyes were stretched wide. Lady Faaldom was staring at the black-haired woman, awe and consternation in her face.

"Korval," Lord yos'Galan said in quiet Trade, "acknowledges a subordinate position in these negotiations. Debts owed Lady Mendoza are by far the greatest and must be met. We support her claims and are guided by her thoughts."

"Just so," Plemia inclined his head, carefully not thinking about the impossibility of what he had just witnessed. Beside him, Sav Rid sat mute and shivering.

"Thodelm Mendoza. I have seen information provided by Mr. dea'Gauss regarding your grievance against Plemia. Also, I have heard privately from my clansman that which convinces me of the justice of that grievance. Without doubt, Plemia owes. The amount must yet be ascertained. I am interested in hearing your thoughts on this."

The black eyes considered him calmly. "Sav Rid Olanek must be removed as Trader on *Daxflan* immediately."

He stiffened. "That is a Clan decision, Thodelm."

"Then it is a decision I require of the Clan," she returned

serenely. "Sav Rid Olanek is unfit. If he were examined by the Trader's Guild tomorrow, sir, he would be found wanting and his license revoked. More." She lifted a hand, forestalling his protest. "I tell you now, sir, your kinsman gave scant attention to the honor of his crew—Liaden as little as Terran. His cargo included illegal pharmaceuticals: Bellaquesa, I will swear to; others I might guess. He is a danger to the honor of your Clan, the honor of your ship . . . and to himself." She glanced at the man on her right. "Is it permitted that I ask Lady Faaldom to speak—as a Healer?"

"If Plemia agrees."

Taam inclined his head. "Plemia agrees."

"Healer Faaldom."

"Lady Mendoza?"

"I feel that Sav Rid Olanek is not—rational. Are you able to form an opinion? Would you tell us what it is?"

The Healer gave the softest of sighs. "My opinion parallels your own. Sav Rid Olanek is deranged. The pattern is one I have only occasionally seen, most often in connection with ingestion of harmful drugs. Bellaquesa addiction, for instance, might cause such a pattern."

"Can he be Healed?" There was hope in the Terran woman's voice. Taam Olanek looked at her in wonder.

The Healer hesitated. "It is beyond my skill."

"Beyond everyone's skill, Lina?" She spoke insistently, and Olanek felt his wonder grow.

"On Liad, perhaps. The path would be a long one, I think, and tedious." She sighed once more. "If Plemia desires, I will provide names, an introduction."

"You are kind, Healer. My thanks to you."

"You will need that list, sir," Lady Mendoza informed him. "My second demand is that he be Healed."

"Thodelm," he said with dignity, "you do not need to demand it. The child shall have what he requires."

She bowed her head. "Forgive me, sir. I meant no offense."

"None was taken, Thodelm. May I know what items further go to balance Plemia's debt?"

"It must be recalled," yos'Galan said smoothly, before the lady could speak again, "that several attempts have been made on Lady Mendoza's life—which is the life of her House, entire. The first attempt must be laid directly upon Sav Rid Olanek, who ordered Dagmar Collier to strike. The second and third incidents must also be laid upon Trader Olanek for his inability to control the actions of one sworn to his service."

"There are practicalities as well," Mr. dea'Gauss put in. "Unpaid wages, contract fee, clothing, hazard pay, recompense of personal indignities suffered while employed on *Daxflan,* family heirlooms lost—"

"Korval," yos'Galan broke in, "owes for the heirlooms, sir. Evidence indicates they were destroyed in retaliation for words spoken by Captain yos'Galan."

Mr. dea'Gauss made a notation. "So then. The sum owed, were there no further balance to be established: two cantra."

Plemia inclined his head. It surprised him that the woman should have drawn so low a wage, that she should have possessed so little. "Plemia agrees to a payment of two cantra in balance for these things."

"Lady Mendoza," yos'Galan said gently, "has declined her right to Trader Olanek's life as balance for his attempts on her own. The life-sum agreed upon by the Council of Clans for a first class pilot is three hundred cantra. It must be remembered that Lady Mendoza is currently the sum of her Line and Clan. It is to be assumed that one in her position would desire to establish a solid base for her House. Three children, I think, is not an unreasonable number. Nor is it unreasonable to suppose these offspring would inherit pilot reactions. Nine hundred cantra, then, for the children unborn."

Twelve hundred cantra.

"A just sum," Plemia murmured around the sinking feeling in his stomach. "Precise balance is intended. However, if Lady Mendoza permits, I would propose this alternate plan: Plemia pays a sum of fifteen hundred cantra, over four Standards, the money to derive from *Daxflan*'s profits—"

"No!" she said sharply. "I want no money from *Daxflan*."

Wearily he raised his eyes to hers. "Lady, I assure you, not all of *Daxflan*'s profits come illegally. A guaranteed payment of three hundred seventy-five cantra per Standard would be made, even should *Daxflan* fail to earn that sum. Is this plan acceptable?"

She looked at him for a long moment, then glanced beyond. "Mr. dea'Gauss."

"Thodelm?"

"If Clan Korval permits, sir, I would like you to take charge of these—details. The sum of twelve hundred cantra at once or fifteen hundred over several Standards is agreeable to me. Otherwise, it would be—comforting—to know that you act in my interest."

"Korval raises no objection," Lord yos'Galan put in, "if Mr. dea'Gauss feels he can undertake the task."

"I accept the commission, Thodelm Mendoza. I am honored to give service." He inclined his head. "Perhaps Delm Plemia and I might meet on the morrow and discuss the matter more fully."

"Certainly, sir. At your convenience."

"We come now," Mr. dea'Gauss said, "to that owed Korval. There is deliberate loss engineered by Sav Rid Olanek. There is the paid attack upon the *Dutiful Passage*—"

"Korval," yos'Galan broke in, "makes the following demands for balance: From Plemia, twenty cantra toward the loss on the mezzik-root purchase. Captain yos'Galan will likewise pay twenty cantra to the ship, to remind him to hear more fully. Also, Korval does likewise insist that Trader Olanek be removed from *Daxflan* immediately and sent home, that Healing may commence.

"Last, Captain yos'Galan would speak with Delm Plemia and Captain yo'Vaade regarding the management of tradeships and the planning of trade routes. Plemia may reap profit from the discussion."

Taam Olanek felt himself adrift. He managed to incline his head. "Plemia agrees to all terms of Korval's balance."

"So be it," Mr. dea'Gauss said formally, and made notation.

"I believe that Master Arbuthnot also holds a just claim," Taam ventured, still unsure of what had occurred.

"Me?" The boy looked up in surprise. "Shan? Does this— does Delm Plemia owe me something?"

"You were in quite a bit of danger through the Trader's mismanagement, you know, Gordy." From the mildness of the tone, yos'Galan might have been discussing a rather mediocre play.

The boy frowned and shook his head. "The only thing he owes me is an apology for calling me 'it.' But if he's going to see a Healer, I guess he'll learn better, so that's okay. Dagmar's the one put me in danger, and she paid as much as she can." Surprisingly, then, he inclined his head, speaking in tolerably accented High Tongue. "Thank you, sir, but I believe our accounts are in order."

Taam bowed his head. "Thank you, Master Arbuthnot. Should you have need, Plemia's name is for you to use."

"Thank you," Gordy said again in response to a glance from Lady Faaldom.

Plemia glanced at the port master. "Madam, I would ask assistance. *Daxflan* must be searched, and all illegal substances must be removed. Is it possible you could instruct me in the proper procedure?"

She nodded gravely. "Delm Plemia, I would be honored to assist you. Allow me to call on you tomorrow midday for the purpose."

"You are kind, madam. I thank you."

"I believe," Mr. dea'Gauss said dryly, "that the meeting may be adjourned." Seeing no dissent, he turned down his papers.

At the head of the table, both tall Thodelms stood, bowed, and glided toward the door. On the threshold the woman turned and raised a hand, tracing an invisible pattern in the air.

"Say Rid Olanek," she announced in the High Tongue, "you may speak now."

Then they passed through the door and were gone.

Taam Olanek felt a sigh pass him, as if a bubble had given way. Beside him, Sav Rid burst into tears.

Acting First Mate Mendoza strode toward the captain's office. Hold 6, empty for the past two months, tantalized memory with the odors of leather, resin, spice. She took a deep breath, then sighed it out with a grin. It was hard to believe that they would establish orbit about Liad in five hours; hard to believe that so much had happened in five months. From pet librarian to acting first mate—she nearly laughed as she laid her hand against the captain's door.

He was frowning at the computer screen, his mental signature laced with irritation. At her entrance he looked up, irritation fading. "Hello, Priscilla."

She smiled, relaxing into the familiarity of his inner self. "You wanted to see me?" He grinned. "Very good. When in doubt, hedge. The captain has several things to discuss with the first mate. Also the first mate was to have discovered what Lina Faaldom was going to do with that damn perfume of hers."

Priscilla laughed. "She's got a buyer in Chonselta City. They're going to package a distillate and sell it for a cantra the quarter ounce. The name is 'Festival Memories.' " She stopped because Shan was laughing.

"Oh, no! Shameless, shameless! She'd have done better to turn her hand to trading than librarying, Priscilla. 'Festival Memories,' in fact! The woman's dangerous." He leaned back, grinning hugely. "She's reserved a quantity for the crew, I hope?"

Priscilla nodded, lighthearted with his pleasure. "Anyone who wants part of their profit in perfume may take it that way, up to two bottles."

He chuckled. "Wonderful, wonderful. Pour yourself a drink, Priscilla, and come sit down."

She moved to the bar. "What are you drinking?"

"Nothing at the moment. But I would like a brandy, if you'd be so kind."

She poured them each a drink, brought him a glass, and settled into the right-hand chair.

Shan sipped, his light eyes on her. "Have you decided what you will do, Priscilla?"

"Do?"

He waved an apologetic hand. "Of course, it's true that you're rather well off now. You might choose to do nothing at all. But I'll tell you frankly, Priscilla, doing nothing is a very boring line of work." He sipped thoughtfully. "Not that there aren't a great many people who don't seem to find it arduous at all. My cousin Pat Rin, for an instance. The first jewels, the most fashionable companions . . . Why, if he didn't play the wheel with suspiciously consistent luck, he'd have no money at all to call his own, and live within his quarter-share he could not."

She smiled. "I don't think I'd do well as a gambler."

"Well, neither do I, frankly. But there are other things you might be about. Buy a house, a bit of land, start talking to people—lay the foundation for possible contracts and alliances."

"To set up my Clan," she surmised.

"Exactly to set up your Clan. Nothing wrong with that, is there?"

She sipped her drink, considering him. Emotive patterns told too little. He was not desperate, but there was a—tentativeness—mixed somehow with the desire she had found herself responding to more and more of late.

"I thought I'd invest my money," she said quietly. "Mr. dea'Gauss kindly offered his services."

Shan raised his glass. "I see that Korval will have to begin casting about for a new man of business. Mr. dea'Gauss is clearly smitten. I had hoped it would prove to be merely a case of calf-love, Priscilla, I confess."

She laughed. "More likely he thinks I'm too young to manage my own affairs! He helped me gain funds and status; how can he leave me alone to botch things now?"

"A fair summation of Mr. dea'Gauss's melant'i in the situation," Shan acknowledged. "But you still don't tell me what you'll be doing, Priscilla."

"Have you heard from Kayzin Ne'Zame?"

The slanted brows pulled together. "She brought *Daxflan* safely home and continues to work closely with Plemia to revise ship's procedures and work out a route that will not unduly tax available resources. I believe she had hopes of showing him the advantages of belonging to a cooperative, with which project I wish her luck. Plemia was rather resistant to the idea when I brought it up in our discussions."

"Does she think she'll be able to finish her work there in time for the *Passage*'s next voyage?" More tentativeness. She knew it for her own.

Shan was surprised. "Kayzin warned me some time ago of her intention to retire at the end of this trip. Most properly, as Mr. dea'Gauss would no doubt agree. In a way, it was good that *Daxflan* and all its troubles came along. It gave her thoughts a new direction, away from—endings." He sipped. "Kayzin's captain was my father, Priscilla. They ran this ship together thirty years. It's not easy for her to see another in his place, even though she helped train me for just that purpose. She only stayed this long to be certain I was able. Her last duty to her captain."

"You'll be needing a first mate and a second?"

"Indeed I will. Which brings us back at last to my original inquiry, Priscilla. Have you thought of what you will do? Your contract runs out in—what? A day?"

"Fourteen hours," she replied, her mind racing. There was so much she did not know, so much training she would need; and there were people on the *Passage* who had been there all their lives, child and adult. Kayzin Ne'Zame, working on the ship for fifty years, at the captain's side for thirty of them, a captain she served even after his death . . .

Shan sipped brandy. She sensed tension in him, and restraint. The decision was hers. Goddess, I'm a fool. How can it be easier to conceive of looking at his face, hearing his voice, sensing his moods for all of thirty years, than to consider myself without those things for even a week?

She licked her lips. "If—I would prefer not to renew my contract as second—" she sensed shocked pain from him, quickly damped, as she hurtled on, "—and to sign a new one, as first mate!"

She was swept by singing triumph and a tangled knot of other feelings, from which she isolated lust, and relief, and joy, and something that seared so she could not find its name before the whole concert was controlled and shackled into the merest background hum.

"Thank you, Priscilla."

Her heart was pounding; she was gasping with the force of his emotions, her own powerfully evoked. Mother, the echo . . . she thought. But it was no echo.

"Priscilla?" He was before her, radiating concern. "Forgive me."

"No." She set the glass aside, hand questing. He took it in his. "Shan . . ."

"Yes, Priscilla?"

She translated it from the High Tongue, because protocol said it was done this way between Liadens, and it was imperative that he understand, that he not think her grasping or unaware of her place as someone all but Clanless. "Will you share pleasure with me, Shan?"

His fingers tightened as astonished joy flickered between them, weighted, though, with something else. Seeking, her inner eye perceived a wall, thick and impenetrable, with only a tiny slit in its smooth surface. As she watched, the slit enlarged, eating the wall until it was gone and there was only— Shan.

The impression was not just sound now, or pattern, or even an occasional whiff of elusive spice. It was all: a woven whole spread before the inner senses—Shan without defenses, open for her to know completely.

Priscilla cried out, jerking to her feet, gripping his shoulders. "No! Shan, you mustn't!"

Then there was sadness, though not despair, and the inner landscape faded, becoming again the barely breached Wall as she sagged against him, craving what she had just denied, and pushed her face against his shoulder.

"Priscilla, I ask your forgiveness yet again." His voice was very gentle in her ear. "I didn't want to distress you."

She drew a shaky breath and stood away. "I—" Words failed her. Goddess, she thought, twice a fool.

He sighed and guided her to the couch. Sitting beside her, he took her hand. "When I came to get you from the precinct house in Theopholis, Priscilla, you said something." She tensed. What *was* real from all she thought she remembered of that night?

"What you said," he pursued gently, "was, 'Shan, there wasn't enough time to be sure.'"

She relaxed. She did remember that. "True."

"It might still be true, Priscilla. There's no need for haste. And many reasons to be . . . sure."

She struggled with it, trying to balance the Liaden concept of pleasure-love with what she felt in him even now, with what she herself felt. "I asked . . . pleasure. And you want it!"

"Priscilla, my very dear." He raised her hand, lips brushing her palm, cheek stroking her fingertips. "Of course I want it.

But not at the expense of your certainty. I'd be a poor friend if I made that trade." He sighed. "And I've already made you angry with me."

"Not angry," she protested, knowing he could read that lack in her. "It's—Shan, it's *wrong* to—to open up so far. To let someone see your—allness."

"Even when that someone is my dear friend? Even when I wish to give the gift?"

She opened her mouth, then closed it. "It is how I was taught," she told him humbly. "I never thought to question it." She had the name of the searingly bright emotion then, and felt tears forming. Too little time, indeed . . .

He sensed her understanding and nodded. "There are other reasons not to rush, as I said. Consider your new position, for one matter. Will you have people say that you are first mate because you and the captain are lovers?"

Her chin rose. "It's our business, not theirs!"

"Theirs," he corrected. "It's a matter of melant'i, and of ship's administration. The crew must know that the two people who run this ship are honorable, are trustworthy—are *capable*. That proved, you may take any lover—and as many!—as you wish. You do have an extensive amount of training to undergo, you know, before you'll be up to Kayzin's level."

Impossibly, she laughed. "As if I didn't know it!"

He grinned, relieved and admiring. "Will you be staying on Liad, Priscilla?"

She nodded. "I'm guesting with Lina until I find a house of my own."

"Good. Then you'll be able to get a firm grounding during the time we're docked. And the next run is the long one—one full Standard. Enough time, I'd think, for everyone to know what works and what doesn't." He squeezed her fingers. "We might not make a very good team in spite of it all, Priscilla. That happens sometimes."

"We're a good team," she said, startled to hear the Seer's lilt in her voice. "We'll be a better one. The best."

The silver eyes glinted mischief. "You sound sure of yourself, Thodelm. Would you care to place a small wager? Say, a cantra? Issue to be decided at Solcintra docking, next runend."

"Done." She grinned, surprised at finding herself so easy, and read the same deep serenity in Shan. On some level, then, they understood each other. The pattern of the Goddess's dance would see to the rest. She gripped the big hand tightly, then let it go and stood. "Sleep well, my friend."

"Sleep well, Priscilla."

She moved to the door.

"Priscilla!"

"Yes?"

"May I call on you at Lina's, Priscilla? It might aid certainty."

She smiled, peace filling her utterly. "I'll be all joy to see you."

ABOUT THE AUTHORS

Sharon Lee and Steve Miller live in the rolling hills of Central Maine. Born and raised in Baltimore, Maryland, in the early '50s, they met several times before taking the hint and formalizing the team, in 1979. They moved to Maine with cats, books, and music following the completion of *Carpe Diem*, their third novel.

Their short fiction, written both jointly and singly, has appeared or will appear in *Absolute Magnitude*, *Catfantastic*, *Such a Pretty Face*, *Dreams of Decadence*, *Fantasy Book*, and several former incarnations of *Amazing*. Meisha Merlin Publishing has or will be publishing four books set in the Liaden Universe: *Plan B*, *Partners in Necessity*, *Pilots Choices*, and *I Dare*.

Both Sharon and Steve have seen their nonfiction work and reviews published in a variety of newspapers and magazines. Steve is the founding curator of the University of Maryland's Kuhn Library Science Fiction Research Collection.

Sharon's interests include music, pine cone collecting, and seashores. Steve also enjoys music, plays chess, and collects cat whiskers. Both spend way too much time playing on the internet, and even have a website at:

www.korval.com

Penguin Putnam Inc.
Online

Your Internet gateway to a virtual environment with
hundreds of entertaining and enlightening books
from Penguin Putnam Inc.

*While you're there, get the latest buzz on
the best authors and books around—*

Tom Clancy, Patricia Cornwell, W.E.B. Griffin,
Nora Roberts, William Gibson, Robin Cook,
Brian Jacques, Catherine Coulter, Stephen King,
Ken Follett, Terry McMillan, and many more!

**Penguin Putnam Online is located at
http://www.penguinputnam.com**

PENGUIN PUTNAM NEWS

Every month you'll get an inside look at our upcom-
ing books and new features on our site. This is an
ongoing effort to provide you with the most
up-to-date information about
our books and authors.

**Subscribe to Penguin Putnam News at
http://www.penguinputnam.com/newsletters**